More Praise for Kinky Friedman and . . .

. . . GREENWICH KILLING TIME

"Hip . . . quirky . . . nonstop action!"   —*Washington Post*

"A 24-carat American original . . . hip and hard-boiled."
—*Chicago Tribune*

"Outrageous . . . gritty charm . . . a swell ending!"
—*Los Angeles Times*

"A fast-paced entertaining book . . . hard-boiled, smart and funny."   —*Chicago Sun-Times*

. . . A CASE OF LONE STAR

"A hilarious winner!"   —*UPI*

"Tough, cool and funny."   —*San Antonio Express-News*

"*A Case of Lone Star* has an effortless charm that eventually grows on you like a catchy country tune."
—*Boston Sunday Globe*

"Ranges from excellent whodunit to high comedy."
—*National Lampoon*

. . . WHEN THE CAT'S AWAY

"Hip, humorous, and tough."   —*Cincinnati Enquirer*

"Vintage Friedman! Bizarre, funny, exciting, crisp, and cynical . . . Kinky keeps getting better!"
—*Richmond News Leader*

"The irrepressible Kinky Friedman is back!"   —*Boston Globe*

"Funny, refreshing fiction . . . sparkles with wit, imagination and hard-boiled humor!"   —*Daily Texan*

KINKY FRIEDMAN

THREE COMPLETE MYSTERIES

KINKY FRIEDMAN

THREE COMPLETE MYSTERIES

GREENWICH KILLING TIME
A CASE OF LONE STAR
WHEN THE CAT'S AWAY

WINGS BOOKS
New York • Avenel, New Jersey

Grateful acknowledgment is made for permission to reprint lines from the following songs:
"WHEN IRISH EYES ARE SMILING" by E. Ball, G. Graffe, & C. Olcott. Copyright 1912 by M. Witmark and Sons, & CHAPPEL & CO., INC. All Rights Administered by CHAPPEL & CO., INC. (Intersong-USA, Pub.) International Copyright Secured. All Rights Reserved. Used by permission.
"HEY GOOD LOOKIN'" by Hank Williams. © 1951 Renewed 1979; Hiriam Music 50% U.S.A. only; Acuff-Rose/Opryland Music, Inc. 50% U.S.A. 100% World Outside U.S.A. 66 Music Square West, Nashville, Tennessee 37203. International Copyright Secured. Made in U.S.A. All Rights Secured.
"I'LL NEVER GET OUT OF THIS WORLD ALIVE" by Fred Rose and Hank Williams. ©1952 Renewed 1980; Aberbach Music 50% U.S.A. only; Milene/Opryland Music, Inc. 50% U.S.A., 100% World Outside U.S.A. 66 Music Square West, Nashville, Tennessee 37203. International Copyright Secured. Made in U.S.A. All Rights Secured.
"SETTIN' THE WOODS ON FIRE" by Fred Rose and Ed. G. Nelson. © 1952 Renewed 1980; Milene/Opryland Music, Inc. 66 Music Square West, Nashville, Tennessee 37203. International Copyright Secured. Made in U.S.A. All Rights Secured.
"KAW-LIGA" by Fred Rose and Hank Williams. © 1952 Renewed 1980; Aberbach Music 50% U.S.A. only; Milene/Opryland Music, Inc. 50% U.S.A. 100% World Outside U.S.A. 66 Music Square West, Nashville, Tennessee 37203. International Copyright Secured. Made in U.S.A. All Rights Secured.
"A MANSION ON THE HILL" by Fred Rose and Hank Williams. © 1948 Renewed 1975; Aberbach Music 50% U.S.A. only; Milene/Opryland Music, Inc. 50% U.S.A., 100% World Outside U.S.A., 66 Music Square West, Nashville, Tennessee 37203. International Copyright Secured. Made in U.S.A. All Rights Secured.
"LOST HIGHWAY" by Leon Payne. © 1949 Renewed 1976; Acuff-Rose/Opryland Music, Inc. 66 Music Square West, Nashville, Tennessee 37203. International Copyright Secured. Made in U.S.A. All Rights Secured.
Lyrics on the dedication page of When the Cat's Away are from the song "Autograph" by Kinky Friedman and Panama Red 1975 by Kinky Music Inc., BMI.

This omnibus was originally published in separate volumes under the titles:
Greenwich Killing Time, copyright © 1986 by Kinky Friedman.
A Case of Lone Star, copyright © 1987 by Kinky Friedman.
When the Cat's Away, copyright © 1988 by Kinky Friedman.

This edition contains the complete and unabridged texts of the original editions. They have been completely reset for this volume.

This 1993 edition is published by Wings Books,
distributed by Outlet Book Company, Inc., a Random House Company,
40 Engelhard Avenue, Avenel, New Jersey 07001,
by arrangement with William Morrow & Company, Inc.

Random House
New York • Toronto • London • Sydney • Auckland

Designed by Helene Berinsky

Printed and bound in the United States of America

Library of Congress Cataloging-in-Publication Data

Friedman, Kinky.
  [Selections. 1993]
  Three complete mysteries / Kinky Friedman.
    p.   cm.
  Contents: Greenwich killing time—A case of lone star—When the cat's away.
  ISBN 0-517-09328-6
  1. Manhattan (New York, N.Y.)—Fiction.   2. Detective and mystery stories, American.   3. Humorous stories, American.   I. Title.   II. Title: Kinky Friedman—three complete mysteries.; aa21
  04-08-93.
  PS3556.R527A6   1993
  813'.54—dc20   93-19513
                                                                             CIP

8   7   6   5   4   3   2   1

CONTENTS

Greenwich
Killing Time

ACKNOWLEDGMENTS

The author would like to thank the following people for their help and encouragement: Tom Friedman, Larry Sloman, Don Imus, Marcie Friedman and Ted Mann; Esther Newberg at ICM; James Landis and Jane Meara at Beech Tree Books; and Steve Rambam, technical adviser.

The author would also like to thank Michael R. McGovern for the use of his mother's Smith-Corona typewriter.

To Min

1

I held the mescal up to the light and watched the worm slide across the bottom of the bottle. A gift from a friend just back from Mexico. The worm was fat and white and somewhat dangerous looking with great hallucinogenic properties attributed to it. You were supposed to eat it and it was supposed to make you so high you would need a stepladder to scratch your ass. We'd see.

I searched my wastebasket for a while till I located a dead, fairly well-preserved, half-smoked cigar and I fired it up. I remembered Winston Churchill's reputed words on the subject: "They're gamier when resurrected." Winston wasn't wrong.

I was leaning back in my chair, puffing a bit, just trying to keep the world at bay, when the phones rang. I was in the habit of keeping two red telephones at stage left and stage right of my desk, both connected to the same line. It sort of enhanced the importance of my calls and when they rang they burned right through you like a red-hot skewer. It was McGovern from the *Daily News*.

You had to like McGovern. He was a very friendly, very large half-Irish, half-Indian who, like every journalist I knew, would take a drink. He nevertheless had many charming and redeeming qualities, some of which were quite noticeably absent in the architecture of my personality. In fact, I often thought that between the two of us, we'd just about make up one fairly adequate human being.

"Get over here right away, man. This is serious. There's a body lying on the floor across the hall. Looks like a case for you." He gave me an address on Jane Street fairly close by in the Village.

I didn't ask him a case of what? Riding up Hudson in the cab I reasoned that it wasn't the kind of case one would like to drink nor the kind one might possibly obtain from any recent unsavory sexualis.

I tipped the cabbie and got out at 42 Jane, opposite the only windmill in New York City, a weatherbeaten but proud remnant of long-ago Dutch masters. I climbed the steps and pushed the buzzer of Apartment 2B, where McGovern had lived since Christ was a cowboy, or at least since I'd known him.

As I cleared the second landing, I could see McGovern's huge form hovering above, displacing a great deal of the narrow hallway. "Over here," he whispered and led me across to the opposite end of the hall from his own place. "In there," he muttered.

I pushed the door open to Apartment 2E. There were several chairs pulled up around a table with a brightly checked red and white tablecloth. On the table was a plate of banana bread and another plate of Brie. There was a pitcher of Bloody Marys in which the ice was beginning to melt and several fairly nice crystal glasses.

One of the glasses was clearly smudged with bright pink lipstick, at least as clear as you could possibly get a smudge. It went with the decor because the man was holding a bouquet of long-stemmed pink roses. He was lying on the floor with a cute little hole right about where his third eye should be. The flowers he was holding were quite lovely but he definitely couldn't care less. On the floor beside the body was a little white card with the typewritten message: "i'm sending you eleven roses . . . the twelfth rose is you."

"There you have it," said McGovern.

2

The cops from the Sixth Precinct came and went in a blue parade. There were a few plainclothesmen. McGovern was, by this time, across the hall on the blower to the *Daily News*.

The cops identified me about the same time they identified the stiff. Neither of us cut much ice with them. They remembered me from my first exploit two years before, which McGovern had written up lavishly in the *News*. The story had carried the gaudy headline: COUNTRY SINGER PLUCKS VICTIM FROM MUGGER.

Since that time I had evolved professionally from "country singer" to "Broadway composer" as I neared completion of my first musical comedy bound for the boards. But with several fortuitous forays into crime solving in the Village, I had also evolved into something between a gnat and a rather motheaten gadfly in the eyes of the officers of the Sixth Precinct.

"You . . . Stay there," said the cop apparently in charge of the case, Detective Sergeant Buddy Fox. We'd met before. He was tall, lean, and mean, and he didn't like country music. He went through the pockets of the deceased. The assistant medical examiner arrived. The police photographer snapped away, kibbitzing with the print men who were dusting the articles on the table and with the assistant medical examiner, who occasionally chuckled and put his two cents in across the bland features of the face on the floor.

"What do you know about this?" Fox asked.

10   "Looks like a warning shot right between the eyes," I said.
"See anyone?"

I shook my head.

"Hear the shot?" he asked.

Again I shook my head.

I won't tell you what he said next. A nicer version of it
might read: "Then what are you doing here, pal?"

It had worked so well I tried shaking my head a third
time.

Detective Sergeant Fox became slightly agitato, but he controlled himself. Trembling only slightly, he impressed upon
me the gravity of tampering with evidence in a homicide. His
partner, Detective Sergeant Mort Cooperman, was shorter
and a great deal stockier than Fox. He was breathing heavily.
I wondered if he'd been out walking his pet stomach. He
took down my address and phone number and then bel-
lowed for me to bug out for the dugout. Actually, those were
not his precise words, but that was the gist.

I left shaking my head, mostly for effect.

I took a cab back to 199B Vandam, cursed the absence of
the freight elevator, and legged it up the four floors to my loft
with the jungle of green plants and the sun-streaked southern exposure that made me the envy of many trendy, back-
to-nature New Yorkers. Actually, the plants were there when
I rented the place, but between thick incessant cigar smoke
and my cat's constant chomping on them, we'd managed to
make a dent or two in the foliage. About every six months or
so I faithfully watered them whether they needed it or not.

I know the exact time because I have a small digital alarm
clock, which I like to think of as a computer, and it keeps me
on the cutting edge of the technological age. I log all incoming calls.

The phones rang at 8:23 P.M. It was McGovern.

"Good news and bad news," he said. "He had sublet the
place for only about six months. His name is or was Frank
Worthington, a part-time actor, part-time bartender, and, ap-

parently, a part-time bisexual. Or should I say a full-time bisexual?''

"Right," I said.

"The bad news is where I'm calling from. I'm calling from the Sixth Precinct. They found the gun in my apartment."

3

I wasted no time getting on the blower to my lawyer, Wolf Nachman. There are no good lawyers. There may be lady wrestlers and Catholic universities. There may be military intelligence. But a good lawyer is a contradiction in terms. When you needed one, you needed one, however, and I needed one. So Wolf was the one I called and he said he'd get right on it.

I brewed some coffee, lit a fresh cigar, and waited. It was a Friday night, the beginning of another fun-filled New York weekend in the Village for teenage hit-run drivers from New Jersey and assorted other Americans.

I turned on the twenty-four-hour all-news station. They had a slogan they kept repeating: "You give us twenty-two minutes—we'll give you the world." No deal, I thought.

They didn't have the story yet. At 11:53 P.M. the phones rang. I listened to Wolf howl at me for a while. He was moving heaven and earth but McGovern would probably be staying in the sneezer for at least the weekend. There was nothing to be done so I decided rather reluctantly to call it a night myself.

The cat yawned and stretched and I yawned and stretched and we both looked at each other. Sometimes I thought there wasn't a man, woman, or child on this planet that I loved as much as that cat. What the cat was thinking was something else of course. I rarely meddled in the cat's personal affairs and she rarely meddled in mine. Neither of us was foolish enough to attribute human emotions to our pets.

* * *

The sounds of garbage trucks awakened me in the morning. Some people wake up to the sounds of church bells. Some people wake up to sounds of birds. But in New York you wake up to the sounds of garbage trucks. Place is still filthy, of course. Can't have everything.

I brewed some strong black coffee and fed the cat. Then I walked the few blocks up to Sheridan Square to get a morning paper. That area is one of New York's throbbing nerve centers of drug-oriented, gay festivity at all hours of day and night. I liked to point out the area to tourists. General Sheridan's statue stands looking over the square but you can tell he isn't liking it much.

I bought a paper and glanced through it in a quaint Fourth Street restaurant that was about as big as my nose and was called The Bagel.

There was nothing. No flowers. No croaked bisexuals. No McGovern. Nary a by-line and nary a bi-line.

Strange.

I paid the check and hoofed it over to Jane Street, stopping only briefly at Village Cigars on Seventh Avenue for a few purchases for the household.

At 42 Jane Street the super was surly. He held a lingering, somewhat unfavorable impression of me from the old days when I used to crash with McGovern for months at a time. The only thing he seemed willing to give me was grief, so I left for a while and circled back, this time employing a set of keys I'd retained from way back when.

I tried one. It was rusty but it worked fine. Like a Haitian curse. I had it in mind to visit somebody on the third floor. I remembered her from a party about seven years ago. She was sort of an ingenue then. Couldn't wait to see her now. Seven years in New York is like a lifetime anywhere else.

I bounded up to the third floor. Carpet was getting a little threadbare up there. I'd have to mention it to the super. I knocked on the door of Apartment 3B, right above McGovern's. After some little cajoling and explaining, I was permitted entry into a dusty, dimly lighted apartment with enough drug paraphernalia to start a store in the East Village.

Adrian looked like a waxen insect.

"You look fine," I lied.

"What do you want?" she said, motioning me with a weary gesture onto the couch next to her.

"I want to know about the guy that got croaked in Two-E. Bought any flowers lately, Adrian?" Sometimes the direct approach was the best.

Now she smiled a little. It wasn't a pleasant thing to see. She was well on her way to acquiring what is sometimes referred to as a "New York face." I think George Orwell was the one who said that by age fifty every man has the face he deserves. Orwell himself was only forty-seven when he died. Well, it can't be helped. But it goes ditto for women, to say the least. And it wasn't a particularly nice direction Adrian's face was taking. Something evil was just beneath the mascara, lurking just behind the eye shadow.

"Have a line," she said, as she stared at the little tray on the coffee table. I shook my head. "How well did you know Frank Worthington?" I asked.

"Frankie?" She smiled. "Everybody knows Frankie."

"Knew."

"Why would I want to hurt little Frankie?" she said. "Bastard owes me eight hundred dollars. You should ask around down at the Monkey's Paw, or ask your friend McGovern, if the cops ever let him go. Sure you don't want a line?"

"No, thanks," I said. "I had an apple on the train."

I left. On impulse I stopped at the second landing and tried McGovern's door. It was locked. I took out another old key and cajoled my way into McGovern's apartment. The place was cluttered and dirty as hell, with record albums, books, newspapers, and news copy all over the place. It should have been clean, at least in the cop sense of the word, but I had a nagging prescience that it wasn't.

The remnants of a two-day-old Chicken McGovern were still wallowing in a blood-red sort of crusty paste in a pot on the stove. I tried some. It wasn't bad. I took a look around and was starting to leave when something caught my eye over by the stereo. McGovern's turntable was very important to him. A guy like me, who'd worked the road and made a living writing and performing music—I hated most music. Only listened to it in elevators. A guy like McGovern, who spent his time covering the seamy, late-breaking side of life, he loved music. Couldn't get enough of it. Music was his life.

He did have some taste, though. Billie Holiday was on the turntable. Through the clear plastic top I saw a pink slip lying suggestively on top of Billie. It was a bill of sale from the little flower shop around the corner on Hudson Street.

The bill came to forty-four dollars for one dozen long-stemmed pink roses.

4

It was a beautiful bright and cold Saturday afternoon in late February. I had pocketed the florist's receipt and locked the door on the way out and was now riding home in a cab driven by a man named Abdul bin Abdul. At least that's what it said on his hack license. He was a non-English speaker or else very shy. Either one was okay. I needed to think.

Could my large, kind, intelligent Irish drinking pal of almost a decade be involved in this bizarre business? He would make a terribly awkward murderer and an even worse bisexual, but who really knew? Somebody was working overtime to set him up and I doubted it would be Adrian. But Adrian clearly knew something and probably more than that.

I looked out of the cab. People behind windows of cozy little cafés drinking their cappuccino, spreading grapefruit marmalade on their croissants. Young couples in the streets shopping aimlessly for flavored toilet soaps.

It almost made you glad to be alive. Almost.

I took out a cigar and began the prenuptial arrangements on it. The cabbie broke the silence, pointed to the sign: "No smoke! No smoke!" he said sullenly.

"Relax, pal," I said, "I wouldn't dream of it." I put the unlighted cigar in my mouth and watched his swarthy visage checking me out in the rearview.

"So much for the Third World," I said, as we snaked our way down Seventh Avenue toward Vandam.

I looked out the window again in silence.

It was a quiet little village. It was home to 250,000 homosexuals, and about 90,000 hard-drug abusers. And occasionally, a rather kinky little murder.

I could see the Village clearly now, but I had the chilling
impression I was a long way from being out of the woods.

5

The Monkey's Paw was not the kind of place Ingrid Bergman might walk into some night. You wouldn't even want to see your ex-wife walk into the place.

It used to be mostly a writer's bar, a crime reporter's hangout, and I guess you could say it still is. McGovern was eighty-sixed from there years ago for peeing on the leg of a patron. It's hard to go downhill from there but the Monkey's Paw tries. Tonight I had business there.

The Weasel arrived at the Monkey's Paw always at six and always alone. He looked like a weasel. If he had a little facial tic or maybe a discernible twitch to his body you could be sure his current batch of weasel dust was the McCoy. I ran out of credit with him long ago, and fortunately, I saw him only rarely now. Like when I wanted to celebrate a death in the family.

The Weasel had a warehouse of information. About the only thing he didn't know was that his name was The Weasel.

He thought it was Max.

"Hi, Max," I said. "Frank Worthington working tonight?"

It was 6:05 P.M. Weasel was running a little behind his schedule.

"Don't you read the papers?" He laid the evening edition of the *Post* on the bar.

"Well! I look in on Nancy and Sluggo occasionally. Why?"

I didn't have to look too far. It was page 1. I sipped my

Guinness and took a casual glance at the story: DAILY NEWS
MAN HELD IN BIZARRE VILLAGE MURDER.

"Your old buddy," said The Weasel, "McGovern."

"Yeah," I said, "I knew McGovern'd come to no good."

Four Guinnesses later I was pumping The Weasel pretty
well. I was buying him Rémys, and each time he left for his
office, which was the men's room, with a client, I'd scribble
down a little more information. It wasn't particularly adding
up but it was a side of the case I was sure the cops didn't
have. From the look of the *Post* story, I didn't even think they
wanted it.

It seemed Worthington was pretty well liked and a fairly
good little church worker, but he definitely had swung from
both sides of the box.

And he got around pretty good too. By the time I left the
Monkey's Paw, I had sort of a hazy, mental picture of four
people. I knew the names of four of Worthington's current
flames. At least they'd been current before last night.

I had hardly patted the cat before the phones rang. It was
McGovern's girlfriend. 8:45 P.M. Cynthia was a little upset
about McGovern's incarceration. I coaxed her down from the
chandelier, cradled the blower, and fished a pretty nice-looking dead cigar out of the trash.

I stoked it up and listened for a while to the rhythmic thud
of the lesbian dance class in the loft above me. It was run by
a girl named Winnie Katz. She was making quite a name for
herself among the diesel-dyke community in the Village.
Might come in handy before this whole thing was over. A
fellow never knew.

It was ten o'clock Saturday night, and the sidewalks of the
Village were crowded with people desperately trying to have
fun and some people actually having it, whatever it is. Almost none of them lived in the Village. They just periodically
descended upon it whenever Brooklyn, Queens, the Bronx,
New Jersey, or the plasticine Upper East Side of Manhattan
became too much for them. Most old-time Village residents

resented them and hoped they'd get mugged. I didn't care what they got as long as it was out of my way.

Andrew had held a table for me at the Derby on MacDougal Street. The Derby is the oldest and best steak house in the Village and maybe the whole town. Andrew was busy seating customers and cursing vegetarians and young people in general for saying bad things about red meat. The trend today was toward vegetables and fish and it wasn't good for America or the Derby.

I told him to try to guess who my dinner companion would be when he came in the door. He said he'd try and I said I'd try a few shots of Jameson.

If Andrew was cursing vegetarians, I was cursing McGovern. McGovern was my main source for information on anything and he was a good one. I wouldn't call him punctual, or reliable, or even sober some of the time, but he was always a steady man in a shaky universe. I had come to think of him as sort of my American Doctor Watson, a notion he once good-naturedly described as "stupid and self-serving." Whatever he thought wasn't going to make too much difference to a tree, however, because he was drinking from a tin cup in the sneezer and I was going to be all alone on this one.

I looked up in time to see Andrew graciously ushering Ratso over to my table. Ratso was an old friend of mine and the editor of a wide-circulation national magazine. He was attired in a manner that was bizarre even for the Derby's rather informal dress code, but Andrew was glossing that one over apparently and ignoring the stares of the other diners. Good for him.

Ratso was wearing his usual cold-weather headgear: a coonskin cap minus the tail. He had on a black-leather motorcycle jacket and sort of off-lox-colored slacks with bright red shoes that had once belonged to a dead man. This was true of almost his entire wardrobe because he did all his shopping among the flea markets along Canal Street.

I'd often mentioned to him that the constant wearing of dead men's shoes might not be his smartest move in terms of hygiene. He always walked away from that one by saying that before goods were sold at the flea market, they had to pass rigid tests for all these things; there was quality control, they sterilized everything, etc.

Then I would take a somewhat more spiritual approach with him, saying that I couldn't be sure but I felt that the wearing of dead men's shoes was probably not particularly good karma. Just wasn't quite best foot forward and all that. He'd always sidestep that one too, and point out some obscure Hasidic commandment that no one on earth had ever believed in, much less bothered to practice.

"Good thing nobody asked you who your tailor is," I said. "He's probably been dead for a hundred years."

"Let's order," he said.

The evening was not a total loss as it turned out. The sliced steak with the Colman's Hot English Mustard was strictly top drawer and the Jameson-Guinness combination was beginning to kick in as well.

One of the few qualities that I admire in Arabian and Turkish peoples is that they never talk serious business until the coffee has arrived. "So, Ratso," I said when the coffee had arrived, "let me fill you in on the McGovern situation." I filled him in.

"Why don't we just call it your new case?" He laughed. "I mean, the cops think McGovern did it and we know he's innocent, right?"

"Partially," I said. "We believe he's innocent, yes."

"Jesus."

"And we know He's innocent."

"Then who done it, Sherlock?"

"Well, not counting McGovern or the little girl who lives upstairs and sells cocaine, we have four current names to run down." I wrote The Weasel's list of Frank's favorites down on a cocktail napkin and Ratso studied them.

"Never heard of any of them. They're all Greek to me," he said, handing back the napkin.

"Yeah, two of them were Greek to Frank, too," I said.

22

We split the list, Ratso taking the two boys and me taking the two girls, and Ratso assuring me he didn't mind "working the homosexual side of the street if it would help McGovern."

Ratso had good connections. He knew Spider Webb, a renowned Village tattoo artist, and he had friends who frequented such places as the Hellfire Club. I told the Rat to get on it very fast. The cops, I understood, always feel that after the first twenty-four hours the bloom begins to fade on a homicide case. After the first few days, if no big breaks develop, the case will probably only be solved by chance. The bloom on this one was fading faster than Frank Worthington's flowers. I paid the check.

6

Sunday morning when I woke up I did not feel like John Denver. The cat was meowing and the phones were ringing but at least the garbage trucks were silent. It was Wolf Nachman on the phone. The computer said 9:17 A.M. "Ah," he said, "you're back from church already."

"Yeah."

"Must have been a pretty short sermon." Humor was not particularly one of Wolf's long suits. He didn't know it though, so I had to play along.

"Yeah," I said.

"I thought you might like to know the gun they found in McGovern's apartment is back from ballistics. It was the murder weapon."

"What was the gun, Wolf?"

"Let's see. It says here a Beretta twenty-five caliber automatic."

"Standard purse gun," I said. I knew that much. I didn't know too much else about guns except I'd never owned one and never wanted to. If anybody ever croaked me, they had damn sure better remember to bring their own gun.

"Kind of looks like some broad may have Sam Cooke'd him," I said.

"Who's that?" asked the lawyer. He wasn't really well-versed in a number of areas, including the area of Negro soul singers croaked by jealous women in hotels in America. But he knew his law. When it came to that he was as brilliant as a barracuda.

"Rather an effeminate weapon for a big boy like McGovern, wouldn't you say?"

Wolf wouldn't say. He'd seen McGovern and proceeded to tell me about it. He said he'd get back to me.

I took the pink receipt slip from the florist shop, stuffed it in an envelope, and slid it to the bottom of the cat litter tray, which I always kept in the shower except of course when I was taking a shower.

Now I was probably obstructing justice or something. At the very least I was withholding and concealing evidence directly related to a homicide case. It was kind of fun actually. And there was no other choice in the matter. If I turned the florist receipt over to Fox and told him where I'd found it, it would hang McGovern for sure.

McGovern was being kept at Central Holding behind the courthouse at 100 Centre Street. Wolf thought he would have him out on bail sometime early in the week. He could be visited only by an attorney or a clergyman and I wasn't either one of them. I didn't even want to be either one of them when I grew up.

This thing was going to take time. I took the cocktail napkin from the Derby out of a cigar box and studied the two names again: Darlene Rigby and Nina Kong.

I knew a little less about women than I knew about guns. Nobody really understood women except maybe bisexual hairdressers. They knew a lot about women but it was obvious they didn't care. In fact, women had very few friends in the world. I'd often felt that a man without a woman was like a neck without a pain.

But maybe I was being a little too harsh. I'd known many women who weren't like other women. Gunner, for instance. I wondered if she'd like to go to the Ranger game with me tonight. She was blond, British, and beautiful, and she'd never seen a hockey game. To live and die on this planet without ever seeing a hockey game was something hard to imagine. People did it all the time though. They did a lot of other things too. Like stab their mother-in-law in the nose with an ice pick.

I tried not to think of McGovern down there at 100 Centre Street in a holding tank quite possibly full of hardened criminals. Gentle, good-natured McGovern, who had once combed his hair before meeting a racehorse.

I hoped he liked baloney sandwiches.

It was still a little too early to try to call Rigby or Kong. So I made some hot chocolate and sipped it for about twenty minutes while I listened to my hair grow. Then I tried information for Darlene Rigby. I knew she was a struggling young actress. Weren't they all. And I knew she lived in some big complex for the arts on Forty-third Street in the heart of Hell's Kitchen. An entire building full of young actors and dancers and the like, all struggling to make it. Well, they certainly picked the right location. In that neighborhood getting to the corner store for a pack of cigarettes was a struggle.

The Weasel had described Darlene Rigby as very talented, very beautiful, and very determined to get to the top of her profession. She might have been very talented, but if she was the one who croaked Frank Worthington, she'd taken the scene right out of a bad movie. There was something rather frightening about the campy way the whole thing was put together: the flowers, the note on the floor, the stagy table setting complete with the Bloody Marys. And the wound that itself was not very bloody, yet was emphatically evil in its perfection. A neat, rather artistic little bull's-eye that told you Frank Worthington had celebrated his very last Ash Wednesday.

If Darlene Rigby had that much determination, God help Hollywood. I picked up the phone.

''Good morning, Miss Rigby. This is Fred Barkin. I was a friend of Frank Worthington's and we're having a little informal get-together tonight at around eight o'clock at Chumley's in the Village. Do you know it? . . . Fine. Then we'll count on seeing you? . . . Fine. Just share a few

26

drinks and a few memories for Frank. . . . Yes it was. . . . Terrible . . . Yes, we all do. We all do. . . . It'll be the kind of evening Frank would have enjoyed. Glad you can make it. . . . See you tonight. Good-bye.''

I was laying it on fairly thick, but I have found that in this business, one of the most important things is sincerity. If you can fake that, you can do just about anything.

7

Nina Kong might be more difficult. She was the lead singer with some new-wave country band that was in the process of signing a big recording contract. I ran her down through my friend Cleve, who was the manager of the Lone Star Café, a country-music place on Fifth Avenue and Thirteenth Street. She'd played there a few times recently, and I'd played there a few times myself back when coffee with a friend was still a dime.

"So when you gonna play here again, man?" Cleve had asked.

"Probably on a cold day in Jerusalem, pal," I'd told him. I missed performing there like I missed having a mescal worm in my matzo-ball soup.

"Come on, man, let's work something out. You don't want people to start calling you the Legendary What's-his-name, do you? Hell, everybody can use a little exposure."

I had forgotten how tedious Cleve could be. That was one of the things I liked about my new life-style—it hardly required my presence. If it wasn't for McGovern, I'd be taking it easy, putting the final touches on my Broadway score, getting ready to start selecting chorus girls.

"I don't want exposure, Cleve. I know people who died of exposure. How about you expose this broad's telephone number to me right now?"

I got it, got off the blower, and was in the process of removing the cat litter from the rain-room when the phones rang again.

Ratso. 10:27 A.M. "Start talking," I said. "And make it fast. I'm a nudist."

"Well, I just wanted to discuss some of the ramifications with you, Inspector Maigret."

"That's cute, but put a sock on it, pal. What the hell do you want?" I was usually pretty grumpy but I was always pretty grumpy in the morning. I was going to make a great old person if I ever lived that long.

We coordinated the Chumley's get-together. Ratso would get his two there and I would get my two there and then we'd throw back a few toasts to ol' Frank and see what happened next. Sounded like fun. It wasn't every night you could be pretty certain you were hoisting a few with a murderer.

I hung up the phone and jumped back into the rain-room. Now there was a place I didn't mind singing.

The sun was flooding into the loft pretty impressively by now. I was feeling better after the shower. I stood at the kitchen window in my purple bathrobe and brown slippers, smoking my early morning cigar. It didn't look like February in New York. If you ignored the garbage trucks, the warehouses, the fire escapes, and the newspapers and crap blowing all over the sidewalks, it was a beautiful view. If you turned your neck at a rather extreme angle you could just see the Hudson River over to the west, but it was hard to keep your head twisted in that position for very long. The fire escapes were hard on the eyes but they were a lot easier on the neck.

I now had to make one of the hardest decisions a person living in the Village ever has to make: espresso or cappuccino. I decided upon cappuccino and walked over to the machine. I didn't have to walk too far. It took up about half of the kitchen. In the brilliant sunlight it gleamed like a small Fascist tank.

As the machine steamed and gurgled, I checked the hockey schedule on the kitchen wall. Obviously tonight was out, but

Wednesday night the Rangers played their archrivals, the Is-landers, at the Garden. The match-up looked brutal enough to warm the heart of any hockey fan. I considered calling Gunner, but I still had this Kong dame to take care of.

I threw a little cinnamon and a little Jameson into the cap-puccino, walked over to the living-room couch, sat down, and dialed the Kong girl's number on the phone there. This was a private line. Only three or four people had this number and I wasn't even sure I remembered who they were. The rocking chair belonged to the cat.

"Good morning. Is Nina there?"

A guy answered kind of gruffly, "Who wants to know?"

"This is Phil Bender. I'm a booking agent working for Cleve at the Lone Star."

Nina picked up the phone.

"That was a pleasant fellow," I said.

"Sorry about that. If this is about a booking, you're wast-ing your time. You can tell Cleve I won't be available for a while."

I could see I'd have to take another tack.

"No," I said, "this isn't about a booking. This is about a croaking. I'm looking into Frank Worthington's murder, and if you don't want a command performance at the Sixth Pre-cinct, I think you should cooperate with me and tell me what you know. Maybe we can keep the cops out of this."

She didn't say anything.

I could see I'd have to take another tack. Pretty soon I wouldn't have enough left to crucify last year's calendar.

"Nina," I said, "this isn't Phil Bender. This is Kinky."

"It sure is," she said. "I know who you are. I saw you play at the Lone Star a long time ago."

"Yeah," I said. "I was probably playing there when you were jumping rope in the schoolyard. Like I said, I'm looking into this Frank Worthington thing. You've heard about Frank Worthington?"

"Y-yes," she said. "It's horrible."

"Terrible," I said. "Look, we're having an informal little

wake tonight at Chumley's in the Village. Can you make it? I'd like to talk to you.''

"Okay. What time?"

"Eight."

"I'll be there. You know," she said wistfully, "I can't believe Frank's really dead. I just can't believe it.''

I took a healthy puff on my cigar. "Pinch yourself," I said.

8

The telephone was an amazing instrument for love, for business deals, and for the
gathering and gleaning of information. But it had its
limits. Even a quasi-legendary detective had to do a little legwork now and then. Put the violin and the cocaine syringe
up on the mantel and fish the old magnifying glass out of the
hope chest. I didn't much like running all over the place
looking for clues but it beat jogging.

If I was one step ahead of the police, it was only because I
knew McGovern was incapable of the crime and they didn't.
Assuming anyone is really incapable of anything.

Maybe Wolf and I would get McGovern out and the very
first thing he'd do would be to come over to my loft and
croak me. Maybe the *Post* would run another headline: COUN-
TRY SINGER CROAKED BY DAILY NEWS MAN. Everybody could use a
little exposure.

It was a beautiful afternoon to joust at windmills so I
walked up Hudson in the direction of Jane Street. Cynthia,
McGovern's latest girlfriend, had told me she'd probably be
over at his place cleaning up a bit and straightening up his
affairs. That was a good one.

I was feeling ambivalent about my visit to McGovern's the
day before. I was glad I'd gone before Cynthia cleaned the
place up. But what the hell was that receipt for the flowers
doing there? I'd have to ask McGovern if I ever spoke to him
again. I'd also like to know how many people besides the
cops, the super, me, and Cynthia had keys to his apartment.

32 Maybe he stood under the windmill and passed them out to street traffic.

Cynthia looked like a slightly weatherbeaten cheerleader. But only slightly. And that was pretty good for New York. She wanted to hug me and I let her. It didn't cost anything and I'd hugged worse in my time. I didn't like it much, though. I felt awkward, impatient about it. Hugging distraught women was just probably not one of my long suits. Of course, the distraught women never knew the difference.

"Cynthia, did McGovern call you anytime Friday evening?"

"Let me think. Yes. He called me twice. The first time he called to make sure I was coming over for dinner that night."

"Chicken McGovern," I said, and nodded knowingly.

"Yes." She was starting to cry again.

"Pace yourself," I said, "this could be a fairly long ordeal for all of us. What was the second call about?"

"He said not to come over. That there'd been a murder in the building. 'Across the hall,' he said. Then he said, 'Do you believe in ghosts?' "

9

I cased the whole apartment and came up with nothing but an old cowboy hat of mine from 1979. Not a particularly good year as I recalled so I tried not to. The hat was about seven sizes too small for McGovern so I really couldn't be too accusatory about the whole thing. I put it on and started to leave, telling Cynthia not to worry, the worst they could pin on him would be a second-degree murder charge and everybody knew you had to kill at least two people in New York before they even thought about putting you away.

That didn't seem to have quite the desired effect, and I wasn't going to get hugged twice on the same day, so I said we'd keep in touch and I left. She was really quite a pretty girl if you liked blondes.

I walked across the hall and took a look, but Worthington's door was locked and an NYPD "scene of crime" seal signed by Detective Sergeant Buddy Fox was firmly in place. The cops used the seal to keep away the curious, the looters, and the ghouls. I guess you'd have to say that I fit into category one there. At least category one. For the whole weekend I'd been having intermittent yet intense struggles with Satan, who'd been urging me to break in there and have a little look in Frank Worthington's closets.

The forces of good triumphed on this occasion. I'd need professional help with the police lock anyway, and Sunday afternoon wasn't the most intellectual time selection for a

34 breaking and entering operation. "Maybe you should come back in the dead of the night," the voice of Satan whispered.

"Now you're talkin' turkey," I said.

On impulse I hoofed it up to the next landing and knocked on Adrian's door. There was a guy just leaving. At least he scurried out of there like a New York rat before I could get into the room.

Adrian looked her lovely self. She was wearing some kind of a black and red leather outfit that didn't do much for her. There wasn't really much you could do. I wished Satan could have been there to get a load of it. "Nice," I said, approvingly.

"Glad you like it," she said, very possibly blushing. I couldn't really tell for sure because of the dim light in the room, the heavy makeup on her face, and my own disinclination to look too closely. It was like staring at a burned-out sun with the naked eye. It wasn't really dangerous, but it wasn't especially good for you either.

"I've been working on stained-glass art," she said, pointing to a small, purplish pane. "It's really time-consuming. It takes forever. I've been working on it for about six months. A friend of mine has a gallery on the Lower East Side and he's going to put it in an exhibition there."

Every drug dealer I'd ever met was not really a drug dealer. He or she was really an artist working with stained glass, or really an author getting ready to do research for a novel about Paris in the twenties, or really a film director patiently waiting for a screenplay that accurately reflected life in Southern California. No drug dealer ever thought of himself as a drug dealer. If you asked him what he did for a living, he couldn't very well answer: "I suck away about seventy percent of your life blood, your spirit, and your energy. Then I suck away about eighty percent of your income. Then I suck away about one hundred percent of whatever little chance you have of finding any happiness in life."

"Nice," I said, holding the stained glass up to what light there was.

I walked home down Fourth Street on a route that would take me through Sheridan Square and down Seventh Avenue to Vandam. The evening was beautiful and crisp, just beginning to chill like a fine imported wine. Or a freshly croaked stiff.

It was like pulling teeth from a buzz saw but Adrian had finally agreed to leave her apartment and join us later tonight at Chumley's. That ought to round out the wake nicely, I thought.

I pulled a cigar out of my hunting vest, from one of a row of tiny pockets stitched into it to hold shotgun shells. I never hunted for anything anyway except maybe trouble.

It wasn't a bad evening and it wasn't a bad cigar either. I began entertaining thoughts of just dropping by the Sixth Precinct and shmoozing with some of the boys. Fox and Cooperman weren't especially big fans of my music. Nor were they particularly inclined to celebrate my brief but thus far successful career in the field of amateur detective work. They had no time for amateurs. When Fox and Cooperman bungled things, it was always in a polished and professional manner.

The press had been more laudatory where I had been concerned. When I had successfully wrapped up a rather grisly murder episode at the Lone Star the year before, it had made page 1 in both the *Post* and the *Daily News*. *The New York Times* must have given the order to "Hold the back pages" when they got the story because it only made page 11. Another reason I never read *The New York Times*.

The *News* had emphasized the fact that the case had baffled the cops for months. The story had gone on to say that my efforts had "cracked the case" and that I had provided the police with the "stunning solution."

The Lone Star was dead in the middle of Fox and Cooperman's bailiwick, and this kind of publicity wasn't calculated to make the three of us fast friends. The by-line, of course, had been McGovern's, but a reporter only writes what he sees.

When I got to Sheridan Square, I stopped in at Village Cigars before heading over to the cop shop. Years ago a guy wearing a cowboy hat in this area would probably have created quite a little stir. People would be yelling "Hey, Tex" and "Cowboy!" You never could tell if they were being derisive or just curious and exuberant, but personally, I never did like it much. If I'd been a real cowboy I probably would have liked it even less. But then, what would a real cowboy be doing in the Village anyway? I thought they always hung out on the Upper East Side.

Of course, today cowboy hats didn't mean very much. You could drive a whole wagon train down just about any street in the Village and people would just think you were a group of happy homosexuals. Time sure changes the river.

I took a left on Tenth Street and walked the two blocks west to the Sixth Precinct station house. A large green globe glimmered on either side of the steps, showing the pedestrians where to enter and the Sunday pigeons where to sit. A sign was posted on one of the glass doors: ALL VISITORS MUST STOP AT FRONT DESK. No problem there.

A Sergeant Bello was at the muster desk. I asked for Fox or Cooperman. I don't know if you could say my luck was in but both of them were. Bello picked up a phone and a moment later Fox came into the doorway behind the muster desk. He was grinning unpleasantly. "Hi, cowboy!" he said. Some things never change.

He gave me what he evidently thought was a coy little wink and motioned Bello to open the drawbridge. I angled under the raised top of the muster desk and followed Fox down a hallway past the detention cages. He opened a pebbled-glass door that said SQUAD ROOM in black letters. There were metal filing cabinets lining three of the walls and there were four desks in the room. Detective Mort Cooperman sat behind one of them, leaning back in a wooden chair, one leg looped over a corner of the desk. He was smoking and smirking at the same time.

"Your boy's not here," he said.

"Yeah," I said, "we knew that."

"We? We?" he said. "What's the matter, you got a mouse in your pocket?"

Fox sat down behind another desk. I remained standing, partly so I could be able to make a quick getaway, but mainly because nobody had asked me to sit down.

"My lawyer and I know where our boy is, but we think our son is innocent," I said, trying to leaven the situation a bit. A guy going through a filing cabinet in the corner chuckled, but Fox and Cooperman weren't having any.

"Did you find out who the gun belonged to?"

"Yeah," said Fox. "The gun was registered to Worthington. But the apartment it was found in was registered to your . . . uh . . . McGovern."

"Could be a clue, don't you think?" said Cooperman, as he crushed a Gauloise into the ashtray. I wasn't going to comment on his off brand of cigarettes. He probably thought he was a special agent for the French Secret Service. "Look," he said, "McGovern will be out on bail soon, probably with a second-degree murder rap; then in a few weeks time, he'll go before the grand jury. He hasn't been talking much, you know."

"What's to say?" said Fox. "It's fairly dead to rights."

"Maybe there's an angle that hasn't really been pursued," I said.

"What would that be," asked Cooperman. "That Worthington shot McGovern?"

"No. It would be that Worthington was a rather promiscuous bisexual with some pretty interesting bedfellows."

"Well, I don't know, guy," said Fox.

"Half the friggin' Village is bi," said Cooperman. "And the other half is pure fruit."

"Present company excluded of course," I said with a friendly smile.

"Yeah," said Cooperman, as he got up and walked over to the hat rack to get his brim.

"Nice rack," I said. "I thought those things went out with the buggy whip."

"Get out," said Fox.

"Then you're not going to pursue the angle?"

"Get out," said Fox again, "and try using your head for something more than a hat rack."

I left, sailing back out under the drawbridge, giving a smart left-handed salute to Sergeant Bello, and stepping out into the street. The pigeons were still nestling on the two green globes. If the wheels of justice were turning, the pigeons didn't know it.

10

Even a wake where you don't know the stiff can be a fairly strenuous thing. Not that it was going to be that kind of wake. I wasn't even sure that any of the wakers really cared. Well, obviously one of them had.

Nonetheless, by the time I got back to the loft on Vandam I was feeling like the Invisible Man on a bad day, except I knew I couldn't be him because I was still wearing the cowboy hat when I walked in. It was almost as if I hadn't got out of bed, and the whole afternoon had been spent in a slow-walking dream.

I hadn't learned much from Cynthia Floyd except that her last name was Floyd.

With Fox and Cooperman it was like I'd never spoken to them at all. Just stopped at the visitor's desk to admire the black, hairy caterpillar that was resting on Bello's upper lip. They listened to me about as seriously as the Trojans had listened when Cassandra had told them, "Don't bring that wooden horse into the city."

If I'd told them about the bill of sale from the florist shop that was now comfortably residing in my cat-litter tray, they probably would have hanged me and McGovern with the same rope. And of course they would have loved to hear about McGovern's ghost. That story probably would have landed the two of us a free suite on the fifth floor of Bellevue.

I decided to take a little power nap, and when I woke up it

40 was dark outside and pushing seven o'clock. I made a double espresso and lighted a cigar. Then I put on some suitable somber clothing, including a tie that said HELLO, HANDSOME but could only be read when you looked at it in a mirror.

I was about as ready as I was ever going to be to see and be seen. I took the freight elevator down.

If you headed up Hudson and then took a right at Barrow and continued until you came to Bedford, you would be at Chumley's, only you still wouldn't be at Chumley's. The place had been a speakeasy during Prohibition and there had never been so much as a sign, a number, or even a light to mark its location on the street. It remains that way today. Most people just walk right by the place, and if I'd known where this whole thing was going to lead, I'd probably have walked on by myself.

As it was, I pushed open the wooden gate and walked into a half-dark courtyard with little else but the moonlight shining on the flagstones. The place is supposed to have been one of F. Scott Fitzgerald's favorite haunts in the Village before he went west and eventually died, a broken man, in Hollywood.

I always made a point of drinking a Jameson with F. Scott whenever I came into Chumley's. Of course, you couldn't tell that Chumley's was even there until you left the quiet courtyard and pulled open another door. Then it always hit you as if you were suddenly entering an older, better world. People at the bar were laughing. A fireplace was burning brightly. Tonight Billie Holiday was on the jukebox. She really got around.

I walked over to the bar, ordered and downed a fast Jameson. Over in a far corner of the room I could see Ratso's glass raised in a toast to ol' Frank. At the table with him were two men whose identities I didn't know but could pretty well guess, and a blond thing I took to be Darlene Rigby.

They looked as if they were getting along all right so I hung out at the bar a little longer and had another Jameson with F.

Scott. He was in kind of a grim mood. Probably been fighting with the wife again. You never knew with old F.

It was a good thing I had stayed awhile at the bar because Nina Kong was just walking in and she appeared hesitant enough to bolt at the drop of a G chord. Nina was dressed in a dark, velvet, spiffily tailored suit, and some women do look good in black. She looked like a sinister, Oriental doll.

She was sinister all right but she wasn't bad. Far from it. And she was doing a few things with her upper lip that I hadn't seen before this side of the Ho Chi Minh Trail.

I walked over to her and took her by the arm. "The others are waiting," I said. "Sorry I had to be so brusque on the phone this morning."

"And I'm sorry if I was rude," she said. "I really don't have the personality of a one-thousand-year-old egg, you know." Her voice and manner were those of a modern American girl, but her eyes were flickering with Eastern mischief. They were terrific. And then there was the upper lip.

She could smile, sulk, beckon, or point in either direction with it. She could probably kill you with it.

"Do you know any of these people?" I asked as we neared the Ratso party.

"I've never seen any of them before," she whispered close to my ear.

"Good," I whispered back. She smiled and her smile looked good, too. Good enough to melt somebody's dream-sicle.

Ratso and the two guys stood up and made room for us around the table as I introduced Nina to the group and Ratso introduced me as "The Kinkster." "Kinky was a dear friend of Frank's," Ratso said, as he avoided my eyes. God knows what he'd been telling these people. Flying by bisexual radar could be dangerous even for an experienced pilot.

Darlene Rigby introduced herself. She was an attractive type but she was still a type. She was an actress and I suppose the question would always be "Is that really her or is she

only acting?'' That is, if anybody gave a damn about it besides her acting coach who was probably just trying to bed
her down himself. I hadn't cared much for actresses since
Jean Harlow had died.

The two guys and Ratso stood up, sat down, ordered more
drinks, and continued to look like themselves. If I'd been
expecting anybody to show any glint of recognition, any
veiled hostility, or any telltale evasiveness, I'd have been
very disappointed. It didn't look as if anybody knew anybody. Everybody was in their own little innocent world.
Even Ratso seemed to be ignoring me.

One of the guys was named Pete Myers, a fairly dapper
Englishman as they go, with a little blue scarf-tie around his
neck. He looked like the type who would have gotten there
on a bicycle, and as it turned out he had. I couldn't really
hold that against him but every quirk adds up.

The other guy, who completed the sandwich around
Darlene Rigby, was a handsome devil named Barry Campbell, who looked like he'd either just come in from the Is-
lands or else had been working the sunlamp overtime. Either
way he looked a shade too healthy and nobody likes that.
Particularly in New York.

Both of the guys looked pretty gay for a wake. I hadn't yet
been able to glean what they did. I mean, I knew some of the
things they did, but what they actually did I didn't know.

I didn't get to find out right then for two reasons. One: As I
started to lean forward, Ratso gave me a little sign with his
hand that I took to mean things were cool, he had everybody
lamped perfectly, and two: Adrian made her slinking little
entrance, fashionably late in keeping with her profession as a
stained-glass artist. It appeared she knew everybody but me,
Ratso, and Darlene. I ordered more drinks.

''How long have you known Adrian?'' I asked Nina.

''We go way back,'' Adrian said before Nina could separate
her lips. Adrian was chatting away like a large, amoral chip-
munk, but it was having the effect of keeping the ball rolling
so I contented myself with a little Nina Kong eye contact.

We'd been sitting there a good fifteen minutes and no one had even mentioned Frank yet. I was waiting to see who'd be first and hoping that nobody would ask me anything. I might step on something and it probably wasn't going to be third base.

"He was a beautiful man," said Nina at last.

"A stunningly beautiful man," said Peter Myers.

"Perhaps too beautiful for his own good," said Barry Campbell.

"How did you know Frank, Kinky?" It was Darlene. Her voice would've carried to the balcony if there'd been one. She had a sort of little happy-sad, expectant smile on her face. I wanted to knock it off with a right cross.

"We go way back, too," I said, a trifle too sullenly.

If you think picking out a murderer from a group of people sitting around a table is easy, you should try it sometime. Nobody was giving anything away. And whoever offed Frank Worthington was methodical, painstakingly careful, and had a nice eye for detail. He or she belonged to the cream of the criminal class. We were dealing with a murderer who had mastered whatever it means to be normal but was really anything but. Thinking about it didn't really get me anything but a few goose pimples. I ordered another round of drinks.

Ratso wanted a screwdriver. Pete predictably wanted a Pimm's Cup Number something or other. Adrian had a Perrier. Darlene ordered some kind of white-wine drink that actresses drink. It was a cumbersome and time-consuming order, and she had to explain it several times to the waiter, much to the irritation of serious drinkers like me and Barry Campbell.

When the waiter finally looked at me, I went with a "Bloody Wetback," a drink an old girlfriend and I had pioneered out on the West Coast. It was a double shot of José Cuervo tequila, a glass of tomato juice, and a lemon. Of course, the whole evening was beginning to look like a lemon.

That was until Barry Campbell laughed and ordered a big pitcher of Bloody Marys. He wasn't looking at the waiter. He was looking straight at Nina Kong, and quite distinctly, I watched him wink at her.

Now the fact that a pitcher of Bloody Marys was found at the scene of the crime was privileged information that the police had withheld from the press. It is routine procedure in a homicide case for them to keep a few things like this up their sleeves. That way, when fourteen sick chickens confessed to killing Frank Worthington, they might all presumably know about the method of death and the flowers, but only the guilty one would know that Frank Worthington had been drinking a pitcher of Bloody Marys with his killer.

This either cleared Campbell completely, I figured, or else he was very stupid or else he was very smart. Take your pick.

Nina Kong said she was ready to leave. She looked as white as she was ever going to. She told us she had a rehearsal for a video they were doing tomorrow.

"I'll help you get a cab," I said.

"That won't be necessary."

I did anyway, and when we got outside I saw why it wouldn't be necessary. A limo and driver were waiting for her at the curb.

"Can I take you somewhere?" she asked.

"No," I said. "What I'd really like is a home video of your upper lip."

She laughed. About half innocently and half knowingly, I thought. She was terrific but I wondered what else she was.

We sat in back for a while swapping phone numbers and hobbies. She took out an enameled Oriental-style snuffbox full of Peruvian-style snuff. We both took a pinch or two.

"This couldn't be Adrian's stuff, could it?" I asked. I knew it wasn't. Adrian's stuff always looked like it'd been stepped on by the Budweiser Clydesdales.

"No, it's from the record company. So's the limo."

"I wish you all the best," I said. I knew as well as anybody what a small step it was from the limo to the gutter. I also knew that we'd all get a limo again when we were dead so I wasn't worried. I never took limos, I never took subways, and I never took private French lessons advertised in the Village.

We nipped a few more little pinches of snuff. "Are you sure you've never seen Barry Campbell before?" I asked.

"Positive. Did you really ever know Frank Worthington?"

"Not until I saw him on the floor," I answered.

I kissed her and we said good night. I'd see her again soon. We had a date for a hockey game on Wednesday night. She'd never seen a hockey game.

By the time I got back inside, things were breaking up. No one could understand why anybody would want to kill Frank. Like all dead people, Frank had been a "warm and human" guy. Like all dead people, he wasn't one now.

We all shook hands and said we'd get together. Ratso said he'd call me in the morning. He was pretty bombed and I was just about walking on my knuckles.

I told the waiter to drop the hatchet, I paid the bill, and I left. The ice had almost melted in the pitcher of Bloody Marys. Sort of had a familiar look to it, like a face in a dream.

11

I was halfway through my first Monday morning espresso and just thinking about breaking out my first cigar of the day when the phones rang. It was Ratso. 9:47 A.M.

"I'm coming over, Sherlock. Tell your landlady . . . what's-her-name . . . to get the kippers ready."

"Mrs. Hudson, like the street. I hope you've got the goods on those guys."

"Pete and Barry and I are like old friends."

"Yeah, well, you better watch yourself, Rat. Sometimes old friends will stab you in the back."

About fifteen minutes later, as I was just embarking on a second espresso, I heard Ratso screaming from the street like a young castrato.

There are no buzzers or names of occupants on the door at 199B Vandam. From the street the whole place looks like an empty warehouse, which it undoubtedly was before somebody got clever and converted the building to loft space.

I am probably less interested than you are in the history of New York real estate. People tell me it is stupid to rent if you can own the property. But I figure it this way. We are living in a time and place threatened by nuclear war, social upheaval, and biblical curses. Kind of keeps you on your toes, I always think. But for a person to actually bother to own property in a place like New York seems to me to be a rather temporal and ephemeral statement to make. Personally, I'd have more confidence in a small boy holding a butterfly's wing.

Of course it would depend upon the deal.

Ratso was yelling from the street again. Not having buzzers and intercoms at the front door had at first seemed a nuisance, but now I preferred their absence. It made it a little harder on visitors, including cops with search warrants. And there were no surprises. I didn't like surprises.

Anyway, I'd solved the problem of letting people into the building long ago when I bought a little Negro puppet on Canal Street and removed its head. The head was about the size of a small grapefruit and the eyes opened and closed. I wedged the key to the front door in its mouth. I'd attached a brightly colored homemade parachute to the head, and making some allowances for wind currents and fire-escape entanglement, I threw the whole thing down to Ratso. Bull's-eye. I was really getting good.

Five minutes later the espresso machine was steaming and humming and Ratso and I were sitting at the kitchen table.

"Monday's the day Mrs. Hudson goes to her video course at the New School," I explained. "Anything I can do for you while we wait for the espresso?"

"You could stop blowing that cigar smoke in my face."

"No problem." I got the espresso. "All right," I said. "Spit it."

Ratso had done his homework pretty well, and he filled me in on these two characters with more information than I had ever cared to know. My chief interest was in Barry Campbell, but I wasn't letting Pete Myers off the hook either.

Campbell was a dancer who worked mainly at a place called the Blue Canary. He was also a male model. Big surprise. I was sure he went way back with Frank Worthington. And I do mean back.

Campbell was a pretty boy, but I had a feeling that his face would be popping up in something pretty ugly pretty soon. Have to keep an eye on him.

48

Pete Myers was a bird of a different feather. His plumage wasn't quite that spectacular. He lived on Barrow Street and made meat pies, British pastries and something he called the "British Knish," in his own oven. He sold them to various restaurants around town that were owned and frequented by his countrymen. Myers was making it, but barely. He saw the British Knish, which he'd invented, as his main chance to trade his bicycle for a Bentley. He was lobbing his knish right at the American fast-food market.

It looked like a long shot but once you could've said the same about the french fry.

Ratso bent my ear for the better part of an hour, gave me the two phone numbers and addresses, asked about McGovern, pledged to stay on the case, and left.

I was sorry he'd mentioned McGovern because I knew less about McGovern's situation than I did about the chances for the British Knish. One thing was for sure—when McGovern got sprung I was going to have a good long talk with him. And if he wanted to tell me a ghost story, I was ready to listen.

The next two days crawled by like a centipede with a bad case of the gout. I read the papers, answered the phones, fed the cat four times, and smoked sixteen cigars. That was a fairly large number even for me, but I only smoked them about halfway down before throwing them away for the first time. I'd always let them age a little while and then select the finest of the lot for resurrection when circumstances demanded.

Wolf Nachman had left a message on my answering machine Tuesday afternoon while I was in Chinatown. I told the cat before I left that she was in charge of everything while I was gone, but apparently she hadn't bothered to take the call from Nachman. Cats, as a rule, don't like lawyers. They have great insight into human character.

The thrust of Wolf's message was not to give up. He'd have McGovern out very soon now. There'd been a few complications but it was all right now. He'd call as soon as McGovern was sprung.

By Wednesday afternoon I'd heard nothing more from Wolf, so I called him at his office. "If we're paying you by the hour," I said, "I'll just be a minute."

"Don't worry; we'll work something out," he said. I wasn't too worried about working something out. I was just concerned with working one large innocent Irishman out of the sneezer. That didn't seem like too much to ask. But Wolf was supposed to be the best, so there was nothing for it but to wait and not let McGovern's sad state of affairs steal the puck from my enjoyment tonight at the hockey game with Nina Kong.

The New York Rangers had not won a Stanley Cup Championship since 1940, which as fate would have it was before my time. It didn't really look like they'd be wrapping one up this year either. The point of the whole thing as I saw it was to immerse yourself in the Madison Square Garden atmosphere: the ice, the fights, the crowd of hockey fanatics. And if that didn't work, there was always the game. It was a good way to leave your troubles behind, and this Wednesday evening I seemed to be having my share.

Things had been going nowhere fast. The cat was out of cat food and the litter tray wasn't looking too good either. It had never looked good but it had looked better. As for me, I was fresh out of charm. I hadn't been sleeping real well, and I hadn't shaved in a few days and was beginning to bear a very slight familial resemblance to Sirhan Sirhan. What was worse, I was beginning to understand his mind. Perfect hockey fan mentality.

I knew that even Sherlock himself used to get pretty gnarly when he was between cases, but here I was right in the middle of one and I was about as frustrated and helpless as Grogan's goat. Too many possible motives, none of which made any real sense. Fox and Cooperman were playing their cards so close to the vest you'd think they were riverboat gamblers.

Well, I knew two things for sure: one, that the lesbian

dance class had just started again in the loft upstairs, and two, that McGovern had not croaked Frank Worthington. I also knew if I didn't get moving soon I'd be late meeting Nina at the hockey game. She'd be sitting in her limo snorting cocaine and wondering what to do. Poor child.

I'd left the cat in charge and my hand was twisting the doorknob to the right when the phones rang. 7:05 P.M. Game time was 7:30 P.M. and it wasn't Wolf Nachman. It was Darlene Rigby making inquiries into my health in a rather breathy voice that didn't really sound as if she cared whether I lived or died.

"Listen, Darlene, I'm on the run," I said. "Can you nut-shell this?"

"Yeah," she said, "I'll nut-shell it. It's something I remembered and it's pretty strange. It's about Frank Worthington."

"Can you get to the meat of it? I'm running later than whoever that *Alice in Wonderland* character was who was running late."

"I remembered something. I saw them together once. And there was something strange."

"Look, Darlene. Will this keep till the morning?"

"Sure. I suppose, but . . ."

"Okay. I'll be at your place at ten o'clock tomorrow morning for croissants or whatever you actresses like to eat. What's the apartment number?"

"It's Forty-three-L."

"See you in the morning. Bye."

I hung up and left, grabbing my hat, my coat, and a cigar for the road.

As it turned out, Darlene's little secret wasn't going to keep till the morning. But how in the hell was I supposed to know?

12

The hockey game was not particularly one for the books but at least it was a hockey game. It wasn't a disco or a seminar on natural childbirth. Nina seemed pleasantly hypnotized by the game and the crowd. We had a few huge cups of beer, which always tasted soapy at the Garden but after a while you didn't care, and we each had foot-long hot dogs that were still barking half an hour after we'd eaten them. At the end of the first period, Nina joined the throng to the ladies' room and I went out into the foyer to make a phone call.

I had to wait while some guy from New Jersey yapped for a while to his girlfriend but that's what love is all about. The whole thing cost me only about eight minutes out of my life so I guess it was a small price to pay. Seemed fairly interminable at the time.

My call was to Cynthia Floyd, who I knew had been camping out at McGovern's place on Jane Street waiting to hear any news at all. She and McGovern had not been an item for all that long but seemed to get on well together. I could still see her little blond puppy face when I'd told her McGovern could get a second-degree murder rap. I felt sorry for her. And she was a damned sight better than McGovern's last broad, who'd been a professional Third World feminist for the United Nations.

"How are you, Cynthia?" She sounded fuzzy. Possibly she'd been getting into the wholesale whiskey warehouse that McGovern was pleased to call his liquor cabinet.

She wanted to know everything so I gave her the lot. It wasn't much. I told her very briefly about the wake at Chumley's. I told her about Nachman's most recent conversation with me. I told her Ratso and I'd be following up on Pete Myers and Barry Campbell. I told her that the struggling young actress, Darlene Rigby, might have something she wanted to get off her chest. Sounded too melodramatic to be anything but I'd probably see her in the morning.

"Cynthia? Are you there?" Maybe I'd put her on the nod.

"Yes. I'm here. What about the other girl?"

"Oh, you mean Nina Kong. She's here with me tonight. I'm getting in tight with her here at the hockey game. I'll definitely be pumping her tonight—for information only of course."

"Oh, God. What am I going to do?"

"Look, we're going to get him out. We're going to find out who really did it. Don't worry and don't start hitting the singles-bar circuit yet. He'll be out of there any minute."

I wish I could have believed what I was telling her, but there are times when almost anything is better than the truth. Of course I didn't even know the truth. And if somebody did know it, he was sure keeping it under his hairpiece. Maybe an old Tibetan monk, or Jesus, or the man in the moon, or the President knew the truth, but none of them was at the hockey game and I was.

The call to Cynthia had taken longer than I'd intended and had been interrupted periodically by roars, chants, and rumbles from the crowd, including several "oohs" and "aahs" indicating narrowly missed goals. By the time I got back to Nina, the Islanders had come back with two goals and the score was now tied 3–3. The fans were in a mood to waste any ten-year-old child carrying an Islander pennant.

It didn't really make you proud to be an American, but it did keep you awake.

In the third period the Islanders scored two more goals, but the crowd got its chance to put in its two cents when an Islander was practically knocked unconscious and had to be taken from the ice on a stretcher. They cheered lustily. They jeered. "You better be dead!" somebody shouted.

"These people are animals," Nina said.

"Let me help you out of the limo, baby," I said.

We left soon afterward, slightly ahead of the exodus of angry Ranger fans from the Garden. As it turned out, I helped her into the limo and got in after her.

As we rode down to the Village we took a few more pinches and I gave her upper lip a little workout but it was nothing that D. H. Lawrence would want to write home about. I wondered what Barry Campbell was doing tonight at the Blue Canary. It was probably something Lawrence of Arabia would want to write home about.

It used to be that it took all kinds. Now it didn't even take two kinds.

13

Nina had the limo driver drop me at the Monkey's Paw on Bedford Street, and she continued on to wherever today's video children play when they deign to part company with their television sets and go out at night. Usually they go to places that have real big television sets. I rarely watched television, I didn't dance to speak of, and I disliked most young people and green plants a good bit more than I feared the nuclear war that might destroy them. So I didn't hit the nightclub circuit much.

Neither did The Weasel. He was too busy popping in and out of the men's room, and tonight was no exception. When he finally saw me, he walked over with a worried look on his face. If you've never seen a worried Weasel, you don't ever want to. He was worried that the Worthington murder case would heat up and some of the suspects I was checking out might get wise to who put me on to them. Like the President, he felt that his job required a fairly high degree of visibility, and the idea frightened him not a little. I tried to calm him a bit. Just a bit.

"Relax, pal. Just keep your eyes open. In your line of work, you can't really call in the police, you know."

He went back to the men's room and I wandered over to the bar. I could hardly walk into the Monkey's Paw anymore without thinking of The Bakerman. I never realized that Tom Baker had been my best friend until after he was dead. Usually works that way.

When The Bakerman's eyes twinkled, you could see the green hills of Ireland where he'd come from but had never been. I motioned to Tommy the bartender for a drink.

Tommy had been working the night a little over three years ago when Baker died. Tommy'd leaned across the crowded bar, looking even more Buddha-like than usual, and asked: "Is it true about The Bakerman? He's gone South?"

"Yeah," I said.

Tom Baker had been an actor, but he'd been a lot of other things too. He'd been a great one in life. But life wasn't the movies. They didn't reissue life. There weren't any reruns.

Now, as I glanced around the bar, everybody looked like gray people in a gray casino. "Do you know The Bakerman?" I said to no one in particular. "He lives in Drury Lane."

I went over to the pay phone and called my friend Rambam at the Brooklyn offices of Pallorium, his security firm. Rambam was a private investigator, although I'd never really seen his license. He had spent two years in federal Never-Never Land where he had picked up several handy trades and made some pretty good connections. He claimed he was still wanted in every state that begins with an *I*. He was wanted by me tonight because I wanted to get past the lock on Frank Worthington's apartment and I was running out of time.

We arranged to meet at 2:00 A.M. at the Corner Bistro, which was only a few blocks from McGovern's place and was open till 4:00 A.M. The Bistro served something called the Bistro Burger that was bigger than your head. I'd always made it a practice never to eat anything bigger than my head but I was hungry and edgy and Rambam usually ran on Brooklyn Standard Time so I ordered a Bistro Burger and told the guy to drag it through the garden.

The guy was still working on it when Rambam walked in, which gives you an idea of how fast the service at the Corner Bistro is. Rambam watched the Bistro Burger sizzling on the open grill, thought it looked pretty good, and so he ordered one too. We had a few beers. I was in no hurry. Two o'clock in the morning was almost rush-hour traffic in this area with people coming home from the bars. Three or even four o'clock would be about the right time for this particular caper, I thought.

I gave Adrian a call. Stained-glass artists, I knew, worked very late and didn't mind calls at strange hours. I told her I might be by with a friend within an hour or so. She said fine. I didn't want to bother Cynthia and I didn't want Cynthia to bother me. Adrian's place on the third floor would be a handy escape hatch if anybody showed up while Rambam and I were fooling around in front of Frank Worthington's door. I sincerely hoped Rambam was as good as he thought he was because I did not look forward to seeing Adrian at 3:30 in the morning.

"You ready, pal?" I asked.

"Yeah," he said. "Let me get my bowling ball out of the trunk."

He walked up the street about a block, opened the trunk of a black Jaguar, and came walking back jauntily with a green army knapsack, about the size of a small accordion, carelessly slung around his left shoulder. "All right," he said. "It's party time."

We walked past the shadow of the windmill and right up the steps to 42 Jane, encountering no one. The building seemed pretty quiet. It was a little after 3:00 A.M.

On the stairwell of the first landing, he handed me a woolen cap, a pair of ordinary garden gloves, and a flashlight about the size of a cigarette lighter. It could be held in the hand or the mouth and was called a bite-light. The plastic over the little bulb was painted red and gave off a soft glow. Rambam stuck an earplug into his left ear. It was attached to a police scanner that he slipped around his belt and on which he monitored all communications between the local precinct and radio patrols in the area.

When we reached Worthington's door, the first thing I noticed was that the "scene of crime" seal had been broken.

Rambam was already chuckling and reaching into his knapsack. He came out with a small putty knife. "This one's for *The Guinness Book of World Records*," he said.

He wedged the knife tightly between the door and the doorjamb, worked it in a little farther, and then gave it a little shove with the heel of his hand. It had taken about twelve seconds if anyone was counting. I'd been too busy counting my worry beads. But he'd opened that door faster than a mob informer could go down Mulberry Street on a skateboard.

We stood inside, closed the door, and turned on the bitelights. Rambam took an elaborate sort of mideastern bow and I patted him on the back. "Cops broke the seal themselves," he said. "They're probably through in here but they could come back. Cops are sneaky."

Every surface in the room was coated with a thick layer of dust and fingerprint powder in about equal proportions. "If this stuff makes me sneeze, don't forget to say 'God bless you,'" Rambam whispered.

"Yeah, the Irishman's tip," I said. "Just don't sneeze."

"Whatever you say," he said and started walking across the room. Everything looked about the same except that Frank Worthington wasn't at home.

I walked over to the closet, turned the knob, and pulled the closet door open a little. I couldn't see a damn thing. I opened the door all the way and we brought the two lights closer and played them around the closet.

What had apparently once been men and women's clothing had been slashed to mere ribbons and lay all over the bottom of the closet. It looked like the floor of Macy's giftwrapping department at closing time. Only it reeked of evil.

I bent down to examine a few remnants on the floor, and something rolled off the top shelf of the closet. It was round and flesh colored and it had hair growing out of the top of it. It bounced once with a loud thud and rolled to a sullen, sickening stop in the semidarkness between us.

"Jesus Christ," I said.

"Not quite my idea of getting a little head," said Rambam.

The head stared up at us out of the gloom. It didn't say anything. It didn't really have to.

"Notice the moss on that dummy," I said.

"So. What of it?" said Rambam.

"Short-hair wig," I said. "Almost identical to Worthington's own hair. Why would he need that?"

"How should I know?" said Rambam. "Why does the pope shit in the woods?"

I stared down at the object on the floor and it glared balefully, eyelessly, back at me like a sentient, grotesque grapefruit.

"Precisely," I said.

Finding the head in Worthington's apartment was not only a fairly hairraising experience, it also raised a few rather disturbing questions.

One was what the hell it was doing there.

Another was what the hell we were doing there.

14

I got to bed at around 5:30 A.M. I got up at 8:30 A.M. Three hours sleep. Napoleon was supposed to have got by on only two or three hours sleep every night. Maybe that was why he was so short. I didn't know and I didn't really care. I made some coffee, drank a few cups, fed the cat, and headed up the West Side to Hell's Kitchen.

You could tell Hell's Kitchen when you got there because there was a junkie hiding behind every garbage can. Sullen-looking kids from every country in the United Nations were milling restlessly about on the street corners even at this early hour of the morning. They looked like they wanted to steal somebody's cappuccino.

I found Darlene Rigby's building. I walked through the lobby, pushed the button, and waited for one of the elevators. There were eight of them in the building but they all seemed to be in perpetual motion. I was running a little late but I certainly wasn't going to leg it up forty-three floors. Sooner or later one of these elevators was going to take it into its head to come down to the lobby.

While I waited I wondered. I thought about what Darlene had said on the phone the night before. "I remembered something," she'd said. So far, so good. "I saw them together once." Whom had she seen together once? Obviously, Frank and one of our little friends. I already knew that. "And there was something strange," she'd said. What could be strange? In New York what could be strange?

I didn't have to wait too long to find out. The elevator doors opened and soon I was hurtling forty-three floors' worth into the heavens above New York City.

When I got out of the elevator, I took a left and followed the arrows to 43L. It was a long and fairly plushly appointed hallway and Darlene Rigby's apartment was at the extreme end of it. When I finally arrived at her door, I raised my hand to knock but that was as far as I got.

The door was already open an inch or two. I pushed it the rest of the way. It was quiet. Too quiet.

It was a pretty big place. I walked through the living room, took a casual turn through the kitchen, and back-tracked again to the bedroom before I saw her.

It was a scene all right, but not the kind a Broadway audience would like to see. Darlene Rigby may have been a struggling young actress, but this time she seemed to have put up the struggle of her life.

The whole room looked as if someone had been changing the scenery on a stage set and had stopped to take a lunch break. Everything was everywhere.

She was sprawled on the bed wearing nothing but a torn nightgown and a number of ugly bruises and contusions. Her face was as white as Philadelphia cream cheese. It was starting to look a little bloated. Both her neck and one of her legs were twisted at what seemed to be quite unnatural angles.

I didn't know when the final curtain had fallen on Darlene Rigby, but she had probably been dead for quite a while. I touched her hand and it was colder than last year's reviews.

As I headed for the telephone on the night table, I stumbled on an unopened bottle of champagne on the floor. There was a little white card attached to the bottle and it had a message typed on it.

"break a leg, baby," it said.

15

With the possible exception of God's, I didn't really know whose jurisdiction this crime came under. But since I already had a rapport with Fox and Cooperman, I thought I'd give them the first fling at it.

I dialed information and asked for the number of the Sixth Precinct in the Village. Darlene Rigby's number would be charged for the information call but I didn't think she'd mind.

I dialed the number. "Sixth Precinct," a voice answered.

"Detective Sergeant Fox, please," I said. The call was then put through to the detectives' squad room. A familiar voice began grating in my ear.

"Special Crimes Task Force. Sergeant Fox speaking," it said.

I spoke to the voice for a little while and the voice spoke to me. Since Fox and Cooperman were a part of the Special Crimes Task Force, their jurisdiction was the whole city. So I'd called the correct number, though the results might still prove to be a bit sticky.

"It definitely looks like foul play?" asked Fox.

"I'm afraid Ronnie Milsap could see this one," I said. He was a blind country singer.

"Who the hell's Ronnie Milsap?" Fox screamed at me.

"He's a blind country singer," I said. I lighted a cigar and waited.

"Listen, guy," he said, "we're on our way. But you are not

to touch anything, you are not to leave the stiff, and you are not to smoke your goddamn cigar around the stiff.''

"Roger," I said, but Fox apparently had already hung up the phone. My cigar and I walked into the living room together. I sat down in one of those comfortable, fan-backed bamboo chairs, put my feet up on the coffee table, and puffed away on the cigar.

The cigar wasn't bad, but I didn't know how much longer it would be able to keep the world at bay.

It took maybe sixteen minutes before the world came barging into Darlene Rigby's apartment on the forty-third floor. It came in the form of a cavalry charge led by Fox and Cooperman, followed by a locust swarm of scientists who bore the resigned expressions of another day at the office. The cheerful, rotund assistant medical examiner brought up the rear.

I wondered why assistant medical examiners were nearly always rotund. Maybe it was the way of their people.

Everybody charged right by me into the bedroom, but Fox came back out after a few minutes to say hello. To look at his face you'd think there was a piece of meat lodged in his throat.

"Okay, pal," he said, "I don't care who you are. Do you understand me? I don't care if your goddamn daddy invented highway reflectors. I want to know what the hell you think you're doing here calling us from this stiff's apartment?''

He sounded fairly serious.

"She called last night wanting to talk to me. It was something to do with Frank Worthington, but I was on my way out to the Garden to see the Ranger game and I was running late. So we agreed to meet here this morning at ten o'clock for breakfast."

"So what the hell happened?" asked Fox. There was now a rather disturbing calmness about him.

"I don't really know," I said. "I guess somebody burned the bacon."

I was trying to think, myself, of who might have offed Darlene Rigby and why, and what Frank Worthington's murder might have had to do with this one. I was trying to think about a lot of things but it became apparent that this wasn't the time or place for much logical deduction on my part. The old gray cells would just have to wait. Before I could use my brain, first I was going to have to save my neck.

Cooperman came into the room and stood stage right of the chair in which I was sitting. I had taken my feet off the coffee table just out of etiquette. The cigar was smoldering in a nearby ashtray.

Cooperman didn't look very friendly this morning either. "Why don't we just run Mr. Broadway in and get it over with?" he asked Fox in a voice as thick as grime on the window of a subway train.

I was starting to feel a long way from COUNTRY SINGER PLUCKS VICTIM FROM MUGGER. How soon they forget.

Cooperman's question, it appeared, was somewhat rhetorical. At least for the time being. Fox preferred to grill me right then and there. I told them the names of the three people, obviously excluding Darlene Rigby, who I felt might know something about the Worthington case. This time, I noticed, they at least took the time to write the names down, but they didn't seem too impressed. They wanted to know where I'd gone after the hockey game. I told them Nina Kong had taken me down to the Monkey's Paw in her limo. This brought a raised eyebrow from Fox but the expression on Cooperman's face remained about the same. Sheer malice.

Cooperman put one foot on the coffee table. His eyes were doing a burn that looked quite a few degrees hotter than my cigar in the ashtray. I picked up the cigar, and probably would have puffed on it, but Fox brought his arm down hard on my wrist and knocked the cigar to the floor. He ground it out with his foot into the beige-colored carpet. It didn't look like something you'd see in *Better Homes and Gardens.*

"Good way to get foot cancer," I said.

"Who did you talk to at the Monkey's Paw?" he asked. Here was another problem.

The Weasel would be too frightened to talk to the police. He'd never go for it. He'd almost certainly deny he even knew me. He wouldn't give me an alibi if my life depended on it. Of course, it didn't yet but the way things were going, who knew?

And if The Weasel part of my alibi was bad, the Rambam part of it was worse. Given Rambam's background and the nature of the little job we'd both done the night before, I didn't want these guys to touch Rambam with a barge pole. No sir. If they even found out I'd had a Bistro Burger with the lad, they'd pull us both in for a lot more than twenty questions.

"So who did you talk to last night? Did you take a long walk in Sheridan Square Park?" This park was only about ten feet wide and it wasn't much longer than General Sheridan's nose.

The air in the room was getting stale and so was the conversation.

"Let's see if we have this," said Fox. "From the time you entered the Monkey's Paw last night until about ten-fifteen this morning when you entered this apartment, no one saw you or spoke to you who might remember you. Right?"

"Right."

"No alibi?"

"No alibi." From where I sat I could see the assistant medical examiner in the bedroom. He was crouching on the floor looking very closely at Darlene Rigby's neck. "Hey!" he shouted, without looking up from his work. "Who won that Ranger game?"

"Islanders, five to three," I said.

"That's a shame," he said.

I was beginning to wonder who I was going to have to screw to get out of this movie, when they finally let me go. "We'll keep in touch," Cooperman said with a very sick little smirk. I wasn't looking too closely, though, because my eyes were already on the door. I figure I got home just a little bit before the stiff got to the morgue.

When you can't win a race with a stiff, you're in trouble.

At the loft there was a message on the machine from Wolf Nachman. I called him back right away.

"What's up, Wolf?" I asked.

"Great news," he said. "I've been trying to reach you all morning."

"What?"

"They sprung McGovern last night," he said.

16

It was a rainy Saturday afternoon in the Village. I was one hockey game and one stiff older and I was watching a Federal Express truck pull into Vandam Street from Greenwich Avenue. The radio station that wanted me to give them twenty-two minutes so they could give me the world had said that it would rain all weekend. That gave me plenty of time to watch.

Rain always made me think of people I wasn't with. Would never be with except when it rained. All my friends today, it seemed, were either dead, born again, or vegetarians. I felt much closer to the dead ones. They always seemed more alive.

The guy with the Federal Express truck was stopping in front of my building. I was thinking of my old friend Slim. Once, a long time ago, some people were giving him grief about his cats knocking over their garbage cans. "Why are your cats always going into our garbage cans?" they'd said. If I live to be thirty-seven, I'll never forget what old Slim told them. "They wants to see the world," he'd said.

The guy was getting out of the Federal Express truck and walking around to the back of it.

I didn't really want to see the world like Slim's cats did, but the way this case was dragging on, I might have to. Two rather bizarre killings in the space of a week. I'd been on the scene before the police both times, and the only thing I'd been able to pick up out of the whole deal had been a shot glass of Jameson.

Maybe I was being too hard on myself. The papers were playing the two murders for all they were worth, which was saying something in a city where murder was almost as commonplace as pastrami.

Even from the limited information they had, the press already saw a fine Italian hand in both crimes. The police were still trying to see a clumsy Irish one. If only the cops and I could somehow pool our information. That didn't seem too likely, but it was essential to finding the killer.

I was looking out at the rain and seeing nothing or everything or whatever people are supposed to see when they look at the rain. The Federal Express guy was looking at a scrap of paper. Then he was waving up at me.

It was too wet for the parachute and the driver was blacker than the puppet so I took the freight elevator down and opened the large metal door in front.

"Package for Four-W. Mr. Friedman. That you?" he asked.

"This must be my lucky day," I said. I signed the receipt and took a narrow brown parcel about two feet long back upstairs with me. There was no return address.

I opened the wrapping paper and lifted the top of the narrow box. It was a pink rose. Attached there was a little white card with a typewritten poem. It read:

> gather ye rosebuds while ye may
> old time is still a-flying
> and this same flower that smiles today
> tomorrow will be dying.

I was pinning the rose to my hunting vest when the phones rang. It was 12:37 P.M. and Cynthia was on the line.

"Have you seen McGovern?" she asked.

"Never could see McGovern," I said. "He's been on the loose since Wednesday night. Hasn't he been home?"

"No," she sobbed. This was terrific. "The police have been here and called several times. They're looking for him too."

"Well, he's probably out getting completely monstered in one of the bars he hasn't been eighty-sixed from yet. That narrows it down a bit. Maybe I can find him."

Three days was nothing for a McGovern binge. "You will call if you find him?" she asked.

"Of course, and you call me if you hear from him first."

She was really holding up pretty well. In spite of my inherent dislike for all blond men, women, and children, I had to admit that Cynthia was growing in my esteem.

McGovern, on the other hand, was running about par for the course.

It looked like it might be time to organize the Village Irregulars and go on a little pub-crawling assignment. But first there were a few loose ends to clear up. I fished the florist's receipt out of the cat-litter tray with a spatula from the kitchen. I didn't cook much anyway. I took the receipt out of the envelope, which was a bit soggy, sprinkled a little Old Spice on it, and put it in the inside pocket of my hunting vest. Then I called the cops.

17

It was raining like hell. Maybe worse.

There wasn't a cab to be found on Hudson Street, so I walked in the rain to the Sixth Precinct.

Rain was a lot like vomiting. One of the few great equalizers in life. It soaked society dames and bag ladies. People and pigeons. Cops and robbers. It was probably even raining on McGovern. Wherever he was.

Fox and Cooperman were next door to civil, which was about as friendly as they ever got. They were as much at sea as I was but they didn't believe in sharing lifeboats. My only chance was to act as if I knew something.

"Somebody's sending me flowers," I said. "One long-stemmed pink rose to be exact." I took off my coat and patted the flower on my vest.

"Goes nice with your eyes. Sit down, pal," said Fox. I put the card with the little typewritten poem on the desk and I sat down. Fox brought out a bottle of Old Overholt and a couple of glasses and he poured me a shot. It went down hard but it cut the phlegm pretty good.

When I got my voice back I said: "The flower and the card arrived at twelve-thirty-five this afternoon. Federal Express. Can you check it out?"

He nodded. He studied the card. "We'll keep this if you don't mind."

"You might also check out the fact that Barry Campbell sent those flowers to Frank Worthington."

"You don't say," said Cooperman. "How'd you learn that if you don't mind my asking? You fat-arm the florist?"

"No. I found this receipt the other day in the hallway as I was leaving. It's from the little flower shop around the corner from Worthington's. I called the place and the girl came up with Barry Campbell's name in the ledger. Anything else on Darlene Rigby?" I laid the pink receipt on the desk.

Cooperman looked at the receipt. Then he looked at Fox. Fox looked at the receipt. Then Fox said: "She was strangled. Trachea crushed . . . leg broken . . . Autopsy shows apparent rape. . . . No traces of semen however . . . Last two calls she made were to you at seven-five P.M. and to Peter Myers at almost midnight. . . . She was killed sometime between two and three in the morning. That's the story, bud."

It wasn't a very pretty one but that was one of the problems with nonfiction. I shook hands with Cooperman and Fox and had almost made the door when Fox brought me up sharp.

"Hold the weddin', pal," he said. "If you should hear from your friend McGovern, we want to talk to him yesterday. Get my meaning?"

I said I got his meaning and I left. It was raining harder, if anything, and there were still no cabs. I ducked into a little bar on Christopher to get out of the rain and to call Cynthia. I put in my two bits and listened to the phone ring at McGovern's apartment. I turned around to look at the bar and saw about thirty men making cocktail chatter and watching the rain. I wondered if they saw what I saw when they looked at the rain. Probably.

"Oh, I'm so glad you called," said Cynthia. This may not have been the first transatlantic phone call but it was definitely the first heterosexual phone call this place had ever known.

"Where are you calling from?" she asked.

"A charming little place called Boots and Saddles, honey; remind me to bring you here sometime. You'd like the ambience. Where's McGovern?"

"I don't know," she said. "I'm getting worried."

"Well, don't," I said. "We'll find him tonight. I promise." It looked like I was going to have to get on the blower and organize the Village Irregulars after all. It also looked like it was going to be one hell of a great night for a good ghost story.

A few of the guys in the bar waved, I waved back, and then walked outside into the rain. "Come again," somebody called after me.

Good luck, pal.

The cat was glad to see me and I was glad to see the cat. "You're the only normal person I've met today," I told her. I made an espresso and was opening the mail with my Smith & Wesson knife when the phones rang. It was now 4:47 P.M. "Start talking," I said.

"Yeah, I'll start talking. This is Detective Sergeant Cooperman. From the Sixth Precinct. Special Crimes Task Force. Remember me?"

"Let me see," I said. "Rather tall, Norwegian chap, very elegantly attired."

"Cut it," he said. "What kind of a building do you think might have a lot of typewriters in it? I'll answer: a newspaper building. Whose typewriter do you think all three of those little white death notes were typed on?"

"You're kidding," I said.

"Yeah, I'm kidding. We're putting out an APB on McGovern. You better hope you find him before we do. I'm finished talking." The line went dead in my hand. For a couple of gumshoes, these guys worked pretty fast.

18

The Village has many faces on Saturday night. None of them are too terribly pretty but nobody looks too close. In a notorious chicken-hawk bar on Tenth Street off Seventh Avenue, an older man who looks like the pastor of some small-town church picks up a thirteen-year-old boy. In a shooting gallery on Cornelia Street, you can get any hard drug you want if you can fight your way through the bloody syringes and the wall-to-wall weirdos. I sat on a couch there once for nearly an hour before it finally moved.

About the only thing you won't see in the Village is a man dancing with his wife. If you want to see that you're pretty sick. Probably a voyeur. In New York people may be jaded, jaundiced, superficial, and lifeless, but they still like to see and be seen. It's as normal as apple strudel.

So that's what I was doing on this particular Saturday night. I was going somewhere on my way to see and be seen. Place called the Blue Canary. I was hoping to see and be seen by Barry Campbell. Somebody knew something and it might as well be him.

Somebody had croaked Frank Worthington and silenced Darlene Rigby before she could open her snapper. Somebody who had at least limited access to McGovern's apartment and to the National Desk of the *Daily News*. Someone who was thorough, imaginative, meticulous, totally ruthless. Someone who was not on the same wavelength as the rest of us. The flesh was slowly beginning to materialize around the grinning Halloween skeleton. But I had an ugly notion that the killer wasn't about to put a sock on it yet. In fact, I was pretty sure of one thing: Whoever this madman was, he was enjoying himself.

Or should I say "madperson"? When you're dealing with murder, it hardly pays to be a chauvinist.

I beat out a young couple for a cab and took it to Fifty-second Street at Ninth Avenue. When I got there, there was still a line of idiots reaching all the way around the corner, braving the drizzle and hoping to be among the few chosen to gain admittance to the city of light.

Well, they knew what they were doing. They'd come all the way from New Jersey; I hoped they knew what they were doing. True New Yorkers would stand in line only at the Carnegie Delicatessen. Or the lottery. Or the soup kitchen on the Bowery.

In New York you've got to know somebody. Or at least you've got to know somebody who knows somebody. I knew somebody who knew somebody and I'd called him that afternoon, so when I walked up to the front of the line and gave my name to a guy who was about four feet wide, he caved right in and unsnapped the purple velvet rope across the sidewalk. I walked in, the envy of several hundred rain-soaked people.

If this kind of thing really made you start to feel smug, you probably needed a personality transplant.

Normally, I wouldn't have gone into one of these places at gunpoint. But tonight was different. Time was running out for McGovern.

And a homicidal maniac was running loose, very probably preparing to strike again. And if there's one thing worse than a homicidal maniac, it's a homicidal maniac with a sick sense of humor.

The place was an ornate, loud, standard, degenerate disco with lights flashing everywhere in such a way that you couldn't see where you were walking. About five hundred people appeared to be frantically dancing with themselves.

All the employees, men and women alike, wore manne-quinlike unisexual tuxedo outfits and looked a little too good. They also looked a little bored, and you really couldn't blame them because anybody that crawled around in a place like that for more than five minutes ought to be bored.

I ordered a beer for five bucks and it was flatter than your little sister, but I couldn't complain because the noise level was about the same as inside a washing machine. I sipped the beer and tried to see where the hell I was going. I kept bumping into people but I didn't know any of them and I didn't want to. I didn't even want to be there. I wished I was outside waiting in line. But it's harder to get out of one of those places than it is to get into one.

I turned a corner and entered another large, crowded room. On the ceiling I could see what looked like light reflected off water. It turned out to be a large swimming pool with a crowd gathered around it. Although I had hoped to find Barry Campbell hanging around somewhere, I didn't think I'd be finding him hanging around quite so literally.

He was suspended from a series of wires attached to the ceiling, and he was going through a series of movements that resembled more than anything else the actions of an emotionally ill ballet dancer. I couldn't be absolutely certain it was Campbell because of what he was and wasn't wearing, but the more I thought about it, who else could it be?

He was dressed as a mermaid. From head to tail.

He looked like a woman and he looked like a fish, but unfortunately, he still looked like Campbell. It wasn't the kind of thing you'd want to see before you had your kippers and toast. It wasn't even real nice right now. The crowd loved it. And "it" was certainly what it looked like. Whatever medication this crowd was on, I was going to need a double dose.

I went over to the cute little poolside bar and ordered an eight-dollar shot of Jack Daniel's. It went down faster than some of the people in the Blue Canary, so I ordered another one.

Eventually the show was over, and although many in the crowd continued to stare at the now empty swimming pool, Campbell swung over to the side and slithered through the throng. He disappeared through a side door. I waited a discreet moment or two and then followed. Nobody tried to stop me, which was fortunate because I didn't know the password unless it was "Get out of my way or I'll kill you and chop you up and put you in the trunk of my Trans-Am."

I walked down a soundproofed hallway, which came to an end at a closed door. It said PRIVATE—KEEP OUT, but I knew it didn't mean me. I turned the knob and pushed and the door opened into a dimly lit, posh sort of office. It looked a bit too swank for Campbell. Most places did. There he was though, still slightly phosphorescent, sitting on a large settee in one corner bending nose first over some kind of alabaster tabletop. He didn't see me come into the room but that was understandable.

"I didn't recognize you at first," I said, "without your wig and tail."

He jumped higher than a porpoise.

"You ever think about taking that act on the road?" I said.

"What do you want, man?" he said.

"I want to know why you sent Frank Worthington eleven roses," I said.

"You've made one of the biggest mistakes of your life coming back here, friend," he said.

"Probably," I said.

"Security," he shrilled. "Security."

Two guys came into the room. One was wearing a pair of sunglasses and the other was wearing a big, sick, but eager smile. The next thing I knew he was holding a .45 caliber Colt automatic in his left hand.

"Another lefty," I said.

"Turn around, Slick," he said.

I turned around and saw Barry Campbell's shy little smile of relief. I think he winked at me, but I couldn't be sure because I pitched forward behind a shattering blow to the back of my head that seared right through whatever the guy had left me of my brain. For a split second every fiber of my body was on fire and the whole world looked like a bad light show at the Fillmore East.

19

I woke up on Fifty-first Street next to a guy selling pretzels from a cart. It was morning, my head was throbbing like hell, I ached all over, and I was freezing to death. Too bad some kids hadn't come by and set my coat on fire. I felt like a used-up whore.

My wallet was gone, but I still had most of my teeth and, more important, my change, so I staggered to the corner pay phone and called Ratso. In New York you've got to know somebody.

Ratso said he'd be right over and I said I wasn't going anywhere. "I had a little hunting accident," I said. "I'll be the guy lying by the pretzel cart on Fifty-first Street." I went back to the cart and waited.

"Jesus," said Ratso, when he got there. "You look like you just went ten rounds with Richard Speck. You all right?"

"Just get me back to my cat," I said, as Ratso bought a pretzel. He hailed a cab, we got in it, and moments later we were hurtling down Ninth Avenue toward the Village. The driver made a point of running every red light and hitting every pothole in the street. There are no Sunday drivers in New York.

Twenty minutes later Ratso and I were sitting at the kitchen table at 199B Vandam. He was pouring us both a second shot of Jameson. The second shot cleared my eyes but didn't do anything for the lump on my head.

It was 10:00 A.M. and everything was pretty quiet on Vandam. The street was a major staging area for garbage trucks, but fortunately for my maltreated medulla, Sunday was their day of rest. It was so quiet you could hear the cockroaches. "It's a good thing there aren't any goddamn churches around here," I said. I was hearing more bells and sirens right now in my head than you ever heard on the streets.

Ratso had brought a copy of the *Daily News* and was poring over the hockey standings when a story in another section caught my eye. The headline read: DIARY OF A MURDER SUSPECT: PART I. The byline was McGovern's and it wasn't in the funnies section either.

My eyes were beginning to blur so I pushed the section across the table and said: "Ratso, here's an article I think you might enjoy. Maybe you'll be kind enough to read it to me."

"Uh-hmn," he said. " 'The *Daily News* in the interest of our readers today begins a five-part series sent to us by secret courier: Diary of a Murder Suspect. The author is a reporter for our National Bureau and is currently a fugitive, wanted by the police in connection with a murder in the Village on February 17. Without our freedom of the press and without the inherent right of a man's innocence until proven guilty, this series would not be possible. . . .' "

"Without our sense of circulation is more like it," I muttered. "Well, at least McGovern's alive."

"Yeah," said Ratso. "Our fugitive reporter is probably holed up right now at the Plaza. We'll never find him."

"We'll find him," I said. "We'll find him. In the meantime, see if you can find a large ice pack, will you?"

Ratso found an ice pack and I found my head and put the ice pack on the top of it. I was becoming increasingly aware that if we did not find McGovern soon, his ass was going to belong to the gypsies. If he was lucky.

Ratso had gone home, I'd given the cat a double order of tuna, and I was sacking out for a couple of hours. Taking a little power nap and trying not to dream. It was around two o'clock. I wasn't in the habit of logging incoming calls when I was on the nod, so I didn't know the exact time Nina rang. But I do remember exactly what her first words to me were.

"I remember something," she said. I thought better of asking her if it would keep until morning.

"It's not too smart to say that around here," I told her. "Could get you croaked."

"You sound terrible," she said. She sounded good.

"Are you all right?" She was really worried.

"I'm fine," I said. "I just came down with a bad case of lockjaw on the way to Fire Island." I was sitting up now and someone had apparently shut down the steam drill in my head.

"Do you want me to come over?" she asked.

"That would be nice," I said. We hung up and I glanced around, thinking maybe to straighten up the place a little bit. It didn't really need much straightening up or else it needed a lot. It depended on how you looked at it. I made the bed and threw out a few empty liquor bottles that were on the table. I set the time right on my cuckoo clock from Leningrad that my friend Boris had given me. It didn't keep the time and the cuckoo part didn't work but it came from Leningrad. Come to think of it, Boris didn't work too much either but he might come in handy yet. He had been a combat karate expert in Russia before he saw the light on the Statue of Liberty. He could kill a man in more than a hundred different ways without leaving any marks.

McGovern and I had taken karate lessons twice a week from Boris in his SoHo studio before somebody'd croaked Frank Worthington. I hadn't got to the lesson yet about how to stop a speeding bullet fired at you by a speeding bullethead. Boris probably knew, though. I warned him never to join the army because if he ever had to salute, he'd probably kill himself. He didn't think that was very funny, but Russians never think that anything is very funny. And they're probably right. Anyway, the clock was a piece of crap but I tried to keep it running. Greenwich Village Meantime, at least. I took the rose from my old hunting vest, put it in a vase on the table, and gave it some water. I could have used a drink myself but it didn't feel like Miller Time. I was chasing a few cockroaches off the cupboard when I heard Nina calling from the street. I threw the puppet head down with the parachute and turned on the espresso machine while I waited for her to climb the three flights of stairs. Even without my bird book and binoculars, she'd looked pretty good standing on the sidewalk.

She looked even better standing at the door. She put her arms around me. "Gently," I said. I didn't have to tell her. Some people just have the touch. She felt great.

"Why don't you lie down on the couch," she said. Her hair was cut after the fashion of a little French newsboy. I didn't go for little French newsboys but it looked good on her. I could imagine a number of things that would look good on her. One of them was myself. I walked over to the couch and I lay down.

Nina was giving me a pretty fair impersonation of a massage when the phones rang. "I'll get it," she said. I didn't log that one either, but I just lay there on the couch thinking about logging something else. "It's Cynthia," she said.

"Tell her I'll meet her at five P.M. at McGovern's."

"You're very popular," she said when she returned.

"Yeah. Look, be very careful what you say if you call me on that phone. I'll lay odds it's tapped, along with McGovern's, and the police'll probably be along to have a little talk with you as well, so just be careful. Somebody's croaked Frank and somebody's croaked Darlene and somebody might just try to croak somebody else."

"I'm very careful," she said. "How does this feel?"

"Better than the out-call service from *Screw* magazine," I said. She wasn't all that good at it but she didn't have to be. "What were you going to tell me?" I asked.

"Well, this was about a year and a half ago. One day I was walking with Frank down Fourth Street, and he pointed off to his right toward that block off Charles Street."

"Did he think he was on a Gray Line Tour?"

"No, he didn't. He said, 'That's where my shrink lives.' "

"He didn't say anything else?"

"That was it. 'That's where my shrink lives.' I'm not sure which side of the street or anything, just Charles to the right of Fourth as you're walking east."

"I'll give that shrink a good checkup from the neck up," I said. "I wonder if he drives a Mercedes and smokes a pipe and has a large dog."

"He could also drive a station wagon," she said. She was working on my head while she was working on my head. I noticed she had a nice little laugh and she knew how to use it. She even knew when to use it. I'd always believed that if you could make a woman laugh you could take her to bed with you.

"Who sent you the rose?" she asked a little too casually.

"That's what we're going to find out. Go easy on my head," I said, touching the lump on top of it. "That's where my shrink lives."

Nina took my hand and held it over her left breast. She didn't really have to hold it but she did. "That's where my shrink lives," she whispered.

I didn't doubt it.

20

By the time I got to Jane Street to see Cynthia, I was feeling remarkably better than I had that morning. Not only were Nina and I getting better acquainted, but I had a much clearer sense of which leads I might want to pursue. I had been treading a tortuous and confused path along which the killer had left seemingly no real clues to his identity. Now, for the first time, I could see a few careless footprints in the clay, and a bent twig or two along the trail, like the twisted synapses of the bent mind I was chasing.

On a Blue Canary cocktail napkin, I had made a little list of what I had to do. It read as follows: (1) Find Barry Campbell, turn him upside down, and use the point of his head to pick up paper with. Also check out the flowers he'd sent to Frank Worthington. (2) Grill Pete Myers to see if he knew about anything besides the British Knish. (3) Check the *Daily News* building's National Desk for access to McGovern's typewriter; check the newspaper morgue for old McGovern bylines over the years. To this, I added number (4) Find Frank Worthington's shrink and get some insights into whatever you prefer to call the mind of a stiff.

This last might require my giving the shrink a healthy jolt of shock therapy, but I liked shrinks only a little better than I liked lawyers, so I wasn't going to worry about it.

I put the cocktail napkin away, pulled a cigar out of my hunting vest, and rang the buzzer to 2B. I lighted the cigar and, satisfying Cynthia that I wasn't Tex Watson, pushed the door open as she buzzed me in. Actually, security of this kind almost never worked. The buzzers, alarms, and chains on the door worked fine. The problem was that no one ever really knew who Tex Watson was until he presented his card. And by that time, it was too late.

On the second floor, I noticed a young couple coming out of Frank Worthington's old place with a little baby in a pram. About the only thing they don't waste time with in New York is renting your apartment once you fall through the trapdoor. They're interviewing new prospects before you even have time to wake up in hell. You go down; the rent goes up.

"Hi, Cynthia," I said.

"Come on in," she said, as she took the chain off the door.

I looked around inside the apartment. She wasn't going to win any housekeeping awards, but the place looked tidier than when McGovern had been there. Of course, the three little pigs probably could've done a better job than McGovern.

I had located some cognac and was searching the kitchen cabinet for an appropriately stemmed glass when I noticed a little white snow seal winking at me from one corner. McGovern never used cocaine, though he used just about everything else.

"Been to see our friend Adrian, I see."

"She came by last night. You must think I'm terrible."

"Yeah, I'm all for clean living," I said. "My body is a temple where I go to pray for drugs." I heard a wrong chord somewhere in my mind but I wasn't sure what it was or who was playing it.

"Look," I said, "McGovern's bound to get in touch with one of us very soon, so we've got to keep in touch. He's probably sorting things out and he's obviously being very careful."

"But why hasn't he called?"

"I just told you, Cynthia. He's being careful. Hasn't it crossed your desk that your phones are being monitored by the police, both here and at your own place? Where do you live?"

"New Jersey." New Jersey was my second favorite place. My first was everywhere else. "Like a drink?"

She shook her head. I was a big enough phony to get by in situations with depressed, distraught women, but that still didn't make it my idea of a good time.

"You see, honey, McGovern is still the number-one suspect in this affair. If you speak to him and don't report it to the police, you're an accessory to the crime. Speaking of which, I want you to be very careful on this phone in general and especially when you're talking to me. Believe me, the cops are watching, listening, and waiting for McGovern to show himself. But he'll find a way of making contact with us, don't worry."

Actually, I was starting to get pretty worried. Why hadn't McGovern found a way of getting in touch with one of us? Maybe he was busily plotting to rub us both out. It happens. In fact, it happens about as often as it doesn't happen. Amazingly few premeditated murders ever involve strangers or casual acquaintances. You have to get to know somebody pretty well before you decide to murder them.

As I left Cynthia's place, something was bothering me but I didn't quite know what the hell it was. She didn't hug me, but she squeezed my hand a few times instead. I could live with it. Something else seemed to be bothering Cynthia besides McGovern. I couldn't even guess what it was. I didn't even know what was bothering me.

I figured I'd draw a bye on seeing Adrian this trip. One dizzy dame was enough for a Sunday afternoon, and I doubted that there would be an appreciable amount of progress in the stained-glass department.

Meanwhile, I was still feeling somewhat in the debit column in the gray matter department. I could've written volumes on what I didn't know if I'd only known what it was. Trouble was, I didn't. I only knew I'd better find the killer before the noose tightened forever around McGovern's seventeen-and-a-half-inch neck.

21

It was about ten o'clock on Sunday night. The weather had become increasingly colder, but at least the rain had stopped earlier in the evening. Charles Street was still there. So was Frank Worthington's shrink, whoever he was.

It was a beautiful street with elegant brownstones and quaint little cafés. If you had to be a shrink and you had to live in the Village, this was the place. It even had what New Yorkers like to think of as trees struggling along here and there up through the sidewalks. But they weren't the kind of trees that would ever prevent you from seeing the forest. It was there. And it was at least as dark as *The Jungle Book*.

I combed the two blocks of Charles Street nearest to Fourth Street for the better part of two hours, weeding out the handful of dentists and the occasional proctologist until I came up with three possible shrinks. It was a nerveracking procedure because many of the little bronze plates were deliberately vague, only saying something like Dr. Stanley Livingstone and requiring my calling up on the intercom to determine the doctor's area of expertise.

I talked to baby-sitters, wives, and housekeepers, most of whom grudgingly gave me a little information and all of whom were ticked off about the late hour. It was a good thing I didn't need a doctor.

I thought of what Albert Einstein's maid had once reportedly told a guy who called up asking if the doctor made house calls. She'd told him: "He's not the kind of doctor who does nobody no good."

By the time I had my three possibles, I felt like a Jehovah's Witness with a rejection complex. Of the three shrinks living in that section of Charles Street, one was dead and one was at a shrinks' convention in Los Angeles. I didn't know which was worse.

The other one was my boy. Dr. Norman Bock. It was 11:45 P.M.

What the hell. I wasn't here for my health. I pushed the button.

A deep, resonant voice laced with thinly veiled irritation said: "Yes."

"Dr. Bock?"

"Yes. Are you aware of what time it is?" He was warming up to me a little.

"Yes, Doctor. I'm sorry it's so late but my name is Marvin Barenblatt and I'm having an anxiety attack." I tried to sound as miserable as I felt.

"How did you get my name and address?" he asked. He sounded thoroughly disgusted with life on this planet. He didn't know it, but he had a ways to go to catch up with me. If I'd had my way, I would've given both of us a kick in the ass.

"I got your name from Frank Worthington, a former patient of yours." He was certainly that.

"Hmmnn," he said. He did a pretty nice job of crowding just a hint of suspicion and just a glint of recognition into that "hmmnn." I couldn't tell which way he was going to go. It made me feel kind of vulnerable. That's probably what they taught them in med school these days. They sure weren't boning up on the bedside manner.

"What was your name again?"

"Marvin. Marvin Barenblatt." I had affected a sort of whiney shrill and I was beginning to feel pretty much at home with it.

"Call me in the morning, Mr. Barenblatt. I'll try to squeeze you in in the afternoon."

I whined a little. "Good night, Dr. Bock" into the intercom, but he'd already gone off to ritually floss his teeth. Well, I'd see him in his office tomorrow.

The human mind was a funny thing, and I was betting my life that Frank Worthington's file, once I got my hands on it, was going to crack us all up.

When I got home it was after midnight. The cat wasn't too happy about how long I'd been gone and neither was I. When you have a cat, you assume certain responsibilities that, in a spiritual sense, may transcend those of a marital or a business relationship. We both felt a little let down.

I made some coffee and I poured a cup and I was thinking about having a cigar when the phones rang. It was McGovern. 12:25 A.M.

"This is Lord Baskerville," he said.

"You dog, you."

"Look, I'm sorry I haven't gotten in touch."

"Don't mention it, pal."

"Listen. You know the one place I haven't been eighty-sixed from in the Village?"

"Yeah." That was an easy one. The Bistro.

"Well, if you can be there in an hour, I'll call you."

"Right-ho, Baskerville, old boy. Been a pleasure talking to you." Less than fifteen seconds. Even phone-company security couldn't trace that one for the cops. I lighted a cigar, fed the cat, put on my hunting vest, and headed out into the night.

It was past one o'clock when I got to the Bistro. It wasn't very crowded for a Sunday night. Maybe that was why they hadn't eighty-sixed McGovern. They needed everybody they could get. Well, they had me tonight.

That was about all they had. Going down the bar, there was one ebony-colored gentleman fighting off the D.T.'s, one recently retired backgammon hustler, one Puerto Rican who looked like a leftover extra from *West Side Story*, one bag lady who'd come in from the cold, and one whatever the hell I was supposed to be.

If you could tell a man by the company he keeps, you couldn't have told me anything.

I ordered a Bistro Burger from my old pal Dave at the bar and I waited to hear from McGovern. "Drag it through the garden, Dave."

"Right you are."

I wondered if I'd miss the Bistro when I was dead. Conceivably. But the older I got, the less likely it seemed. I wasn't going to miss much else either at the rate I was going.

Of course, most people didn't know what they were missing. And they sure didn't know what they weren't missing. Nor did they know that there was any difference between the two.

"That's why everybody else in the world is happy and I'm as lonely as a lighthouse," I thought.

Of course it wasn't true. It was just something that happened to people who had to wait too long for their Bistro Burgers.

So I ordered a Canadian Mist for a Canadian I missed and I bought a drink for the bag lady. "Cheers," I said.

"Mind your manners," she said.

I was hungry enough to eat pork tartare by the time the Bistro Burger arrived. And I had all five pounds of it in my hands en route to my choppers when the phone rang. I set the burger down and walked over to the pay phone, which was the only phone in the place and was located in the middle of the room right next to the jukebox. It wasn't very private, but then neither was the men's room at Grand Central Station. And a lot of business was conducted there.

It was McGovern.

"Hey," he said, "I've missed you."

"Yeah, where are you?"

"I've been riding the couch circuit for a while. I'm at Costello's." Costello's was the drinking newspaperman's bar on

Forty-fourth Street. And what newspaperman didn't drink? "Been staying with Brennan and here and there." Mick Brennan was a charming, high-powered, wild, and well-connected British free-lance photographer. Two of his many claims to fame were that he'd covered the Falklands War from mainland Argentina, and that he was a personal friend of Michael Caine's. I liked him anyway.

"McGovern, how long can you keep this up before you get nailed?" Hell, for the right money, I was ready to turn him in.

"Hey, I'm making it. Did you read my column today?"

"Yeah, I did, and I'll bet the ranch you'll be back in the sneezer before they can run part five. 'Diary of an Idiot.'" McGovern sounded fairly monstered. Couldn't say I blamed him.

"Tell Cynthia I'll drop by and see her at the place one night this week."

"That's real smart," I said.

"How's she holding up?"

"About as well as you are. She'll make it. I'm not so sure about you."

I took a quick look to see if my Bistro Burger was intact. Nobody'd touched it, but I could see the heat disseminating from it with alarming rapidity.

"Do you want me to come up there?" I asked.

"No. I've got to be on the move. You know how it is."

"Yeah. This fugitive underground journalist thing is going to your head. Better tell me about this goddamn ghost you saw, just in case I never see you again."

"The ghost. Yeah, the ghost. Look, I didn't tell anybody but you and Cynthia about this."

"It's a good thing. You tell the cops and you'll wind up in wig city for sure." I didn't tell him, but that might be better than being sentenced for second-degree murder. Hanging out with guys who thought they were Jesus and Napoleon would probably be preferable to being in a cell with a large black man who called you Louise.

"It was a little while after you'd left and a little before the police came across the hall to my apartment and found the gun. That's when I saw the ghost. It was standing there by the stairs in the hallway, and then it just disappeared."

"Well, I got two questions for you: Number one is, why didn't the cops see the ghost? And number two is, were you drinking?" Actually, I knew the answer to the second one. It was the same answer you'd expect if you'd asked "Do fish fart underwater?"

"The cops probably didn't see this ghost because they were busy in Worthington's apartment and also because they weren't looking for this particular ghost."

"I see. Was the ghost anybody you knew?" This was starting to get good.

"Yes, it was. That's the funny part. I'd had a few drinks, you know, but as drunk as I've ever got, I've never seen a ghost before and I never want to see one again, I can tell you."

"Well, come on, McGovern, how the hell did you know it was a ghost? This ain't *The Twilight Zone.* I don't have to stand around here all night listening to this crap. How do you know it wasn't somebody in the building going out for a pizza?"

"Because while the cops were in the other apartment with Frank Worthington's body, I saw the ghost in the hall. It was coming right toward me. . . . It was carrying a flower. . . . I know this sounds crazy . . . you're going to hate me for this. . . ."

"Don't worry." How could anyone hate a large, personable Irishman whose brain was slowly turning to Silly Putty? "Just tell me how you knew what you saw was a goddamn ghost."

"Because I knew who it was."

"Who, then? Who was the ghost?" I was starting to feel a little uneasy in spite of myself.

"It was Frank Worthington," he said. "I saw Frank Worthington's ghost in the hall after he was murdered."

22

If my conversation with McGovern hadn't sufficiently taken away my appetite, the figure darkening the door was more than enough to finish the job.

It was Detective Sergeant Cooperman, and he didn't especially look as if he'd been having a good day. That made two of us.

It was what could be described as a close call.

"Who you calling, pal? Fixing up a late date with Greta Garbo?" This guy was funny.

"Yeah," I said. I drifted over to my Bistro Burger, and Cooperman drifted right with me. He sat down on the other side of me from the bag lady. "I'd like you to meet a friend of mine," I said to her, gesturing toward Cooperman.

"Watch it," she said.

It didn't take a rocket scientist to figure out that Cooperman was running a stakeout on McGovern's place. The question was, what was I doing here?

"What are you doing here, pal?" he asked.

"What am I doing here? I'm a regular. I'm always here on Sunday night. Right, Dave?"

"Right you are," said Dave.

I wasn't feeling very hungry, and Cooperman said he was, so in a rare display of brotherhood, he and I decided to split my Bistro Burger between us. He looked up at Dave the bartender. "You got a knife, pal?" he said.

"Why don't we just use the one in McGovern's back?" I said. Cooperman chuckled at that one.

"Say, your old pal must be getting just a little nervous in the service right about now."

"I wouldn't know," I said.

"You haven't talked to him, eh?"

"No." The hamburger was going down like lead. Cooperman was smiling and chomping away at his half of the burger at the same time. I'd hate to have to watch him eat every night.

"Well, I'm sure he'll turn up pretty soon," he said. "Maybe belly up if he isn't careful." Cooperman was starting to really enjoy himself. It was past time for me to get the hell out of there.

I paid the check, left Dave a good tip, said good night to him, to Cooperman, and to the bag lady, and walked out. I figured that it must be just another one of those wonderful little coincidences of life that Cooperman and I had run into each other in that place at that time. Next time I ran into Cooperman, I hoped I'd be driving.

When I got back to 199B Vandam I put on the sarong that I'd got from Borneo, made some camomile tea, drank it, and went to bed. But sleep came slower than a frigid woman.

I played the same hand over and over again in my mind, but the cards just weren't stacking up right. I knew the other players. I knew the odds. But somehow I didn't trust the look in the dealer's eyes.

Anything could happen, and if I knew anything it probably would.

Funny bumping into Cooperman . . .

It was a small world, but I'd hate to paint it.

23

When I got up Monday morning I felt like I'd been run over by a bookmobile but otherwise I was fine. It was too early to call the shrink's office for my appointment so I made some coffee and was just starting to look over the score for the Broadway show I was working on when the phones rang. It was 9:07 A.M. Ratso.

"Start talking," I said.

"Well, I was born in a small Texas town. My family didn't have much money so I went to work at a very early age pumping gas in a whorehouse and then . . ."

"Give it a rest, will you?"

"Sure," said Ratso. "Just thought you'd want to know that one of our friends is performing tonight at the Ear Inn. Good ol' Peter Myers." The Ear was a little bar on Spring Street that went in for literary and artistic endeavors in a big way. The neon *B* in the word *Bar* had burned out in several places and for years had read *Ear* and that's the reason they call the Ear the Ear.

"Knowing our friend," I said, "I'm afraid to ask what he's performing. Is it of a sexually explicit nature?" Maybe he was sticking it in his own ear.

"Oh, no," said Ratso, "it's quite legitimate. Myers has been on the calendar there for over a month. He's giving a poetry reading. You know, 'Gather ye rosebuds while ye may,' that kind of thing. Not really your cup of tea probably, but considering he may be trying to kill you, I just thought you might like to attend. It's at eight o'clock tonight.''

The only guy I'd ever want to go hear read poetry was Dylan Thomas and it wasn't bloody likely because he'd been dead for thirty years. At least I hoped he was dead; they buried him thirty years ago. ''Okay, I'll meet you there,'' I said.

''Sounds delightful, doesn't it?'' said Ratso.

''Sounds pretty goddamn weak to me,'' I said and hung up. I had another cup of coffee, lighted my first cigar of the new day, and thought about a lot of things. I even thought about watering the plants but didn't get much further than that. It was time to see if Dr. Norman Bock could squeeze me in. When it came time for me to level with this guy, it was probably going to turn pretty ugly.

I picked up the phone. Got a young secretary's voice. ''Doctor's office. May I help you?'' she said.

''Marvin Barenblatt here,'' I shrilled. ''Dr. Bock said he'd try to squeeze me in this afternoon. I'm a new patient.'' Poor Marvin.

''Fine, Mr. Barenblatt. How does three o'clock sound?''

''Fine,'' I told her. And that was that.

I called Cynthia and I called Wolf Nachman to keep them abreast of the situation such as it was. Cynthia sounded like she hadn't slept since I'd seen her last. Wolf sounded the way all lawyers sound—like life never quite touches them. Maybe lawyers just never have any personal problems of their own. They just spend their lives giving gray hair to other people.

It was now five days since somebody had torpedoed Darlene Rigby's career. It was ten days since somebody had snuffed Worthington. He hadn't even had a career to torpedo, but they'd croaked him just the same. Obviously Worthington was croaked for a deeply personal reason, one which Darlene Rigby had apparently been privy to. She had known something and it had been something that hadn't kept till the morning.

No murderer could be said to be truly sane but there was always a reason, real or imagined, for a killer to kill. This killer struck me as rational, methodical, and lucky, but he was pushing his luck. All I could really do was try to get an in-depth look at Frank Worthington's mind, and a firmer grasp of where Nina, Campbell, Myers, and Adrian were coming from. And keep my fingers crossed for McGovern. Get out my lucky shamrock for the boy. God knows he was going to need it.

Two-thirty on an unseasonably mild Monday afternoon found me walking Marvin Barenblatt's sick brain down Fourth Street on its way to his psychiatrist's office. I was whistling a tune. It was a tune from an old Broadway show and it was jarred only occasionally by some teenage idiot with a ghetto blaster or by the honking of traffic behind a car that was hopelessly lost in that Ariadne's maze that is the Village.

An obsidian young man flew by backward on a skateboard. A homosexual couple was patching up an argument on the corner. One was holding the other to his chest, stroking his head. It looked like spring was just around the corner.

I didn't care what a young man's fancy turned to in spring. My mind was on murder. Two murders to be exact. And this was going to be a long winter. Even Marvin knew that the appearance of spring in New York was phonier than a French waiter. And Marvin was a phony himself.

I put murder on the back burner and stopped whistling when I reached Dr. Norman Bock's office on Charles Street. If Marvin had a problem, so did I.

Being Marvin Barenblatt at all was a nauseating experience and about another five or ten minutes was all that I was going to be good for. I'd always made it a policy of intensely disliking anyone named Marvin. Now I knew why. Marvin was getting on my nerves. I couldn't wait for him to meet Dr. Bock and leave me alone.

I pushed the buzzer, the little voice said, "Doctor's office," and I said: "Marvin Barenblatt here to see Dr. Bock." I gained entry.

The little voice that had said "Doctor's office" was sitting behind a desk in a container that must have weighed in at two hundred pounds. Only a shrink or an undertaker could have afforded to have a receptionist as wide as her desk. And for a fat lady, she wasn't all that friendly. Neither was I. Fortunately, neither of us had to wait too long.

Bock opened the door into the waiting room and said, "Mr. Barenblatt." The receptionist said, "You can go in now," which was a little unnecessary because I was already going in. I shot her my best Marvin look of cloying reproach, but she only looked at me with pity in her eyes. I followed Bock into his pastel basement shrinking parlor and walked around a bit looking at the abstract crap on the wall that somebody'd seen fit to frame. If it wasn't the work of his patients, it should have been.

"I feel like I know you already, Marvin," he said.

"Yeah. Sorry about last night, Doctor."

"Oh, don't worry about it. That's what we're here for."

"Beautiful day out there today, isn't it?" It was hard to tell if you lived in a pastel basement. Molten lava could've been coming down Charles Street and he wouldn't have known it.

"Yes. I'd say it was spring if I didn't know better," he said. "Well, what seems to be bothering you, Marvin? You started to tell me last night, I believe."

"Yeah. Sorry about that, Doc." I thought I'd start to repeat myself a time or two. Might be worth a jot on a pad.

"Don't mention it," he said, a little curtly, I thought. I'd seen better eye contact in drunks.

"Have you been in touch with Frank Worthington lately?" I asked.

"No. I haven't seen Frank in several years now. How's he doing?"

"Not too well," I said.

"That's a shame. Does pipe smoke bother you?"

"Not at all. I like it, in fact. It reminds me of my old Grand-dad Barenblatt. He used to smoke a big old briar pipe. Do you have a dog?"

"Yes, I do," he laughed. "Why do you ask?"

"You look like a dog lover."

"Do you have a dog, Marv?"

"No, I have a cat." At a hundred and twenty-seven dollars an hour somebody was getting hosed.

"Cats are nice, I understand," he said.

"They can be a lot of trouble sometimes."

"So can dogs, here in the city," he said. Of course, anything was a problem here in the city. The care and upkeep of a ball-point pen could be a problem. This was going nowhere pretty quickly. Time to put some cards on the table. Assuming that this guy could really shrink a head, mine was going to be about the size of a LeSueur pea before I learned anything useful about Frank Worthington.

"Look, Doc," I said, "there's a few things I ought to tell you before this goes too far."

"What's on your mind, Marv?"

"Well, for one thing, someone's threatening to kill me."

"Okay, Marv." He really believed that one.

"For another, while Marvin Barenblatt is a very melodic name, it's not mine." Bock sat up straight and put down his pipe. He seemed to be running down a few deep-breathing exercises.

"What name would you like to use?" he asked finally.

"I'd like to use the name Frank Worthington," I said. "He won't be needing it anymore. Somebody croaked him eleven days ago. That's why he's not doing too well. I'm working unofficially but I am in touch with the cops in charge of the case. Can I see his file?"

"Out of the question," said Bock hotly. I got up and walked over to his desk. "Especially," he said, "after the totally fraudulent way in which you've presented yourself."

"Now, Doc, don't let old Marvin get your goat. I thought he was a woosie of the first water myself, but you'll find that I'm not and I want to know all there is to know about Frank Worthington two years ago. What were his problems? Was the boy out where the buses don't run? I mean, had the date on his carton expired, or what?"

Bock just screwed up his mouth and shook his head. He started to light his pipe. I took out a cigar and fired it up and waited.

"Frank Worthington . . ." said the shrink softly. A dreamy sort of expression came into Bock's eyes. Dreamy and maybe something else. Even psychiatrists had their dreams. And their secrets.

"Frank Worthington was a man of great physical beauty," he said. "He was attractive to many women. And to many men. He seemed almost to drift through life like a fragile and beautiful butterfly just beyond everybody's reach. People saw him and they wanted to . . . they wanted to . . . to collect him . . . but nobody ever could. . . ."

At this point Bock stopped to relight his pipe. Then he looked right at me and said in an almost wistful voice: "Nobody ever could. . . ."

"Looks to me like somebody pinned his wings pretty good, Doc," I said.

"I'm going out of town Wednesday," he said brusquely, "and my schedule is really very crowded. So I'll have to ask you to please leave now, Mr. Barenblatt. Immediately." He stood up abruptly, walked across the room, opened the door, and held it for me.

My appointment was obviously over.

Wednesday night, however, I planned to be back with Rambam and his little putty knife. But I could see that getting into Frank Worthington's head was going to be a lot bigger operation than getting into Frank Worthington's apartment.

Dr. Bock nodded curtly at me as I walked by him into the

waiting room, then he disappeared into his office, closing the door behind him. I walked past the receptionist who stared at me with disgust.

"For the initial evaluation, sir," she said, "we charge . . ."

"Bill me," I said.

24

I took a cab up to Costello's bar on Forty-fourth to meet Mick Brennan and have him take me over to the *Daily News* building just two blocks away. Mick was at the bar drinking a creative gin-based concoction of his own invention and reading "The Diary of a Murder Suspect: Part II."

"McGovern's a bit more out there than I quite thought, mate," he said. I didn't disagree. When the cops did catch him, they were going to be so mad they'd throw him in the back of the pen.

"Mick, do you have a Minox?"

A Minox was a small Japanese surveillance camera much favored by spies, counterespionage agents, and people who wished to photograph the files of anal-retentive shrinks.

"No, I'll have a Heineken," he said.

A Heineken was a Dutch beer much favored by Mick Brennan. On occasion, he would favor more than one.

"Mick," I said, "I know you only like to plan half an hour ahead, but I have an important assignment for you late Wednesday night that is almost as dangerous, not to say stupid, as it was for a wiseass Brit photographer to be caught hanging around mainland Argentina during the Falklands War. Or should I say skirmish?"

"War," he said.

"War," I agreed, and ordered a Bass ale along with a Jameson to keep it company. For nothing in this world looks quite as lonely sitting on a bar as a pint of beer without a shot of Jameson unless it's a shot of Jameson without a chaser.

"Let's drink to war," I said. "Peace can be so tedious."

"Spoken like a man who's never seen one," said Brennan.

"You participant-observers of life must get a little world-weary sometimes. Can we pencil you in for Wednesday night?"

"Let's drink to penciling me in."

"To penciling you in." He joined me in a shot. "Cheers, mate," he said.

"Are you sure you'd like to know what I'm penciling you in for?"

"Not particularly. But let's have it before I die of ennui."

"We're going to break into a shrink's office in the Village and photograph the confidential files of a recent bisexual murder victim. The killer has struck twice now. And he's not very nice. He's still on the loose, you know. Could be me or you. Where were you last Wednesday night?"

"I was visiting your friend Gunner." Brennan smiled impishly. Brennan said just about everything impishly. When he wanted to be, he could be as bad a troublemaker as Jesus.

"What were you doing over there? Helping her adjust her light meter?"

"Why don't you break into her apartment and photograph her little diary and find out?" he said. When he wasn't being impish, Brennan could get a little testy. If there was one thing I hated, it was a testy Brit. It just didn't wear well on them.

"I'll drink to that," I said, and we ordered and downed a couple more shots. I wanted to be sure we weren't walking on our knuckles when we left there because I wanted to be fairly sharp when we got to the *Daily News* and however sharp you have to be to attend a poetry reading. I didn't really think a poetry reading would be all that dangerous. In fact, it sounded so exciting I wondered if I could stay awake through it. Which goes to show that the books are filled with stuff I didn't know. But I would be learning. The hard way.

We left Costello's still walking upright and headed over to the *Daily News*.

As my father once remarked when he got back from a trip abroad, "If you've seen one Sistine Chapel, you've seen 'em all." That was particularly true of big-city newspaper offices. There is a certain trapped spirit of resigned cynicism that you can catch like a virus if you stay there too long. Probably it was reality. I wouldn't know. But my respect for McGovern grew. To survive as a maverick in the truth business was no mean feat.

One of the first things that grabs you when you walk into the *Daily News* building is the giant blue globe of what we are sometimes pleased to call the planet earth that is sunk into the lobby and is as big as a St. Patrick's Day hangover. Emanating from it are mosaic markers on the floor of the lobby to show the various distances away of major cities of the world. If you said that the distances were all measured from Costello's bar, you probably wouldn't be wrong.

Brennan and I circled the globe a couple times along with a few visitors from Japan and several guys who looked like professional loiterers. A guard kept a wary eye on the group of us. If anyone had been thinking of going to Nome, it was 3,781 miles away. If you wanted to bang your head against the Great Wall of China it was 6,882 miles away in Beijing, but if you couldn't stand to wait that long, you could bang your head against the Wailing Wall, which was only 5,696 miles away in Jerusalem. Or you could just move to Cleveland, which was only 404 miles away but would make you feel like banging your head against a wall. Piccadilly Circus was 3,475 miles away in London and the Moscow Circus, if it hadn't defected yet, was 4,665 miles from here.

The circus that I had to deal with was on the seventh floor.

Brennan and I negotiated the elevator all right but ran into immediate trouble on the seventh floor. The guy at the desk there appeared not to know Brennan from Adam and he looked right through me like I wasn't there.

"You sure this is the lingerie department?" I asked Brennan. He silenced me with a severe glance.

"Is Bob Miller here?" he asked.

"You want to speak to the city editor?" said the guy at the desk. "Are you kidding? He wouldn't pick up the phone for God."

Mick maintained his dignity, which is something the British do very well when they want to. They have more of it than they need to start with. "Tell him Mick Brennan is here to see him."

Rather grudgingly the guy called the city editor, and before you could have cooked a two-minute egg, the waves were parting, the wheels were turning, the metaphors were mixing, and the two of us were shaking hands with Virgil and following him down into the circles of Hell. Miller led us through a paper-strewn, workaday mazeway of human ratholes, cubicles, and plush offices and into the huge, smoke-filled, bustling city room. As the name implied, it looked like a small city.

"I'd like to have a look at McGovern's typewriter," I said.

"That's no problem," said Miller. "It's one of the few old heirlooms we've got left." It was true. Everywhere you looked, at almost every desk in the city room, reporters worked with computer screens instead of typewriters. Miller showed us around.

"About seven years ago these buggers started taking over. Video-display terminals. VDTs. Typewriter's practically a dinosaur. Sorry to say it, but it's true. There's McGovern's desk. Where the hell he is, I don't know. Make yourself at home. I'll be back in a few minutes."

"Nice guy," I said.

"That's what you think," said Brennan. "Even Jesus hates a city editor. And usually for good reasons."

I was hardly listening to Mick by then. I was looking over McGovern's typewriter. The old dinosaur that had helped the cops hang two murders on him. I knew the city room wasn't humming with action all the time, but it was hard to conceive of someone coming in here on several occasions and using McGovern's machine without someone seeing him. I doubted if the cops had even bothered with that possibility. I wasn't even too sure I believed it myself.

I put a piece of paper into the old Underwood and typed "break a leg, baby." Then, under it, I typed "i'm sending you eleven roses . . . the twelfth rose is you." I used no caps, just like the original notes to Frank Worthington and Darlene Rigby. Everything the murderer had written was in lowercase letters. "It's interesting," I told Brennan, "and it raises the shocking possibility that the murderer was e. e. cummings."

"That's cute," said Mick. "Better get cracking on whatever it is you're doing because Miller may change his rabbit mind and chuck us out of here at any moment."

"It was probably the last thing either of them ever read," I continued, half to myself. They certainly hadn't had time to read the writing on the wall. Well, maybe Darlene had. I felt a small twinge of guilt but it passed quickly.

Every typewriter, especially an old baby like this one, has its own set of fingerprints that it leaves on every typed page. I put the page down under the desk light and Brennan and I pored over it. If I had been Sherlock I could've left the magnifying glass at home. I wasn't even going to need "gather ye rosebuds while ye may." The *l* on McGovern's machine was visibly flawed. You could have driven a *Daily News* truck through it without scratching the paint. I was sure of that *l* on Worthington's note, and I remembered it in Darlene's original note and in the poem sent to me. A bit too obvious, but there it was, as they say, in black and white right before my eyes.

No question about it, the notes had been typed, all three of them, on McGovern's Underwood. Also there was no question in my mind that McGovern himself hadn't typed them. Almost no question.

* * *

I sent Brennan home and told him to get his equipment and his act together for what could be a fairly nasty Wednesday night. Someone pointed me through a long narrow hallway and I followed it right up to the desk of an old lady who sat guarding the *Daily News* morgue. Nice work if you could get it.

I told her I'd spoken to Bob Miller and I was looking for any and all bylines by McGovern. Her eyes widened a bit. "I'll see what I can find," she said.

"How far does the morgue go back in time?" I asked.

"June of 1919," she said.

"That was a good year for Château de Cat Piss but it's a bit farther than I want to go. How about going ten years back? Everything by McGovern that you can find."

"Well, it's all here," she said. I could see that. I could also see that this would be an exercise in tedium if I couldn't light a rather large bonfire under this nice old lady's ass.

"Ma'am," I said, "right now the police are looking frantically for McGovern and they believe he's a prime murder suspect as you've no doubt read." She nodded. She might've been nodding off for all I knew, but I continued in a brisker tone.

"Anything and everything by McGovern. We've got to find something that connects up to these murders. It's got to be here somewhere. Okay, let me have it."

She had some kind of a VDT there too and she stoked it up. As something came onto the screen she'd get that issue off the shelves and toss it on the table for me.

The first thing she came up with was a story by McGovern about six months old and datelined Dallas. PET PYTHON SWALLOWS EIGHT-MONTH-OLD BABY. Nice item.

"Keep 'em coming," I shouted. She did. An article about five years old concerning Senator Baker's wife going into surgery. It was headlined BAKER'S WIFE UNDER KNIFE.

"No," I said. I thought of McGovern's attitude toward his

profession. He'd summed it up in one sentence: "I don't do long leads and I don't work in the rain."

McGovern had felt that there was a built-in cynicism about the newspaper business. If twenty-four Mexicans were killed in a bus wreck, it was worth a short paragraph. If nine hundred people were killed in a ferryboat disaster in India, it was worth about two sentences, and so forth.

"Here's a recent one," the old lady said. I took a wary look. HIT-RUN DRIVER KILLS ALTAR BOY.

"We're getting warmer," I said. The old lady was trying to be nice. It was just the situation that was starting to look ugly.

"Eight years ago," she said. I looked. JAPANESE SWIM TEAM NIPS U.S. That wasn't it.

"Ten years ago," she piped. It was another story from India. The headline was STORM RIPS CEMETERY—500 FOUND DEAD.

"We're getting warmer still," I said. I was about ready to squash this kindly old lady like a bug and cut her into microfilm when she laid another dusty piece of newsprint before me. What was the use? The whole damn place was full of yesterday's fish wrappers anyway. I took an apathetic half glance at the paper on the table. Then my eyes lit up like a Christmas tree in Las Vegas. I jumped up and practically hugged the old lady.

"I need a copy of this," I said.

Ten minutes later I was leaving the building with a renewed confidence and a large brown folder under my arm when I ran into Bob Miller, the city editor, in the hall.

"You think they'll nail McGovern?" he asked.

"I sure hope not," I said.

"I sure hope not too," he said. "He's selling a hell of a lot of goddamn newspapers."

25

It was after six by the time I got back to Vandam Street and I was hungry and so was the cat. I fed the cat some tuna, and for myself I located an old Italian salami that had fallen into the back of the refrigerator and had been there since about Purim of 1974. Those things will keep forever. Life is short but Italian salamis are long. I ate the son of a bitch with a little leftover shredded wheat that was hanging around and washed it down with some white wine. I wasn't sure what year the wine was but whatever it was, the salami was older. There wasn't much in the house. Had to go shopping one of these days. Right now I couldn't be bothered with food. I was shopping for a maniac.

Unfortunately, he was also shopping for me.

I had a few hours to kill so I thought I'd reestablish commo with Cynthia and Nina, whom I hadn't forgotten about, and try to run down a two-legged arachnid named Barry Campbell. Adrian, I knew, would always be where she was both figuratively and literally. Coke dealers I had known were invariably creatures of narrow habit. They were a lot like cats except that cats had more soul.

Some coke dealers would travel into Harlem at four o'clock in the morning to deliver half a gram and others wouldn't venture across the street because they didn't believe in giving curb service. Whatever their habits and ways were, you could bet they would never dream of changing them to save their lives. Or your life.

So I lit a cigar and I dialed Cynthia's number through the smoke. She sounded like hell but I really couldn't blame her. Why did women ever fall in love with guys like McGovern? Why not find some nice slick advertising guy with pleated pants? This was New York, for God's sake. Men were everywhere, and at least some of them weren't homosexual. I wasn't. At least I didn't think so.

"Hi, honey, how're you doing?" I said.

"I'm here," she said. "I haven't heard from McGovern."

"You will," I said. I was hoping it wouldn't be through the obits or the police blotter, but all I said was "You will" again very sagely. Maybe she would.

"I just wish this was over," she said.

"It will be over soon," I said. "And I do mean o-v-e-r. I found something in the newspaper morgue today that may be pertinent. I am making headway, believe me." I didn't know if I believed me but it sounded like she did.

"Don't forget McGovern's a big boy. I'll see you tomorrow." McGovern wasn't just a big boy. He was also a big nerd. I was just waiting for him to crack like the ceiling plaster underneath a lesbian dance class.

I dialed Nina Kong's number. She wasn't home and pretty soon I wasn't either. I was on my way to meet Ratso at the Ear Inn to hear some kind of iambic pentameter drivel from Peter Myers.

I knew I was getting into deep waters. I didn't reckon, though, that it was going to be the bottomless lagoon.

26

The evening was crisp and beautiful, a particularly horrible night to have to sit while some pompous lisping self-righteous buffoon bent your ear at the Ear. The moon was up and the cobblestones were beckoning so I took a little walk through the Village. These modern poet-type people were usually so long-winded I doubted if I'd be missing much if I got to the Ear an hour late. If I never went there for the rest of my life I doubted if I'd be missing much.

But Ratso would be there. And of course Pete Myers.

I had just about settled the age-old dilemma of espresso versus cappuccino in favor of cappuccino when the Blue Mill Tavern loomed up in front of me and I walked in and ordered a Jameson. The Blue Mill was a place where a lot of old people usually congregated and the demographics were such that no matter who you were, you always felt young there. McGovern never much favored the place. Said it was the kind of place where Irish bartenders take their families on weekends. Not enough action for McGovern. But Monday night at the Blue Mill was perfect for me. I downed the Jameson and ordered another one with a Prior's dark and went to the telephone to call Nina.

"Hey," she said, "you just caught me. We're going into the studio tonight to start on the video. Why not come by some night this week?"

"Okay, I'll do it," I said. I got the name of the place and the directions. I remembered music when it was still music but I wasn't going to paddle against the wave of the future. Not on one Jameson. "Maybe tomorrow night," I said.

"Great," she said. "We'd be honored to have you."

"I'd be honored to have you," I said and hung up.

I went back to the bar, finished the drinks, ordered another round, and took an old newspaper clipping out of my hunting vest. I put it on the bar in front of me, and when the bartender returned, he put the shot of Jameson on the left of the article and the glass of beer on the right.

"Nice placement job," I said. I looked over the article again just to be sure I hadn't been dreaming, and it was still the same one I'd gotten from the lady in the newspaper morgue. The story was about four years old. If it had been a Havana cigar, a racehorse, or a French wine, it probably would be coming into its own about now and boding well for all. As it was, it was an old news story that didn't bode especially well for anyone. It was written by a *Daily News* reporter who appeared to have cracked a gay drug ring in the Village.

The reporter, of course, was McGovern. One of those charged was, of course, my old pal Barry Campbell.

Why didn't people ever tell me things before I went chasing after mermaids?

I left the Blue Mill Tavern feeling a lot better for what I'd been thinking and what I'd been drinking. I took a fresh cigar out of my hunting vest and paused by a doorway on Barrow Street to light it. As I rolled the cigar around between my thumb and fingers, always keeping it well above the actual flame, I glanced around me. I was good enough by now to light a cigar in my sleep and probably I would have if it weren't for the fire hazards.

My eyes went to a poster on the wall a little bit above my head. It showed four people in what could only be described as hideously contorted positions. Either they were war victims of some sort or the whirling dervishes were back in town. Underneath that it said WINNIE KATZ'S EXPERIMENTAL DANCE CLASSES FOR WOMEN.

It wasn't something you'd ever want to laugh at out loud, but I did chuckle a bit as I walked off in the general direction of the Ear Inn. "So that's what they call it," I said.

27

I entered the Ear as surreptitiously as a stray Q-Tip but was captured by Martin, the owner of the place, before I got by the bar. "Cheers," he said, as he laid a shot on the bar for me. Martin was a Brit too. Or maybe he was Irish. They all looked the same to me.

I stared into the main room of the Ear where some guy was spouting forth and the ten tables in the place were full of people listening raptly.

"Bit of culture never hurts anything but the cash register," said Martin.

"You know how I love your poetry nights, Martin," I said, indicating with my thumb the poet on the stage. "I'd like to buy that bastard a muzzle for Christmas. How many more are left? They all recite the Yellow Pages, don't they?"

"There's about three or four more who'll be giving readings. Have you ever heard Peter Myers?"

"Yeah," I said, "he's terrific. He's the bee's knees."

It was a quaint place all right, with a giant skylight, pictures of old battleships on the walls, and crayons at the table for customers to draw on the paper tablecloths when they got bored with the poetry readings. I took a few steps into the main room. A figure was slumping semicomatose in a chair at a corner table. Almost all of his body was under the table except for his head and his feet. The prehistoric shoes looked familiar. They'd obviously once belonged to a person who was no longer with us. I couldn't see how the figure was clothed, but I checked the head and it was Ratso's. There were a number of empty bottles on the table. He'd apparently been there since eight o'clock and he did not look pleased.

I walked over and sat down. "Kind of exciting, isn't it?" I whispered.

"Keep on your toes," he whispered back.

"Why?" I asked. "They raise the urinals in this joint?"

The guy standing on the tiny stage never missed a chance to take a simple idea and intellectualize it until it disappeared completely. I didn't know what he was yapping about and I didn't much give a damn. I wished I could get a forklift to get him out of there.

Ratso was sitting up now. "Keep on your toes," he whispered, "because Barry Campbell's sitting over there in the far corner."

"Good," I said. "I'd like to harm that child." I signaled the waitress and she took our order. Four shots of Jameson and a cup of coffee for Ratso. Had to keep the boy straight.

The drinks arrived about the time Pete Myers hit the stage, which was a good thing because the guy was a driving bore. You couldn't've told that to Barry Campbell though. He was hanging on every word. I'd like to have seen him hanging from a shower rod.

Myers went on interminably and Ratso and I drank. What else could a sane person do? Finally it was over. It was about 10:45. To this day I have no idea what he was reading. The people who weren't brain dead after two and a half hours of poetry recitations applauded politely, and the room broke up into small clusters of people.

"Keep your eye on Campbell," I told Ratso. "I'm going to have a word with Myers."

Myers was talking to an eager young couple. "Excuse me, Pete, can I have a word with you? It's rather important," I said. Everybody in this frigging town thought that what they were doing and saying was important so I might as well lie like the rest of them.

"Glad you could get by," he said. "How's the Frank Worthington thing going?"

"Well, now that you've asked, maybe you can help me. 'Gather ye rosebuds while ye may.' Who wrote that?"

I'd already checked it out and it was Robert Herrick, one of the lesser-known British poets, 1591 to 1674. "Gather ye rosebuds" had been his one big hit apparently.

Myers stroked what there was of his chin for a moment and then offered ponderously: "I'd have to say John Donne." Some expert.

"I'd have to say Pete Myers," I said. I was about half drunk. When you're half drunk, it's hard to tell if you're drunk or sober. I don't really know what I was trying to prove. Maybe nothing. Maybe just get some reaction. Whatever I was trying to do, it didn't work. Myers laughed and made small talk and told me the two of us should stay in touch. By the time I got back to the table Ratso was gone. I looked across the room and so was Barry Campbell.

I looked in the men's room, the ladies' room, and under a few tables, and finally I walked outside hoping to catch a glimpse of someone I knew.

I heard a noise like a car backfiring. I'd heard cars backfiring almost every day of my life but this time I was fresh out of luck. Something sang through my left shoulder and sawed a nice ragged section out of the other side. A swarm of killer bees were buzzing around in my brain as I sank into one of the less populated sidewalks of New York. It was raining blood.

28

I came to in the meat wagon. I wasn't sure if I was on the way to the hospital or to the morgue, and I didn't give a flying Canadian which as long as I got there in a hurry. The gestapo sirens weren't doing my nerves a lot of good but they weren't as bad as the potholes.

It wouldn't be too unpleasant to be lying on a nice sunny beach right now instead of a meat wagon. But something was always happening to put a crimp in one's vacation plans.

The nurses at St. Vincent's were very nice except that one of them looked like The Weasel. Maybe I wasn't seeing too well. It felt like I had a fork sticking in my left iris. Maybe it was The Weasel's sister. Have to make a note to ask him if he had a sister who was a nurse. Better a nurse than a nerd, I thought. My mind was beginning to clear but it was still about as lucid as tripe soup.

Ratso came walking through the fog in a pair of red pants that hurt me. He sat down in the chair next to my bed.

"It'll take more than Barry Campbell's little gang of killer fags to nail you, won't it, pal?" he said.

"Oh, I don't know," I said. "I thought they nailed me pretty good this time."

"Nah, it's only a flesh wound." Unfortunately, it was my flesh.

"What day is it?"

"It's Tuesday morning."

"Gotta get out of here."

"Look, the cops are onto the Campbell thing already. They'll probably be wanting to talk to you. But right now there's a visitor outside that's been waiting to see you. She's been very worried. If it's okay with you I'll get her." Ratso left the room and a few minutes passed before the door opened again. It was Cynthia.

She sat down and took my hand without saying anything for a while. I had to admit it felt good to have her there. Nina was probably too busy or else she didn't know yet. It didn't matter. Maybe video was Nina's life. Cynthia was a woman. And she was here.

Funny how getting nearly blown away could make you appreciate someone.

"Cynthia," I said. For a moment I entertained a fleeting thought of jumping her bones but I soon realized what a sick chicken that would make me both physically and spiritually. She looked ravishing. Maybe I was sicker than I thought.

"Are you in great pain?" she asked.

"No. It only hurts when I get excited. Like when I think of how I'm going to rip out McGovern's lungs when I see him."

"You know, I'm not going to be a guilty woman and say it's all my fault and everything. It's not all my fault. I know. But if McGovern had trusted me more, had believed in me like I believed in him, this wouldn't have happened. He wouldn't have been drinking so much, having nightmares, shouting curses in his sleep. He wouldn't be seeing ghosts in hallways and running from the police. I wouldn't be worn to a frazzle and this would never have happened to you. If he'd only trusted me."

"Cynthia," I said, "did you know that McGovern was the yo-yo champ of the state of Utah when he was only twelve years old?"

She laughed incredulously. "He wasn't," she said.

"It's the God's truth. He was. And the bastard's still a yo-yo as far as I'm concerned. First of all, I was minding my own business one afternoon when he called me to come over because there was a stiff in the apartment across the hall. A week later there's two stiffs. And last night I damn near made it a ménage à trois. Now the bastard's pulled his patented disappearing act, which he might have gone and done even if the cops weren't looking for him. He will do that, you know."

"I know," she said with a wistful smile.

"And he's made the case extremely difficult to make head or tail of even for an experienced veteran sleuth like myself." I was worn out from talking. I preferred just looking at Cynthia anyway. This time when she hugged me I didn't mind.

I held her for a moment and just at that moment Ratso came back in the room winking at me lasciviously. Cynthia got off the bed, whispered good-bye, and said she'd check on me the next day.

Ratso walked her out the door and when he came back into the room he was smiling. "I've been waiting for the love interest to come into play. Maybe she'll nurse you through your illness and you two will fall in love."

"If she's not careful, I may try nursing her first," I said. "Help me get out of here, pal, will you?"

"Yeah, I'll help you get out of here. But I'm coming with you and moving in with you for a while. I can sleep on the couch. I just don't trust this whole situation. I'll tell you the truth, Sherlock, your latest case really gives me the heebie-jeebies. So you've got a new roommate until the case is solved."

He seemed adamant and I was feeling too weak to argue with him.

It was a rare case of a rat joining a sinking ship.

29

It was Wednesday afternoon and a light rain was falling on the Village and the town. This was my favorite kind of weather because it reminded me of Vermont or Seattle or some place I'd just visited once and never stayed long enough to learn to hate.

Mick Brennan was futzing around with his camera equipment in my living room and simultaneously overseeing the brewing of some tea in the kitchen. He was a man of many talents.

Ratso and I were having coffee at the kitchen table. He was poring over the documents of the case, i.e., the article on Barry Campbell and Parts 1 to 4 of "Diary of a Murder Suspect." I was monitoring the rain and trying to recall what it was I was trying to recall. Whatever it might have been, it remained like a Japanese fishing boat just beyond the territorial waters of my memory and nothing I could do seemed to bring it any closer. I felt fine as long as nobody frogged me in the shoulder.

"You know," Ratso said as he started knocking down a toasted bagel with nova, cream cheese, onion, and tomato, "in Part Four here . . ."

"Diary of an Idiot?"

"Yeah, Diary of an Idiot, Part Four, the author really begins to positively crow like a rooster in heat."

"Sure. It's very self-aggrandizing. First he thinks he's Gandhi writing from a South African prison, and then when he's on the run from the cops, he progresses to sort of a Jack

London presence in which he describes a type of freedom that only he can attain and a life-style that only he can appreciate.''

"You do a disservice to Jack London and Gandhi,'' said Ratso.

"What are they? Your family's patron saints or something?''

"I knew you weren't going to make a good roommate,'' Ratso said, as he located some pickles fresh from the Carnegie Delicatessen.

"Just as long as you don't complain about the room service,'' I said. "Actually, there's not one solid fact in any of McGovern's first four articles that brings us one step closer to solving the killings.''

"Maybe Part Five will be the blockbuster.''

"Yeah. Maybe I'll start riding the subways tomorrow.'' I looked out the window at the rain slanting down onto the fire escapes across the street. The Japanese fishing boat was still out there too somewhere, but its outline wasn't coming any more clearly into focus. Why were the Japanese always fishing so close to our fire escapes?

"Two friends of yours here, mate,'' said Brennan looking down at Greenwich Street from a far window.

"Impossible,'' said Ratso. "He doesn't have two friends.''

"Actually, I have a great many friends,'' I said, "and they come from all walks of life. If you're a very nice, pleasant person and you always think of others, then if you have a lot of friends it's practically meaningless. But if you're an eccentric, self-directed sort like I am who voyages through the dark and troubled waters of life and doesn't give a damn about anybody and you still have a lot of friends in spite of all that, that could be seen as a sort of tribute to you.''

Ratso got up and walked across the room to where Brennan was standing. "Yeah, well, these two friends appear to have just emerged from an unmarked squad car.''

"Get back from the windows. Maybe they'll go away.''

"I think you ought to talk to them,'' said Ratso. "They've

certainly grilled Campbell by now, maybe even hauled him in. Obviously you were getting too close to something connected with the case or Campbell wouldn't have been so desperate about taking a potshot at you."

"My dear Ratso, this case is beginning to smell like the shithouse door on a shrimp boat. Now whether Campbell himself took a shot at me, which I doubt, or whether he hired someone to scare me off, which I think is more likely, neither of those actions fit the peculiar modus operandi of the first two killings. Surely you can see that. Campbell's obviously a bit het up about something and I intend to find out what it is. But it could just be something quite extraneous to the case. What we in the detective business sometimes refer to as a 'red herring.'"

"Well, you've got a couple of nice seagoing images there anyway," said Ratso, "red herrings and shrimp boats."

"You leave those two cops out there in the rain much longer and they'll be seagoing too," said Brennan. "What's the drill, mate? It's your house."

" 'Mate' itself is a nice seagoing salutation," I said. "If I can bring calm and equanimity to my two houseguests by throwing a goddamn puppet head out the window, I'll damn sure do it." With my good arm I raised the window and chucked the parachute device down to Fox and Cooperman below. "They're not going to be too pleased," I observed.

"Yeah," said Brennan. "What do you want me to do with all this photography equipment? Break it down into its component parts?" I thought about it for a minute or two. It was going to look pretty suspicious having all Brennan's surveillance gear scattered around the place. "Ever taken group photos?" I asked as Fox and Cooperman pounded on the door of the loft.

Ratso went to the door and let Fox and Cooperman in. They were about as damp as the reception I gave them. "How you doin', hero?" asked Fox.

"Like the dinosaur said, 'I'll survive.' But if I find Barry Campbell, I'm going to spray his brains all over Gay Street."

"Let's not get too trigger-happy, pal," said Cooperman. "We talked to Campbell. He's got an alibi for the time you were shot and it checks out fine."

"Yeah? Where was he? At the Turkish baths?"

"No," said Cooperman, "he was at a recording studio on Eighth Street watching them make a rock video. Name of the singer was Nina Kong. You ever heard anything by her?"

My shoulder had started to hurt again. "Yeah," I said.

"Everybody smile," said Brennan, and he snapped our picture.

30

I stood Fox and Cooperman to a cup of coffee each and eventually they took their leave.

The new wrinkle about Barry Campbell and Nina Kong didn't bother me too much. I didn't have to make the bed, but I might still want to lie in it occasionally.

Meanwhile, it was growing dark outside and I had an appointment to keep at my psychiatrist's. Too bad he wasn't going to be there.

We had a few hours to kill before Rambam arrived, so Ratso and Brennan went out for a drink and I stayed home for a drink. For a change of pace I thought I'd have a shot of Jameson and a cigar to go along with it. I found a Havana cigar I'd bought for eleven dollars several years ago in Vancouver. I was sort of saving it for a celebration, but if you saved anything too long these days you'd wind up in the bone orchard and other people would be doing your celebrating for you.

I lopped off the end of the cigar with my Smith & Wesson knife and carefully singed about an inch of it with a wooden match. Always keeping the cigar well above the flame. Lighting a cigar was like wearing a hat or making love. You either knew how to do it or you didn't. And if you didn't know, you didn't know that you didn't know so it was all right as long as I didn't have to watch you.

Of course, when you paid eleven bucks for a cigar, you expected it to stay all night and bring you a warm washcloth when you were through.

Actually the cigar wasn't bad but it was starting to get kind of brittle. A couple more years and it'd be as brittle as my nerves. I heard Rambam yelling up from the sidewalk so I went over to the window, opened it, and threw down the puppet head. I stood there awhile and watched what was left of the rain. The cool, damp air felt good and cleared some of the cigar smoke out of the place, but it didn't do much to clear up what was bugging me about this whole McGovern business.

I could see that Campbell had a revenge motive for framing McGovern, but he still had no motive for whacking Worthington or Darlene Rigby. And why would Nina Kong lie to me about never knowing Barry Campbell? Did she think I was as trusting and innocent as I looked? And there was something else that was bothering me too. Something deeper and more sinister in its nature. There were several key pieces to this psychological jigsaw that were doing their dead-level best not to fit.

A sudden chill caught me and I closed the window but I still felt the chill.

There was a knock at the door and I went over and opened it. There was Rambam dressed all in black, with a knapsack slung over one shoulder and a big smile on his face.

It was after midnight, and from the way this shrink break-in was being plotted, you'd have thought it was Watergate II. Brennan and Ratso had returned and the big smile on Rambam's face had left.

"Very bad idea," said Rambam, "very bad idea. You never told me we were going to take these two meatballs with us. We're talking coded key pads; we're talking motion detectors. I think you're crazy to go with four guys. Why don't we bring the Gay Men's Chorus down there while we're at it?"

"Look," said Ratso, "you see what shape Sherlock's in. If he goes down there tonight, I'm going with him."

"That's very moving," I said, "but we're not particularly joined at the hip, you know."

"That's all right," said Rambam. "I've got something for Ratso to do." He was smiling again, but this time it was a smaller, more malicious smile.

"Yeah, I've got something for you to do, too," said Ratso.

"Look, fellas," I said, "this bickering is unseemly. We've got a job to do—get a copy of this shrink's file on Frank Worthington—and I only hope it's worth the risk we're going to be taking. If I can get a clearer picture of his mind, it'll help me a lot."

"How about a stiff one for the stiff?" said Brennan cheerfully. I poured the whole house a shot and we all drank one to a dead bisexual we'd never met. A worthy subject for a toast if there ever was one.

"Okay," said Rambam, "I'm going on a brief scavenger hunt. I'll be back in about two hours and then it's off to Never-Never Land."

"Don't let the door bang your ass on the way out," said Ratso.

When Rambam had left I said to Ratso: "Look, pal, for your own health, education, and welfare don't upset this guy. He's not doing this for you, he's doing this for me and he's absolutely crucial to the operation."

"He may be crucial," said Brennan, "but I'm indispensable."

"Do me a favor, will you, Mick?" I said. "Just for tonight try snapping your shutter and shutting your snapper." I saw Rambam's point. If Moses had been a committee, the Jews would probably never have gotten out of Egypt. On the other hand, I didn't see any other way around it. So I retired to the bedroom to take a little power nap before the night's entertainment. I nodded off thinking about Dr. Bock's pipe and the little leather patches on his elbows and feeling better about the whole thing. That's what happens when you mess around with Marvin Barenblatt.

31

I don't know exactly what time it was when Rambam got back, but I did remember who it was I was dreaming about. It was Cynthia. I also remembered what she was wearing and it wasn't much. Just a pair of cute pink house slippers and a little pajama top that didn't go down too far but went a long way toward helping the two of us get a little better acquainted.

When Rambam walked in holding a pair of pink house slippers, I thought I was having some kind of a Peace Corps flashback. Two years in the jungles of Borneo will stay with you for a while.

As it turned out, the slippers weren't for me but for Ratso. Rambam gave them to him, went to the closet, and located a bright purple bathrobe and threw that to Ratso also. "Put 'em on," he said, "you've got a friend waiting for you in the car." It sounded crazy at the time. I thought Rambam had lost touch with the mother ship. But it was a stroke of genius.

Ratso put on the slippers and the robe and finished what he was doing, which was pouring coffee for all of us.

"You're going to make some lucky guy a pretty gnarly housewife," I said. Brennan packed his equipment up and we all drank the coffee.

"This is it," I said. "Let's go." It was after two in the morning. No one was on the street. The rain had stopped completely. A few newspapers swirled by in a small gust of wind. There were several parked cars on Vandam, one with a hand-lettered sign in the window that said "No Radio." There were about five empty garbage trucks parked in a row, and right in front of them, leading the parade, was Rambam's black Jaguar with what looked to be a little white miniature poodle yapping at us from the front seat. "He belongs to my aunt," said Rambam. It was the kind of dog that even a lonely old lady would have to think twice about. My cat could have eaten it for breakfast but she didn't like French cooking. We got in.

Rambam gave Ratso a small walkie-talkie to put in the pocket of the bathrobe. His job was to walk the poodle up and down Charles Street and look like he belonged and to call us if he saw suspicious cop activity. We let Ratso and the dog out at Fourth and Charles. "His name is Dom Pérignon," said Rambam.

"Thanks," said Ratso, "that'll help a lot."

We parked the car a little farther down the block, and the three of us got out. Rambam looked around a little bit. Then he took out a small tension bar and something else I couldn't see and he was through Bock's Segal lock in under a minute. It might have been faster than that. Time seems amplified when you're standing on the street in the middle of the night watching a guy in pink carpet slippers walking a miniature poodle.

Inside the foyer we heard a soft "click" and the little red light of a motion detector went on and sent Rambam scrambling. "Oh, shit," he said, "we've got sixty seconds tops." That meant before the call went through to the security service and from there to the cops. Rambam jimmied the keypad box off the wall and, with breathtaking speed, took two wires that looked like miniature jumper cables from around his neck and short-circuited the box.

Three minutes later we were inside Bock's office, and Rambam was sizing up the filing cabinets. "That wasn't bad, was it, mate?" Brennan said to me.

Bock had old-fashioned wooden filing cabinets, and

Rambam shoved the bottom drawer down and in with a deft movement and that was all it took. In no time I had Worthington's file out and Brennan was setting up the Minox.

It was fortunate that we'd brought Brennan along because the file was about fifty pages in length and the guy's handwriting looked like it was written by a horseshoe crab that happened to be left-handed.

Mick was working as fast as he could but Rambam was starting to get a little nervous. That made me nervous.

"You got it, Mick?" I asked.

"It's a wrap," he said.

"Okay, boys," I said, "let's call in the dogs and piss on the fire."

"What was that, mate?" asked Brennan.

"Speed-read my lips, pal," I said: "Let's get the hell out of here."

We left the building, got in the car, and located Ratso and Dom Pérignon on the corner where they'd met a blonde with a German shepherd. We dropped Brennan off on Bedford Street at the Monkey's Paw, but I extracted a promise that he'd have the film developed and blown up for me by the following day. Twenty minutes later Ratso was asleep on the couch, the cat was out cold on the rocker, and I was in bed hoping it had all been worthwhile. I was also hoping that Cynthia would come back again. I had a feeling that she would.

32

When I got up Thursday morning it was after eleven and Ratso had gone to work. When he wasn't wearing humorous-looking clothing or running around the Village helping me commit felonies, Ratso went about the high-pressure business of his job as an editor. But the important thing about him now was that he was gone.

I dialed Cynthia's number. Lighting a cigar the correct way while dialing a telephone can pose a problem but I managed.

I wasn't really fickle in my attitude toward women; I just didn't care. I'd loved five or six women in my life but I'd only been in love maybe once. And when the person you love more than anyone else in the world kisses a windshield at 95 mph in her Ferrari, everything else falls into perspective.

"Hello, Cynthia," I said.

"How are you?" a sleepy voice answered. "I was going to call you."

"Well, I called you first. How about joining me for a dim sum this morning in Chinatown?" "Dim sum" was sort of a Chinese breakfast of many small dishes. The words, so I'd been told by a Chinese girlfriend once, meant "to touch the heart lightly." That wasn't too bad a description of the effect Cynthia was having on me.

A half hour later I'd picked Cynthia up on Jane Street and we were in a taxi heading up Houston Street toward Chinatown. Traffic was so bad that the driver skirted Broadway and Mott Street and went all the way to the Bowery before hooking a right toward Canal. He explained it would be faster this way. He would also make a few bucks more on the meter, but it was a beautiful day and I could afford to spend a few more simoleons without winding up washing chopsticks.

It wasn't any faster going down the Bowery. Traffic was tied up like a junkie's arm. So I paid the cabbie and we got out about five blocks from Canal Street, which was where Chinatown formally began. Winos hoping for a tip were washing windshields of the stalled cars. Panhandlers were strung out all along the sidewalk like costume jewelry in a gaudy necklace you wouldn't want your girlfriend to wear to a dogfight.

"This area always bums me out," I said to Cynthia.

She smiled. If you could make a woman smile, you could probably make her laugh, and if you could make a woman laugh, you could probably . . . and then there was McGovern. I tried to put him out of my mind but it wasn't easy.

I took Cynthia to a dim sum place called the Silver Palace at Bowery and Canal where you take an escalator up one floor and you're suddenly confronted by the sight of half the population of Shanghai gnawing on chicken feet. We were seated at a large round table, which we shared with what looked like an extended Chinese family—babies, kids, old folks—everything but the family dog. That was probably one of the things being served on the dim sum carts. These carts were pushed by Chinese women who circled the room like giant birds, squawking the names of their particular dishes over and over again.

If you saw something you liked such as fish lips or eye of newt, you pointed to it and they gave you the dish. When you were finished, they charged you by the number of dishes on the table. There was good dim sum and there was bad dim sum and you never knew which you'd had until about an hour later when if it was good you felt good and if it was bad you walked around for the rest of the day with a bowling ball in your stomach and a baby squid climbing into your upper intestine.

We ordered several dishes, including a few round objects about the size of golf balls that were filled with shrimp meat; the dim sum lady called them "shrimp balls."

"They're from a very large shrimp," I told Cynthia.

"You know I heard from McGovern," she said.

"Speaking of a very large shrimp."

"And he gave me a message to give to you and said he'd call you soon. But I'm supposed to give you the message. I warn you he sounded pretty crazy and so does the message, I'm afraid." Big surprise.

"Spill it," I said. I got a good grip on my chopsticks.

"He told me to ask you if you remembered the ghost that you didn't believe he saw."

"Yeah," I said, "I remember it."

"Well, he said to tell you that he didn't see it again."

33

I took Cynthia Floyd home with me to Vandam when we left the Silver Palace. After nearly getting blown away the other night, I didn't enjoy being alone as much as I used to. Maybe I was being paranoid, but it was becoming quite obvious to me that there was somebody out there, in addition to Dr. Bock and Detectives Cooperman and Fox, who didn't particularly think I hung the moon.

Or maybe someone really did admire me but just had a funny way of expressing himself. I didn't want to find out. But it looked like I was going to have to.

"Wait'll you see the place," I told Cynthia as we rode up together in the freight elevator.

"I can't wait," she said. She still had her sense of humor. And I still had most of my shoulder.

Seeing the warehouse-baroque outer facade of 199B Vandam all done in dismal battleship gray with occasional touches of graffiti, then passing through the dingy, dust-laden hallway into the freight elevator with its one exposed light bulb did not lead visitors to expect much. It was always a pleasant surprise when I opened the door to reveal a spacious, comfortable, beautifully appointed loft. It wasn't really beautifully appointed but compared to the freight elevator it could have been the Plaza.

Cynthia was impressed. I told her to look around and make herself at home. "My loft is your loft," I said.

I stoked up the espresso maker and checked for messages on the answering machine. As often happens, I'd gotten calls from almost all the wrong people. Creditors, anxious, worried women I couldn't care less about, acquaintances who were just in town for a few days and I couldn't remember who they were, old dope dealers trying to tempt me back into the fold, and Ratso, whose current residence was my couch so I didn't desperately need to talk to him on the phone.

There was no sense waiting for the call that was going to change my life. It would come all right. But those kinds of calls always come about seven minutes too late to make any difference.

The only two calls worth remembering at all were from Brennan and Pete Myers. Brennan's message was something to the effect that he would drop the very explicit photographs of the young boys by my place around three o'clock.

Myers wanted to talk with me about the other night. I wasn't even sure which "other night" he was referring to. I'd had quite a few of them lately.

Cynthia and I sat down at the kitchen table and I poured us each an espresso. She took out a pack of cigarettes and I bummed one. "Us Merit smokers gotta stick together," I told her.

I noticed her eyes for the first time really. They weren't just blue. They were fire-engine blue. They looked intelligent, lost, and worried, with maybe a side order of bored. They also looked plenty frightened.

"Relax, kid," I said. "Stay here as long as you like. Maybe together we can shed some light on this unfortunate affair." Things like this McGovern-Worthington business were always happening to girls like Cynthia Floyd, it seemed. Sordid affairs never did seem to quite get hold of slinkier dames like Nina Kong. Of course, both of them had fared a damn sight better than Darlene Rigby. If you wanted to look at it that way.

Outside the rain was falling again but the sun was still shining. "The devil's beating his wife," she said in a small voice.

"Yeah," I said. "Or at least he's giving her a hard time. Do you understand what McGovern's message to me might have meant?"

"I haven't understood anything McGovern's said for a long time," she said. "Even before anything happened to that man across the hall. I don't understand how anybody could murder two people in such a horrible fashion. I don't understand why someone would want to go and take a shot at you."

"Hey," I said, "there's a jungle out there, Jane." I took off my jacket.

"Let's have a look at that shoulder," she said. It was still kind of painful to take my shirt off, so she came over and helped me with it. "You really ought to have that dressing changed. Here, I'll do it for you." Regular Nurse Ratched, this girl.

She changed the dressing very efficiently and she stood close to me while she did it. She wasn't at all squeamish. From coroners and lab assistants who'd worked at various stiff hotels, I'd learned that most women, indeed, were not very squeamish when viewing gore and dead bodies. The fainting incidence ran about five to one in favor of men over women. Broads could be tough as nails when they wanted to. They could also be soft as the space between McGovern's ears.

But knowing what they could be didn't tell you what they would be. It didn't even tell you what they should be. If you really thought you understood women, you were probably already a latent hairdresser and you needed to make an appointment with Dr. Bock. Unfortunately he was out of town.

"I like your cat," she said, as she slipped her shoes off.

"My cat speaks very highly of you," I said. The cat was already in her lap. I wouldn't have minded being there myself.

Looking at the two of them I realized, not for the first time, that women and cats had a lot in common. For one thing, neither of them had a particularly well-developed sense of humor. For another, they both went through life governed only by things that either comforted them or intrigued them. They both liked to be stroked and cuddled and they both could pounce when you least expected it. On the whole, I preferred cats to women because cats seldom if ever used the word "relationship."

I went over to my desk and got a cigar and I poured out a few more espressos and I fed the cat a late breakfast and Cynthia and I discussed the case.

She said she hadn't really known Frank Worthington at all except to say hello to or in this case good-bye to. She'd seen both Pete Myers and Barry Campbell coming and going from the building on Jane Street and knew they were friends of Worthington. She'd found Campbell attractive and had even exchanged a few heated words with McGovern about him. She'd never seen Nina Kong or the Rigby girl before.

I probed gently her relationship with Adrian. I didn't really feel there was that much there but it was hard to tell. For one thing, Cynthia had that look of innocence about her. It wasn't just something she'd been born with, it was an achieved innocence, the kind a prostitute has who turns a trick and gives the money to her boyfriend.

Adrian, on the other hand, worked the opposite side of the spiritual fence. Maybe she wasn't the most jaded person I'd ever met, but she did have degeneracy fairly well staked out. I couldn't see the two of them having much to talk about, but opposites will attract a lot more often than they'll repel. Unless it was a simple case of Adrian's repelling me, which she always did very effectively.

A little of her went a long way.

I thought I'd try hitting Cynthia with a broadside. "How much are you into Adrian in the weasel-dust department?" I asked. Any severely stepped-on cocaine I always referred to as weasel dust, taking the name of course from the original Weasel at the Monkey's Paw.

Around the Village they said that if John Belushi had only done weasel dust he'd be alive today. And then there were those who said that if Karen Carpenter and Mama Cass had only shared that ham sandwich, they'd both be alive today.

I wondered what it would have taken for Darlene Rigby to be alive today. What would she have to have not seen? To have not heard?

Cynthia was looking down at the cat and I was beginning to wonder if it'd gotten her tongue.

34

If Cynthia Floyd was having a bit of a hard time with a drug problem, I could empathize with her under the circumstances. The cops were ready to believe McGovern had croaked two people, and the longer he stayed on the lam, the more they were convinced he was guilty. Cynthia didn't know what to believe, and the more weasel dust she consumed, the more serious the whole affair was going to become. At least in her mind. It was a pretty serious affair even outside of her mind, which was exactly where she was going to be if she kept snorting weasel dust.

You couldn't tell anybody about drugs and booze. I'd been there myself, and every time somebody broke out the hard stuff around me, it was still touch and go. I could very easily be there again if I wasn't damn careful. Of course, it was hard to be too careful when you were dealing in the life-and-death business the way I apparently was now. I guess everybody has to deal with the life-and-death business sooner or later, but there was no point in rushing to the downstairs bedroom.

What I wanted to tell Cynthia but didn't was that you had to decide for yourself about cocaine. You had to hit whatever was the bottom for you before you realized there was nowhere left to fall. The bottom for me had come about five years before on a brittle January morning when I was lugging an ounce of the stuff from one place to another place somewhere on the Upper East Side. It could have been any time but it was probably around nine o'clock in the morning. I didn't have my computer with me. I'd been up for six days and it felt like a week.

I'd been standing in some street that should have been a bad dream but it wasn't. I passed by a down-at-the-heel Negro who was hopped up on heroin and talking to himself. I saw a total no-hoper stagger by, smashed completely out of his mind with nothing left to hold on to but the bottle in his hand. "Another satisfied customer," I remember thinking.

I was numb. I was ticking like the stopwatch they used on *60 Minutes*. I was so high I was starting to get lonely.

Apparently I'd forgotten just about everything including the fact that my cigar was lit and I'd put it back in my breast pocket. I didn't feel hot or cold because I didn't feel anything. That was about the time I hit the bottom.

The precise moment, I think, was when a small kid came up to me and said, "Hey, mister, your coat's on fire." I looked at him and I felt like the oldest living veteran of the War Between the States and at that moment I just didn't give a shit whether or not I ever woke up in Kansas.

I wanted to tell Cynthia this.

But now it was a Thursday afternoon and we were standing in my kitchen on Vandam Street in New York City and we were desperately, make it passionately, clinging to each other. We were still on planet earth but you wouldn't know it.

We kissed each other. It was not a friendly kiss. It was the way you kissed somebody when you knew that in a matter of moments you'd be torn from each other's arms forever and thrown to the fish.

"Don't get too attached," I said.

With reluctance I took her by the hand and walked down the stairs with her. Someone else in the building was evidently using the freight elevator. I walked her to the corner and as I was putting her in a taxi a blue-eyed ocean rolled across a brown-eyed shoreline.

"Who is this dame?" I asked myself. "How can we possibly

have found ourselves in this situation?'' She was, after all, McGovern's girl. McGovern was, after all, one of my best buddies. I didn't exactly have character staked out, but next to her I came off like a spiritual Green Beret. And yet . . .

"Will we see each other?" she asked.

"In our dreams," I said, and as the cab pulled away I found myself fervently hoping that dreams came true.

35

On my way back to the loft I met Mick Brennan. Good. It saved wear and tear on the puppet head. We went up together in the freight elevator, which was now yawning like an open tomb in what passed for the lobby.

He had the goods with him right under his arm and I couldn't wait to get at them.

"I hope you appreciate my staying up half the night processing these bloody bastards," he said.

"I'd like to see what you got first. Maybe you left your finger over the lens cap or something."

As I was fooling around with the lock on my door, I could hear the phones ringing inside the loft. By the time I got to them, I felt like I'd just done forty squat thrusts in the parking lot.

"This is the Shadow," a familiar voice said. It was McGovern. 3:17 P.M.

"Go ahead, Shadow, I read you," I panted. I looked around for another cigar to help me get my wind back. "Make some tea and some crumpets or something, will you, Mick?" I shouted.

"Righty-ho."

"Meet you tonight late. Place where Charlie Parker and Edith Piaf used to hang out. Down the street from where I urinated on the lady's leg. Okay?"

"See you there, pal. Are you all right?" I asked.

"Does a chicken have lips?" He hung up.

I knew the place he was referring to. It was a seedy interracial jazz bar down the way from the Monkey's Paw. It made the Paw look chic.

I joined Brennan for a spot of tea. He took out the prints he'd made of Bock's file on Frank Worthington and we looked them over. The physical clarity was remarkable. What clues I might find in a two-and-a-half-year-old shrink report that might pertain to a two-week-old croaking, I wasn't sure.

"Got to be going, mate," said Brennan. "The prints and the processing are all on the house, by the way."

"Well, at least the price is right," I said. "Thanks, Mick." I closed and locked the door behind him as he left. Couldn't be too careful these days. Then I got busy on the blower. First I called my friend Boris, the Russian karate master.

"Boris," I said, "can you help us with a job tonight? It could get rough. We may have to put on our lobster bibs."

"I don't understand," said Boris, in a deep, thick, and very dangerous accent.

"You will. I'm going to see a guy named Barry Campbell tonight. The last two times I saw him I needed a hospital immediately afterward. Tonight I want to find out what he knows and maybe pay him back if necessary."

"Good," said Boris. "I will choke him."

"Yeah, but you'll have to be careful. He's got the entire Polish army working for him, and I don't want anybody to end up in the croakee's condominium."

"I don't understand," said Boris.

"You will," I said. I doubted if he would. I didn't understand either. I set the time for ten o'clock at my place and rang off.

I puffed on the cigar and watched as my digital-computer alarm hit 3:47 P.M. Actually the whole situation was alarming but nowhere near as alarming as it was soon going to be.

In a dusty cabinet beneath the sink, I found a shot glass made from an old bull's horn and into it I poured a healthy slug from a new bottle of Jameson. Something old and something new. The something borrowed would have to be my couch, which was still loaded down with Ratso's crap even when Ratso himself wasn't parking his torpedolike body there. And the something blue was my shoulder, which was, to quote Amory Blaine in *This Side of Paradise*, "blue as the sky, gentlemen."

Everything was running about par for the course.

I took the shot glass, the bottle, the cigar, and the shrink's report over to my desk, upon which the cat was already putting down roots. I started going over the report. The first thing I noticed was that Frank Worthington's date of birth was in mid-February. Whether he was an Aquarius or a Pisces I wasn't sure, but something fishy was going on here that I should have been alert to before now.

I checked back on the calendar and found the day and the date Worthington had gotten croaked. It was his birthday. Many happy returns, pal.

There was plenty of sickological drivel in the file all right. Dr. Bock had seen to that. Worthington was having some problems with his sexual identity, some problems with his interpersonal relationships, and some problems with just about everything else. So what else was new?

I was in the act of pouring another tot of Jameson into the bull horn when I tripped and fell over a twenty-dollar word in one of Dr. Bock's nagging little footnotes. It read: "The patient at times appears to be living in irrational fear of his doppelgänger." I called Ratso.

"*National Lampoon*," the secretary said.

"Yeah. Ratso, please."

"Just a moment, please."

"Editorial department."

"Yeah, Ratso, please."

"Just a moment, please. May I tell him who's calling?" By all means.

"Yeah. This is Dr. Felch calling."

"One moment, please, Dr. Felch." A little more time elapsed. Someone was probably going into Ratso's office to shake him awake. In another moment he came on the line, businesslike and brusque as he always was when he was in the office.

"Yeah, Felch. What can I do for you?"

"Well, I've come across a rather large but kraut word in this shrink's report."

"What is it?"

"*Doppelgänger*. 'The patient at times appears to be living in irrational fear of his doppelgänger.' "

"It means he's afraid of his double," said Ratso.

"Is that all?" I said.

I must have dozed off. My shoulder had been throbbing and I'd been feeling a recurrent chill down my spine but the Jameson had apparently kicked in. I was having a nightmare about doppelgängers and the cat was sitting on the shrink's report right in front of me and about equidistant between the two phones on the desk when they rang. The cat went up like a rocket at 6:17 P.M. and went down like an oil well about five seconds later.

The phones ringing scared the hell out of me, too. But they didn't scare me half as much as what I heard next.

My answering machine was rolling to screen my calls and I got the message down on tape so it wasn't just a part of the nightmare I was having. It was a nightmare, though, just the same. Except that this one wasn't a dream.

It was an unfamiliar, disembodied, pay-phoney sort of voice, and it didn't sound particularly earthbound.

"This is Frank Worthington," it said.

36

I had about half an hour before Ratso got home to my couch from work so I downshifted from Jameson to coffee, phased the cat gently out of the rocking chair, and tried to take stock of the situation as it was at 6:25 P.M. Thursday night, the chilling, rattling caboose of a frozen February in this year of our landlord 1985.

I had two stiffs, one doppelgänger, one dangerous fruitcake to grill, one fugitive friend to meet. If it had been a poker-hand I would have passed.

If you looked at life in pokerhands, another hand might have been the four suspects—Campbell, Myers, Nina, Adrian—and five would be McGovern if you wanted to count him. One of these cards was quite a joker all right, and I was determined to weed that joker out even if I had to borrow Old McDonald's threshing machine to do it.

I got up and played the phone machine message a few more times. "This is Frank Worthington . . ." "This is Frank Worthington . . ." I'd only met him once and that was as a stiff on the floor, but now I was starting to understand his mind, his problems, his dreams, and I also had what purported to be his own voice on my answering machine.

It also crossed my increasingly cluttered desk that if Worthington had been a part-time actor, there might exist a recording of his voice. Maybe a television commercial like "Honey, this frozen quiche is delicious!" or "Honey, these plates really sparkle!" or in Worthington's own particular case, "Honey, I'm going out bowling with the boys tonight."

If something like this existed, it could easily be matched with the tape I had to determine my message's authenticity. I was thinking over the possibilities when I remembered I hadn't called Pete Myers back yet. So I did.

"I've identified your poet," he said.

"What the hell are you talking about?"

" 'Gather ye rosebuds while ye may,' my friend. It was Robert Herrick, a British romantic poet who wrote in the sixteenth century."

"Seventeenth," I said.

"Well, sixteenth and seventeenth, I'd say."

"He must have been a goddamn prodigy then. He was only about eight and a half years old when the sixteenth century burned its last few witches and ground to a close."

"Touché," said Myers. I liked people who said "touché" about as much as I liked people who said "ciao." I didn't even like Italians who said "ciao," though if they didn't say it, I could see how they'd probably have a pretty rough time trying to leave a room.

"Look, Myers, did Frank Worthington ever do any voice-overs or television commercials or anything like that, to your knowledge?" I was taking a little chance here that Myers could himself be the one behind my crank call, but that's what life was all about, wasn't it? Taking chances. It was also, of course, what death was all about.

"He did. Yes, he did. When I was . . . uh . . . seeing him, he was with some advertising agency. I think it was called Umbrella, Incorporated, or something like that."

"Thanks," I said. "You want to fall by here sometime to-morrow afternoon?"

"Sure. How about threeish? We can discuss Robert Her-rick's development as a poet."

"Fine. I'll be here. One-ninety-nine-B Vandam. Look up to the fourth floor and holler." At least Myers was a good sport. I wondered if he was a good shot.

As it turned out, for reasons quite beyond my control, no one but the cat would be here tomorrow afternoon at three o'clock. And the cat knew enough never to let strangers into the apartment.

I was just ciao-ing off with Myers when Ratso walked in.

"Somebody left a message on the machine for you, Ratso," I said and I played him the tape. "This is Frank Worthington. . . ."

"Jesus," he said. "What is that? Somebody's idea of a sick prank?"

"I prefer to think of it as the hand of Satan moving in the world," I said.

"Looks like somebody out there's sure trying to jerk our chain, doesn't it?"

"Yes, yes, it does, my dear Ratso," I said. "It's certainly beginning to appear as if there's a doppelgänger in the woodpile."

37

At ten o'clock sharp a voice louder than a garbage truck shattered the peace of Vandam Street and I hastened to the kitchen window to fling forth the puppet head into the February night. Boris was nothing if he wasn't punctual. Well, actually he was something. He was deadly.

"Ratso," I said, "why don't you turn that crap off and get ready to go." Moving in with me had meant that Ratso had had to make the extreme sacrifice—leave his cable T.V. and his beloved Ranger games and make do with my small, shabby, dusty black-and-white set that required a screwdriver to turn it on or off or to adjust the volume because the knob had been lost through the carelessness of one of the previous owners. I did supply the screwdriver, but Ratso was still not very happy having to watch *So This Is New Jersey* and *Meet the Black Mayors*.

"Great stuff," he said as he turned off the set with a screwdriver and a good deal of disgust.

"Programming isn't what it used to be," I said.

Boris was pounding on the door. I walked over and let him in. He had a bottle of vodka, a large loaf of Russian rye bread, and about five pounds of caviar on him, all of which he deposited onto the kitchen table.

"Good," I said, "if we get back alive tonight, we'll have a little midnight snack."

I picked up my Smith & Wesson knife and started to slip it into the old hunting vest but Boris stopped me with a rather decisive and unpleasant gesture. "Do not take it. You will not need it," he said.

"You're sure?" I asked.

"I promise," he said and as he rolled his *r* in *promise,* I rolled my eyes at Ratso. It looked like a fun-filled evening ahead.

The three of us drank a little vodka toast to warm our spirits and then I left the cat in charge and locked the door. On the way down the stairs, Boris said to us, "You have never seen Boris in action?"

"No," said Ratso, "but we've heard stories."

"Tonight you will see," said Boris, "that the stories about Boris are true." I was sure they were. Boris, blindfolded, putting out lighted matches with a bullwhip. Boris unarmed and single-handedly demolishing a twelve-member street gang in Brooklyn. Boris teaching karate to the school for the blind in Russia. Boris teaching secret North Vietnamese techniques to the NYPD SWAT team. No doubt about it, the boy was good. Also, I admired people who always spoke of themselves in the third person.

We piled into Boris's beat-up little car. "The heater doesn't work," he said with some irritation, "thanks to Rambam."

"Rambam really gets around," I said.

"Where to, Sherlock?" asked Ratso.

"Tenth Street and Waverly," I answered. I'd done a little personal surveillance on Campbell and I knew his movements like the back of my shoulder. His movements weren't real complex. When he wasn't dressed up like a mermaid shimmering across the waves and flapping his tail at the denizens of the Blue Canary, he was running a fairly steady tattoo back and forth from his home on West Tenth Street to the gay bar on the corner called Julius's. Some life.

If you plumbed deeply enough into the triple-decker sandwich of the mind until you reached that Land of Oz, the subconscious, you'd find that every homosexual was a heterosexual and that every heterosexual was a homosexual.

You'd probably also find that neither group was too fond of
Sigmund Freud.

Boris parked the car on Waverly in the middle of the block.
Julius's bar was in plain sight on the corner. The place was
practically a Village landmark. It had been there since Adam
and Steve.

I told Boris and Ratso to wait in the car and if I wasn't out
of there in twenty minutes to send in the Marines. What a
scene that would have been.

I walked into the place tough and assured, feeling kind of
like the Marlboro Man. Fortunately nobody asked me to light
their Lucky. There were about a hundred guys in the place
already, laughing, drinking, and making whatever passed for
gay cocktail chatter. Sounded like somebody was mastur-
bating tiny little baby chipmunks.

"Turkey on the rocks," I told the bartender. I wanted a
suitably masculine drink. Not that there was anything wrong
with Jameson. Hell, no.

I casually glanced around through the cigarette smoke and
over the bobbing heads of Julius's clientele. I was a man
among men all right. Not a dame in sight unless you wanted
to count the middle-aged queen at the end of the bar and I
didn't. Barry Campbell was not there.

I fished through the crap in my pocket and came up with a
scrap of paper with his number on it. I walked over to the
pay phone and plunked in a quarter. I let the phone ring
about nine times. No Campbell. I checked information for the
number of the Blue Canary, called there, and learned Campbell wasn't working tonight.

I hung up and walked back to the bar and ordered another
Turkey on the rocks and waited.

About seven minutes later Campbell came into the bar.
There were the usual greetings: "Hey, Barry," "Hello,
sweetie," "Hi, big fella." He was quite a popular character,
well liked by his peers. He walked over to the bar and the
bartender said: "Will it be the usual, Barry?" I was dying to

know what the usual was. Probably a pink lady. A brandy
Alexander.

The bartender poured him a Turkey on the rocks.

"So much for appearances," I said.

Campbell looked over at me, registered shock, started to
bolt, apparently thought better of it, stayed put, and took a
slug of Wild Turkey.

"What the hell are you doing here?" he asked belligerently.

"Thought I'd have a drink with the boys," I said. "Join me
at a table?"

Campbell looked furtively around the bar. "All right," he
said. "Let's get this over with."

We threaded our way through the fashion plates, the truck
drivers who weren't truck drivers, and the longshoremen
who'd never seen a ship up close unless it was a ferry.

There were even a few guys who looked like insurance
salesmen or accountants. I didn't know if they were the real
thing or not, but I wasn't going to find out. We found an
empty table in the back and sat down.

"Campbell," I said, "we're going to pass for the moment
on what happened to my mind and my left shoulder last
Monday night. We'll take that up later, I assure you. But
right now I want you to cast your mind back nearly two
weeks ago to a Friday afternoon when you sent Frank Worthington some flowers. How many flowers did you send him
and why?" I took out a cigar and started to fool around with
it preparatory to lighting. Before I could strike a match, he
blurted the answer.

"A dozen roses," he sneered. "It was his friggin' birthday,
that's why. Anything on the books against that?"

"Nothing on the books," I said. In my book Campbell was
one under-the-weather chicken.

"What're you drinking Wild Turkey for?" I asked. "I
thought you were big on Bloody Marys."

"I like a little variety," he said.

"Yeah," I said, looking around the place, "I can see that."

"What else is on your mind, big guy?" said Campbell.

"Where were you that Friday, Campbell? Did you attend a little birthday party for Worthington?"

"Yeah. I was over there."

"Bring the roses with you?"

"No. I had them sent in the morning. I stopped by about two o'clock to party a little with Frank."

"Remind me not to invite you to my next affair," I said. "Did anybody else stop by while you were there? How long did you stay?"

"I stayed about an hour. Pete Myers was just arriving when I left. He was carrying the banana bread. He's a great cook. Quite a fine poet, too."

"Sounds like a real all-around guy," I said. "You didn't notice if he was wearing any lipstick, did you? We found some on one of the glasses."

"That's very funny," said Campbell. "No, he wasn't. Is that all now?" Campbell stood up to leave. He was starting to look a little nervous.

"What's the matter, Campbell? You're looking a little green around the gills if you'll pardon the expression."

"I don't have to take this shit from you. I don't have to take this shit from anybody," he said and he strode out of the place like an angry little rooster. My twenty minutes were up anyway.

"Whatever did you say to Barry?" somebody in the crowd asked me as I headed for the door.

"I told him his pants were on fire," I said without turning around or slowing my pace. I wanted to get out of there in at least the same lousy shape I was in when I had first entered the joint.

It didn't look like anybody was following me. Didn't really hurt my ego though. I stood out on the sidewalk for a moment. I looked around but Barry Campbell was as gone as a goose in winter. It was a good thing he was gone, too. He was starting to get on what was left of my nerves.

I took out a cigar and was going to light it when a beautiful young woman walked by. I put out the match and watched her as she moved farther down the sidewalk. A rather willowy young man was leaning against the doorway of the club smoking a cigarette and gazing desultorily at the girl. He killed his cigarette. I lit my cigar.

"Almost makes you wish you were a lesbian, doesn't it, pal?" I said.

38

I looked up and down the street. It was as peaceful as any little village you ever saw. The clock in the old church tower on Tenth Street said eleven-thirty. If it could've talked it would've said a hell of a lot more.

The sleepy little village was just waking up. It was what they call a "late town." Many of the trendier clubs hadn't even opened yet. Pretty soon all hell would break loose, I figured. Actually, it broke loose a little sooner than that.

I walked back up the block to where Boris and Ratso were shivering in the little car. "It's about time, Senator," said Ratso. "I was beginning to think you were turning over a new life-style." I got into the car. It was colder than a hockey puck in there and it was almost as small.

As Boris started her up, a big new Lincoln pulled up on the street in front of us to double-park. It appeared to have a full complement of adult white males inside as far as I could see, which evidently wasn't far enough.

Boris backed his little car up as far as he could and cut the wheel. He probably would've tried to honk a few times except that his horn worked about as well as his heater. The big Lincoln inched forward a bit as if to let us out, but then it swiftly glided back again in one smooth motion like a graceful urban shark. The situation didn't look too promising. I didn't really want to get my last supper served to me on New Jersey plates.

"Too bad we don't have the other kind of heater either," said Ratso.

"What do you mean?" asked Boris.

"Later," Ratso said distractedly from the back seat, "later."

"That's being a bit presumptuous, isn't it? You're assuming there'll be a later." Being right there next to Boris made me more cocky than usual. It was clearly going to be a tension convention of some sort, and I knew from recent experience that I wasn't bulletproof, but I still felt pretty confident about handling the situation.

The guys in the car, what I could see of them, looked like well-dressed, fairly bored professionals, but they were large specimens and there was something about their demeanor that was serious as cancer.

I couldn't really be sure that these birds had any connections with Barry Campbell, but the last two times I'd seen the guy something unpleasant had happened to me and this time it looked like he was going for the hat trick. These goons obviously wanted to take our parking place but the trouble was that they seemed to want us to still be in it.

Ratso made a move to open the door. "Stay in the car," I said. That's usually good advice in these situations. The only better advice would have been to stay in bed that morning. He wasn't going anywhere anyway. It was a two-door car. He was a trapped rat if these guys got out. All three of us were. But one of us was Boris.

This thought cheered me ever so slightly, as if I'd just snorted about a half gram of courage heavily cut with stupidity. I hollered, "Hey, move it!," but the guys in the Lincoln didn't even turn their heads. They looked as dangerous and amoral as store mannequins but not quite as sensitive.

Something had to break and I knew that whatever it was, it wasn't going to be my heart, so I rolled down my window and stuck my head out of the little car and yelled at the driver: "Hey, pal! You want to move your father's mortgage?"

It worked like a signal from the Old North Church. Four

haircuts in aluminum suits piled out of the Lincoln and came right at us.

''Holy shit,'' said Ratso.

''Tell me about it,'' I said as I frantically tried to roll up the window.

Moments like these you'd be surprised how much can go through your mind. Not that your whole life flashes before your eyes or anything like that. Nothing that tedious. But you do have time for a few little irrelevancies here and there. I thought about guys like Barry Campbell. There are guys that look gay and there are guys that don't look gay and there are guys that you can't tell if they're gay or not when they're walking down the street until they turn and go into the Caffé Sha Sha. Campbell was one of this last group of guys. But once you knew he was gay, it became pretty obvious and you usually convinced yourself that you'd known all along.

I thought in a fraction of a second about Nina Kong. She didn't seem like the type to turn into a lying welcher. Maybe all women had the potential. Maybe all people had the potential. Horrifying thought. Why would Nina lie to me and tell me she didn't know Barry Campbell and then I get some lead lodged in my shoulder blade and his alibi is that he's watching her make her video? Maybe he was just a fast worker. But I remembered the knowing way he winked at her that night at Chumley's. It seemed like another world. Another lifetime. Guess I wouldn't be getting down to Texas to see the folks this summer. I might get to see some interesting coral formations or some exotic fish or whatever you see at the bottom of the Hudson River when you're wearing cement wheels or a nice Italian suit of scrap iron. Come to think of it, they probably didn't have coral formations or exotic fish in the Hudson River. But they might have mermaids swimming in and out of sunken Japanese fishing boats.

And Cynthia. Hard to believe that a beautiful blonde could have wormed her way into my gypsy heart. Probably should have hosed her when I had the chance. Would have if it hadn't been for McGovern. McGovern. McGovern was the root of all evil. . . .

I was still cursing McGovern when the door on my side of the car was torn open like a can of sardines. There was a man out there standing on the sidewalk and I came about eye level to his kneecaps. If he was wearing a head I couldn't see it.

Whatever he had on above his neck, there wasn't time for him to get complacent about it. I heard a number of repeated explosions somewhere on the roof of Boris's car, and when I looked around for Boris, he wasn't there but at least two other sets of kneecaps were. Later I heard from a homosexual bystander who shall remain anonymous probably for his whole life that Boris was on top of the car pounding the head that belonged to my guy's set of kneecaps into the metal roof while the other guys were running around furiously grabbing for Boris. From my vantage point all I could see really clearly was a number of teeth skittering down over the windshield and bouncing a couple of times on the hood. It looked like somebody had sabotaged a Chiclet factory.

I leveled a solid kick between one of the sets of kneecaps and a little above, and apparently I connected because I heard a howling noise a few stories up. I saw daylight and I scuttled out and backward on the driver's side like a frightened crab ready to pinch the world. I looked over the top of the car and saw Boris field-stripping a guy on the sidewalk. I turned around just in time to catch a freight train right between the eyes and I had to take the mandatory eight count. Several shots rang out across the barroom floor and I saw a face that looked a lot like Ratso's receding rapidly in the window of a spaceship. I could still see, I just couldn't quite pick myself up off the canvas or the sawdust or the ocean bed or wherever the hell I was currently deep-sixed.

Boris was doing some sort of sinister ballet moves. His partner was a big blond fellow, but by the time Boris had tapped the guy behind his left ear with a few fingers and rammed his nose about halfway through his brain, the guy was a redhead and he was lying next to me on the street. The reason I say left ear was because that was the only ear the guy had left.

Ratso was now out of the car and helping me up and either the big black shark was receding or else my hairline was.

39

As we drove away, Boris was laughing deeply and heartily and ranting against peasants, soldiers, fools, and cossacks. Ratso was laughing too, but a little nervously, I thought. I would've been laughing but I tried it a few times and it made my head hurt, so I just smiled serenely like a Moonie on LSD. It felt good to be alive when very recently you didn't think you would be.

"Hey, Ratso," I said, "you really got out there into the thick of things."

"I couldn't get the goddamn seat to go forward."

"If the seat had not been broken, you would be dead," said Boris gravely.

"We don't know that," I said.

"Yes, we do," said Boris. "You were very lucky."

I didn't know it then but that was about as lucky as I was going to get that Thursday night. Lady Luck had other commitments apparently. Maybe she was in Atlantic City or Monte Carlo. Or maybe it was just something I had said to her.

It was midnight. It had almost been a damn sight later than that.

Boris drove around the Village a bit and parked the little car next to a handy hydrant on Fourth Street. We walked over to the Monkey's Paw for a beverage or two and I noticed The Weasel was tying up the pay phone with one of his business calls and I'd forgotten to bring my crowbar.

I made a mental note to speak to Cynthia the following morning. I didn't need anybody else to know that I was in contact with McGovern, so I didn't tell Ratso or Boris both for my protection and for theirs. And I wanted to warn Cynthia about talking to Adrian. Adrian was on a search and self-destruct mission in life and she didn't give a damn who she took with her. And Cynthia was just the kind that could get taken.

It was easier to spill your heart to a coke dealer than it was to a bartender or a shrink or the man at the Greyhound station. If Cynthia needed a confidant, she could talk to me. Discretion was my middle name.

After a few shots I was feeling better than I had in years. It always seemed that way for about an hour. I even started listening to Ratso's account to Tommy the bartender of the evening's little fracas. It didn't sound like the same evening.

I told Boris to collect Ratso in a little while and I'd meet them around two-thirty in the morning at my place for vodka and caviar. If you've got to have vodka and caviar, two-thirty in the morning is as good a time as any. And I didn't want to hurt Boris's feelings.

Boris was smiling a big, satisfied smile as I ankled it out of the joint. As I slipped out the front door I could hear Ratso telling the whole left side of the bar: "So I says to the guy, 'You're not gonna push me around like a little red apple. . . .' "

It was raining in Sheridan Square, which made it look all the better because it cut the visibility. In the rain it looked lonely and crowded at the same time, and all the people looked just like people in the rain. They say the rain washes everybody clean, but the rain had its work cut out for it in Sheridan Square.

I was just enjoying the negative ions out on the sidewalk when I turned to see a pair of beady, nervous little orbs knifing their way into my back. It was a face that managed to look frightened, threatening, desperate, and predatory at the same time, as well as reflecting several other sicker emotions. It wasn't a bad appetite depressant but just about everything else about the face was bad. And the voice behind the face was worse.

"You're a liar. You're a scumbag!" it said.

"Mr. Scumbag to you, pal," I said. It was The Weasel. He hadn't wanted to create a disturbance in his place of business, so he'd followed me out there in the rain. Mean little bastard would have probably followed me into hell just so he wouldn't make waves in the marketplace.

"What's distressing you, Max?" I asked. "Haven't you gotten enough money together yet to go to Rome and paint your masterpiece?"

A mask of cold hate fell across his mean little countenance and it gave me a turn, but I figured I'd finish the thought. Might as well, he hadn't shot me yet.

"After all, you have had a broad range of experience. Not everybody's spent ten years in the men's room of the Paw and lived to tell about it. And I think you've got a certain artistic flair . . ."

"Shut up!" he screamed like an emotionally disturbed little girl. What a tragedy for me to escape four haircuts in aluminum suits only to be drilled by a weasel.

"You-set-me-up," he stammered. "The cops are onto me. Those names I gave you. They want my blood. . . ."

"What's in a name, Weasel?" He was already so convulsed it was hard to tell if he even heard me.

"We're not friends. I don't like you," he shouted. Hearing a middle-aged man talk this way was frightening. I turned and walked toward Village Cigars, quite aware that the Village Cigar sign might well be the last thing I was ever going to see on the short little merry-go-round ride some of us call life.

I took about twelve steps and then I turned to look. There was no Weasel. There was only the rain where The Weasel had been. He'd either disappeared like some demon in a dismal night or he'd gone back into the men's room from whence he'd sprung. I was surprised to find my hands were trembling and the flesh was creeping a little on the back of my neck. "Nothing like a good cigar on a rainy night," I thought, and I walked briskly across a rain-swept Seventh Avenue in the direction of the old Village Cigar sign.

There was a guy on the corner trying to collect money to fight AIDS. He shouted: "Money for AIDS—not for war!" Over his head hung a rain-drenched banner that said: IF THE WORLD BLOWS UP YOU CAN'T BE GAY.

That was certainly true.

40

I was smoking an expensive rope from the Dominican Republic when I walked down the three steps into the joint called the High Five. It was pushing one o'clock. I bought a shot of snake piss and I looked around through the smoke. McGovern was there all right, about twice as big as God, sitting at a little table in the corner. I walked over and sat down across from him.

"Hey, pal," I said.

"Hey, pal," he said.

"While we're doing a little sober time here together in such intimate surroundings, you'd better spill your little ghost story first."

"You know Edith Piaf and Charlie Parker probably sat at this same little table."

"Yeah," I said, "they must've been quite an item." I was running fresh out of charm. "Spit it," I said.

"You know Cynthia once told me the kind of man she loved was the kind that could never attend a black-tie dinner."

"Some broads today still have a little class," I said. "Cynthia's one." Cynthia was one all right and look where it'd gotten her. She was as miserable as Edith Piaf or Billie Holiday. Sensitivity, character, intelligence: These were little hurdles you had to overcome if you wanted to get anyplace in life. Now take The Weasel, for instance . . .

"Same ghost," said McGovern. "Following me. It never

says a word, but when I turn around sometimes it's there. Pretty spooky, I'll tell you."

"McGovern, do you know how silly it sounds to hear this from a grown man?"

"I can't help it. Drunk or sober I still keep seeing the damn thing. I'm snapping my wig. The cops are after me. Maybe I'll just turn myself in."

"Or you could try pissing up a rope, pal," I said. I looked in his eyes and immediately felt bad for saying it.

"Jesus Christ, McGovern," I said. "Give me till Monday. Give me three more days to solve this thing. We'll turn the goddamn Village upside down and shake it. If I haven't caught the killer by Monday, do what you feel you have to." This whole thing was getting hairier than the guy in ZZ Top.

"Deal?" I asked.

"Deal," said McGovern. He looked as shaky as I felt.

"Better stagger our departures," I said. "You go first. If there's a ghost waiting out there, there's no point in him scaring the hell out of both of us."

"Okay," said McGovern as he got up to leave. "It's just a good thing that I'm so tall."

"Why is that, McGovern?" I asked.

"Because I think I'm in some deep shit," he said.

The cab let me off on Vandam Street between two garbage trucks. It was two-thirty in the morning, the time a Chinaman goes to his dentist. I looked up from the street and saw that the lights were all burning on the fourth floor. Some bastard had taken the freight elevator again, so I legged it up the stairs and got my key out to unlock the door. Even then I knew that something was wrong. When I opened the door I knew what it was.

Detective Sergeants Fox and Cooperman were standing in my kitchen. Ratso and Boris were at the kitchen table. It didn't look like they'd made much of a dent in the vodka or the caviar. The cat was nowhere to be seen.

"Don't bother taking off your hat," said Cooperman, "because you ain't stayin'."

"Is there a problem, gentlemen?" I asked.

"Yes," said Fox, "there is a little problem. Somebody whacked Barry Campbell tonight. Nice professional little job. Two slugs in the back of the head. Body was found in the gutter on Waverly about a block and a half from Gay Street."

"Remember Gay Street?" asked Cooperman.

"Should I?" I asked. I walked over to the table and picked up the bottle of vodka and put a lip-lock on it. It burned its way down my throat and it felt like Napoleon's whole army was down there retreating in front of it.

"Well," said Cooperman, "let me refresh your memory for you. A few days ago you stood in this same room and swore to me and my colleague here that when you found Campbell you'd spray his brains all over Gay Street. Now here we are a week later and we get this report and we go out and who do we find croaked and hugging the gutter? Campbell. Where do we find him? A block and a half off Gay Street. And they were short blocks. Now that's close enough for cop instinct."

"When I said that, I'd just gotten winged by one of Campbell's goons. I was angry. It was just a figure of speech."

"Yeah," said Fox, "well, you figure a speech out on the way to the precinct. We're taking you in for questioning, pal. Let's move it."

I caught a brief glimpse of the cat hiding under the sofa and peering out nervously at me as I was escorted through the door.

Cats were pretty smart.

41

"Western Union prefers not to transmit that type of message, sir."

"What the hell. Well, send the first one anyway. Thank you." I cradled the blower and picked it up again. It was now more than twelve hours later and I had been to hell and back and I hadn't seen Audie Murphy anywhere. Wolf Nachman had finally gotten me out of a hotbox between Fox and Cooperman that had provided an enormous amount of heat and damn little light. I was now engaged in a flurry of activity to try to pull together what few frazzled threads I could find in this mess and weave them into enough of a straitjacket to keep McGovern from turning himself in to the cops on Monday. If McGovern did that, I felt, it would be tantamount to an admission of guilt on his part.

It was 3:47 P.M. on a cold, brisk Friday afternoon, the last Friday in February. I lit a handsome-looking new cigar and took a slurp of hot black coffee. The cat was sitting under her private heat lamp on my desk and watching me as I dialed the number of the ad agency Frank Worthington had once done some commercials for, Umbrella, Inc.

"Umbrella. May I help you?" came the no-nonsense secretary's voice.

"Yeah," I said. "Let me speak to Bill Johnson." Ratso had run down the name for me. The guy was head honcho at the ad agency.

"Who's calling, please?" I didn't like this secretary already. I told her my name.

"What is the call in regard to, sir?"

"Look, all I can tell you is that the matter is very urgent and may possibly involve a life-or-death situation. Now will you find Mr. Johnson for me?"

"But what is the call in regard to, sir?" Poor woman, she was running out of patience with me.

"Don't dreidel me, lady. It's about the umbrella he's going to need to keep the crap off his head that's going to come down on him if I don't get to talk to him now. . . . Tell him it concerns Frank Worthington," I said as kind of an afterthought, but apparently those were the magic words.

"Just a minute, sir," she said rather curtly. I waited a little more. Peter Myers was due over any minute, and tonight I intended to dissect Nina Kong like a laboratory frog. The cops were of the opinion that either McGovern, myself, or the mob had croaked Campbell. Anyone that started with an *M*. I knew I was innocent and I was almost as certain that Mc-Govern was, so, as I told the cops repeatedly, Campbell was obviously hoisted on his own petard, rubbed out by some faction of his own mob-style killers. You lives by the water-melon, you dies by the watermelon.

The cops weren't buying any watermelon, however. Nor were they buying any red herrings. I carefully avoided using that expression during my interview with them so as not to increase my amateur standing in their eyes, but privately I felt more and more certain that Campbell's death was unrelated to the other two and that if some break didn't come very quickly, Campbell's death was going to be unrelated to the other three. Because there would probably be another croaking. Trouble was, I didn't have any idea who the croakee was going to be. I did have an idea about the identity of the croaker but it wasn't the kind of thing the cops would take seriously if I told them. It wasn't the kind of thing anybody would take seriously.

By the time Bill Johnson came to the phone, I'd almost forgotten who the hell he was and Peter Myers was hallooing me from the sidewalk below. I told Bill Johnson to wait, threw down the puppet head to Myers, and then proceeded to explain to Johnson my close working relationship with the police and my immediate need for a tape copy of the voice of the deceased.

"Frank Worthington, you say? Couldn't forget him. Horrible thing to happen . . ."

"Terrible," I said.

"I'm sure we have a tape somewhere," he said. "When do you need it?"

"Yesterday, pal," I said, "yesterday."

"I'll call you back within the hour," he said.

"Roger," I said. "This'll make the boys at the precinct very happy." You couldn't lay it on too thick for these advertising guys. In fact, you had to lay it on pretty thick because their skulls were so thick.

"I've brought you something," said Myers as he came in the door to my loft. I retrieved the puppet head from him and put it back on top of the refrigerator. You never know who might come calling on you these days. Best to be prepared.

Myers took a small, round, hard object about the size of a hockey puck out of a paper bag he was carrying. He set it down squarely in the middle of the kitchen table.

"Know what that is?" he asked.

"Somebody's lost their hockey puck," I said. Myers laughed heartily. He sounded like some kind of British Sten gun. "That's good! That's good!" he said.

"Yeah, it's pretty goddamn funny." This guy was too much.

"You Americans are too much," he said. "This is a pork pie. You do eat pork, don't you?"

"No. Our leader, Mohammed, forbids it."

"Pity."

"Listen, pal," I said, "I've got a busy weekend ahead and I got no time for small talk. I'm going to make you a nice cup of tea and I want you to sit down here and spill it and I don't mean the tea." I made Myers a cup of tea. I even made my-self a cup of tea so I could be on the same wavelength with him.

I got the teacups, sugar, cream, and Myers in place around the table, and I went over and picked up the shrink's report off the desk. I sat down across from Myers, who was taking tentative little sips of his tea and making little expressions like somebody was jabbing him with a hatpin.

"Well," I said, "everybody's here but the Mad Hatter. He, apparently, couldn't make it today but we do have his confi-dential shrink report. It requires a great leap of faith but I'll assume, only for the sake of discussion, you understand, that you did not kill Frank Worthington."

"Big of you," he said.

"Yes. Now, you see that at the beginning of the shrink's notes, Worthington is discussing his troubled relationship with 'C.' Then we flip a few pages and Worthington flips out a few more times and we come to somebody named 'N.' Now toward the end of the whole megillah we have mention of a character referred to as 'M.' That would be you, my lad, cor-rect?"

"Whatever you say."

"So if we draw a flow chart on a Carnegie Delicatessen napkin, we go back a little over four years to 'Campbell,' come to 'Nina Kong' about a year later, and finally, as Wor-thington ends therapy with this shrink about two and a half years ago, we find that he leaves his mind at your doorstep."

Myers's upright posture had deteriorated to that of a large fishing worm. "I didn't kill the poor blighter," he said, "though God knows there were times I'd have liked to."

"Your dear departed friend Barry Campbell claims he was leaving Worthington's apartment about when you were ar-riving. It looks like you were among the last to see Frankie Boy alive. If not the last."

"I didn't kill him."

"Fine."

"And Campbell was no friend of mine. That cunt."

"May he rest in peace," I said. I had disliked Campbell at least as much as Myers had, but still, it was an interesting choice of words. The British, of course, often referred derogatorily to both men and women as "cunts." Homosexuals used the word often too, usually but not always applying it to men and meaning about the same as when they called a man a "bitch." I thought suddenly of McGovern. He used the word to describe any man, woman, or child that got in his way. "Cunt" was not a word I often used in my own vocabulary, but it was a word that would come back to haunt me before this sordid business was over.

There was only one more loose end concerning Pete Myers that I wanted to tie up before I let him go. I still had to see Johnson, the guy from the ad agency, about the tape of Worthington's voice, and I still planned to pay a visit to Nina Kong at the recording studio that night. I looked Myers right in the eye and he looked into his teacup.

"What're you doing," I asked, "reading the leaves?"

He looked up at me sullenly. "What else do you want?" he said.

"How many flowers did you see there at Worthington's?"

"A dozen. A dozen roses."

"You sure, Myers?"

"Sure as I could be. I left my abacus at home, you see." He was one smug item.

"Just one more thing, Myers. What did Darlene Rigby want from you when she called you just before midnight on the night she was murdered?"

He looked right at me and he didn't bat an eye. Then he smiled and he leaned back in his chair.

"She wanted my recipe for pork pies," he said.

42

Just before five o'clock that evening I went by Umbrella, Inc., to pick up the tape I'd ordered. You don't get to be head of an advertising agency in New York by being a nice guy but Johnson wasn't too bad for a guy in a three-piece suit. If I'd had to dress that way every day for the past twenty years, I probably wouldn't have been much better.

I walked out of there twenty minutes later with a cassette and a smile. I thought I had friends in the advertising business and Johnson thought he had friends at the Sixth Precinct. So much for friendship.

I called Ratso at his office to find out when he'd be back at the loft. I wanted to get his opinion of the tapes.

When I finally got through to him he said, "Dr. Felch. Is that you?"

"Yeah. When are you going to be at the loft?"

"Can you give me half an hour?" he asked.

"I can give you a lot longer than that, pal."

"Okay, don't get snippy. I'll be there a little after six."

I stopped off at a little grocery on the corner and did my shopping for the week. Cigars, coffee, cat food, toilet paper. I also bought some wine, cheese, and a rather vile-looking Italian sausage. You never knew when you were going to have guests.

As I was ankling it up Vandam, I noticed a cab pulled over to the side of the street with the driver's door open. The driver was standing behind the door taking a leak on the street and it was too late to pretend I hadn't seen him.

"How's it going?" I said. He didn't answer but he did give me a little sneer. This kind of thing happened quite often on Vandam. It was a quiet street but you paid the price in other ways. I couldn't blame the guy. I'd been there myself. If you didn't have a wad of bills, credit cards, and a hotel key, you were going to have a hell of a time trying to urinate in New York. It was easier to cop a plea than it was to cop a pee.

By the time I got home Ratso was already there, screwdriver in hand, cursing the television set.

"I'll tell you, Sherlock, the sacrifices I make for you."

"Not everybody has Manhattan Cable, pal. Now you see how the other half lives." I put the groceries away, such as they were, and poured a mean jigger of Jameson into the bull's-horn shot glass. The cat had a late brunch so I didn't bother with feeding her just then. She wasn't knocked out about it, I could tell, but she took it stoically. On balance, she was handling herself better than Ratso.

"Come over here, Rat, I want you to hear something. This is bachelor number one," I said as I rewound and played back the tape on my answering machine. We heard again the same sober, anomic voice: "This is Frank Worthington . . ."

I popped the cassette out and put in the one that Johnson had given me. "Now this is bachelor number two." The voice we heard was vibrant this time and decidedly earthbound, but there was no mistaking its identity. It said, "Are you a hemorrhoid sufferer? If you are, this message is for you. Painful, inflamed hemorrhoidal tissues . . ."

"Enough!" shouted Ratso. "No question about it."

"I agree," I said. "Bachelor number one and bachelor number two are clearly the same person."

We had a match all right but it looked like a match that had been made in hell.

"Well," said Ratso, "if Worthington is dead, which we know he is, why in the hell is he still calling us?"

"There are certain other possibilities that suggest themselves, my dear Ratso," I said, as I put on my hunting vest and reached for a few cigars.

"Where are you going?" he asked.

"Out," I said. "The game is afoot."

I wasn't sure who the game was or what the game was. All I knew was I was going to try to bite it before it bit me.

43

I walked down Eighth Street on my way to the studio where Nina Kong was finishing her rock video. It was Friday night again, exactly two weeks to the day since Frank Worthington had gotten himself croaked and had gotten me into this ungodly mess. As I walked I took stock of the situation. No one had been croaked now in almost twenty-four hours. That was saying something. Maybe this was the end of it, but I really didn't believe it. The more I thought about it, the less likely I thought it was that Worthington and Rigby's killer had murdered Campbell. For one thing, Campbell's death looked like a garden-variety hit to me. It wasn't cute. Where was the flair? Where was the killer's sense of humor? No, Campbell's death had come about because he was getting too big for his stylish little suspendered britches. Maybe I indirectly helped his demise. Maybe he was snuffed out by a couple of disgruntled haircuts in aluminum suits. It just didn't fit with the other two croakings. I didn't see the fine Italian hand.

I wasn't through with Myers, I was just getting ready to tackle Nina, and tomorrow I intended to put what Adrian was pleased to call her mind through a Deering blender. If she was squirreling anything, I was sure as hell going to find out. Earlier in the day, before Myers and I had had our little tea party, I'd spoken to Cynthia. It hadn't been an easy call to make. She was already in the throes of a deep depression. I told her that time was running out, that I'd be talking to everybody involved this weekend, including herself. I told her to brace up as best she could and keep her powder dry. Better yet, I said, avoid the powder, avoid Adrian if possible, and be damn careful about letting any information slip to her. Adrian was a cocaine dealer, not a father confessor. I also invited Cynthia to join me for dinner Sunday night at the Derby.

That was about where things stood when I half trampled a Moonie who was selling flowers in the middle of the sidewalk at Eighth and University. He never stopped smiling all the way to the pavement. Bouquets of flowers all wrapped neatly in cellophane fell to the sidewalk, too. That was how you could always tell a Moonie—lots of smiling and lots of cellophane. I didn't hate Moonies but I didn't like them either, so I just kept walking and the Moonie just kept smiling. Never even said "Watch where you're going." But I figured I'd better watch where I was going anyway, because where I was going there lurked a psycho killer just waiting to make me a part of a nice burgeoning little corpse collection.

They say the grass is always greener over a corpse but I certainly wasn't dying to find out if it was true.

I gave my name to the Philip Morris midget at the door of the building and he waved me into the elevator. Four floors and one crushed cigar stub later, I strolled into the studio lobby where hordes of hangers-on were milling about and walked up to what looked to be the mission-control desk. The guy behind the desk had an inflated opinion of his own importance, but anybody could have developed that just by being exposed to the flotsam and jetsam drifting around the rest of the lobby.

"Who the hell are these people?" I asked the guy.

"They're the 'audience' we're using for the video. Who wants to know?" he said.

"I think I've spoken to you before, pal," I said. "It wasn't overly pleasant that time either." I gave him my name.

"Oh, yeah," he said, "I remember you said you were some kind of booking agent last time you called." This guy obviously wasn't a Moonie. If he was, he sure wasn't smiling too much.

"Anything's possible," I said. "Where can I find Nina?"

"Right through that door," he said, pointing into the studio. "She's working on close-ups now, but she wants to talk to you."

I walked through the soundproofed double doors of the recording studio into a room filled with acrid yellow smoke and hot lights. The guys with the smoke pellets were working overtime. A couple of video types were directing operations. From the way they acted, you'd think they were directing a crowd scene in some mammoth biblical epic. Well, we all had our dreams.

The music was loud and unintelligible. Even McGovern wouldn't have liked it. And the same eight bars or so were being repeated over and over at top decibel level. I'd been in worse places, but this one was certainly in the running. It wasn't a bad approximation of my idea of hell.

My eyes were beginning to clear a little bit and I could see that there was a sound stage with some people on it. One of them was Nina Kong. One of the makeup crew was dusting Nina's face with a little powder, but her face wasn't the most interesting part of Nina. I squinted my eyes to be sure I was seeing things right. I was.

It didn't take a pair of opera glasses to tell that Nina Kong was dressed entirely as a man.

44

We were in a posh little room off to one side of the sound stage. It had low lighting, comfortable furniture, soundproofed walls, and a good lock on the door. It looked as if it had been designed for what Nina was doing, which was laying out a pretty fair quantity of cocaine onto a large glass tabletop.

"That's a lot of fish ice cream you got there," I said.

"Is it?" she said without taking her eyes off her work.

"Before we burn too many synapses here, why did you lie to me about not knowing Barry Campbell?"

"I was hoping you wouldn't ask any hard questions. It's a long story," she said. Her upper lip was trembling a little as she lowered a nicely shaped nostril in for a landing onto the glass tabletop.

"Try to nut-shell it," I said.

"I wouldn't know where to start," she said.

"Start with why you lied to me about Campbell." I started to bring a nostril in for a landing myself but hesitated and made a last minute flyover instead. The tower told me to circle for a while.

"I knew Barry. Of course I knew Barry. I didn't tell you for two reasons. One was that I loved him once. And the other was that I thought he'd killed Frank. At least up until last night I thought he'd killed Frank." I watched as a few more light planes came in. She knew how to handle an aircraft all right. Of course, there wasn't much chance of missing the field, but still, a case of pilot error could be pretty expensive.

"I've been lonely most of my life," she said. I brought in a big transcontinental Concorde. The kind with its nose pointed down. "My parents were never able to show me that they loved me. . . ."

"You know what this is?" I asked. I was moving the index finger of my left hand back and forth across the thumbnail of the same hand.

"No," she said. She was sulking and she looked great when she sulked. Just sitting there pouting with that little tie on and dressed as a man she was something to see. Maybe I was subconsciously a homosexual. I'd have to ask Dr. Bock when he got back.

"You don't know what this is?" I said. "Well, let me tell you, honey. It's the smallest violin in the world and it's playing 'Hearts and Flowers.' "

"You're an insensitive prick, you know that?"

"Mr. Insensitive Prick to you, honey," I said. "Pray continue and don't let anything I might say ruffle your beautiful feathers. Life is tough and it's a funny old world and I just don't feel sorry for you. I've seen people who clean their teeth with steel wool in Vermont." I felt like grudge-jumping her right there on the spot but I thought better of it.

"It's not something I'm exactly proud of. Barry and I both were involved with Frank. First me and then Barry."

"Jesus," I said. "Frank dumped you for Barry." No wonder Worthington was seeing a shrink.

"That's a nice way of putting it," she said.

"Go on," I said. The jets were starting to come in on the little landing strip. Air traffic was getting pretty heavy.

"Frank dumped Barry, as you say, for Pete, though I don't think Pete was that interested. Barry and I were both rebounders. But when a woman is rejected by a man for another man, something happens to her. I'd never had much love in my life and I sort of went off the deep end. It was a low point for me. It hit me really hard. Barry picked me up and I'll always be grateful to him for it. I was rebounding terribly, and then he was rebounding, and we both just sort

178

of rebounded together at a crucial period for me. Later we drifted apart and went our own ways but I've never forgotten. Maybe you don't know what it's like. Maybe you've never been a rebounder."

"Everybody's a rebounder, honey," I said. "If there weren't any rebounding in this world, there'd be one hell of a lot of missed hoops." I was such a wise, understanding person.

I wanted to hug her but I took a Carnegie Delicatessen napkin out of my pocket instead. "Look at this," I said.

"So what?" she said. "So he makes a gooooood sandwich?"

I looked at the napkin. There was a little cartoon logo of my friend Carnegie Leo holding up a big pastrami sandwich and saying his famous slogan: "I make a gooood sandwich."

"That's not what I meant," I said. "Look over here." I showed her the flow chart of Frank Worthington's bisexual history as Dr. Bock had recorded it. On the napkin I'd written the following: C.——N.——M.

She studied the three initials for a moment and then said: "No, that's wrong. It should read: N.——C.——M."

"Okay," I said. "Nina, Campbell, Myers." I put the changed order of the initials underneath the old grouping.

"Curious," I said.

"Is that supposed to be a clue or something?" she asked in a pose of sexy mock innocence that was really quite fetching, I thought.

"No," I said, "it's in case you spill something on your tie. That's a nice outfit, kid." She blushed a little or maybe the blood was just rushing to her head.

"You wouldn't dress like that out on the street, would you?" I asked. "Out on Jane Street?"

" 'No' is the answer to both your questions. I'm shy."

"That's funny; you don't look shy."

"I'm shy," she continued as if I hadn't interrupted. "I'm dressing like this for the video. I'm not some kind of dyke, if that's what you think. I did not kill Frank Worthington. I'm

sad about Barry and I'm sorry about that actress girl whatever her name was. . . ."

"You sound it."

"I am sorry, damn it," she said and she stamped her little
foot. She looked, in spite of her clothing, like a woman
through and through and she looked dangerous as hell. "I'm
not sorry Frank was killed," she said as an afterthought.

"Yeah," I said, "he was a pretty popular guy all around."

"Look," she said, "I've got to get back in there for about
ninety-seven more hours of close-ups. You do some of this
special stuff." She took out the little ceramic snuffbox that I'd
seen before in the limousine. My hands weren't trembling
yet, so I thought I'd go ahead and give it a try.

"Knock yourself out," she said.

"I wish you hadn't said that," I said. "I was just starting to
like you again."

She shrugged; then she smiled and went over and opened
the door. As we walked back toward the sound stage, she
suddenly took my hand and led me into a little empty hallway somewhere behind the stage. She turned and I was
aware that she was standing very close to me. We grabbed
each other at about the same time, and I held her for a moment very tightly. If anyone on the street could have seen us,
they would probably have thought nothing of two men
standing together with their bodies caught up in a passionate
embrace. "What do you expect?" they would have said. "It's
the Village."

After a moment or two I whispered to her, "Don't say
'Knock yourself out,' honey."

"Don't say anything," she whispered. I didn't.

Later, after I'd straightened her tie and I'd said good-bye to
her in the little hallway, I was walking out toward the lobby
when she called after me. "I could be getting jealous," she
said. "Ever find out who sent you that rose?"

"Yeah," I said, "I think I have."

45

Saturday morning broke colder than The Weasel's smile. It was snowing outside and the falling flakes reminded me that I had to call Adrian. Ratso was still asleep on the couch, so I made some coffee and the cat and I sat by the window and watched the snow fall while I screwed up my nerve to hear Adrian's voice in the morning.

She was the kind of girl that older dentists find attractive. She had a nice set of teeth, a fair set of knockers, and a lousy set of values. She was a chemical puppet. I could picture her now after a night of wheeling, dealing, and tooting her own horn, out cold on the couch in some parody of a lingerie getup that even the perviest guy in the universe wouldn't find too exciting. Perrier spilled all over the floor probably. A few pieces of pizza spot-welded upside down on the couch next to her.

Well, like they said about the guy who stabbed his wife thirty-seven times with a screwdriver, nobody's perfect.

I called Adrian. I let the phone ring about nine times and hung up. Maybe she'd disconnected it. I frankly doubted that she was out bird-watching in Central Park.

It was now 10:00 A.M. I gave Mick Brennan a ring.

"Umhmmmm . . ." said Brennan.

"Leap sideways, pal," I said. "I need that information I asked you for. No later than this afternoon. Ask Bob Miller. Ask around in the city room. I've got to have it and fast."

I hung up and called the little florist shop on Hudson

Street. When I had called two weeks earlier, a young girl had been working there. She'd been very sweet and cooperative, checking the ledger and informing me that it was Barry Campbell who'd ordered the flowers for Frank Worthington. Now, two weeks later, the phone was answered by a mean old lady who didn't sound like she'd give me the time of day. Maybe the young girl had grown up.

It was not a pleasant phone call. The old lady bitched. I badgered. I threatened. She cackled. I cajoled. She grudgingly gave.

Worthington's flowers had gone out at 9:45 A.M. First delivery of the day.

"Are you satisfied now?" she asked smugly. "Do you want to place an order?"

"Yeah, lady," I said. "I want to order you to hang up your telephone."

I tried Adrian's number again. No answer. I walked back over to the window. The cat was still sitting on the sill. The garbage trucks looked very tranquil in the snow. A few big flakes drifted against the windowpane and the cat observed them with deep curiosity. I didn't know whether the cat could see the pattern in the snowflakes or not, but I was finally starting to see a few patterns myself. And what I saw I didn't like.

It was crowding 11:30. The snow was still falling, the cat was still watching, and Ratso and I were having an espresso at the kitchen table. Much to Ratso's displeasure, I was smoking my first cigar of the day and the smoke all seemed to be drifting directly into his left eye. There was nothing I could do about it.

I took out my old napkin from the Carnegie Delicatessen and spread it on the table in front of Ratso. "I want to show you something. Do you know what this means?"

"What's it mean?" he asked. "You don't get linen anymore?" He was referring to the Carnegie's tradition of giving linen napkins to their special customers. When a celebrity or a favorite customer came into the place, Carnegie Leo would shout to the waiter, "Give 'em linen." So you'd sit at a big table with the guy on your right and the guy on your left using paper napkins and you had linen. It was one of the few true rushes left in life.

I explained to Ratso the first little chart that I'd made according to the shrink's notes, and then I showed him the second one underneath it that was Nina Kong's version.

"Curious," he said.

"That's what I said," I said. I wasn't even sure that Nina's elevator went to the top floor, but if it did and her version was correct, it raised a rather unaccountable discrepancy. We decided to talk it over at lunch and what better place to have it than at the Carnegie.

I left the cat in charge, and we walked along in the crisp, white snow through the Village for a while. It was a beautiful village. Especially when it was blanketed with newly fallen snow. Of course, give it about two hours and it would look like crankcase oil. But beauty never lasts in this world. God and man and large dogs see to that.

We took a cab up to Fifty-fifth and Seventh and joined the long line waiting for tables inside the Carnegie Delicatessen. Leo spotted us in the line, pulled us out, found a table for us, and told the head waiter, "Give 'em linen." We ordered two bowls of matzo-ball soup. Ratso stuffed his linen napkin into the neck of his shirt so the neighboring diners couldn't miss it. We had a couple of pastrami sandwiches, which Leo claims are the best in New York and he won't get a beef from me about it. We had some seltzer, Dr. Brown's Creme Soda, coffee, cheesecake, and Ratso topped things off by ordering a pope's nose. The waiter said he'd ask the guy at the counter if they had one. They did. It was the rear end of a turkey. Quite a delicacy in deli circles, I'm told.

We did not discuss the case and I didn't think about Mc-Govern once until we got home and there was a message on the machine from Mick Brennan. I rang him up right away.

"Spit it, Mick," I said.

"It's just as you thought," he said. "Friday morning around eleven o'clock was one time. That wasn't the only occasion either. But I still don't see what it means."

"These are deep waters, Brennan. And at the bottom lurks a creature that's going to make the Loch Ness Monster look like a cute little E.T. Say nothing about this to anyone if you value your life."

"Right, mate."

"Even if you don't value your life," I added as an afterthought. It was hard to tell sometimes with Mick.

I knew how the murderer had committed the crime. I had the timing down now. I could even see the motive beginning to crystallize in the back of my mind. All I needed was for the mask of death to drop and show the even deadlier face behind it.

46

By ten o'clock Saturday night the Monkey's Paw was beginning to twitch pretty good.

Outside, the snow was still on the ground, but if you'd built a snowman out of it, he would've died of toxic poisoning. I was standing by the bar nursing a Guinness and quietly piecing together a mosaic of murder in my mind. I was playing a cat-and-mouse game with myself and it was proving to be an exasperating experience. I was the cat. Whoever or whatever the mouse was I couldn't quite tell, but it was peeping at me from every dusty corner of my mind. Several times as I stood there, I thought I had him, but he always managed to scurry away just beyond the reach of my memory. Damn! Six more inches and I would have been king.

This little mental mouse I was chasing through the rusty convolutions of my brain had something to do with drugs, something to do with the voice of a dead man whom I'd never met, something . . . something else . . . but it was gone again . . . like a ghost in a hallway . . .

I'd have to talk this over with my cat when I got home. What would the cat do if it were in my place? How do you catch a mouse when you're not even sure it's really there?

I ordered another Guinness from Tommy, who was not smiling like a Moonie. He looked a little harassed tonight. I wasn't experiencing the even-mindedness of the ol' Mahatma myself. I reached through a well-dressed young Saturday night couple for the Guinness.

"Pardon my boardinghouse reach," I said.

"Don't mention it, chief," said the guy.

"Fine."

The second Guinness was bringing out the mouse a little better. I had to go on the assumption that McGovern was the victim of a fiendishly clever frame-up. Of course, I could be wrong about that. Invariably the neighbors of mass murderers were wrong about them. So were their teachers, parents, gym coaches, best friends. Maybe it took a psycho to know a psycho. Maybe I was such a wonderful trusting American that I'd had McGovern lamped wrong the whole time.

As my old friend Slim used to say back in Texas, "You never know what the monkey eat until the monkey shit." Crude, but appropriate. Possibly very appropriate.

When I got heavily monstered I could often remember things I thought I couldn't remember. For example, I had repressed many things in my past. One of them was California. But when I got truly hammered, sometimes I could vividly recall just about every loving, bloody, Technicolor detail of Yesterday Street. I could reel off the phone numbers of hotels in L.A. and Santa Monica, of half-a-dozen long-forgotten coke dealers, of old girlfriends and lost loves who'd gone on to whatever they go on to. Probably making a mess of some other guy's life. Did they stop a second to think of me as they stood in the patio with the kids all around and the husband standing by the barbecue pit? I hoped not.

I could even speak fluent Malay and a little Swahili when I was drunk.

"Uh-oh, here comes trouble," said a familiar voice with a thick British accent.

"*Hujambo, bwana,*" I said. It was Mick Brennan, and from the look of him he'd already covered Yesterday Street like a Fuller brush man.

"What're you doing tomorrow night, mate? We're having some roast beef with Yorkshire pudding over at a friend's place. We need a token American."

"Can't," I said. "I'm taking Cynthia to the Derby."

"Ah," he said, "while the bloody cat's away the bleeding mice will play, eh?"

"Closer than you know, pal."

"Cheers," he said and ordered another round for us.

"Where is he tonight, Mick?" I asked.

"Who? McGovern or The Weasel?"

"I already don't know where McGovern is," I said. "I'm talkin' Weasel, man. Where is that miserable little porch monkey?"

"He was here earlier but he left. Said he wouldn't be back tonight. Looked to be a bit upset. Said he thought his source had dried up."

"Jesus," I said. On instinct I went to the pay phone, dropped a quarter, and dialed Adrian's number. There was no answer. I let it ring about eleven times but I wasn't really listening anymore.

It fit together too well. It probably had been going on for years and I hadn't known. Hadn't even guessed. But now I knew as surely as I was standing there with the receiver in my hand.

The Weasel had been getting his stuff from Adrian.

All the time it had been literally right under my nose.

47

It was with a certain chill of premonition that I hailed a cab up Fourth Street to Adrian's place. Many thoughts were suddenly hurtling through my mind and none of them was "Have a nice day." I didn't have the key with me to the building on 42 Jane Street, but there was no time to go back to the loft to get it. Adrian hadn't answered the phone from the first time I'd tried her at ten o'clock that morning until just minutes ago when I'd called again from the Monkey's Paw.

That was a long time between dreams.

Especially for a coke dealer who rarely left her apartment. Maybe she was visiting her mother in Teaneck. Or her brother in Redneck. Did coke dealers have mothers or brothers? I supposed it was possible. I knew The Weasel didn't have a mother in Teaneck. The rock he'd crawled out from under was on the third ring of Saturn.

Career coke dealers had no real friends in the world; why should they have family? The architecture of their lives came down to nothing but straws and mirrors. They were spinning ghosts in the land of the lost . . . spinning ghosts . . .

It would have been a hell of a lot faster if I'd hoofed it up Fourth, I now realized. The Saturday night Village traffic was a honking, crawling nightmare in itself. But it gave me a little chance to think.

I noticed there wasn't any "No Smoking" sign in the cab so I reached into my old hunting vest and came up with a good two-dollar and twenty-five-cent Partagas cigar. What this country needed was a good two-dollar and twenty-five-cent cigar. That and a couple of other things.

I lit the cigar and I leaned back on the seat and puffed a bit. I thought of what I might find at my journey's end.

"You smoke the cigar?" asked the driver. "No smoking the cigar," he shouted. "No smoke!"

"Fine," I said. The cigar cost more than the goddamn fare. I got out in the middle of the street and paid the guy, giving him a tip that was appropriate to the services.

I'd just about decided that it wouldn't pay to go rushing into Adrian's place as if I expected something to be amiss. For one thing, it was just possible the cops might be there already. For another, the neighbors might see me and tell the cops a guy with a big cigar was running through the building after midnight and that he wasn't Ernie Kovacs. And for a third thing, maybe nothing at all was amiss and my whole intrusion would just amount to a social embarrassment. I could survive dropping the salad fork.

So I slowed my pace a little. But just a little.

I walked past the Corner Bistro and I saw the little thatched roof on top of the green windmill across from 42 Jane Street. I stood and looked at the building where McGovern had lived and had first seen Frank Worthington's ghost. Where Frank Worthington had lived and died a violent death. I hoped that Adrian, whatever tense she was currently in, wasn't there. Not that she and I went way back or anything; I just hoped she wasn't there. I hoped she was attending a coke-dealers convention this weekend in Vail, Colorado, and had forgotten to mention it to anyone.

Like the commercial for Holiday Inn, I wanted no surprises.

I looked both ways before crossing the street. It was a little trick I'd learned in Singapore. There was nobody on the street at all unless you wanted to count the kid on the bicycle or the guy going through the garbage cans. It was a quiet reflective moment in the life of Jane Street before the lights changed or the bars closed. I crossed the street.

I climbed the four steps, opened the door into the little hallway, found Adrian's buzzer, and leaned heavily on it. I listened for a voice but it was quiet as a picnic in the country. Quiet as a funeral in the suburbs. It was so quiet it almost made you want to scream. It was deadly quiet.

I stepped back out to the sidewalk to get some air and to test my auditory responses. Maybe I'd hear a guy arguing with his wife. Maybe a car going by or a junkie walking down the sidewalk talking to himself. Maybe even a garbage truck . . . Nothing. It was the same frightening sensation you'd get if you were walking in the jungle and suddenly all the birds stopped singing. You knew the leopard was going to pounce; you just didn't know which shadow it was going to pounce from. And at times like these you wouldn't really be considering whether or not the leopard had changed its spots. I certainly wasn't.

I scrambled back up the steps and practiced a little Morse code on McGovern's buzzer. With any luck Cynthia would be there. Nothing . . . Where the hell was Rambam when you needed him? Where was anybody when you needed him?

I walked over to the Bistro. I even had a hard time getting the bartender. The Bistro was jumping on a Saturday night.

"Dave," I shouted. "Dave! Give me a shot of something."

"Right you are," said Dave and he gave me a shot of something. It tasted like some Benedictine monk had forgotten to put the cork back on it for a couple of years but I wasn't going to complain. I went to the pay phone, which cringed on the wall next to the blaring jukebox, and I did my best to call Cynthia's number. She wasn't home but Southside Johnny was. I ordered another shot of whatever it was I'd ordered the first time, and it tasted better the second time. Kind of like love except it was cheaper.

I went back to 42 Jane and pushed Adrian's buzzer—more nothing. I camped out on Cynthia's buzzer for a while. I practically pushed the damn thing through the wall and I kept repeating "Cynthia" in a loud voice that was beginning to sound like a guy pulling the starter cord on a busted lawn mower. At last I heard a small voice and I didn't think it sounded like my conscience.

"Yes. Who is it?" it said.

"Cynthia, it's me. For Christ's sake, let me in." The door buzzed and I pushed the damn thing open and went up to McGovern's. Cynthia was alive and well and apparently just getting out of the shower.

"I was just taking a shower," she said. "Was that you on the telephone too?"

"Yeah." She was wearing a housecoat with red and blue parrots that looked as if they were about to fall off their perch. I was about to fall off mine too, only I didn't know it at the time.

"I'm going upstairs in a second; got a shot of something?" I asked. Some women were at their very best coming out of the shower. She looked troubled and damp and ravishing. But it was a rather obvious case of time does not allow. And then there was the specter of McGovern lurking out there somewhere in the night. There was also my growing dread of whatever the hell I might find upstairs. But that was another story.

Cynthia brought me the drink. It was better than the Bistro's and the service was too. I caught a quick glimpse of myself in the bathroom mirror and I knew I needed a bracer. I looked like the loneliest man I'd ever met. I looked like an out patient who needed to get back in.

I downed the rest of the drink. "Thanks," I said. "Have you seen Adrian?"

"Not since two days ago. No. I haven't seen her."

"Well, don't hold your breath. Stay here—I'll be right back. I'm going up." I didn't want to leave Cynthia and about half of me didn't want to know what was up there on the third floor, so I kissed Cynthia on the forehead and lightly over her closed eyes. She kissed me on the lips and held on to me for dear life.

"I've got to get up there," I said and I took her arms from around my neck and held her in front of me until I could see the parrots real well. "I'll be right back," I told her, and I went out the door and up the stairs to the third floor.

A couple of those parrots had looked like they wanted a cracker bad, and they didn't look like they really cared whether or not that cracker was me.

48

I knocked on Adrian's door not like I was expecting any answer but like I was checking to see if the room was hollow. It wasn't. But it was dark as some unlit corner of hell. The door had opened much too easily for my blood.

My hand crept along the wall for the light switch and the flesh crept along the back of my neck. I didn't know where it was creeping to but I wished it would stop. It didn't. I found the switch and I hit the lights. I blinked a few times and took a step forward. I was almost on top of her before I saw her. She was lying facedown on the floor right between the light green sofa and the dark green coffee table. I turned her over and her face was a bad lavender.

She was colder than a frozen margarita. There were little bubbles of foam still clinging to the corners of her mouth. Her eyes were caught in the act of trying to tell something to someone, only whoever the someone had been, he was gone and I wasn't. Not that I didn't want to be gone. I wanted to goose-step right out of there, but I forced myself to stick around like an unwanted guest at a party of one.

Adrian was the second stiff I'd seen in this building in just a little over a fortnight. It was a case of history starting to cause ennui. Served me right for not staying at the Holiday Inn.

As I stood up and took a step backward, something made a little crunching sound under my left foot. When I picked it up, I saw that it was a small fragment of pink glass. I looked around on the floor and found a few more pieces in several pastel colors that reminded me of something. Oh, Christ. It was what was left of Adrian's poor, pathetic pane of stained glass. Someone had done a pretty thorough job of smashing it all to hell, and it hadn't been a kid with a baseball. The girl had spent an eternity working on her own little masterpiece and the only gallery it would ever see was this floor of dusty death. Art imitating life. And life was the strangest monkey of them all.

It was enough to bring a tear to a stained-glass eye.

I looked down at the coffee table for the first time. There was maybe half an ounce of cocaine swirled out across the coffee table in the stark, determined configurations of a word. The clumsy white letters against the green background were vaguely reminiscent of the scribblings of a child on a blackboard someone had erased along with the other fragile memories of forgotten youth.

But this writing was not the work of a child. One word was written in cocaine on top of the little table.

The word was "Cunt."

"So that's the story, Sergeant. I haven't pinched anything but my own arm to see if I was dreaming." There were three of us in the room—Sergeant Fox, myself, and Adrian's stiff—and I seemed to be the one who'd been doing most of the talking. "So it's getting late and I'd like to check out the alibis of a few Americans before the trail gets too cold. Can I talk to you guys in the morning?"

"Jesus, you country-singer types are something, aren't you?" said Fox, as he picked up a small sliver of stained glass with his handkerchief.

"I'm not a country-singer type anymore," I said. "Now I'm in the the-ah-tuh." I gave Fox the most friendly, engaging smile I could find in the warehouse. He just kept studying the piece of glass like it was the key to everything man didn't know in the world. Maybe it was. If anybody had come into the room, it would have looked like he was holding a tiny piece of ice in his handkerchief and seeing how long it would take for it to melt. It reminded me of Bat Masterson's last comment on life. He had been a sportswriter on the New York *Morning Telegraph*, and his colleagues had found the following message in his typewriter after he died: "I have found the secret of life. It is ice. The poor folks have it in the winter and the rich folks have it in the summer."

The poor folks evidently had it now because it was as cold as a warlock's nipple outside. And inside the apartment building at 42 Jane Street, you couldn't get much poorer than poor Adrian.

"Poisoned," said Fox, as he walked around the room and stopped at the coffee table. "Either in the Perrier or maybe cut right into the product here. Poisoned cocaine. A poison within a poison." He looked at the four-letter word on the coffee table. "That's nice," he said.

"Yeah, I thought you'd like that," I said. "Look, I think I'll be going now. I forgot to feed the cat."

"You're staying with me, pal," he said. "We're gonna get real close before this thing's over. If one of us eats a piece of watermelon, the other one's gonna be able to spit out the seeds."

Before I could say anything else—not that there was much to say—Cooperman came hustling into the room. When he saw me he didn't know whether to shit or go blind.

But he recovered nicely. "Goddamn, Fox, this guy's a regular advance man. The longer it takes to find McGovern, the better this guy looks to me. But I don't think it'll take that long to find McGovern. Not after what his broad's been telling me downstairs. Come on down for a minute. I want you to hear this."

The police photographer and the print man had arrived and were setting up. A uniformed cop was at the door. It was one-thirty in the morning. Adrian was wearing high heels, a rather risqué, black, see-through-but-you-wish-you-hadn't sort of negligee affair. She was also wearing a very twisted, cyanide smile. She would not be dealing tonight. She was in for the evening forever.

Cynthia was sitting on McGovern's big stuffed easy chair and looking very fragile. She'd been crying, she'd been drinking a little, and I didn't know what else she'd been doing. Fox was standing over her with one foot on the radiator, which, as usual, was cold. Cooperman was standing by the fireplace warming himself by the nonexistent fire. I gathered a few old newspapers from McGovern's own personal morgue that threatened to block out what little sunlight ever crept into his living room, then grabbed a few small logs and made like a boy scout for a few minutes. Soon I had a fair approximation of a fire going. It wouldn't have warmed the hearts or the hands of a band of gypsies, but by New York standards it wasn't bad.

I walked into the kitchen and made a drink for myself. Cynthia already had one. Fox and Cooperman weren't drinking; they were reconstructing the past twenty-four hours with Cynthia's help. It looked like it was going to be a long night.

I couldn't help but wonder if we were doing the right thing standing here yapping with Cynthia about McGovern and Adrian and letting The Weasel weasel away. And had Nina been working in the studio the past twenty-four hours? And had Pete Myers been busy cooking pork pies or had he been doing something else? It would all have to be checked out.

"Now, Miss Floyd, would you go over again what you told us earlier about what happened late last night?" It was Cooperman asking the questions as if he were talking to a child. Cooperman was taking his time. He was putting down roots there right in front of the fireplace, preparing for the long assault on Cynthia's defenses.

As it happened, it wasn't going to take the hordes of foot soldiers, the catapults, or the battering ram to get results. Cynthia's castle was already crumbling. Tears were coming again. Fox gave her a handkerchief. I hoped he'd remembered to take the piece of glass out of it first.

"Well, last night I just couldn't sleep," said Cynthia. "It was about two o'clock in the morning and I was just sitting here listening to the r-radio." I wandered over to the little kitchen while she was talking and made like I was looking for a drink in the cabinets. There were two or three more little snow-seal packages tucked away in the corner of the cabinet. I tucked them a little farther away out of sight, and as long as I was already there, I pulled down a bottle of Bushmill's Irish whiskey and went through the charade of pouring a hefty jolt and drinking it. I could see why Cynthia was having trouble sleeping. I'd had trouble sleeping for years. It's hard to count sheep when you're grinding your teeth.

"I tried r-reading a book." Cynthia was wiping her eyes with the handkerchief. "I kept thinking about McGovern. Suddenly the door opened and he was right here in the room."

"What time was this?" asked Cooperman.

"It was about two-thirty in the morning. I couldn't believe my eyes. I just don't want to . . . I don't want for him to . . ."

The fire crackling was the only sound in the room. I went to the kitchen and got Cynthia a brandy and walked over and gave it to her. She took it like a little girl receiving a gift.

"Cynthia," I said, "we know what McGovern means to you. If he's innocent, anything you say can only help to clear him. So tell us the truth. Tell us what happened last night."

McGovern's timing was impeccably bad as usual. The guy stays away for the better part of two weeks while the whole NYPD is looking for him, and then he comes in at an ETA of almost precisely the time somebody croaks Adrian. He hadn't lost his touch.

Cynthia had stopped crying. She sniffed a few times and took a little gulp of the brandy. "He'd been drinking and he was acting very strange. Sort of growling to himself about something. We went to bed around three in the morning and when I woke up it was already eight o'clock and he was gone. But I had had trouble falling asleep, and while I was tossing and turning, sort of half out of it, I remembered him talking, kind of snarling in his sleep. He'd done it before so I was kind of used to him talking in his sleep but this time it scared me."

"Could you understand anything he said?" asked Cooperman.

"He was sort of cursing and growling to himself," she said.

"And?" said Cooperman.

Silence.

"What did he say, Miss Floyd?" said Fox.

A few of the parrots had evidently gotten their feathers ruffled and she was smoothing them out. She stared down at the floor.

"Let's have it, Cynthia," I said.

She raised her head and looked straight in front of her. Her eyes were dry and empty. She spoke in a low monotone but nobody had to ask her to repeat what she said.

"He said, 'Cunt . . . cunt . . . I'll kill the cunt. . . .'"

49

It was Sunday afternoon, bright and cold in New York. The cat, the Rat, and I were all sitting around watching Doug Flutie and the New Jersey Generals play the Arizona Heroin Addicts. USFL football was not very exciting to a lot of people and it wasn't very exciting to me either. I just liked to kind of relax, meditate, have a cup of coffee, and watch the players tump over on the field. In a world that had already lost its meaning to many folks, USFL football had to be the most meaningless facet of life on this planet. That was why I watched it.

I was heading into my third cup of coffee when the phones rang. I walked over to the desk and picked up the blower on the left. It was 3:13 P.M. It was Cooperman.

"Well, well, well," he said. "I've got a little news flash for you."

"What's that? They find a cure for herpes?"

"No. But that was pretty good. Want to guess again?" I didn't like the vitality I was hearing in Cooperman's voice.

"Christ," I said. "I don't know. Bisexual bites dog?"

"No. It's a little hotter than that."

"Well, what the hell is it, Sergeant?"

"Your pal McGovern turned himself in. About two hours ago. Like they say in Hollywood, it's a wrap. In fact, it's three raps. Murder One times three."

"He didn't do it," I said.

"Oh, yeah?" said Cooperman. "He did it all right. And

now all he's going to have to do is figure out who's going to look after his cockroaches while he's gone."

I cradled the blower and put down the cigar I had been thinking about lighting.

Now things were starting to look bad.

Needless to say I did not take Cynthia to the Derby that Sunday night. I didn't take anybody anywhere for a long time. I didn't even take my laundry to the cleaners. I just hung around the loft adding a few layers of cigar smoke to the atmosphere in the daytime, and at night I would hit the Village bars and work a little more on developing my tavern tan.

It was like somebody had died. Not just the covey of stiffs I had hardly known who had shuffled off to Buffalo in varied and violent fashion with their name tags stuck on their big toes and who could be discussed like some sort of parlor game in a random and haphazard order. In New York nobody really regarded anybody as dead; we just thought of them as not currently working on a project.

But McGovern was somebody close to me. And McGovern was not McGovern anymore. Whether he was dead or not, I suppose, was arguable. Clinically, I knew, he was still alive somewhere in a monkey cage eating baloney sandwiches. But his mind and his spirit, I was afraid, were damn near as dead as Dumbo's mother.

I seemed to be about the only person in New York who still clung feebly to the notion that McGovern was innocent. Actually, there was another person who knew of McGovern's innocence—that was the killer. But the killer wasn't talking. The killer, having killed, had moved on to something else. He had diversified.

Weeks passed in a glum fashion. The Mets had opened their season and the Rangers had closed theirs. Ratso had been making flapping noises about flying home like a sparrow to nearby SoHo. Then one day I looked at the empty couch and I realized he was gone.

I ran into Mick Brennan a few times in the Monkey's Paw and struggled through a few rounds with him. I noticed with a perverse satisfaction that The Weasel was back in the men's room. All was well with the world.

The mills of the Lord may have been grinding slowly and they may have been grinding exceedingly fine, but I wasn't planning to use their product in my coffee machine.

50

One grim anonymous evening I was stroking the cat and what was left of my ego when the phones rang. It was Ratso. 8:15 P.M.

"Sherlock," he said, "it might be a good idea if you got out a little more. Why don't we meet at Big Wong? Say about eight-forty-five."

"Yeah," I said. "Okay."

Half an hour later we were feeling as snug as two snowpeas in a pod, ordering pork lo mein, soy-sauce chicken, roast duck, and bok choy along with hot pepper sauce, duck sauce, ginger sauce, and mustard sauce. For years Big Wong's had been a mainstay for Ratso and me. It was located about halfway up Mott Street in the heart of Chinatown. We'd been there so often that, though we didn't know most of their names, the waiters were like old friends to us.

We discussed various things. Ratso's screenplay was nearing completion. My Broadway show was still on track for the fall. Ratso's job at the magazine was going along. Life was going along. Both were having some circulation problems.

We discussed women. "There's nothing wrong with any woman that a hand grenade or a Quaalude can't straighten out," said Ratso. I thought of how women sometimes came into our lives and left again like sleek nameless little jets equipped with heat-seeking missiles and all the latest feminine radar, landing on the decks of a creaky and battle-scarred old aircraft carrier alone in the middle of a deep and troubled sea. Sometimes the decks were clear enough for shuffleboard. Was the war over yet?

"This goddamn pork lo mein is great," said Ratso.

"Killer bee," I agreed.

"You know," he said, "it's hard to believe that an old pal could, in reality, be a psycho killer. I mean, we've known McGovern . . ."

"I don't believe it."

"Come off it, Sherlock. You're letting your reputation lead you down the garden path. This is one time the cops are right and you are wrong, I'm sorry to say."

"Then don't say it. Just pass the soy-sauce chicken." Neither of us said anything for a while. The waiters poured more hot tea into our glasses and carried hot trays of food over the heads of the customers shouting all the while at the other waiters to get out of their way. The chopsticks were clicking but very little else was.

"Pass the doppelgänger lo mein, will you?" asked Ratso.

"That's cute, pal." I signaled the waiter to drop the hatchet and a few minutes later he brought the check over.

"Of course McGovern killed those people," said Ratso. "He just had us going with all that ghost shit. Sort of like Son of Sam saying that his dog told him what to do. Of course there wasn't a ghost."

Ratso performed a rather complex financial transaction involving myself, the waiter, and the guy at the cash register, which resulted in my getting screwed out of about seven dollars. It was no big deal. Three cigars.

As we left Big Wong's and walked up Mott Street to Canal, Ratso was still mumbling to himself.

"There never was any fucking ghost," he said.

"Oh, but my dear Ratso," I said, "there was a ghost."

There was also an ugly picture coming together in my attic. As we walked, some of the dust was coming off it. It was sort of an abstract work, and each time I tried to look at it, it looked like something quite different.

It was part mouse and part Japanese fishing boat. No, it

wasn't a mouse. It was a weasel hiding behind a vase of flowers. There was also a mirror in the picture somewhere with a distorted face in it. It was a spectral, almost diabolical face, a witch or a demon to the superstitious eye. If I could just get out the old screwdriver and adjust the focus a little bit . . .

That night it rained like a bitch with a charge account. It let up a little around midnight, and I was feeling pretty restless so I left the cat in charge and legged it a few blocks over to the Ear. My shoulder wanted to see the place again.

"Let's get drunk and be somebody, Martin," I said. "There's no poetry reading tonight, is there?"

"Not on your life," he said.

"Good." I started with Bloody Wetbacks and Martin went a few rounds with me. The first shot of Cuervo Gold cut my throat like a bowie knife and I chased it quickly with tomato juice and a chomp of lime. Round two went better for me, and I was also looking pretty good in rounds three and four. Martin was starting to neglect his customers and some of them were yelling for service. My head was starting to feel pretty good. Kind of like a pink balloon that had gotten away from somebody at the county fair.

I thought of Nina Kong all decked out as a man in her coat and tie, leather pants, and tough guy lid. Getting dumped by Frank Worthington for another guy really twisted her head around, she'd said. I remembered the carved statues in the jungles of Borneo that the natives had worshipped and called "hantus" or ghosts. The hantus all had their heads twisted around backward.

I thought of Cynthia getting out of the shower and into my arms. Maybe she was wearing the little housecoat, maybe she wasn't. If she was, I had ways to make those parrots talk.

I thought of Gunner. I hadn't called her in weeks. The only hockey action she was likely to see this season might be a power play by me. Give her a couple of good body checks. Might slip one in her net if she wasn't careful.

I thought of Pete Myers, The Weasel, McGovern. I thought of myself. I looked at myself in the bar mirror, trying to keep my balance on the stool. I knew I wasn't as stupid as I looked. No one was. I let my eyes go out of focus so they could see what they wanted to see.

There were red lights blinking at me from the bar. It was the red neon bar sign that hung high above the sidewalk out in front of the place. It was reflecting on the rain-wet sidewalk and throwing double images at me through the mirror on the bar. And it was flashing the words EAR . . . BAR . . . EAR . . . BAR . . . EAR . . . BAR . . . right through my tequila-ized brain and out the other side. Suddenly I was sober as a judge. A warm wave rolled over me and I might even have smiled. I had it. I knew who the killer was.

Now if I could get someone other than the cat to believe me.

51

I was holding a postcard from Florida that the postman had just brought. It showed a beautiful girl in a little blue bikini walking along a sunny, sandy beach. The girl had a very nice bucket and it wasn't the kind you hold in your hand. Maybe if you knew her pretty well . . .

On the back of the postcard was a message from Cynthia. It read: "Wish you were here. It's beautiful. Thanks for helping me through a hard time. Love, Cynthia. P.S. Coming home Tuesday night. Arriving at ten o'clock at La Guardia on Air Florida. I'm not an easy pickup but why not give it a try?"

Nina had called earlier that morning. She had finished working on the video and was wondering if I'd like to get together with her. Rambam called and wanted to know if I wished to go shooting with him. He didn't say shooting what and I didn't ask. My old friend Ted Mann called from California. He'd been in Hollywood for six months, writing movies to amuse Americans, and he was coming back this week. Wanted to go out and burp in the Indian restaurant where they had the sitar player. One of the things I could do was say the phrase "I like Indian restaurants" in one belch. Ted said for me to round up McGovern and Boris and some of the boys.

"Might be a little difficult to get McGovern," I told him.

"Why?" asked Ted.

"He's on a vacation," I said.

"When's he coming back?" asked Ted.

"He's on a long vacation. We'll have to go to Indian restaurants without him for a while."

No point in telling Ted yet. He'd find out soon enough. Everybody in New York except for him and the sitar player knew about McGovern already. And sometimes I wasn't so sure about the sitar player. He had a kind of smarmy, knowing look about him on occasion.

Brennan called and wanted to meet at the Monkey's Paw. Ratso called and wanted to meet at Big Wong's for lunch. Boris called and wanted to unload five pounds of caviar on me for a very reasonable price. Pete Myers finally called to express his sympathy about McGovern.

"Bit of hard luck, old man," he said.

"Yeah."

Even Dr. Bock's office had called. The large secretary wanted to know why I hadn't paid the large bill.

It never fails. You're always in demand when you want to be alone.

I wound up spending the afternoon with the cat. There wasn't any rain so I couldn't watch it. The cat chased a few cockroaches and I chased my tail around the room waiting for Cynthia to get back the following night.

Maybe I truly missed McGovern. Maybe I was outraged at what I knew to be a thorough miscarriage of justice. Or maybe Ratso was right and my ego was just a little bruised from having Fox and Cooperman show me up so badly. Whatever it was, I wasn't quite through yet. I had one more card to play.

The monkey wasn't dead and the show wasn't over.

By 9:45 Tuesday night, Ratso and I were standing at the Air Florida baggage carousel at La Guardia Airport. He was wearing his coonskin cap without the tail and a black leather coat that was loaded to the gills with nonfunctional buckles and snaps.

"Don't fall asleep," I said. "Somebody might mistake you

for their nice Italian luggage. You could wake up at the Hotel Pierre."

"I could do worse," he said.

We watched the carousel going round and round. It was completely empty except for a frilly, bright-red hatbox with a pink sash that looked like something Miss Kitty might carry in *Gunsmoke*. We watched it go around about twenty times.

"What comes around goes around," said Ratso.

A frail, androgynous-looking young man came by, picked up the hatbox, and stepped primly away with it.

"Not always," I said. "Life's full of little surprises. Sometimes God throws you a slider."

I turned around and saw Cynthia coming down the walkway toward us. She was a vision and a half. Some girls shouldn't be allowed to go to Florida. I would always be a sucker for a suntan on a beautiful woman. I took a deep breath in spite of myself.

I thought of somebody else I'd gone to meet at an airport once. She was coming back from Mexico and I was coming back from Mars. The girl was different of course. The times were different—it had been almost eight years ago. The airport had been in Los Angeles. Good old LAX.

The only things that were the same were the suntan and, I suppose, my heart.

"Oh, guys," she said, "what a sweet reception committee."

"After what you've been through," said Ratso, "we couldn't do less."

"You look great, Cynthia," I said.

Ten minutes later we had the luggage stowed in the trunk and the three of us, with Cynthia in the middle, were rolling out of La Guardia in a Checker. "Forty-two Jane Street," Cynthia told the driver, "in the Village." We settled back for the ride.

We sped down the Grand Central Parkway to the Brooklyn-Queens Expressway, and when the Williamsburg Bridge, which would take us into the city, came into sight, I took a ragged piece of paper from the pocket of my coat. It was the napkin from the Carnegie Delicatessen.

"Have a look at this," I said.

"Jesus," said Ratso, "not the old Carnegie Delicatessen Napkin Trick again."

"He makes a goood sandwich?" asked Cynthia. She laughed.

"Best pastrami in the city," I said. "Now I'd like to call your attention to the symbols on this napkin." I showed them to Cynthia. I pointed out the first three initials:

C.———N.———M.

"This first is from the notes made by Frank Worthington's psychiatrist. It's my little 'flow chart' and it shows the sequence of Worthington's relationships for what it's worth.

"Directly below we find another grouping of initials that an old girlfriend of Worthington's, Nina Kong, considered to be a more correct sequence. They are as follows:"

N.———C.———M.

I underlined the letters with my finger.

"Now the Rosetta Stone, it ain't. But it did fool us for a while. You see, it doesn't really matter which version is the correct one. The point is that we always assumed the 'C.' stood for 'Campbell' as in 'Barry Campbell.' But what if, just for the hell of it, we say that the 'C.' stands for 'Cynthia,' as in 'Cynthia Floyd.' What if we say that you were once sadly, passionately, hopelessly, in love with Frank Worthington? I think you were. I think you were more than just in love with Frank Worthington. I think you wanted to *be* Frank Worthington."

"What are you saying?" asked Cynthia.

"I'm saying I know you Sam Cooke'd him, baby," I said.

"What is that supposed to mean?" she sniffed.

"You can look it up when you get home," I said. I reached inside my hunting vest and pulled out a small parcel wrapped in an old page from the *Daily News*. I handed it to Cynthia. "I got you a little present," I said. "Go ahead—open it."

She put the package in her lap and tore off the newspaper

wrapping. The three of us stared down at a frayed and fragile, worn and withered pink rose.

"I think it belongs to you," I said. "Kept it in the refrigerator for you." Ratso looked at me, but Cynthia kept her eyes on the rose.

"Now cross-dressing and dressing identically can be a fun thing for a girl to do with her fella," I said. "But it gets to be a drag when the clothes start to make the man. Or the woman. And I do mean a drag.

"Watching her lover slowly evolve into a homosexual right before her eyes can't be much fun for a girl. It could even twist a girl's head around. But you carried the torch and you kept carrying it until that eternal flame burned your mind.

"Then one morning you walked down the hall and you saw the flowers that Barry Campbell, another man, had sent to Worthington on his birthday. The heat became too intense.

"You went to the *Daily News* as McGovern's girlfriend picking up some notes for him that he'd supposedly left at his desk. You typed your own little note at his typewriter. You returned home later, had a farewell drink with Frank, dispatched him to the happy homosexual hunting ground, left the card, took one flower, planted the receipt, and hid the gun in McGovern's apartment. Later you sent the flower to me with another note you typed on McGovern's typewriter. Are you with me so far?"

Cynthia sat there like an autistic child but she had something in her eye and it wasn't the sort of thing that was ever going to be removed by a nice gentleman's handkerchief.

"Darlene Rigby was a problem," I said. "She'd inadvertently seen one thing she shouldn't have in her short life. The thing she saw was you and Frank Worthington together, possibly in your 'twin' getups. She was dying to tell me. But I made the mistake of mentioning it to you. Well, like it says on the wall above the bar at the Monkey's Paw, 'Loose lips sink ships.' Only you fixed it so that Darlene Rigby's whole goddamn harbor sank.

"I doubt if McGovern was onto you, but he did see a ghost. And the ghost was one of the things that drove him to turn himself in. You were the ghost, Cynthia—dressed as Frank Worthington. Just like the old days, right?

"Then, of course, you told the truth to the cops about overhearing McGovern's vague threats as he talked in his sleep. You couldn't tell a lie. But it gave you something to think about, and you used it that same night when you murdered Adrian. I congratulate you. It was very fast thinking and it was clever as all hell. Even more clever than using Worthington's voice on his old answering machine to scare the shit out of me and Ratso.

"You poisoned Adrian's Perrier, or was it the cocaine? The point is rather moot but, out of curiosity, which was it?"

Cynthia said nothing, but her eyes could have whipped up on somebody in the dart contest at the local pub.

"It doesn't matter," I said. "Say you cut Adrian's cocaine with something stronger than the Ajax she normally used. You came back later to check your handiwork. Now here is the clever part. I didn't get it myself until a couple of nights ago when I saw how the burned-out neon in a sign could change the word BAR to the word EAR. Anyway, as I was saying, you came back to check your handiwork and you saw that Adrian, in her death throes, had managed to write something in cocaine on the coffee table before she cashed in her chips. She'd written the word 'Cynthia.' The name of her killer.

"In a flash of diabolical brilliance, you, Cynthia, found a straw and snorted the little tail of the letter 'y' in Cynthia, thereby changing the 'y' to a 'u.' Then you Hoovered the 'hia' and that left only the word 'cunt' which would lead straight to McGovern once you told the cops what you'd heard him say earlier that night. The whole snorting operation must have given you quite a bit of satisfaction. Not to mention a little buzz.

"You killed two birds and got stoned. You snuffed Adrian who you thought was beginning to lamp you for what you were, and you put the final twist into the noose you knew would hang McGovern. But it won't, Cynthia. It'll allow me, instead, to tie up this whole unpleasant affair in a sailor's knot and hand it over to the police. I'm sure that Fox and Cooperman will be grateful for justice having been done, aren't you, Ratso?"

"Jesus," said Ratso in a low voice.

Cynthia was laughing now. But her laughter sounded so canned you could almost taste the botulism breeding in it. Suddenly she stopped laughing. She spoke in a sweet, melodic voice. A little girl's voice.

"Perr-i-er," she said. "It was the Perr-i-er."

A high keening noise emitted from her lips. It was the kind of sound you could only pray would end up on the cutting-room floor of your nightmares. Like listening to a hundred Arab women mourning in your Walkman.

Cynthia's eyes had now turned backward into her head. What she saw there God only knows. And he wasn't even clueing Moses.

I leaned forward and rapped on the partition of the cab.

"The lady looks sick, buddy," the driver said. "You want I should take her to a hospital?"

"Sixth Precinct, pal," I said.

I took a last long look at Cynthia as we were coming down Seventh Avenue. The pink rose still lay in her lap like a languid lover. But all the color had drained completely from her face.

You can lose a tan pretty fast in New York.

52

"Sir, your coat's on the floor," said the irritated young waitress in the little Greek coffee shop.

"Oh, thank you," said McGovern.

"Just like old times," I said. McGovern looked pretty good considering.

"I really feel like a chump," said McGovern. "She had such a nice, wholesome, innocent look about her. . . . When did you first suspect it was Cynthia?"

"Well, there were a number of little things that didn't quite ring true about her. Don't feel too bad about being a chump. I was taken in too. In a manner of speaking.

"When she came to visit me in the hospital, she was upset about your not trusting her more. Said it was partly her fault you were drinking and running from the cops and seeing ghosts in hallways. Now at that time, you still hadn't talked to her since you phoned her after finding Worthington's body. All you said to her was 'Do you believe in ghosts?' That sounded pretty weird in itself when she told me about it. But the point is, you never told her about seeing ghosts in the hallways. 'How could she have known that?' I asked myself. There were only two possibilities. Either she'd seen the ghost in the hallway herself. Or—something I could hardly believe —she was the ghost in the hallway. Of course, the latter possibility was correct.

"Then I asked myself: 'Who could have plausible access to your typewriter at the *Daily News?*'' Who could have slipped the gun into your apartment undetected?' Cynthia had the means to do both, but I still couldn't be sure. So I borrowed a page from my old friend Sherlock Holmes, and I sent out a few telegrams to get a rundown on Cynthia's background. Her mother has had bouts with severe schizophrenia for years. Cynthia's mother's turbulent emotional history makes Zelda Fitzgerald look only as if maybe her guppies had died.

"For the past seven years her mother's been living in the monstro-wig ward of a Des Plaines, Illinois, mental hospital. And she ain't gettin' out soon."

"Never knew a thing about it," said McGovern. "Cynthia never mentioned it."

"It's not exactly the kind of thing she'd want to put in her résumé, but it does account for a great deal of Cynthia's bizarre, distorted, murderous frame of mind. Cynthia came by it honestly at least. Her father left home when Cynthia was very young. I understand he did a little time on the rock, too."

"It's still hard to believe," said McGovern.

"Well, I hate to be the one to take the flyswatter to Tinker Bell, but the girl was clearly a psychopathic liar, McGovern. And that was one of her more endearing qualities. She bullshitted me the first time I talked to her about how Adrian dropped off some cocaine for her. Adrian was pathological about not giving curb service. Many dealers are. Adrian wouldn't have brought it to you if you were standing in her kitchen.

"Then, after she'd croaked Adrian, Cynthia wanted some time to get her thoughts together. I tried for about two hours that night to get into the building and Cynthia pretended she wasn't there. When I called she said she'd just gotten out of the shower. . . . She looked the part all right, but I remembered seeing my face in the bathroom mirror just before I went upstairs to find Adrian's body. Later I wondered, 'How could I have seen my face in the mirror? Why wasn't it steamed?'

"You know the rest from what you've read and written in

the papers. Cynthia'd waited a long time to take her revenge on Frank Worthington and you're a sweet, trusting kind of guy with a little bit of Gullible's Travels going for you. She just saw you coming and decided to hang her albatross around your neck."

"She damn near did, too," said McGovern.

"She felt she had to silence Darlene Rigby. She felt threatened by what she thought Adrian might have known, and being paranoid as all hell, she thought she had to silence her, too. No doubt about it. Cynthia was definitely cookin' on another planet, pal. I was probably next on her shopping list. We'll never know."

"I'll buy you lunch," said McGovern. "I owe it to you. I hear you had a hole in your shoulder big enough to drive a truck through."

"Maybe a Japanese import," I said.

McGovern paid the cashier and we took a stroll through the Village. It was a cold afternoon but it was clear and sunny and we passed a pretty thing or two walking down Hudson.

We were almost to Jane Street when McGovern pulled up short at 634 Hudson. He pointed out a brand-new awning that read: MYERS OF KESWICK.

"I'll be damned," I said. "Pete Myers did it."

"The place is a hit," said McGovern. "I come in here all the time. Pete's a very decent chap and the pork pies are the best in town."

"They're also about the only ones in town," I said, as we walked into the place. I had to admit the assortment of steak and kidney pies, Irish sausages, pork pies, and curried beef looked great even if you weren't British.

Pete was behind the counter. He came out and shook hands with us. "Congratulations, Myers," I said.

"And congratulations to you," he said. "You've beaten Scotland Yard again, Mr. Holmes." He laughed. He still had the same laugh. "Can I help you lads?" he said.

"Yeah," I said, "I'll have a British Knish."

"Would you believe," said Myers, "out of everything I make here, that was the only product that didn't sell."

"Too bad," I said. "Seemed like a natural." We bought a few pork pies from Myers, promised to be back again soon, and left the place.

"You see," said McGovern, "Myers is a straight arrow after all."

"Don't wish that on anyone, McGovern," I said. "I think it's important for all of us to explore our bisexual feelings."

"We don't have to do it right now, do we?" asked McGovern. The question did not dignify an answer so I didn't give it one. Instead, I looked back at the sign on the awning.

"Myers of Keswick," I said. "That's the place in England that all the poets are from, isn't it?"

"That's right," said McGovern. "I didn't know you knew that."

"Oh, I know a lot of things, McGovern."

"Do you know that the *w* in *Keswick* is silent?"

I was silent myself for a moment. Then I took out a cigar and fired it up. "Goddamn Brits," I said.

When we reached the old windmill across from his apartment, McGovern shook his head. "Man, I'll tell you," he said. "That cocaine on the coffee table was a stroke of brilliance on your part."

"It wasn't too shabby on Cynthia's part, either."

"I still can't believe that Cynthia was capable of doing all that she did."

"Oh, it's not so hard to believe," I said. "Just look up into the dark twisted limbs of that gnarly old family tree, pal. Blood will tell, McGovern. Blood will tell."

"That's comforting," said McGovern. He stood hesitating at the door of his building. "You know," he said, "I'm almost afraid to go inside."

"If you see another ghost in there, you're in trouble, pal," I said.

53

It was a Tuesday evening or maybe it was a Thursday. It had been two weeks since we'd picked Cynthia up at the airport and nothing much was happening. The newspapers were already back to covering hit-run incidents, subway muggings, and child abuse. The usual stuff.

Ratso, the cat, and I had been just sitting around the loft looking at each other like three guests in a Roach Motel. I wandered over to the kitchen, picked up a bottle of Irish whiskey, and poured a long shot into the old bull horn. They say God created whiskey to keep the Irish from taking over the world. Maybe he created black-and-white T.V. to keep Ratso from taking over my couch. At any rate, Ratso was leaving.

"Wickedly clever. My hat's really off to you for solving this one. I never thought you would, to tell you the truth."

"It's all in the wrist," I said.

"I'll bet the cops never even thanked you."

"Well, let's just say that all the publicity over the past two weeks hasn't exactly been brick and mortar to my relationship with Detective Sergeants Fox and Cooperman."

"They'll get over it," said Ratso. "Look, Sherlock, I want you to take care of yourself. Stay away from The Weasel and his weasel dust. I know you're very vulnerable when you're between cases. I'll call you tomorrow."

"Thanks, Rats," I said. I let Ratso out, fed the cat, and sat back down at my desk waiting for the worm of happiness to turn my way. There are worse things in this world than being lonely, but I didn't ever want to find out what they were. I was used to lonely. Lonely fit me like an old hunting vest. I would wear it in good health.

I thought of McGovern. He was probably down at Costello's now, making up for a little lost time. Tomorrow morning Ratso would be back in his office taking meetings, goosing the secretary, going about the business of being an editor.

Calling Nina Kong wasn't in the cards. Three days before, I'd run into her, quite inadvertently, in the hallway of my building. I was taking out the trash and she was coming down from Winnie Katz's experimental dance class.

You can't win 'em all.

54

I got up one morning several weeks later feeling rested and optimistic about what the future might bring. The events of the past few months were well behind me. Cynthia was in some prison psycho ward where she belonged, all ghosts and doppelgängers had been banished, and my shoulder was about back to normal. I could shrug again.

I fed the cat, made some coffee, poured a cup, and stood at the kitchen window of the loft watching one of nature's greatest wonders, New York sunshine. I took out a handsome-looking, fresh cigar and was just starting to light it when the phones rang. I walked back to my desk where the phones were and noted it was 10:17 A.M. I lit the cigar. Never answer phones too quickly. Somebody might think you need work.

I took a puff or two on the cigar. The phones kept ringing. Being left-handed, I'd always had a little penchant for the phone on the left, but now I reached across and picked up the blower on the right. Thought I might diversify. Change my luck. Try something new.

"Start talkin'," I said.

The voice I heard was strange and disembodied, yet faintly, and frighteningly, familiar.

"This is Frank Worthington," it said.

There was the sound of silence on the line and it wasn't the one by Simon and Garfunkel. Then I heard muffled laughter. It sounded like a squirrel or a rat. I couldn't be sure but I leaned toward the rat.

"Very cute, Ratso," I said.

"It's heartening to see you haven't lost your powers of perception, Sherlock," he said.

"Oh, it was very goddamn elementary, my dear Ratso," I said. "You bootlegged that tape from my loft."

"Yeah, but how can you be so sure it was me?" Ratso shouted indignantly.

"Dead man's shoes," I said.

A Case of
Lone Star

ACKNOWLEDGMENTS

The author would like to thank the following people for their help and encouragement: Tom Friedman, Earl Buckelew, Dylan Ferrero, Dr. Jay Wise, and Larry "Ratso" Sloman; Esther "Lobster" Newberg at ICM; James Landis, Jane Meara, and Lori Ames at Beech Tree Books; and Steve Rambam, technical adviser.

When Irish hearts are happy,
All the world seems bright and gay,
And when Irish eyes are smiling,
Sure they steal your heart away.

For Tom Baker
1940–1982

1

I opened the window and reached for the puppet head on top of the refrigerator. That was where I always kept it. It was once a little Negro puppet that I'd bought at a flea market on Canal Street. Now it was an indispensable part of my life. I had removed the head of the puppet, wedged the key to the front door of the building in its mouth, and attached a colorful, homemade parachute to the whole operation. The front facade of 199B Vandam appeared for all the world to be nothing but an abandoned, gray, graffiti-strewn warehouse, which, in fact, it had once been before somebody got clever and converted the whole building into loft space for people like myself and like Winnie Katz, who ran a lesbian dance class in her studio one floor above me. I listened to the rhythmic thuddings of Winnie's girls starting up over my head, and then I remembered Downtown Judy had been waiting on the sidewalk below. I looked down and she was still there. Getting a little colder maybe, but still there. I threw down the puppet head and closed the window.

It was Thanksgiving in New York, and about the only thing I was thankful for was that I didn't live in New Jersey.

My spacious, wind-swept loft was cold as hell. Maybe colder. It depended on what season it was in hell.

The cat had been hunkered down next to the coffee percolator most of the afternoon. It was now almost midnight. I was looking forward to doing a little horizontal mambo with Downtown Judy.

There was Downtown Judy and there was Uptown Judy, and neither knew the other one existed. I liked to keep it that way.

The day had been a typical gray blurry Thursday with damn little going on to get excited about. Earlier that afternoon I'd gotten into an ugly altercation at a vegetarian restaurant on Seventh Avenue over whether the smoke from my cigar was harmful to the patrons eating their bean curds.

That was the high point of the day.

Downtown Judy and I hadn't been in bed long when the phone rang. It cut through the two of us like a shrimping knife. I turned in the general direction of the sound, reached across the darkness, and collared the blower in my left hand.

"Start talkin'," I said.

"Yeah. Hey, man, this is Cleve at the Lone Star." Cleve was the manager of the club and a friend of mine. He'd started out as a road manager with my band.

"What is it, pal?" I asked. "I'm right in the middle of someone."

"I've got a problem over here," said Cleve.

"What is it? You run out of tube socks for the gift shop?"

"It's a little more serious than that," said Cleve. "It's Larry Barkin." Larry Barkin was an old acquaintance of mine, a good-looking prima donna of a country star I'd known in Nashville back before both of us were nothing. In the past few years he'd sold a lot of records to a lot of lonely housewives. He was currently appearing with his two brothers, Randy and Jim, at the Lone Star. Larry Barkin and the Barkin Brothers.

"What's the matter?" I asked. "He won't go on for the second show?"

"He won't ever go on again, man," said Cleve. "He's dead."

2

I ankled it over to Hudson Street and nailed a Checker right off the bat, which was lucky because I was beginning to feel like the inside of a Dreamsicle. Being in a warm Checker cab in the New York wintertime is like being back in the womb, even if the womb is hurtling across Fourteenth Street at fifty miles an hour. I wouldn't say that it provided an opportunity to meditate, but if you tried you could almost think.

That's what I was trying to do, but it wasn't really working out. Ever since I'd plucked a beautiful young victim from her would-be mugger at an all-night cash machine in the Village my life as a simple, broken-hearted country singer was over. COUNTRY SINGER PLUCKS VICTIM FROM MUGGER, the headline read at the time. Then with several fortuitous forays into crime-solving in the Village, I'd become a hero to my friends and family. With the help of my friend McGovern, a reporter for the *Daily News*, I'd become good copy. And, with all of this, I'd become a nuisance to the cops of the Sixth Precinct. You can't please everybody.

It was two-thirty in the morning when the cab jerked to a halt at the corner of Fifth Avenue and Thirteenth Street. The Lone Star Cafe. At one time or another, everyone from the Rolling Stones to the Blues Brothers had jammed there. To-night was a different kind of jam. I paid the cabbie and headed for the revolving door in the front of the place. Cleve was standing there looking fairly cadaverous himself.

"Fox and Cooperman here yet?" I asked. They were two

detectives who worked out of the Sixth Precinct, and they liked to try to work me over every chance they got. They didn't like country-singers-turned-amateur-detectives. Or anybody else.

Cleve shook his head and led me up the back stairs of the Lone Star past the balcony and to the third floor, where the dressing rooms were.

"Let's make it fast, pal," I told him as he unlocked the door to the third floor. "This may be the Village, but I don't want to have two dicks leaning on me if I can help it."

We walked down the narrow hallway of the third floor past walls that were strewn with graffiti—the names of musicians and bands who had played the Lone Star in the past. Some of them were famous now, some of them were dead, and some of them were both. Like Larry Barkin.

Cleve unlocked the door to Barkin's dressing room. I still didn't like dressing rooms. Dressing rooms, amplifiers, booking agents, fans, groupies, coke dealers, bass players from L.A.—it was enough to make an insurance salesman out of anybody. I'd seen that dressing room when every inch of the floor was soaked in beer and every tabletop was strewn with cocaine. No joy actually. No joy at all.

There wasn't a hell of a lot of joy in the place right now, come to think of it.

Larry Barkin had been an old friend of mine. Old friends are ones you may not really like but you're stuck with because you're old friends. You can pick your friends and you can pick your nose, but you can't wipe your friends off on your saddle.

Whether I'd liked Larry Barkin or not was apparently rather a moot point. He was slumped over a folding chair in the far right corner of the room.

It was a good thing he wouldn't be needing his Gibson guitar anymore because somebody had evidently bashed in the back of his skull with it. The broken guitar was lying on the floor beside the chair. Rusty blood was already doing a nice job of congealing in his straw-blond blow-dried hair. A yellow cowboy shirt with silver sequins picked up light like a miniature Milky Way. Face was a little off-color—California suntan on a sluggish freeway to chartreuse.

Boots by Larry Mahan. Had a pair myself but not quite as nice. "What are those?" I asked. "Brontosaurus foreskin?" Cleve said nothing. He was looking at the little pink cowboy scarf around Barkin's neck. Whoever had tied it for him had been a trifle overzealous with the job—about seven notches worth.

"Shit," said Cleve.

"You can say that again," I said. "Bashed with his own guitar and then strangled with his own bandanna. Charming."

Cleve fidgeted nervously. Death will do that to you. It's almost as bad as going onstage.

"Who the hell could've done something like this?" asked Cleve. My eyes lingered for a moment on Barkin's sweet and swollen face.

"Somebody who didn't like his last record," I said.

I hauled my old snot rag out of my hip pocket and reached across to the breast pocket of Barkin's yellow-fringed cowboy shirt. Something green was sticking up out of the pocket, and it wasn't Kermit the Frog. I took a quick glance at it and I put it right back the way I had found it, just peeping out at me over the top of the pocket. It was a two-dollar bill.

"Curious," I said.

"What do you make of it?" asked Cleve. I shrugged.

"Two rides on the subway," I said.

3 From Cleve I was able to obtain a fairly complete list of the people who'd been in the dressing room during the evening. Of the five people he mentioned, one was a beautiful blond British photographer, one was a mysterious bald-headed lawyer who'd been dispensing cocaine, and three were close, personal friends of mine. With friends like these, I thought, who needed murder suspects?

And then, for all I knew, Randy and Jim could've croaked their more celebrated sibling themselves. These country music family acts had been known to get a little biblical at times. Cain had set the precedent some years back when he'd gone a step beyond mere sibling rivalry and lunched his brother. If this was what had occurred, it was going to make for fairly deep waters, and not the kind that were going to part very easily.

These were the thoughts going through my head when the large, surly form of Detective Sergeant Mort Cooperman blackened the doorway behind me. The snakelike figure of Detective Sergeant Buddy Fox lurked a few steps behind him like an unhealthy shadow. Cooperman's little eyes roamed the little room. They took in the corpse and Cleve and came to a bumpy landing when they reached me.

"Oh, Christ," he said, "it's another goddamn case of déjà vu!"

"I don't speak Italian," I said.

* * *

I never found talking to cops all that amusing. I told them the little I knew, but clearly I was the wrong person in the wrong place at the wrong time, and they grilled me like a blackened redfish. It made for an unpleasant nightcap to an unpleasant evening.

It was a quarter after who-gives-a-damn when the cabbie dropped me off at the corner of Hudson Street and Vandam. I walked the final couple of blocks to no. 199B.

I took the freight elevator with the one exposed light bulb up to the fourth floor, unlocked the door to my loft, found a cigar and the old bull's horn that I sometimes used for a shot glass. Then I found a handy bottle, poured it into the bull's horn, and discharged it into my mouth like Ernest Hemingway's shotgun. I didn't know if old Ernest had had a cat or a telephone, but I did, and both of them were complaining to me. I walked over and picked up the cat and the blower. The cat hated to be picked up but the blower didn't seem to mind. It said, "Hi. Where have you been? I've been calling for ages."

It was Uptown Judy. I looked around into the bedroom sort of as an afterthought and noticed that Downtown Judy had apparently vacated the premises. My heart did not skip a beat.

"I've been over at the Lone Star," I said.

"You're kidding," she shrilled in my ear. "That's where I'm calling from, baby."

I was still holding the bull's horn but I'd deposited the cat on top of the desk.

"That's Mr. Baby, to you," I said.

It was agreed that Uptown Judy would come over to the loft. I hung up the phone, poured another shot, and lit the cigar. Always keeping it well above the flame. My mind was not on the two Judys, however. It was on the two-dollar bill.

Even with inflation, Larry Barkin had gotten more than he'd bargained for.

4

When I woke Friday morning Uptown Judy was already uptown. Nothing too earth-shattering about that. Some people worked for a living. I jumped into the rainroom and took a shower, then stood around in my purple bathrobe slurping a hot cup of coffee, smoking my first cigar of the day, and watching the garbage trucks moving in slow motion through the freezing drizzle that was slanting down onto the world below. The old rusty fire escapes were still there across the street. They weren't much prettier than the garbage trucks but they were quieter. Vandam Street was a major garbage-truck staging area for the city. Nonetheless, the street was still filthy as hell. That was probably because it was where the garbage trucks came from and not where they went to. I thought about this almost halfway through my second cup of coffee, but I wasn't a city planner and I wasn't a philosopher and I didn't really give a damn anyway. Fortunately, I didn't have to put on a conservative tie and a three-piece suit and drink a little Brim with a mean-minded, vacuous wife and head out for the gray, spirit-grinding office. All I had to do was get dressed and feed the cat. Not a bad life.

I got dressed and fed the cat.

I sat down at my desk and tried to decide what to do next. It was still only ten o'clock in the morning. Whether that was early or late depended on how you looked at it, and I preferred not to. I put my feet up on the desk, smoked my cigar, and winked at the cat, who had now joined me and was sitting about equidistant between the two red telephones that I always kept on my desk at stage left and stage right of my brain. They were both attached to the same line, and when they rang it seemed to enhance the importance of my calls.

The phones rang that Friday morning at 10:17 A.M. I know the precise time because of my custom of logging all incoming calls on my digital computer alarm clock that I keep on my desk. There was nothing alarming about it except for the cat, who was directly in the line of fire and jumped over the moon, the cow, and the fiddle, and my Statue of Liberty thermometer, which read forty-six degrees Fahrenheit inside the loft. The landlord was really on the ball. Great guy. Probably in Florida.

I picked up the blower and watched the cat settle into a hunkering-down position beside the coffee percolator. She was smarter than some people I knew.

"Hey, man, I was just going through the mail on my desk this morning and there's something here I think you ought to see." It was Cleve, and whatever it was I didn't want to see it.

"I saw enough last night, pal," I said.

"Come over here, man. Do it for ol' Cleve."

"Hang ol' Cleve from the green apple tree."

I was already in this thing up to my uvula, but if there was a way to get out of it I was sure as hell going to take it. One way was to stay away from the Lone Star. Draw a bye on the Five-Alarm Chili for a while. Country music these days had lost whatever appeal it had had for me. It was hard to believe I'd once been in the thick of it. I was now thinking more along the lines of working on a score for a Broadway musical. Something with class, dignity, intelligence. No steel guitars.

"Don't let me down, man," said Cleve with a whine in his voice like a blue-ball trucker topping a hill. "Just come over here one last time . . . All right. If you won't come over here, I'll bring the damn thing over to you now."

While I waited for Cleve, I paced restlessly back and forth

in the kitchen of the loft wishing I were as extinct as the saber-toothed tiger. I just didn't like this business. Give me a nice clean sordid affair to pry into. Murder cases could be hazardous to your health. And it was bad to be cracking heads with Fox and Cooperman before the stiff had even cooled to room temperature. Very bad.

I went to the door and let Cleve in and listened to his grumbling for a while, and then he took a large manila envelope out of his briefcase and placed it on the desk in front of me. It was addressed to Mr. Larry Barkin, c/o The Lone Star Cafe, 61 Fifth Avenue, New York, New York.

"Note the date," said Cleve. "It was sent last Monday. It arrived in our office on Wednesday, the day before Barkin played the Lone Star. We just assumed it was fan mail, and I hadn't really looked at it until this morning."

Cleve pushed the envelope closer to me and I noticed his hands were trembling slightly. "What the hell is in it?" I asked. "Hate mail? IRS? Greetings from his long-lost ex-wife?"

"Better than that," said Cleve quietly. "Why don't you open it and see for yourself?"

I opened the envelope and extracted a colorful piece of sheet music. It was the old Hank Williams song "Hey, Good Lookin'." Cleve looked over my shoulder and together we read the lyrics:

Hey, hey good lookin', what cha got cookin'
How's about cookin' somethin' up with me.
Hey, sweet baby, don't you think maybe
We could find us a brand new recipe
I got a hot rod Ford and a two-dollar bill
And I know a spot right over the hill . . .

There was a sudden chill in the loft, and I felt pretty sure that it had nothing at all to do with wintertime in New York.

5 Cleve had taken his leave. I was taking a little power nap and trying not to dream. I was doing all right. I had succeeded in turning my mind into a small-town drive-in movie screen during the off-season. New York did not exist. It had been there for only a second, like a vaguely familiar bag lady passing quickly by the window of your cab in the rain.

The telephone by the bed seemed to be ringing, so I picked it up.

"Start talkin'," I said in a deep sandpaper voice that would've made Kenny Rogers sound like a castrato. I was in a fairly vicious mood. It was a case of power napus interruptus. I looked outside and it was damn near dark. Then a rather rodentlike voice started yapping at me from the phone. It was Ratso.

Ratso was flea market flamboyant. New York, New York. He was loyal, intelligent, and thrifty enough to make Scrooge McDuck jealous. He was the editor of *National Lampoon.* Ratso had been right there with me on the first few cases I'd worked on, and I'd almost come to think of him, in my weaker moments, as my American Dr. Watson. What went on in Ratso's mind I would not like to hazard a guess, but I liked him so I always gave him a little extra rope. Figured he'd either hang himself or start up a rope factory.

"Hey, man, how you doin'?" said Ratso.

"Could be worse," I said. "Could be snortin' Tide and drinkin' Aqua Velva."

"Yeah, well, did you see the papers today? You read what happened to Larry Barkin at the Lone Star last night?"

"I didn't need to read the papers, pal. I caught all the action live last night. Or rather dead last night." I filled Ratso in on the Hank Williams song and the two-dollar bill that I found on Barkin.

"Shit," said Ratso, "I must've come too early."

"Yeah," I said, "that's what Uptown Judy told me last night."

"Seriously, man, I can't believe somebody killed the guy. I saw the whole first set myself and the guy was great. So vibrant. So alive."

"Yeah, well he was a little stiff by the second set. Look, Ratso, did you notice any strange people hanging around the Lone Star last night during the first show?"

"You kiddin', man?" said Ratso. "This is New York."

"I know what it is," I said. "I still think you can help me. Maybe it was somebody who didn't look strange."

"That helps a lot," said Ratso.

"Look, meet me at the Monkey's Paw in an hour. Is that okay?"

"That's fine," said Ratso. "I just hope I can pick you out in the crowd."

"Bring your bird book and binoculars," I said and hung up. I walked over to the window and looked down at a dim and nearly deserted Vandam Street. Even the garbage trucks were gone. Tucked away in their little garage-apartments dreaming of coffee grinds and old typewriters somebody'd left out in the snow.

Friday night was the night most people thought they were supposed to have fun. Trouble was most people didn't know what fun was or how to have it, so things usually ended up pretty ugly.

Maybe Daddy'd taken everybody's T-bird away and they just didn't know it yet.

I put on my hat and coat, grabbed a few cigars for the road, and told the cat she was in charge while I was gone. Then I locked the door to the loft, legged it down four flights of stairs, and headed left on Vandam past Hudson to Seventh Avenue. It had gotten colder, if that was possible. The place looked like an excited penguin colony. Everybody was in a hurry but the winos. Newspapers were swirling around all over the sidewalks like somebody's old love letters to yesterday's world.

I smoked a cigar as I walked toward Sheridan Square and the Monkey's Paw, with my hands in my pockets to keep them at least lukewarm. If the Monkey's Paw had been a few blocks farther away I was going to need somebody to help me melt my cold, cold heart.

I thought very briefly about what the back of Larry Barkin's head had looked like the night before. Sort of like some half-rotten, hybrid garden vegetable. I found myself humming "Hey, Good Lookin' " as I crossed Seventh Avenue, but it seemed inappropriate so I forced myself to put a sock on it.

The Monkey's Paw was just across Seventh on Bedford Street, one of the few heterosexual bars in the area. It had always had pretensions about being a literary bar. I wasn't so sure of that. It was so cold that heterosexual was good enough for me.

Ratso was standing at the bar. He was wearing green leather pants and a red sweater with little hockey players weaving and checking all over it.

"Hi, Sherlock," he said.

6

The waitress pointed us to a table about the size of a skateboard. It had a nice view of the garbage cans piled up right outside on Bedford Street.

"Great table," Ratso said to the waitress.

"Yeah," I said, "it looks like the Last Supper table for Jesus and the Seven Dwarfs."

"Sorry," said the waitress cheerfully. She was about the sorriest thing I'd seen on ten toes.

The Monkey's Paw was always crowded with tourists on weekends. Intrepid travelers from distant lands like New Jersey. Young couples all the way from the Upper East Side. Like most Village residents I instinctively disliked these people. Half of them thought they were here for a big night in the city, and the other half thought they were slumming. I didn't like either half, but it doesn't cost anything to be nice.

"You want to move your chair, pal?" I asked a guy who was flapping his mustache to some broad about "what a dreadful season we're experiencing on Broadway" and blocking my way at the same time.

"Certainly," he sniffed.

"Yep," said Ratso in a loud voice as the waitress seated the two of us at the little table ridiculously close to the guy, "looks like the theater's really dead."

"Modulate your voice, will you," I said to Ratso. "This guy gets hostile and he'll beat us both to death with his cookie duster."

Ratso ordered a vodka and soda and I ordered a Prior Dark

with a shot of Old Grand-Dad to keep it company. The table was starting to get a little crowded, but if you live in New York you don't go out looking for elbow room. You just try to get your shot glass from your hand to your mouth. Sometimes it's harder than it looks.

"Hey," I said, "that's McGovern's drink you ordered." McGovern was half Irish and half Indian and worked on the national desk of the *Daily News*. He'd been eighty-sixed from the Monkey's Paw years ago for urinating on the leg of a patron.

Ratso smiled. "As long as it's not Elijah's drink," he said. Who Elijah was was hard to explain, except that I doubted if he worked for the *Daily News*.

"You know," said Ratso, "they say the lady that McGovern peed on has never been back here."

"Neither has McGovern," I said.

"Neither has Elijah," said Ratso.

"I'll drink to that," I said and we ordered another round. Things had cleared a little by now. The theater crowd, so to speak, had left, and I eased my chair back a little.

"This was Dylan Thomas's drink, you know. Drank eighteen straight shots of Old Grand-Dad down at the White Horse Tavern before he fell through the trapdoor into the downstairs bedroom."

"Okay," said Ratso, dismissing the subject, "how can I help?"

"You can stop me at seventeen," I said. I signaled the waitress for another shot. Ratso nursed his drink.

"You were there," I said, "in Larry Barkin's dressing room." Ratso nodded. "What did you see? Who did you see?" I had a pretty good idea from Cleve what the list of suspects looked like, but I wanted to hear it again from Ratso.

"Cast your mind back," I encouraged him.

"Certainly, Monsieur Poirot," he said. "There was a blonde. A photographer. Her name was Gunner."

"That's a funny name," I said.

"So's Kinky," said Ratso.

"Go on," I said.

"There was a bald-headed lawyer passing out cocaine to everybody—"

"That description could fit just about everyone I know."

"Now listen to this," said Ratso. "Your old pal Chet Flippo was there. Very chummy with Barkin. Very chummy. And of course your rapierlike memory bank will recall the title of Chet's latest book. . . ."

Chet was an old friend of mine from Texas who had written a book recently that had turned Nashville and country music lovers in general into at least three armed camps. One group loved it. One group hated it. One group thought it was a little ho-hum. I hadn't read the book yet myself but I knew the title: *Your Cheatin' Heart: A Biography of Hank Williams.*

"A bit obvious, wouldn't you think?"

"I'm just tellin' you who was there, Sherlock. You put it in your pipe and smoke it." I lit a cigar.

"There was also your friend Mike Simmons. He was playing Barkin's guitar, I think, trying to show him a song or something."

"I'll bet he was," I said. Simmons was one of the best country singers I'd ever heard, but he would take a drink. He was crazy, talented, and frustrated. Like everybody else in New York.

"Simmons was pretty bombed all right," said Ratso. "I was kind of worried he was going to break Barkin's guitar."

"Yeah," I said. I puffed on the cigar thoughtfully. I killed the shot and ordered another one. Ratso ordered another vodka and soda.

"Okay," I said, when the drinks arrived, "what've we got?"

"We've got," said Ratso, "the blond photographer, the bald-headed lawyer who was dispensing cocaine, Chet Flippo, and Mike Simmons."

"What about Bill Dick?" I asked.

"Bill Dick owns the club," said Ratso.

"My dear Ratso," I said, "I've worked with a great many

club owners, and I've found that they're capable of anything."

"Well, then," said Ratso, "we've got five suspects. It looks pretty easy."

"Right." I killed the shot and signaled the waitress to drop the hatchet.

"You're stopping at five Old Grand-Dads?" asked Ratso. "I'm quite disillusioned."

"I'm sure you are," I said as I paid the check and watched Ratso pretend to look for his money. "What's the matter, pal, you got fishhooks in your pockets?"

We walked outside.

"Well, thanks for a lovely evening," said Ratso. "I'm going home to spank my monkey."

"Fine," I said. "Let's keep in touch on this thing. It could turn fairly ugly."

As I walked home in the cold I thought the whole business over. Getting into a murder investigation was a little like getting into drugs or alcohol.

As my old friend Slim used to say back in Texas, "sometimes you gotta find what you like and let it kill you."

7

Early Saturday morning I was sawing away on a particularly peaceful Perma-Log when the phones rang. The voice came over the wire like a chain saw that had cut its teeth in Brooklyn.

"We can't have it. We just can't have it. Right or wrong, Kinkster?"

"Right, Bill," I said sleepily. It was Bill Dick, the owner of the Lone Star. He might've had a weak last name but he had a strong set of lungs. Maybe it was the hour.

I sat up in bed and looked first at the cat and then at the clock. The cat yawned. The clock said nine-thirty.

"What can't we have, Bill?" I asked. I eyed the coffee percolator in the kitchen like a long-lost lover.

"We can't have a maniac running loose around the Lone Star," he said.

"Where were you Thursday night, Bill?" I asked a bit too abruptly.

"I was sailing, for Christ's sake. Out in the goddamn boat. Got back last night. Never thought anything like this could happen. I like to sail. Get away from the rat race. Man's got a nice boat. Man likes to sail. Can't work all the time. Right or wrong, Kinkster?"

"Right, Bill," I said.

"Look," he said, "you helped make the Lone Star what it is, Kinkster. You performed here many times and you profited from those performances. The cops have been here. Been here several times. But they're lost at sea without a sail.

Will you take the wheel, Kinkster? Will you find who murdered Larry Barkin? Will you do it for the Lone Star?''

''Well, Jesus, Bill,'' I said, ''since you put it that way. I
guess I'll do it for God and country music.''

''That's the spirit,'' said Bill Dick. ''We'll get to the bottom
of this. Right or wrong, Kinkster?''

''Right, Bill,'' I said. I hung up. I put some coffee in the
percolator along with a bit of old eggshell for flavor, and
while I waited for it to perk I fired up a cigar.

''Home is the sailor,'' I said to the cat. ''Home from the
sea.'' I gave her some tuna for breakfast.

I didn't figure I owed God much. And I didn't think I owed
country music the time of day. I didn't even owe anything to
the Lone Star except maybe an old bar bill from way back
when. About all I owed was what I owed to McGovern, fifty
dollars, and since he would no doubt put the fifty dollars to
ill use, I was really doing him a favor by not paying him for a
while. Not that I didn't have the assets.

I was on my second cup of coffee and slightly past the
midway point of the cigar I'd lit after I'd talked to Bill Dick. I
didn't usually like to smoke a cigar past the midway point. I
liked to store them for a while in the wastebasket and fire up
the remaining portion at a later date. In the manner of a fine
wine, you had to let a half-smoked cigar age a bit. Had to let
it breathe. A lot of people didn't understand this, but I didn't
understand a lot of people.

I smoke as many as ten cigars a day and I expect to live
forever. Of course I don't inhale. I just blow the smoke at
small children, green plants, vegetarians, and anybody who
happens to be jogging by at the same time that I'm exhaling.

You have to work at it if you want to be a good smoker.
Especially today with all the nonsmoking world constantly
harassing you. It's enough to make you drink. I poured a
shot of Jameson Irish Whiskey into a third cup of coffee and I
sat down at my desk.

I thought of what Charles Lamb, the renowned British essayist, had said when someone asked him how he could smoke so many cigars and pipes. He said: "I toil after it, sir, as some men toil after virtue." Not bad, Chuck.

I placed a call to Sergeant Cooperman at the Sixth Precinct but he was out protecting the public. The desk sergeant said he'd get back to me. I called Mike Simmons.

"Hey, Mike," I said, "how about a little liquor drink for the heat?"

"The heat is right," said Simmons. "This Sergeant Cooperman character's been covering my ass like an Indian blanket."

"That's hardly the way to speak of New York's finest, Simmons," I reminded him.

"Where?" he asked.

"Where what?"

"The liquor drink for the heat."

"City Limits. Ten o'clock."

"See you there," he said.

I decided to take a litle power nap, but when I woke up it was almost eight o'clock. As luck would have it, I didn't dream. Or if I had dreamed, I didn't remember anything, which is almost as good. I jumped into the rainroom and took a shower. Sang a little Hank Williams medley. "Cold, Cold Heart," "Your Cheatin' Heart,"—Hank apparently had had a thing about hearts—and "I'll Never Get Out of This World Alive." The lyrics to the chorus of the last song went:

> *"No matter how I struggle and strive*
> *I'll never get out of this world alive."*

That seemed like a good place to stop. I dried off with a towel I had inadvertently taken from the Chelsea Hotel. It said YMCA on it.

They say Dylan Thomas died while he was staying at the Chelsea. Many places claim Homer's birth and many places claim Dylan Thomas's death. What does that tell us?

Nothing, I thought. I decided against shaving. Go for the Yes-sir You're-a-fart Look. Very in these days.

I spread the towel out on the cold, cold radiator to either dry or mildew as the case might be. John Lennon, Nina Simone, Abbie Hoffman, and Sid Vicious had also stayed at the Chelsea, and so had the guy who wrote the song "Tubby the Tuba." Quite a clientele.

I got dressed, threw on my old hunting vest, left the cat in charge, and split. I headed up Hudson and then snaked over toward Seventh Avenue. On Grove Street there was a young woman sitting on a wooden chair on the sidewalk playing a cello. The big cello case was open in front of her. It looked like a coffin for a large child. There were a few quarters and dimes and nickels in it and that was all. Chump change in anybody's league. I stood there in the cold and listened for a moment. She sounded pretty good, but what I knew about the cello you could put in a ukulele case and rattle it around a bit.

On the brick wall above her I noticed a bronze plaque. It was a bust of Thomas Paine, who'd died on this site in 1809 after being tortured on his deathbed by clergymen. On the sides of the plaque, slightly grimy but still readable, were two of Paine's credos: "The world is my country" and "To do good is my religion."

I gave the girl a five-dollar bill. I figured anyone who could play the cello in this weather deserved something. She nodded thanks to me. Kind of world-weary. Kind of sweet.

I headed over to City Limits, a rather funky country music bar in the heart of the Village, to meet Simmons. At Seventh Avenue I turned back to look at the girl, and she was playing the cello as if I were still standing in front of her. Never get to Carnegie Hall, I thought.

'Course, why would you want to go to Carnegie Hall when you could go to the Carnegie Delicatessen?

8

City Limits was the place you went when you'd had all the fun you could take at the Lone Star and it was still only two o'clock in the morning. When it was four o'clock in the morning and you'd had all the fun you could possibly stand at City Limits, you'd put your brain in a wheelchair and navigate over to the Zodiac, an after-hours bar that resembled what all the concentric circles of hell would look like if they were suddenly compressed into one large, dark, loud, rather tedious pancake. After having fun at the Zodiac, you'd walk out into the blinding sunlight and grinding traffic of Canal Street at 9:00 A.M. of a workaday morning and you'd know what it meant to wish you were dead. Fun was hard work in New York.

I nodded to Glen, the bouncer who worked the door at City Limits. Glen was a big guy with a long ponytail that nobody ever pulled except a little old lady from Idaho one night who thought it was her scarf.

"Is Mr. Simmons here?" I asked him.

"Not for long," he said ominously. He waved me in and I put the two bucks cover charge back in my pocket. Fifteen years dying slowly on the road so I could get into dumps like this without paying the cover. Us big celebrities had it made.

Simmons was standing at the bar. He was drinking Jack Daniel's on the rocks.

"Hey, man," he shouted at me, "now that you're in the black, I'll buy you a drink." It appeared as if he'd had a few already.

"Okay," I said. "I'll have a Lone Star beer for three dollars and fifty cents."

"Shit," he said, "you can do better than that."

"All right," I said, "give me a Chivas on the rocks with a little splash of New York tap water in it. Cuts the bite."

"Naw," said Simmons, "that's too complicated."

"Courvoisier," I said.

"Naw," said Simmons in a loud voice. "That's too sophisticated for this goddamn low-life dive." I looked over my shoulder and saw the large bartender wearing some kind of biker's vest, a cowboy hat, and a scowl.

"Give us a moment, pal," I said. He turned away in disgust.

"Simmons," I said, "this may look like a goddamn low-life dive to you, but actually, what these people are trying to do is re-create the ambience of the early country and western honky-tonk. Also," I said, "you might want to modulate your voice or they might try to re-create it on the bridge of your nose." He laughed.

"Give me a Jameson," I said.

"Naw," said Simmons, "that's too damn ethnic, man. You don't want a Jameson." I'd made the mistake of giving Simmons a cigar, and he was now gesturing with it and precariously waving the lighted end in front of the eyes of nearby patrons. I turned for a moment and watched the band on the little stage across the room. I recognized a few of the pickers. They were pretty good. They had talent. And talent was its own reward. It had to be. That was about all they were going to get playing three brutal sets for jaded strangers from the Upper West Side and people waiting for the Zodiac to open. But the band was playing and the people were dancing.

I saw that the drummer was a guy who'd played a few concert tours with me in the bleary past. He looked over at me, waved a stick, and shrugged, as if to say "Help! Get me out of here." He was a talented drummer. But most landlords I'd known didn't take talent when the rent came due. I needed a drink.

"Simmons," I said, "order me a drink or I'll kill you."

"Barkeep," Simmons shouted, "two double Black Jacks. Rocks. Walking now, make 'em fly."

The bartender, in a slow and surly fashion, brought two double Jack Daniel's over to us. Simmons was having trouble holding his glass, but he raised it now rather precariously in a toast. He clinked the bottom of it against the top of mine and said, "Never above you." Then he clinked the top of it against the bottom of mine. "Never below you," he said. Then he put his arm around my shoulder and slammed his glass dangerously against my glass and said, "Always by your side."

"Don't link our karma, pal," I said.

We both took a slug of the Jack.

I disengaged my shoulder from Simmons' arm and walked a little closer to the bandstand. The guitar player had reversed the strings on his guitar and was playing it left-handed. It wasn't unheard of. I'd seen it before. But it did make me think of something that had been nagging at me since I'd visited the late Larry Barkin in his dressing room at the Lone Star. I picked up a handful of peanuts from a barrel in the middle of the floor and walked back over to Simmons at the bar.

"Mike," I said, "you wouldn't be a southpaw, would you?"

"Who wants to know?" he said belligerently.

"Who the hell do you think wants to know?" I asked. "Who do you see standing here talking to you?"

"I see Spade Cooley," he said. Spade Cooley was a country singer who stomped his wife to death, served time in prison, and passed on painfully to hillbilly heaven.

The band had taken a break, and I went over and talked with them for a while. When I looked over at the bar for Simmons, I could see an altercation taking place. Simmons was struggling with a well-dressed woman. The big bartender had him around the neck, and Glen the bouncer was hurrying over in the direction of the trouble.

They wouldn't hurt Simmons inside the bar but I'd seen some of City Limits' Neanderthals work over rowdy patrons in the alley down the street from the club. I figured I'd meet them right outside the door and take Simmons off their big, remorseless, country music hands. Not that he didn't deserve it.

I stood out on Tenth Street in the cold and waited. The door to the place burst open and Simmons came flying out onto the sidewalk. Shaking with rage, he picked himself up and started back toward the club. I grabbed his arm but he managed to pry the door open, and with me holding on to him, he staggered a few steps back into the place. Glen and his ponytail started toward us, then stopped. Simmons roared over the noise and din of the bar.

"You'd throw Hank fucking Williams out of here!" he said.

9

I put Simmons in a cab and told the driver to take him to Marylou's on Ninth Street, where the atmosphere was friendlier. He would not go home, and I knew there was no way to make him. Home was a meaningless word in New York. Sometimes it was nowhere. Apparently it meant little to Simmons. Except for the fact that the cat was there, it didn't mean a hell of a lot to me either.

I had learned nothing from Simmons except that I shouldn't go back to City Limits with him again. I didn't even learn if he was left-handed.

I went to a pay phone across the street from Village Cigars and called Chet Flippo at The Writers' Room on Waverly. It was a quiet place he sometimes went to work on his current projects and to hide from the noise and disruption that was New York. I wondered if there could be anything else he was hiding from.

I had only five suspects to work on at the moment, though I might be narrowing or enlarging the field once I knew more. Ratso and Cleve were probably out of it. Ratso made a fairly adequate modern-day Watson and I couldn't really afford to lose him, and Cleve had been the one who'd gotten me involved in the Barkin affair to begin with. Bill Dick had been on his goddamn boat. Chet Flippo and Mike Simmons were both friends of mine, but when I thought about it, that didn't really put them in the clear. Where murder was concerned, you had to be a little more analytical about people than you would if you were merely sending out bar mitzvah invitations.

Then there was the bald-headed, cocaine-dispensing lawyer and the lovely limey shutterbug. Couldn't overlook them. But I was already getting an ugly feeling about this case.

I bought a couple of nice ropes at Village Cigars and walked briskly across Sheridan Square. In this weather you had to walk briskly. If you didn't, you might freeze, and some avant-garde SoHo artist might try to mount you in his gallery as an ice sculpture. You had to be careful crossing Sheridan Square in any season. Somebody might try just to mount you.

The High Five was a step down from the street and from a lot of other places, too. It was a jazz-oriented bar that took "seedy" to a whole other level. The High Five had a liberal sprinkling of interracial couples around for local color. Most of them appeared to be heterosexual, but you couldn't have everything. One of the nice things about the joint was that no matter who the hell you were, you never looked out of place.

Flippo was sitting at the bar when I got there. He looked at me with colorless eyes through steel-rimmed glasses. He did not look happy. "Sit down," he said.

I hadn't seen Chet Flippo in a long time. When I thought about it, maybe I'd never seen Chet Flippo. "Have a drink," he said. He looked harmless enough, but I'd been on the circuit long enough to know that harmless enough was always dangerous. Since 1982 I hadn't even trusted the Easter Bunny.

I ordered a shot of Irish whiskey and a Bass ale to keep it company on the mahogany. "Used to be a nice place," I said. "Charlie Parker and Edith Piaf used to hang out here." Flippo looked around a little at the squalor with disbelief in his eyes.

"That's what they say," I said. He sipped his draft beer nervously. "Cops talk to you, Chester?" I asked.

"Affirmative," he said, nodding his head sharply once.

"What'd they want to know? They ask you about your old parking tickets?"

"I told them I didn't drive," he said.

"Quite sensible," I said. Even A. J. Foyt took a hack in the city. "Okay, Chester," I said, "what happened Thursday night in Barkin's dressing room? Spit it, pal." I killed the shot and looked right at him.

"Barkin and I've known each other on and off for a long time," said Flippo. "I've reviewed a few of his shows for various magazines. I never liked his sugar-coated music and he never liked my acid-toned journalistic style, but we both had a grudging professional respect for each other's work."

"Okay," I said, "spare me everybody's résumé. Nut-shell the damn thing."

"Well, I'd been up there a little while talking with Barkin. Maybe fifteen minutes. That photographer, I believe her name was Gunner something or other, she was there the whole time, snapping away. The bartender, Cleve, and the bouncer, they all came in and out at various times while I was there. This was after the first set. Pretty good show, actually."

"Glad you enjoyed it. Pray continue," I said irritably, as I ordered another shot.

"Your friend Ratso had managed to worm his way in there. I think Barkin wanted him out of the dressing room for some reason."

"Quite understandable," I said.

"Ratso was still there when I left the first time to go to the cloakroom and get a copy of the book for Barkin."

"The book?" I asked.

"My book on Hank Williams. I gave a copy to Barkin."

"Curious," I said.

"Not really," said Flippo, "I give copies to any number of—"

"That's not what I meant, pal. You missed the harbor on that one. I meant it was curious because the book was gone when I got there. The body was there but the book was gone."

"Yeah, well, I autographed one for him and brought it back up to him. They'd gotten rid of Ratso by then. And that's about it."

"You didn't notice a bald-headed lawyer distributing cocaine to everybody?" I asked.

"No, I didn't," said Flippo. "I've got a fine eye for detail. I would've noticed something like that." He chuckled to himself, but the chuckle didn't quite reach his eyes. They were still colorless, emotionless through the steel-rimmed glasses, like a Nazi villain's in a late-night movie.

"Excuse me," I said. "I'm going to hit the ladies' room." He raised an eyebrow but I let it pass. I walked to the back of the place to a tiny hallway where the bathrooms and the pay phone were. The men's room at the High Five I knew from experience was invariably in such a state of extreme disarray so as to make it highly unsuitable for even casual usage. It went way beyond "out of order." You wouldn't want to straighten your bow tie in the place.

One deal had apparently just transpired in the ladies' room because when I walked in, three very cool, noncommittal guys walked out. Didn't even nod at me.

I didn't linger very long, but it was long enough to notice that somebody had whizzed in the sink. That in itself was nothing new. People had been doing that since Lenny Bruce became the first modern man to piss in a sink and to attach a certain amount of importance to it. Doubtless somebody in some primitive Australopithecine culture had probably pissed in a sink before Bruce. But could you call it a sink? And could you call it culture?

By the time I got back to Chet Flippo at the bar, he'd already paid the bill and was taking a copy of his book out of a briefcase on the floor. The bartender picked up the money from the bar, and as he counted it I thought I saw a two-dollar bill flash by between a sawbuck and a single. I didn't say anything.

Flippo autographed the book and handed it to me. He'd signed his autograph left-handed. As we walked out, I looked at the cover. It read: *Your Cheatin' Heart: A Biography of Hank Williams.*

"Catchy title," I said.

10

Sunday was the Lord's day. He could have it. Sundays were lonely, family-oriented, and fairly unproductive in the investigation of murder. Most people went to church on Sunday. Even Bill Dick, who belonged to the Church of the Latter-Day Businessman, probably went to church on Sunday. If he wasn't out on his goddamn boat. Afterward, most people would do Sunday kinds of things like jog, go for a picnic in the park, or drive their cars slowly.

Of course, you didn't see too many picnickers in New York. The parks in the area were not real conducive to picnics. Also, the weather was as cold as Chet Flippo's eyes.

But the good thing about Sundays that almost made up for all the other crap was the total, unearthly absence of garbage trucks. You could grind your teeth in peace. You could really get into a hangover. You could cling to the tattered fabric of your dreams.

Sunday was also a great day for reflections. I looked in the mirror. Decided not to shave.

I made some coffee. I fed the cat. I took a kitchen match and lit a two dollar and twenty-five-cent Partagas cigar. Always keeping it well above the flame. I paced around the loft in my purple bathrobe.

I made a little bet with myself. Who would call first, Uptown Judy or Downtown Judy? The smart money was probably on Downtown Judy. She was possibly a little lonelier and a little unhappier at this time in her life, but who knew? Christ, I thought, maybe I'll call one of them.

The time seemed right to conduct a small Sherlockian experiment I'd been thinking about since I'd seen the left-handed guitar player at City Limits. I got my guitar case out of the closet, knocked off a few cobwebs, and opened it up. My guitar was an Ovation, the kind with the big, rounded back to it that, when you played it, always made you look fatter than you were. It had a wide fingerboard, about the same size as the one on Larry Barkin's Gibson.

The experiment I was attempting was not a strictly scientific one, but I hoped it would shed some light on the gloom of what I was pleased to call the investigation. I leaned the guitar against my desk and walked purposefully into the kitchen. I took the little black puppet head from its place on top of the refrigerator near the kitchen window. I placed it squarely in the middle of the kitchen table and walked back to the desk to get the guitar.

The only ways you could kill somebody with a guitar were to hit him with the sides of it or to bash him, mortar and pestle-like, with the fat tail end of the sound box. One other method commonly used was to bore the victim to death by playing it. Such was not the case here, however. Nor, from the appearance of Barkin's guitar, was the mortar and pestle method employed. The killer I was looking for had used the most common approach to guitar murder—the Mickey Mantle method, in which the guitar is swung like a baseball bat in an effort to take the victim's head downtown. All this, I felt, was clearly indicated. Even the cops knew it.

The point of contact on Barkin's Gibson had been the top side of the sound box. I'd seen that in the dressing room. Some country singers tape cheat sheets on this part of their ax, with song titles, jokes, and maybe the name of the town they're in if they've been on the road for a long time. I never taped cheat sheets to my guitar. Always used the inside of my hat.

I took a few trial swings at the puppet head from the left-hand side. I held the guitar with both hands around the fingerboard. I held it close to the neck. Faceup. That was the way Barkin's attacker had probably done it. The guitar felt comfortable in my hands. I took a whack at the puppet head just for the hell of it, swinging from left to right. Sent it flying across the room. The cat jumped onto the desk. The cat detested violence of any sort.

"Relax," I said. "This is just a test." I retrieved the puppet head and put it back on the table. Now came the crucial part of the experiment. I turned the guitar facedown and took a few trial swings from the right-hand side. The fingerboard felt awkward, nearly slipping from my grasp. The steel strings cut into my fingers. It was almost a chore to hold the guitar level because of the rounded shape of the guitar neck. It would be exceedingly difficult, I thought, to take a solid swing from the right side with the guitar in a facedown position. In other words, if a righty had croaked Barkin, he would have held the guitar faceup. But then the guitar would have been smashed on the bottom part of the sound box. The guitar was damaged on the top part of the sound box. Therefore, unless I'd missed my guess badly, Barkin's murderer was left-handed.

I went directly to the phone and dialed Mike Simmons' number. It was 3:17 P.M. but I woke him from a dead slumber on the fourth ring.

"Mike," I said with some urgency, "leap sideways."

"Huh?" he said.

"Mike," I said. "This is Kinky. Look, are you left-handed?"

"Yeah," he said, with some little irritation. "Why?"

"No problem," I said. "It's nothing."

"Then why the fuck did you wake me up and ask me if I'm left-handed?" It was a logical question, and I hadn't been wholly unprepared for it. But I still had to think on my feet. I took a healthy puff of the cigar I was smoking.

"We're having a Lefty Frizzell look-alike contest, Simmons," I said, "and I wanted to be sure you qualified." I hung up the phone.

Lefty Frizzell was a great country singer who died a number of years ago. But he still worked fine in a pinch.

I dialed the number of the Lone Star Cafe. I heard the sound of music and laughter in the background. Business might be down because of Larry Barkin's murder, but the Lone Star seemed to be doing the best with what it had. Probably take a hydrogen bomb to put a sock on the place.

"Lone Star Cafe," came a sweet, insipid voice.

"Yeah," I said, "is Cleve there?"

"Who's calling, please?" she asked.

"Tell him it's Kinky," I said.

"Oh, Kinky," the voice gushed, "when are you going to play the Lone Star again?"

"Not for a while," I said, "under the circumstances."

"Oh," she said. "Just a moment." Saccharine, recorded country music came on the line while I waited. Sounded like a Larry Barkin song. Then Cleve picked up the phone.

"Cleve," I said, "can you help me with something?"

"This ain't Opportunity Hot Line, but I'll see what I can do," he said.

"That's the spirit," I said. "What's that British bird's name, luv, and will you give me the number of her telly?"

"You want the number of her television set?" Cleve asked.

"No, goddammit," I said. "Give me the number of whatever they call their telephones." He gave me Gunner's full name and phone number.

"She left-handed?" I asked.

"Beg pardon?"

"You heard me," I said. "Is she left-handed?" It didn't take me long to get short with Cleve.

"Wouldn't know," he said.

"I'll find out," I said. Even if she was right-handed, it didn't necessarily put her in the clear. She might have had an accomplice who bashed Barkin. Maybe she only garroted him with his little pink cowboy tie. But that was unlikely. In fact, the whole damn thing was unlikely.

"What about the bald-headed lawyer who dispenses co-caine?"

"What about him?" asked Cleve.

"Is he left-handed?"

"I don't even know who he is," said Cleve. "But he does offer you the coke straw with his right hand."

"Inconclusive," I murmured. I thanked Cleve and cradled the blower. Either I had a lot of work to do or I didn't have a damn thing to do. I didn't know enough about the case to know which.

I walked over to the kitchen and found a bottle of Jameson and my old bull's horn shot glass and took them both back with me over to the desk. I poured a fairly liberal amount into the bull's horn. I had made the polite gesture of a toast to the cat and had managed to manipulate the bull's horn almost to my lips when the phones rang.

Delicately balancing the bull's horn, I reached for the blower on the left. "Start talkin'," I said rather curtly.

"Hi, honey," said the voice on the phone. "What's going on? What did you do today? I missed you."

It was Downtown Judy. I downed the shot.

11

The next few days went by in what some are wont to call a mindless blur. Actually, that wasn't quite accurate. Some of the tedium was pretty well defined. Like my meeting Tuesday afternoon with Bill Dick at the Lone Star Cafe. Cleve sat in on the meeting. We had a three-Lone Star beer lunch.

"Jesus Christ," said Bill Dick, "these bozos are only on the road three hundred ninety-seven days a year. You'd think they might find some other place to get themselves bumped off. Maybe Nashville or Austin or someplace. They've got country music down there, don't they?"

"Yeah," I said. "It's probably better, too." Dick glared at me.

"Well, maybe not Nashville," I said.

The bartender brought us three bowls of Five-Alarm Chili and another round of beer.

Dick hoisted his bottle of Lone Star in the air and looked me right in the eye. "No matter how successful I get," he said, "no matter if I own this place or what, I still drink my beer from the bottle. That's the kind of guy I am. Right or wrong, Kinkster?"

"Right, Bill," I said. I took another drink from my glass.

"I'm not a phony. I never bullshit you. Right or wrong, Kinkster?"

"Right, Bill," I said.

"And I'm worried. I'm real worried. If we don't catch this

killer, we can bring down the big top . . . drop the curtain . . . set our horses free . . . cut the mainsail . . .''

He took a drink from his bottle and mixed another metaphor or two. Then he was through. I looked on silently and stirred my chili.

If the meeting at the Lone Star hadn't been a raging success, I was having even more trouble getting in touch with Princess Di. Maybe the British photographer broad was hiding in her darkroom trying to develop her alibi. I'd left five messages on her machine in the past three days and I was running out of charm. I was also running out of cat food. All I had left was one can of sliced veal in gravy. The cat hated sliced veal in gravy. I'd found her one wintry night back when she was just a little kitten lost in an alley in Chinatown. If she had made it across Canal Street into Little Italy, she probably would have liked sliced veal in gravy.

I figured I'd give my British bird call one more try, and if that didn't work I'd probably have to go on a field trip. It was 6:07 of a Wednesday evening by the computer clock when I finally connected with Gunner.

"Hello," she said very briskly. Sounded like she was in a hurry to set up a tripod. Like she had to rush to catch something before it went away. I was used to that. All photographers sounded that way. Except the ones who worked for the morgue.

"Sixth time's a charm, eh what?" I said.

"Who is this?" she asked. I wasn't Professor Higgins, but her accent sounded good to me.

"F. Stop Fitzgerald," I said. Thought I'd try a light-hearted approach.

"Who the bloody hell is this?" she stormed. An accent, like so many other components of a woman, is really more attractive when the woman is a little angry. You shouldn't point it out though, unless you want the woman to get really angry, which is never attractive.

"Look," I said, "my name is Kinky. I got your number from Cleve at the Lone Star. I'm doing some work for them on this Barkin situation. I need to talk to you."

"The police have already spoken to me."

"I know that. I still want to talk to you."

"You're not a detective, are you?" she asked.

"I'm not from the Yard," I said, "but I am a close friend of Mick Brennan's." Mick was a celebrated British freelancer, who had, among other exploits, covered the Argentine mainland during the Falklands War and lived to tell about it, which he often did. Brennan was also a friend of Michael Caine's, for what it was worth.

"You know Mick Brennan?" she asked. She was interested now. Probably saw a good career move.

"Sure, I know Mick," I said. "Saw him a few weeks ago. Tavern on the Green, I think it was." Men's room at the Monkey's Paw was actually where I'd seen Brennan, but far be it from me to destroy a young girl's illusion. One tavern's as good as another.

"Kinky," she said, "a man has been murdered. I don't give a damn about Mick Brennan or about you. If I talk to you it will be because I feel a moral responsibility to help apprehend a vicious, brutal, cold-blooded killer, not because of who you are or who you know."

"Sounds like fun," I said.

"We may as well get this over with now," she said with a rather British-sounding sigh. "Do you know where I live?"

She gave me the address.

Ten minutes later I was hacking it up Third Avenue to Thirty-eighth Street.

Another ten minutes and the doorman at Gunner's building was giving me the old fish eye and calling up to see if I was who I said I was. Or at least if who I said I was was who she was expecting. It was and I was. I took the elevator up to the fourth floor.

Gunner came to the door. She was handsome, blond, British, and, it emerged, right-handed. She made some tea while

I looked around the living room. It really wasn't a living room at all; it was a photography studio with two teacups in it.

The tea seemed to thaw her out a bit, but she didn't tell me much that I didn't already know. And that wasn't much. She'd already turned over to the cops all the rolls she shot in the Lone Star dressing room. She'd briefly met Chet Flippo, Mike Simmons, Ratso, and, of course, Larry Barkin and his two brothers, both of whom had apparently used a smaller dressing room down the hall. She had shot the pictures of Barkin for a European fashion magazine, which either demonstrated that country music was getting very trendy or that European fashion editors were pretty slow out of the chute. She had seen, but did not meet, the bald-headed lawyer.

Her cat was named Dennis.

"Look, Gunner," I said, "I know you don't give a damn about me or Mick Brennan, but why not come join us for a drink at least. I'm on my way to meet him now."

"Well, Kinky . . . ," she said. It was a coy, hearty, sort of well-bred come-on, and I liked the inflection she was starting to give to the "Kinky" part.

We walked up Third Avenue to Forty-fourth Street and halfway down Forty-fourth to Costello's Bar. Costello's was the haunt of practically every newspaperman in New York who would take a drink, and that was practically every newspaperman in New York.

We went in and walked to the far end of the bar. I noticed a fair number of heads turning. The shutterbug wasn't bad in the visual department. I didn't know how bright she was, how devious she could be, or what she was like when she took her camera off, but she did have the strength of character not to give a damn about me or Mick Brennan. And she was making a few waves at Costello's.

Brennan was sitting at the very end of the bar accompanied by a Heineken and by my old pal McGovern from the *Daily News*. McGovern was working on an extremely large vodka and tonic. Neither glanced up as we came over.

"Here's trouble," said Brennan. They both looked fairly heavily monstered.

"Gunner," I said, "this is my friend McGovern from the *Daily News.*"

"And I'm Jimmy Olsen from the *Daily Planet,*" said Brennan.

"And this is my intrepid young photographer friend, Gunner," I said. McGovern laughed a loud, almost obscene laugh. Gunner ignored it.

"I admire your work, Mr. Brennan," said Gunner, "and I've seen your by-line quite often, Mr. McGovern."

"That's more than he can say for himself," said Brennan.

"Charmed," said McGovern.

Gunner and I sat down at the bar next to the two of them. She ordered a glass of red wine and I ordered a shot of Jameson with a pint of Victoria bitters. Gunner and Brennan ran a little compulsory photography shoptalk, and I had a chance to ask McGovern for a little favor.

"Can you help me with something, McGovern?" I asked politely.

"No," said McGovern.

"It's important," I said.

"Out of the question," said McGovern. I ordered another round for the four of us.

"I'd like to know what you have in the files on Chet Flippo. He's a music journalist. Has a book out on Hank Williams. I'd like to know what else he's done. Also everything you have on Larry Barkin, the country singer who got himself croaked last week."

"Call me tomorrow afternoon at the city desk."

"You're a real pal, McGovern," I said.

"Don't I know it," he said.

"Want to see some shots of the creature?" asked Gunner as she reached into the large bag she was carrying.

"I've already shot plenty of McGovern," said Brennan.

"I mean the creature on top of the Lone Star Cafe," said Gunner.

"The iguana," explained McGovern to Brennan. The iguana was a famous fifty-foot-long metal monster that had been created by an artist friend of mine, Bob Wade, from Dallas. It was so hideous-looking that the squeamish Fifth Avenue Merchant Association got the city to order the monster taken down. But by that time the iguana had become so famous as to almost be a tourist attraction, and the city reversed itself and ordered the creature reinstated, to Bob Wade's extreme gratification and the Merchant Association's extreme mortification. Today its huge head glares triumphantly over Fifth Avenue.

All you have to do to get a closer look at the iguana is to wait until the security guy at the club goes down to the men's room. Then you get up to the third floor and worm your way into the dressing room at the end of the hallway. Ask Ratso how it's done. Then pry open the unlocked metal door that leads on to the roof, and you're right there standing about even with the iguana's somewhat unkempt toenails and looking up right into its giant Fifth Avenue-hating eyes. Pleasant spot for a mint julep. Had a few other things there myself, including one of the waitresses at the club.

Gunner took out a contact sheet and a loupe and put them both on the bar. Brennan and McGovern leaned forward to have a look. I took my time about it, having already seen the iguana almost every time I'd played the Lone Star and also in some of my milder nightmares.

"When did you take these?" I asked Gunner.

"Last Thursday night," said Gunner. "The roll's just of the iguana and a few shots of some men playing chess in Washington Square Park, so I didn't bother to develop it until this morning. The police wanted everything else I shot that night."

I leaned forward toward the contact sheet with only a lukewarm interest. I didn't see it at first. I picked up the loupe and gave a cursory glance at several frames. Near the middle of the sheet I stopped the loupe. I'd almost missed it.

When I backtracked with the loupe one frame, it hit me

like a haymaker from Joe Palooka. The door that led out to the roof was open, and on a distant wall of the dressing room was what appeared to be a blurry shadow.

"What do you make of it, Mick?" I asked Brennan.

"It's a picture of a man making a hand shadow of a duck, mate," he said. I heard a sharp intake of air as Gunner looked at the shadow on the frame. She'd recognized it also.

"No, I'm afraid not, pal," I said as I threw down a final shot of Jameson. I wasn't sure if it was the Jameson or what I'd just seen through the loupe that caused me to speak in a soft and husky voice, scarcely above a whisper. Maybe it was a little of both.

"It's a picture of a man murdering another man," I said.

12

"The trouble is that it's a right-handed shadow," I said to Ratso. We were sitting around the kitchen table at 199B Vandam waiting for the coffee to perk or for something else to happen. Whichever came first.

The coffee perked. I poured us both a cup.

"I see you're left-handed yourself," said Ratso as he ransacked the kitchen looking for cream and sugar.

"You're extremely observant, my dear Ratso," I said. "Of course I'm left-handed. Isn't everybody left-handed?"

"I'm not left-handed," said Ratso.

"No, you wouldn't be," I said.

The cat jumped up on the kitchen table and began walking toward Ratso's coffee cup.

"Get down," said Ratso to the cat. The cat didn't say anything.

"Ratso," I said, "just imagine that you're the guest, and the cat and I are your hosts, and we're all riding in Dr. Dolittle's giant pink sea snail."

"All right," said Ratso, "we're on this giant fucking pink sea snail and we're traveling back to last Thursday night to investigate the murder of Larry Barkin. What do we see?"

"We see a preponderance of left-handers, a right-handed shadow of a murderer, and a two-dollar bill."

"Okay," said Ratso, "you find a two-dollar bill in Barkin's pocket at the murder scene. The Hank Williams song 'Hey,

Good Lookin' ' comes in the mail addressed to the victim and postmarked prior to the murder. Right?"

"Right," I said. I got up and poured us both another cup of coffee. The cat hopped off the table and onto the desk and curled up under the desk lamp. "She's in Miami Beach," I said.

"Who is?" asked Ratso.

"The cat," I said.

"Now the song makes mention," said Ratso, "of a two-dollar bill in the lyric. 'A hot rod Ford and a two-dollar bill.' So whoever gave Barkin the two-dollar bill, or placed it in his pocket afterward, is the murderer and the sender of the song. But why does he want to give us this deliberate signature, this clue? Why this connection to Hank Williams?"

"These are deep waters, my dear Ratso, for the pink sea snail. Hank Williams has had an almost magical effect on millions of people for a great many years now. I know something about the power he can exert, even dead, over people. He's one of my patron saints, you know."

"Really?" asked Ratso.

"Sure," I said. "Just like Jesus, Hitler, and Bob Dylan are your three patron saints, I have three also."

"Oh, yeah," said Ratso, "who are the other two besides Hank?"

"Anne Frank and Ernie Kovacs," I said.

"I see," said Ratso. "But what about Sherlock?"

"I am Sherlock," I said.

"So who the hell am I?" Ratso asked. "Dr. Watson or Dr. Dolittle?"

"Dealer's choice," I said. "They're the only two doctors who still make house calls."

It was two cups of coffee later and Ratso was standing up and looking around for his coat, when the phones rang. "Stick around a minute," I said as I walked over to the desk and picked up the blower on the left.

It was Detective Sergeant Cooperman, and his low, grating

voice was coming down the line at me like somebody's run-away bowling ball. Apparently Gunner had given him the contact sheet.

"Well," I said into the receiver, "maybe he kills left, photographs right."

I won't repeat what Cooperman said to that, but the essence of his thought pattern was why was I asking everyone in New York if they were left-handed when Cooperman was right now looking at photographic evidence that clearly indicated the killer was right-handed? He said a few other things, too, then he hung up. Ratso had walked over to the refrigerator, opened the door, and was looking inside.

I had already told Ratso about the shadow on the contact sheet, and now I went into some little detail about the guitar experiment I'd done in the loft on the previous Sunday. "You see," I said, "I still believe the killer's a southpaw. Something's wrong somewhere."

"Well," said Ratso, "a right-handed shadow is better than no shadow at all."

"Not if there's a left-handed lunatic running around plotting who he'll kill next," I said.

"Oh," said Ratso, "so you think we'll be hearing from Hank again."

"I'm sure of it," I said. "Nothing's more dangerous than the arrogance of a clever killer. And I haven't been able to prove a damn thing. The investigation's going nowhere extremely fast."

"Don't be so hard on yourself," said Ratso. "You've got a negative attitude."

I lit a cigar thoughtfully with a kitchen match. "That's it, pal," I said softly. "You've just said it. I've got to get my hands on that contact sheet again. The old men playing chess in Washington Square Park."

I walked quickly over to the far end of the loft. "Come over here, Ratso," I said. "Look at that picture on the wall." It was a framed photograph of an older man playing chess with a small boy. "That's Samuel Reshevsky, the world grand master, when he came to Houston, Texas, and played fifty people simultaneously and beat them all. The kid was the youngest person Reshevsky played that night. I think the kid was only seven years old at the time, so this picture made the front page of the *Houston Chronicle*. Reshevsky later told the kid's dad he was very sorry to have beaten his kid, but he had to take the match seriously because losing to a seven-year-old wasn't good for a grand master's reputation."

Ratso looked up at the picture for a while. "So how do you know all this?" he asked.

"I was the kid," I said.

Ratso looked at the picture again. So did I for a moment. The face reflected an innocence and a keen, childlike intensity of spirit that I no longer saw when I looked in the mirror, and I only hoped had been consigned to my heart.

"That picture," I said, "has something important to tell us about the shadow who murdered Larry Barkin."

"Let me guess," said Ratso. "The killer comes from Houston?"

I took a few patient puffs on my cigar and I looked at Ratso. "Not quite," I said.

13

I spent most of Thursday trying to locate the bald-headed lawyer, but I couldn't find hide nor hair of him. It was hard to believe that nobody I'd talked to could tell me his name. That they'd all assumed he'd gotten into the dressing room with somebody else. You'd think people would pay closer attention to a bald-headed lawyer who was dispensing cocaine.

Late that afternoon I called the city desk of the *Daily News*.

"City desk," came a busy, distracted voice.

"Is McGovern there?" I asked.

"I don't see him," said the voice.

"Never could see McGovern," I said. "Well, when he gets in, will you ask him to call Holmes?"

"Will do," said the voice. I fed the cat and fielded a brutal, unrelenting series of stray phone calls, full of sound and fury and signifying nothing except that my phone was still working and that a guy named Joe in Little Italy was delivering an espresso-cappuccino machine to my loft the following week as a token of gratitude for my helping with a little situation the previous year. I never refused tokens of gratitude. Especially when they came from Little Italy.

The other calls, in a random and haphazard order, were from Downtown Judy, who said she was coming over. I said okay. From Bill Dick at the Lone Star, wanting to know how I was progressing. I said okay. From Uptown Judy, who said she was coming down. I said okay. And from Ratso, who wanted to know what the picture of me playing chess with Samuel What's-his-name meant. I said "Reshevsky."

In between the calls I walked over to the kitchen window and watched the dismal darkness settle over the dismal November gray of New York City. New York was the kind of place where you could hide from anything. Possibly even yourself.

At seven-fifteen, I called the *Daily News* again. McGovern answered.

"City desk," he said.

"Why didn't you call me, precious lips?"

"I didn't get a message from you," said McGovern.

"I left a message for you to call Holmes. Sort of a pseudonym. Thought you might pick up on it."

"Shit," he said, "the message I got was to call home. I knew that couldn't be right." McGovern was a devoted bachelor and had lived in a small apartment on Jane Street for as long as I'd known him. He had no family living, and very little of it dead.

"You're not kiddin'," I said.

"Hey, I've got something for you," said McGovern.

"Spit it," I said. It was about time somebody had something for me. Not that I'd ever expected the solution of the problem to be easy. If the killer was someone I didn't know, possibly didn't even suspect, then how in the hell was I going to find him? If he was somebody that I did know, he was one pretty sick item.

"First, Flippo," said McGovern. "Apparently Flippo's some kind of literary ghoul. Only writes about dead people."

"That's not so strange, McGovern," I said. "You told me yourself that you're the *Daily News'* number one man when it comes to writing obits for the living. That's not only ghoulish, it's cynical."

"Yeah," said McGovern, "but it requires a lot of imagination. You ought to see the obit I just finished on Bob Hope. Want to hear it?"

"Maybe some other time," I said. "It'll keep."

"Yeah, but will Bob?" asked McGovern.

"Back to Flippo," I said.

"Here's part of a review on Flippo's book *Your Cheatin' Heart*: '. . . The thing that makes this work different from other books on Hank Williams is that thoughts, emotions, scenes, and incidents are herein described that only Hank Williams himself could have known.'"

"That's bizarre enough to make me want to read the book," I said. "Of course I never took the Amelia Earhart Speed Reading Course or whatever it's called, so at my remedial pace I probably won't finish it until it's too late."

"Too late for what?" asked McGovern.

"I'd rather not say."

"Sure," said McGovern. "Top secret. Classified. I understand." I was hoping McGovern wouldn't go into a snit. That could only slow the flow of information. And there was precious little of that as it was. "Okay," he said finally, "on to Barkin."

I felt a small wave of relief that my main source for background information was not being shut off to me. McGovern wasn't exactly Deep Throat, but he did have remarkable access to almost any facet of American history. Right at his Irish fingertips. The wave of relief was not big enough to make me feel very good about how the case was going. It was just about enough for me to lean back and light a fresh cigar. With a Bic.

Using a Bic made it extremely difficult to keep the cigar well above the flame. I wondered what Charles Lamb would've thought about my lighting a cigar with a Bic. Of course, they didn't have Bics in those days. And these days, we didn't have Charles Lamb.

"Larry Barkin and the Barkin Brothers," said McGovern. "Seven gold records . . . twice named country singer of the year . . . two brothers, Jim and Randy . . . born in the little Texas town of Medina . . . Christ, all country singers were born in a little Texas town."

"Hank wasn't," I said.

"No?"

"No, sir," I said. "He was born in a little town in Alabama."

"I see," said McGovern.

"You can skip the part about Barkin buying his mother a big house outside of Nashville," I said.

"How'd you know he bought his mother a big house outside of Nashville?"

"All country singers buy their mothers big houses outside of Nashville."

"You oughta be tellin' this shit to me," said McGovern.

"Is there anything else now?" I asked. "Any problems? Legal? Marital? Anything shady or questionable about this all-American boy?"

"Yeah," said McGovern. "There was a pretty ugly lawsuit about five years ago. Barkin and a former manager of his. Bit of country music mud-slinging involved."

"Was this guy screwing Barkin?"

"Sexually? Financially? Spiritually?" asked McGovern.

"Financially, McGovern," I said. Sexually, I doubted. And all managers screwed country singers spiritually.

"Looks like he was screwing Barkin financially. Barkin won a big settlement from the guy—the guy was also a lawyer. Not that all lawyers are crooks."

"Of course not," I said shortly. "What's this lawyer's name?"

"Murray Fishkin," said McGovern.

"Bald?"

"Come again?"

"Is the goddamn lawyer bald?"

"Just a minute. I think there's a picture here." There was silence on the line for a few moments while McGovern went away to flip some pages or adjust some microfilm or whatever they did. Then he came back on the line. "As an eagle," he said.

"Thanks, McGovern," I said, "I definitely owe you one."

"Yeah, well, how about telling me what this is all about? I

mean it's obvious you're looking into the Barkin murder. Let's see. Barkin was bumped off exactly a week ago at the Lone Star. Okay, I understand your involvement in that, but what's Hank Williams got to do with this mess? He's been dead for twenty-five years."

"Thirty-three years," I said. "And look, I really can't tell you just now. I'm not sure I even know what the connection is myself."

"C'mon, man," he said. "Give me a little hint. I'll figure it out for myself."

McGovern and I had met on the gangplank of Noah's ark. But in a murder investigation you had to be very careful what you told old friends. Especially old friends who were members of the Fourth Estate.

"Ask Bob Hope," I said.

14

I didn't think it'd be a good idea to put my feet up on Sergeant Cooperman's desk. The way I looked at it, just coming down to the precinct station house had been fairly testicular. I knew I wasn't going to be working hand in glove with the cops on this one, but I thought maybe I'd get a look at that contact sheet again. All I could see at the moment was Cooperman's fiery little eyes. They were boring right through me like two piss holes in the snow.

"Fox!" shouted Cooperman. Fox detached his serpentine frame from a nearby filing cabinet, walked over to the desk, put both hands down on top of it, and leaned as far as he could toward me. I could see why they called them the fuzz. If he got much closer he's be growing out of my chin.

"What do I do with this guy?" asked Cooperman in a very soft whisper. Soft as a down pillow just before it smothered you to death. "I call him and let him know he's screwin' up, and he takes it as an invitation to come here to the squad room for a chat."

Cooperman eased his large body backward in his chair. He picked up a yellow pencil and tapped it slowly on the desk. Fox stood up, folded his arms across his chest, and glared down at me. The three of us held our respective positions for quite a few pencil tappings. It reminded me of a B movie. Unfortunately, it wasn't. It was a B world.

"I'd like to have a look," I said, "at the photographic evidence that shows the killer is right-handed."

"Fox, get him the contact sheet," said Cooperman. "You look, then you leave," he said to me. He'd stopped tapping, but his orbs were still working overtime on me.

"Fine," I said. Cooperman lacked certain qualities that were essential in a good host.

Fox went into another room. "Let me tell you something, friend," said Cooperman. He used the word "friend" in the same way that a Turk, or an Arab, or a redneck used it when he wanted you to know you were not his friend. "If it weren't for your pal, that manager of the club—"

"Cleve," I said.

"Cleve," he said, "alibiing for you, you might just have made a prime suspect yourself."

"Cleve called me after Barkin was croaked," I said.

"Save it," said Cooperman.

Fox came back in the room. He put the contact sheet on the desk and pointed demonstratively at the frame that contained the shadow. I followed the moving finger.

"Right-handed beyond a shadow of a doubt," he said. "You don't agree, Tex?" Fox had seen me sometime in the past when I was wearing a cowboy hat, and he'd managed to retain the image.

I wasn't looking at the shadow anymore. I was looking at the bottom of the page at the last three frames on the roll. A couple of old guys playing chess in Washington Square Park.

"No, I don't," I said. "I've thought for a while that something was wrong with this contact sheet. Look at this chessboard." I held the sheet up to where both Cooperman and Fox could see.

"The black square is at each player's right-hand side," I said.

"So what?" asked Fox.

"So the *white* square is supposed to be at each player's right-hand side."

"We'll check on it," said Cooperman.

"This is no time for puns, Sergeant," I said.

Cooperman looked at me. Then he jerked his head rather

violently toward the other room, and Fox took the contact sheet from the desk and walked away with it.

"What about the Hank Williams song that came in the mail?" I asked.

"You country singers got country music on the brain. We're looking into it. You see this pile right here?" Cooperman nodded his head to indicate a stack of papers on his desk. I nodded my head to indicate I could see the stack of papers. "You know what that is?" he asked.

"You're getting an early start on your income tax?" I asked.

Cooperman smiled a sweet, smirky, patronizing little smile. Fortunately, it did not reach his eyes. "These are twenty-four unsolved homicide cases sitting right next to a cold cup of coffee," he said brusquely. "Take a walk."

I took a walk.

15

Late that night I witnessed the most exciting and harrowing experience of the week, excluding, of course, the murder of Larry Barkin. It involved the two Judys and it happened at the front door of my loft. It was a nerve-wrenching near miss. Uptown Judy was going down in the freight elevator at the same time as Downtown Judy was coming up the stairs.

One moment I was saying, "Good night, Judy. Take care," and twenty seconds later I was saying, "So Judy, where the hell you been?"

Friday morning I was sitting at my desk. Both Judys had come and gone, in a manner of speaking. Neither of them was any the wiser. Neither was I. Larry Barkin was still dead, and I had the sickening suspicion that no matter what I did, I'd be barkin' up the wrong tree.

I was wearing my purple bathrobe, drinking coffee, and opening the day's correspondence with my Smith & Wesson knife. The cat was lying on the desk under the lamp. The cat and I were engaged in a little contest. We were trying to see which of us could display the least emotion every time I opened a bill.

I was studying an invitation to a roller-skating party at a discotheque, when the phones rang. It was 11:37 A.M. I picked up the blower on the left.

"We got another one," the voice said. It was Cleve calling from the Lone Star. There was a strange note in his voice, and it took me a moment to figure out what it was. It was what a shiver would sound like if you could hear it.

"Relax, pal," I said. "You got another what?"

"Another song, man," he said. "Another Hank Williams song came in the mail."

16

It was pushing three in the afternoon and I was standing at the kitchen window of the loft waiting for the messenger to bring over the Hank Williams song from the Lone Star. I didn't know what the song was, or to whom it'd been sent. Cleve had been too upset to even hum a few bars. From time to time I picked up the puppet head from the top of the refrigerator and gave it a little anticipatory juggle from hand to hand, but no messenger.

Why was I waiting here? It was a gorgeous day, as we say in New York. Hell, I could've been out in the sunshine kicking the garbage around on the sidewalk.

I started to pace back and forth across the length of the loft, periodically gazing hopefully down at the sidewalk. Sometimes pacing back and forth helped me take stock of things. The cat, some years back, had followed at my heels as I paced up and down with cigar in hand. The cat had now given up such kittenish games. I continued to pace. I was a creature of narrow habit, and I was somewhat disappointed in the cat, but I never let it show. No doubt, the cat had her reasons to be disappointed in me as well. Somehow we managed.

I stopped pacing. I wasn't getting anywhere, figuratively or literally. I looked at the cat. She was curled up asleep on the rocker. The loft was as close to home as either of us was ever likely to get. It wasn't home, but how could it be? Everybody knew that home was in Kansas. And it better stay there if it knew what was good for it.

I poured a cup of coffee and prowled around the loft like a battery-powered tiger trying desperately to burn bright with a knowledge I didn't possess. What did I actually know? I thought about it for a moment. A country singer had rather unpleasantly gotten himself unsung eight days ago. Prior to the murder, someone had sent him the Hank Williams song "Hey, Good Lookin'," which contained the reference to a two-dollar bill in the lyrics, the same two-dollar bill having found its nefarious way into the dying breast pocket of the sequined suit of the young cowboy. Right out of the Old West. But East was East and West was West. Who'd want to croak a saccharine-tongued, good ol' boy, housewife's dream anyway? Besides myself, of course. I didn't have an answer.

And now, to show it was nothing personal against Larry Barkin, another song had arrived. The cops, according to Cleve, had dusted it for prints. Unsuccessfully. Even murderers watched enough television to know about fingerprints. The cops' interest level in the new song had, apparently, not been high. Cooperman had told Cleve and Bill Dick that there were fifteen million nut cases sitting around the New York area with nothing to do but clog the mails with letters, threats, and solicitations directed at well-known people.

I wasn't sure that Fox and Cooperman even knew who Hank Williams was. I knew Hank didn't know who Fox and Cooperman were. He'd been dead for thirty-three years.

But even that narrow little fact wasn't exactly true. In a far more important sense, Hank Williams, like Jesus or Joe Hill, in a random and haphazard order, never really died. People still listened to Hank's words and Hank's voice, and there was a magic about the man that had conquered the mortal boundaries of geography, culture, and time.

And there were people like Chet Flippo who kept Hank alive. I wondered very briefly if Flippo also could be making people dead. I didn't really believe it. He'd given the bartender a two-dollar bill at the High Five. He was a Hank Williams nut, but so was Mike Simmons. If Ratso had known a little more about country music, he'd probably be a Hank

Williams nut, too. There were literally millions of them. And a Hank Williams nut was a hard nut to crack.

Flippo, in his distant, unassuming way, was a friend of mine. Was there a killer switch somewhere in that artichoke heart? I didn't see it. But then, if it were there, it wasn't the kind of thing you were likely to see.

Simmons was more hot-blooded, more frustrated, more capable of violent murder. And he was left-handed. He loved Hank Williams more than God. "You'd throw Hank fucking Williams out of here," he'd shouted to the philistines at City Limits. A revealing line, I thought. But it was too flimsy a line even to snort from the smooth, domed top of Murray Fishkin's head.

And what of Fishkin? The mysterious lawyer-manager-crook whose reputation and profile were both lower than a whale turd? I'd have to get on to him. When the law offices opened on Monday morning, I'd open him like a forty-two-cent can of cat food. Where there's a will, there's a lawyer.

I even wondered about Gunner, the trusty girl photographer. There was something about her that didn't quite fit the picture. And for some reason I trusted her even less than I trusted most attractive women I'd met. Was it just male chauvinist prejudice? Was it? Maybe it was male intuition. No, it couldn't be that. Everybody knew there was no such thing. Okay. Who was left? Had to be left . . .

I heard a shout from below and I threw down the puppet head on the parachute. I watched it as it glided gracefully down to the sidewalk. It was really a thing of beauty to see.

Moments later I heard a continuous rapping at the door of the loft. It was either a very insistent person or a pretty tall woodpecker. And by this time I didn't care which as long as it was carrying a Hank Williams song in its beak. I opened the door.

"You Kinky?" asked the messenger. In his right hand was a manila envelope, and in his left was a large carton that looked like it could hold more ice cream than I wanted to think about. I nodded. "What's in the carton?" I asked.

"Man said it was Five-Alarm Chili," he said.

"That Bill Dick thinks of everything," I said. "And now, the envelope, please." He handed me the envelope and I took it over to the desk.

"Come on in," I said. "I may want to send this back where it came from." The messenger came in and stood by the door.

"Pour yourself some coffee or something," I said. The guy wasn't doing anything, but sometimes it's more annoying to have somebody not doing something than it is to have somebody doing something really obnoxious.

I looked at the outside of the envelope. Same big block letters as before. But this time it was addressed to Bubba and Blane, c/o The Lone Star Cafe.

Bubba and Blane Borgelt were two big friendly Texas brothers with a string of catchy country hits as long as their tour bus. I'd even worked a few shows with them on the road. What I liked to call the early days. "When Jesus was our savior and cotton was our king," as Billy Joe Shaver put it. 199B Vandam was still a warehouse back then. I didn't have a cat. I didn't even have intimations of an espresso machine.

I opened the envelope. It contained the sheet music for the Hank Williams song "Settin' the Woods on Fire." If I remembered correctly, Bubba and Blane were playing the Lone Star on Monday night.

"Watcha got there?" asked the messenger.

"Somebody's swan song," I said.

17

On Saturday afternoon Ratso and I were sitting in the Carnegie Delicatessen on Seventh Avenue and Fifty-fifth Street. Outside it was snowing. The Carnegie Deli was a good spiritual place to be when it was snowing. So was a bar. Or any place in the Village. Actually, when it snowed in New York, every block took on the aspects of a little village. The snow blocked out the tall buildings and seemed to bring people closer together. It created a blanket of peace and tranquility over the city. Strangers talked to one another. You almost felt like you were in a small town. Fortunately, it never lasted.

I was working on a matzo ball about the size of McGovern's head and looking forward to renewing my acquaintance with Bubba and Blane on Monday night. I didn't think, however, that I should get too attached. Ratso was eating a large number of pickles from one of the buckets that were always on the tables. Leo had brought us linen napkins, treatment reserved only for celebrities and special friends.

"What did you order, Ratso?" I asked. The matzo ball was killer bee.

"Pope's nose," he said.

"What the hell's a pope's nose?" I asked.

"Turkey's ass," he said.

Ratso handled several pickles in the bucket, and finally settled on one that met his culinary approval.

"Ratso, I don't want to put you off your appetite for your pope's nose," I said, "but I'd like for you to look over something with me." I took the sheet music out of my coat pocket.

We looked over the lyrics together to "Settin' the Woods on Fire." They were as follows:

> Comb your hair and paint and powder
> You act proud and I'll act prouder
> You sing loud and I'll sing louder
> Tonight we're settin' the woods on fire
>
> You're my gal and I'm your feller
> Dress up in your frock of yeller
> I'll look swell but you'll look sweller
> Settin' the woods on fire
>
> We'll take in all the honky-tonks, tonight
>   we're havin' fun
> We'll show the folks a brand new dance
>   that never has been done
>
> I don't care who thinks we're silly
> You be daffy and I'll be dilly
> We'll order up two bowls of chili
> Settin' the woods on fire
>
> I'll gas up my hot rod stoker
> We'll get hotter than a poker
> You'll be broke but I'll be broker
> Tonight we're settin' the woods on fire.

"The song's a field day for a criminal mind," said Ratso, shaking his head in a disbelieving manner. He reached around in the bucket for another pickle.

"It's not all that bad," I said. "You see, I don't think the murderer is actually revealing his methodology with these songs. How he's going to do it, why he's going to do it, we don't know. All we know for sure is he's going to do it. And there'll be a clue in the song that connects it to the crime.

He's playing with us. He's inviting us. What we're looking at is really the killer's calling card. The fact that he uses ol' Hank as his vessel of communication may be the most revealing thing we know yet about the person we're looking for.''

"Let's look at the song," said Ratso. "Okay . . . here— 'We'll get hotter than a poker.' What about that?''

"My dear Ratso," I said, "this is not an English hunting lodge. This is New York City."

"Right, Sherlock," he said. "I forgot." He looked down at the song again. "How about this? Two bowls of chili. 'We'll order up two bowls of chili.' ''

"So don't eat the chili," I said.

"Hell," said Ratso, "the regular chili at the Lone Star could kill you."

"Not a chance," I said. "You're just an urban woosy, Ratso. But I need you there Monday night. You bring a kind of naïveté to the investigation that already is suggesting certain possibilities to me."

"You're a pope's nose," he said.

As we got into the cab to go back downtown, Ratso told the driver to hurry, he was late. "Everybody's late," said the driver as he threw the meter. "In this town, everybody's late."

I looked out the window of the hack and watched the snowy sidewalks slide past in a dream. I wasn't late yet. But I was starting to run scared. And I had a feeling Monday night was going to come faster than a nymphomaniac.

18

Cleve was the first person I saw at the door of the Lone Star on Monday night. He was wringing his hands like an unctuous funeral director. I had a few words with him, walked over to the downstairs bar, and took a seat on the only empty barstool—right next to the cash register. The businessman's piano.

I ordered a Jameson and looked around for either strange or familiar faces. I didn't see any. Everybody at the downstairs bar looked vaguely familiar. Like you could almost place them but you didn't really want to. They looked like people who habitually shopped the generic aisle of the supermarket. Maybe some of it had rubbed off on them.

I turned around on the barstool and watched the opening act. I'd seen this band thousands of times over the years. Different places, different faces, same old song. Their current favorite was ''Luckenbach, Texas.'' Probably once it had been ''Bad, Bad Leroy Brown'' or ''Are You Going to San Francisco?'' if they'd been old enough to go, and it looked like they had been. They'd always changed, if not with the times, then just a little bit behind them. They'd learned to ''roll with the bullets,'' as my friend Doug Kenney used to say before he fell off his perch in Hawaii. I missed Doug. I signaled to the bartender for another Jameson, and when he poured it I didn't miss Doug so much.

The band was going through the torturous twenty minutes of musical foreplay that is sometimes known as tuning up. Should take under a minute, but these guys wanted all the stage time they could get. Didn't want to leave a rhinestone unturned in the limelight. What the hell. Wherever there were barflies there had to be lounge lizards. It was a law of nature.

I turned back to the bar and finished my drink. Why was I being so hard on these guys? They were just trying to earn a living. "Hell, everybody can't be Hank Williams," I said. "Everybody can't die in the backseat of a Cadillac on the way to Canton, Ohio."

"What was that?" asked the bartender.

"Put it on the tab," I said.

The band had started to play and I had started for the stairs to the balcony. It gave a better view of the whole place and it wasn't quite as loud. Nothing on the planet was quite as loud as sitting at the downstairs bar of the Lone Star Cafe and listening to a country rock band.

The second floor of the Lone Star was usually where most of the action was, always discounting, of course, the executive men's room. I wasn't halfway up the stairs before I regretted not having had a few more drinks before attaining that second Dantean level. Somebody was yelling "Kinkstah! Kinkstah!" at me. Once you heard that voice you never forgot it. It was Ratso. I'd wanted to keep a slightly lower profile, but I now saw that was going to be rather difficult.

Ratso was holding forth with some people at a table on the far side of the balcony. I gave him a little Hitler wave, like an Italian waiter carrying a tray, except without the tray. It was a gesture that clearly indicated "Cut me some slack, pal," but as I reached the second-floor landing I heard the dread macawlike tones once more. "Kinkstah . . . Kinkstah!" I chose to ignore them for the moment. I had to because I ran right into Mike Simmons at the top of the stairs. I'd been trying to turn left and he'd come charging out of the ladies' room at the top of the stairs. There were angry shouts emanating from the ladies' room and Mike seemed a little out of breath.

"Sure isn't Marylou's," he said. "They've got a much more

progressive attitude over there." Simmons had been known to enter ladies' rooms occasionally and offer the ladies controlled substances if they would take their blouses off. It worked about half the time. The other half it could get pretty ugly.

"Mike, I don't have any strong moral feelings about this one way or the other," I said. "I just wish you wouldn't come scooting out of there like a goddamn dog."

"I'll try to remember that," he said. It looked like he'd already had the drinks I needed. We walked over to the upstairs bar for a couple more. I couldn't see Simmons killing anybody but himself. And he'd been working on that for a long time. Hadn't we all.

I thought I'd have one drink with Simmons, check out the upstairs bar area and gift shop, and then join Ratso at the table he was holding on the balcony rail. It gave a good overview of the whole place.

Security looked pretty good. Patrick, the bouncer, was circulating like a rather large, anxious society hostess; Norman, the sweet-voiced and obviously very dangerous, androgynous black belt, was standing at the top of the stairs. When Norman smiled, it was obvious that he was pretty ill. His smile told you he'd love to dice up your Adam's apple for kicks. Mal, the former cop who ran a limo service on the side, stopped by the bar to take a little topper off my drink.

"Have a nice day," he said.

I lit a cigar. Simmons went to the men's room on the right of the bar if you were facing away from the bar on a barstool, which I was. I puffed thoughtfully on the cigar as I watched a cowboy from New Jersey. He'd had a long ride over to the Lone Star that night. Probably somebody's dope dealer. Ridin' 'cross the desert on a horse with no legs.

I downed the Jameson and let my mind wander the range a bit. Visions of two-dollar bills, left-handed swingers, Hank Williams songs. I thought of what Hank must have looked and sounded like playing the Grand Ol' Opry those many years ago. A troubled, leaning Jesus who sang with the sadness of a train and the beauty of a whippoorwill. It was said that on a number of occasions he'd actually cried while he sang on that stage. Over two decades later I played the Grand Ol' Opry myself a few times. I remembered walking on the stage in front of thousands of people at the old Ryman Auditorium looking for Hank's teardrops. But they, like my own, had long since dried. At least that's what I thought at the time.

I looked up just as a blinding light flashed in my eyes. I heard the sound of British laughter. Reticent, almost clipped.

"Very unprofessional of me, I'm afraid," said Gunner as she put her camera down on the bar next to me.

"Very tedious," I said. It was always hard to look indignant in the face of a beautiful face.

"You were such a study in . . . in introspection," she said. "Where were you just now when I took the picture?"

"Oh, Nashville," I said. "Nashville and Vancouver."

"That's a long way to travel on a barstool," she said softly.

I downed the fresh shot of Jameson that the bartender had poured. "I get around," I said.

The opening band was still thrashing through their first set as I took Gunner up the back stairs. They led up to the third-floor dressing rooms. As a performer myself, I was always hesitant about bugging entertainers just before a show. This time I was prepared to make an exception to my rule. Bubba and Blane might not be around afterward.

"The security people were very sweet," said Gunner. "They let me take a photograph."

"I let you take a photograph, too," I said.

"You couldn't have stopped me if you'd wanted to," she said tauntingly. Beneath the royal blue of her eyes I saw more than a taunt. More than laughter. I saw a challenge to mankind.

"Who would want to?" I asked admiringly. She nodded her head once in agreement.

We walked down the little hall on the third floor and I

knocked on the dressing room door. A big Nashville type with long sideburns and a Billy Graham hairdo opened the door.

"They're okay," Cleve shouted to him from the far side of the room.

"That's good to know," I said to Gunner. We walked in and the guy closed the door behind us. Bill Dick was standing next to Cleve and talking with Bubba and Blane. Patrick, the bouncer, had attached himself to the wall by the door like a red-bearded barnacle. He nodded at me. There were several other people in the room busy seeing and being seen. I didn't know who they were. A table of drinks had been set up by the open door to the patio. I looked through the door and could see the green metal scales of the iguana gleaming in the cold moonlight. Gunner followed my gaze and shivered slightly.

"Cold?" I asked.

"No," she said. "I was just thinking . . ."

"Well, don't do it again," I said. "Thinking can be dangerous. At least I think it can." The mood in the room was quiet. Maybe a little tense. That could just be opening-night jitters, I thought. Especially for country acts, playing New York City and the Lone Star Cafe was a big thing. It didn't mean a flying Canadian to me, though. When you live close to the pyramids you become acclimated to them.

I walked over to the table with the drinks and procured a couple. If Gunner didn't want one I'd drink two. As I walked over to the Borgelts, Bill Dick went over to Gunner. Club owners like to rub shoulders with the stars, but even more than that, they like to rub anything they can with pretty girls. Some people who don't own clubs like to do that, too.

I shook hands with Blane and Bubba. A few guys in the band were tuning up instruments over in a corner, getting ready for the first set. "Long time between dreams," I said.

"Haven't seen you in a coon's age," said Bubba.

"In a coon's age," agreed Blane.

"Let's keep race out of it, boys," I said. Blane laughed.

Bubba adjusted his "Go Texas" bow tie with the two se-quined strands of material running down his chest. The bow tie was a clip-on job. Smart after what had happened to Larry Barkin. I took out a cigar and lit it. Then I took out two more cigars and offered one to each of the Borgelts. They both turned them down. Almost everybody did. That's why I of-fered them to people.

"You guys nervous?" I asked.

"About the show?" Bubba asked.

"About the other thing," I said ominously. "Why the hell did you guys take this gig? If I'm not being too personal."

"Just a crackpot," laughed Bubba. "You can't hide from life. Besides, a gig's a gig."

"Can't hide from life," said Blane. "A gig's a gig." Sounded like he'd spent too many years in the echo chamber.

"That's the spirit," said Bill Dick as he hurried back over and put one arm around each of the boys. "How about a few shots, Gunner?"

Gunner obligingly shot away. At Dick's request I got into the act and stood next to Bubba. Then Cleve slipped in next to Blane. Pretty soon everybody'd gotten into the picture but Mother Maybelle Carter. That was country music, all right. One big happy family. Almost.

When my eyes came back into focus again I saw two blurry figures lurking in the doorway of the dressing room. Fox and Cooperman. Gunner had stopped taking pictures but Dick still had his arms around Bubba and Blane.

"I'd like to see somebody try something tonight," he said.

19

Gunner and I joined the Ratso table on the balcony rail. Ratso's date for the evening was porn star Annie Sprinkle. She wore her wristwatch around her ankle and her heart on her sleeve. Sometimes that was all she wore.

We had survived two brutal sets by the opening act, and one moderately entertaining show by Bubba and Blane. We'd been up to the dressing room one more time. More drinks. More pictures. More hand-shaking, more hugging, more rubbing shoulders with the stars. Nobody'd ordered two bowls of chili.

Now we were back at the table on the balcony waiting for the final set by Bubba and Blane. A new sound man was working. He was setting up the stage for the Borgelts. Cleve stopped by our table. "Where's Round Man the Sound Man?" I asked. He was the club's regular sound man. Weighed in at close to three hundred pounds.

"Let him have the night off," said Cleve. "This guy's a little green, but he'll get the levels set perfect just about the time the show's over." He smiled.

"Hey," he said, "your buddy Flippo was asking about you. He's in the gift shop setting up a display for his book."

"I'll just see what he wants," I said, getting up to leave.

"I'll just keep an eye on Gunner for you," said Cleve.

Flippo was autographing somebody's book in the gift shop. "Be careful," I told the young woman whose book he was signing, "his autographs are bouncing."

"Hey," said Flippo, "just who I was looking for. How's the book going?" It was moving about as fast as the Barkin murder case, but I had to say something.

"The thing that makes it work," I said, "is that it contains thoughts, incidents, scenes, emotions that only Hank Williams himself could have known."

"Glad you're enjoying it," said Flippo.

"Yeah," I said. "Look. The other night at the High Five when you gave me the book—where'd you get that two-dollar bill you had?"

"Larry gave it to me," he said. "Larry Barkin."

"Fine," I said. I went back to the table. Cleve was gone, but Simmons had taken his place. The Borgelts were coming on to the stage to raucous applause from the crowd. I pulled up an empty chair from another table and sat down. A waitress came by and we ordered a fresh round of drinks and sat back to watch the show.

Bubba Borgelt was at center mike. He played lead guitar and sang. Blane was on the mike at his right. He sang harmony. Sometimes the two would get together on the center mike, and the vocals really came across then. The sound man was beginning to get his act together. The band—a drummer, bass player, fiddler, and steel player—were all smooth, slick, right out of Nashville central casting.

"They ain't the Everly Brothers," said Ratso, "but they're not bad."

"Their long suit's recording," I shouted over the next song. "Their studio work's very commercial. Neither one of them's exactly Mr. Charismo onstage."

"They're not Kinky, that's for sure," said Ratso.

"Who is?" I asked.

"Good question," said Ratso.

"I've got to water my iguana," said Simmons as he got up and headed for the men's room.

Gunner took a few shots of the band with the camera balanced on the rail, looking right down at the stage. We had a pretty good view of the whole club from where we sat. I gazed into the crowd on the first-floor level and I thought I saw the gleam of a bald head. It was either Daddy Warbucks or Fishkin, Barkin's former manager. I slipped out of my chair and headed around the balcony to the stairs. I took the stairs down to the first floor at a fast clip. The band was playing a country rock tune and I came close enough to the stage to touch Blane Borgelt.

I stood to the right side of the stage and looked carefully over the audience.

"Sit down," shouted an angry woman.

"Relax, lady," I said. I walked farther back into the club. The only familiar face I saw was Cooperman's. He gave me a grudging nod.

"You see a bald-headed guy come by this way a minute ago?" I asked.

"No," said Cooperman. "What happened? He snatch your handbag?"

"Look, Sergeant, as long as we're here like this, I'd like to know something."

"I'll bet you would," he said with just this side of a snarl.

"If something happens tonight—" I started to say.

"It won't," he said. He didn't look at me.

"If it does though," I continued, "that's two songs and two murders, right?" I figured even Cooperman could tally that up.

"Enjoy the music," he said.

I walked back to the table. The band was into their last song. It was after two in the morning.

When I got back Gunner wasn't there. "Your bird has flown," said Ratso. "She said she'd call you later in the week."

"Great," I said. The band had left the stage, but the hardcore crowd had gathered around on the dance floor below us and was pushing for an encore. There was a double shot of Jameson and a cold Lone Star beer at my place at the table. "Compliments of Bill Dick," said Ratso. "He stopped by the table when you were away. He was damn relieved that the Borgelts made it through the night."

"He thinks we dodged the bullet, eh?" I took a healthy jolt of the Jameson. I smiled at Annie. She smiled at me.

"Sure looks that way," said Ratso. "If there ever was a bullet."

"There was one," I said. "Let's hope we don't have to bite it." The band came back on the stage for the encore. "Hey, Annie," I said. "I've been meaning to ask you. Why do you wear your wristwatch on your ankle?"

She looked up at me and laughed, her eyes a study in prurience and innocence. "What a strange thing to ask," she said.

Bubba Borgelt had come up to the center microphone, and a soft light was falling on him. He was saying what a great time we'd all had at the Lone Star tonight. He was thanking everybody in New York for being so beautiful.

"Shows what he knows," said Ratso. I was wondering what the hell time it was, but I didn't really want to ask Annie.

Bubba had one hand lazily draped over the neck of his guitar, and he reached out with the other to bring the microphone closer to him. The next thing I knew he was jumping around the stage like an epileptic shaman from New Guinea. He was still holding the guitar and the microphone, or rather they were still holding him. For maybe fifteen seconds everybody in the place froze like players in a macabre tableau. Everybody but Bubba.

For what seemed like an eternity, a crackling, popping noise emitted from the house speakers at a high decibel level. It didn't sound like country rock. A figure darted across the front of the stage to the soundboard where the new sound man was sitting, staring at the stage like a hypnotized puppet. The whole place was plunged into blackness except for little pinpoints of light made by people holding cigarettes. The points of light did not move. Nothing moved. It looked like the Old Chisholm Trail on a starry night, I remember thinking.

When the lights came back on, Cleve was standing by the wall switch he'd thrown to cut the juice and end the horrifying spectacle. His face was very white.

There was a smell in the place like tires burning, only not so heavy and a little sweeter. It stayed with you. The sound was something you weren't likely to forget either. Sounded like a short-order cook working overtime on a large order of french fries. But it had killed everybody's appetite.

And it had killed Bubba Borgelt.

20

Somewhere around eight-thirty Tuesday morning the phone rang by my bed. I'd been dreaming of somebody nice. Somebody from long ago. I'd been in several movies with her. Lots of excitement. A few memorable love scenes. The kind you could pop into the VCR unit you are sometimes pleased to call your brain, and play again and again and again . . .

Where was she now? In the bone orchard pushing up somebody's state flower. If they had state flowers in Canada. Like Al Capone once said: "I don't even know what street Canada's on."

No, they didn't seem to be making those kinds of movies anymore. What the hell. You couldn't expect more out of Hollywood than you could out of life. . . .

On about the fifth ring I collared the blower with some intensity. "Start talkin'," I said.

The voice on the phone was shouting, kind of like a football chant. It was Ratso. The chant went as follows: "Dim sum! Dim sum! Numbah one! Numbah one! Dim sum!" I had heard the chant before. It meant that Ratso was up early and feeling pretty good and wanted me to join him for dim sum, which was a form of Chinese breakfast. The location of the proposed breakfast was apparently the Number One Chinese Restaurant on Canal Street in Chinatown. It was my morning office when I was in Chinatown. In the afternoon, my office was Big Wong's on Mott Street. Actually, my office was anyplace that had a phone and a halfway hygienic dumper.

I looked at the clock. It was still eight-thirty.

"You participant-observers of life got it made, Ratso," I said. "Last night you see a guy deep-fried on a stage right in front of you, this morning you're ready to eat braised duck feet." Actually, I was getting kind of hungry myself.

"That's what I want to talk to you about," said Ratso. "Last night. We'll get the morning papers and you bring that song with you, 'Settin' the Trees on Fire.' "

" 'Settin' the Woods on Fire,' " I said.

"Yeah, that's the song."

"Ratso, that sheet music is now evidence in a homicide. It wouldn't be exactly prudent for me to go schlepping it all over New York. The cops'll be wanting it back now."

"What? They check it for prints yet?"

"Yeah, Starsky, they did," I said.

"Then bring the song," he said. "Maybe we'll find the clue."

"Maybe you'll find a pearl in your bean curd," I said.

The idea of a dim sum postmortem with Ratso was not something you'd want to look forward to every morning. But if you were going to have a dim sum postportem with Ratso, Number One was the best place to go.

I walked up Vandam to Sixth Avenue. There was still some snow around, but it wasn't the kind you see in the story-books. It was black and gray and it had cheap wine bottles, dog turds, and off-track betting forms in it. Make a pretty unpleasant-looking snowman.

I crossed Sixth Avenue, leaned left, and continued the few blocks up Prince Street where Ratso lived. Past a day-care center, an Italian bakery, and an all-night moonie vegetable stand, in case you had to have a rutabaga at four o'clock in the morning. It was a nice neighborhood. If you liked neighborhoods.

I walked into Ratso's building and pushed his buzzer.

"Who's there?" he asked.

"Son of Sam," I said pleasantly.

"Be right down, Son," he said.

When Ratso came down he was wearing his coonskin cap without the tail, and he was walking very fast. "C'mon," he said, "we'll pick up the papers at Bennie's, then we'll catch a cab to Chinatown."

Ratso was walking so fast that I found myself walking behind him a good bit of the time. "Ratso," I said, "slow the hell down, will you. I feel like a baby duck walking here behind you."

"That's called imprinting," said Ratso. "Ask a psychologist."

"*You* ask a psychologist," I said.

We went into Bennie's, where Ratso bought all three newspapers: the *Post,* which I always read and Ratso hated, *The New York Times,* which Ratso loved and I didn't believe in, and the *Daily News,* which we both read to see if the Russians were attacking the Alamo yet.

Bennie always treated Ratso like Frank Sinatra when he came in the place. Ratso loved it. Bought three papers there every morning. That was probably why Bennie treated him like Frank Sinatra.

As we headed toward West Broadway, Ratso carrying the *Times* and the *Daily News* and me carrying the *Post,* I said, "They really treat you like Frank Sinatra in there, Ratso."

"Yeah," he said.

"You know, Ratso," I said, "ol' Bennie could be camping with the clan of the dimly lit. Maybe he thinks you *are* Frank Sinatra."

Ratso considered it for a moment. "I tell you what," he said. "Don't spoil it for him."

21

"What city?" asked the information operator.

"That's what they all say," I said.

"What *city*, sir?"

"Nashville. For Randy Barkin." From the pay phone where I was standing, I watched a baby squid go from Ratso's chopsticks into his mouth.

"The number is 589-2328," said an electronic voice with about the same amount of animation as the information operator. You couldn't blame the operator, though. Imagine living out your days and finally, on your deathbed, looking back and your whole life flashing before you, and all you see is you sitting on your ass saying, "What city?"

I put the quarter back in the phone and dialed the Nashville number.

"Thank you for using AT&T," said the operator.

"Yeah," I said. "I'd like to charge this call to my office. That's 688-4070."

"And your name, sir?"

"Ratso," I said.

"Will you spell that, sir?" I looked over and saw Ratso eating a chicken's foot with his hand. They were kind of hard to nab with the chopsticks unless you knew what you were doing.

"R-A-T-S-O," I said.

"Thank you, Mr. Ratso. Just a moment, please." I figured

I'd charge the call to *National Lampoon.* Let him carry his own weight a little on this deal.

I waited. A number of Chinese men in business suits passed by me on the way to the men's room. A guy in white overalls came by with a dead pig on his shoulder.

"Go ahead," said the operator.

"Randy! Leap sideways, hoss. This is Kinky."

"Hey, brother, how are you?" said Randy in a sleepy voice. No matter how they overdubbed and remixed it, Nashville would always sound sleepy next to New York. Nashville had other things going for it. Pat Boone was from Nashville.

"Look, Randy," I said, "this may be important. It also may be nothing. What was the deal with your brother always carrying two-dollar bills?"

"Oh, that," said Randy. "He started that sort of as a gimmick with disc jockeys and fans. He'd give 'em a two-dollar bill for good luck, I guess, and to remember him by. He stopped doing that a long time ago, though.

"I remember one time he gave one to a colored street preacher, and the colored preacher said, 'Bless you, child'— he didn't even know who Larry was, you see—'and may the baby Jesus hold you in the palm of His little hand.' We all said 'Amen' to that."

"Yeah, that's nice," I said. The only thing wrong with Southern Baptists was they didn't hold them underwater long enough.

"It was almost like bein' in church," said Randy.

"Yeah," I said, "I can imagine." A woman came by hustling a tray of octopus beaks or something. I didn't get a good look at it.

"Where you callin' from?" he asked. I looked across the sea of Chinese faces placidly reading Chinese newspapers and eating chicken feet in the heart of the swirling madness that was New York City.

"Far away," I said.

22

One would think that Bubba Borgelt's demise would be a hard act to follow. But I was afraid that the killer was going to try. I was basing my judgment on the viciousness of both crimes, and the macabre nature of the "clue" I believed I saw in "Settin' the Woods on Fire."

Trouble was, I was a day late and a two-dollar bill short. I knew the clue but I didn't know the killer. Or rather I knew the killer but I didn't know that I knew him.

In the words of Hank Williams, I was going to have to piece together "a picture from life's other side." It was hard enough to know what you were doing on this side.

I just didn't want to take a disastrous wrong turn this early in the game. You may think that two stiffs in two weeks is not early in the game. But if you think that, believe me, you've taken a disastrous wrong turn somewhere. Pull over to life's other side and look in your glove box for your topographic map of the criminal mind. Anyone capable of doing murder, of consciously crossing those human boundaries that demark the lives of civilized men, was probably just beginning to get his second wind. And it looked like he might be going to blow Bill Dick's house down.

I stood at the window. I paced up and down. I sat at the desk. Finally, I had a heart-to-heart talk with the cat. What do we really know? The killer has sent two songs. He's killed the recipient of each. Each one a country singer performing at the Lone Star. The killer is left-handed. Knows enough about electrical wiring to arrange for a short in the system. Knows Hank Williams backward and forward. Every nuance of every lyric. He has a terminally ill sense of humor. He's very good at what he does. Any clues he's left, he's left intentionally. No face. No name. No apparent motive. And one more thing. He's got a cold, cold heart.

"What do you think?" I asked the cat. The cat didn't think too much of it apparently, because she yawned and went back to sleep.

"That's what I think, too," I said. Neither of us knew at the time that we were getting very close to him. And soon, standing up on two legs, he would turn on us with the furious, unspeakable evil of a trapped rat.

23

Friday may have been the end of the week, but it was the beginning of a nightmare.

Not that the two previous weeks had been egg creams. But things could get worse.

They did.

I was in the middle of a fitful dream Friday morning when a persistent honking from the street woke me up. I dreamed that I'd found a little baby on the sidewalk out in front of Village Cigars. It was much smaller than a baby should be. Maybe four inches long, with a diaper about the size of a commemorative stamp.

I'd picked the baby up and was holding it in my hand when a large group of familiar faces began to gather around me. Both Uptown and Downtown Judys were standing there together like demented Doublemint twins. Bill Dick was an admiral. Ratso was in his usual Sonny Bono hand-me-downs. Cleve, like a presidential assistant, was trying to keep the press away from me and the ridiculously small baby. Flippo was an SS officer. There was a guy with a haircut like Harpo Marx. He was offering cocaine to Sergeant Cooperman and Sergeant Fox, who were walking side by side, swinging their nightsticks in sync with each other.

Gunner was the Red Queen. She was carrying a gigantic tray upon which were two miniature bowls of chili, one for me and one for the baby. Mike Simmons stood a little off to the side. He wore a big white hat over his thin face. His shoulders were slightly hunched as if over a microphone. He was wearing a resplendent cowboy outfit that reflected the sun like a million tiny mirrors. For a brief moment I got a glimpse of him, and then the light became too bright. He looked like the spitting image of Hank Williams.

McGovern was dressed in a David Copperfield cap and ragged clothes. He resembled a giant newspaper boy, and in fact he was holding up a newspaper and shouting something I couldn't hear. Then my eye caught the headline. It read EXTRA! KINKY MURDERED AT LONE STAR! There was a big smile on McGovern's face.

The crowd was getting out of hand. They were all beginning to close in on me. I feared for the safety of the child. The crowd began chanting a rising, deafening chorus in unison. They shouted: "Change the diaper! Change the diaper! Change the diaper!"

Finally, Sergeant Cooperman worked his way through the crowd to where I was standing. He slapped his nightstick into the palm of his hand two or three times. The sound echoed loudly throughout the city of New York. Then, in a surprisingly gentle voice, Cooperman spoke to me. "What's the meaning of this?" he asked. "What's the meaning of this?"

I didn't know what the hell it meant. All I knew was that somebody was honking his horn and it sounded like his car was double-parked in my bedroom.

I got out of bed, put on my purple bathrobe, and walked over to the kitchen window in the general direction of the honking.

I opened the window. The honking was coming from a car that someone had driven right up onto the sidewalk directly in front of 199B Vandam. The car had a green Kojak bubble light on the dash.

"Ah, Christ," I said. The cat jumped up on the windowsill. "What do they want with us, now?" I asked the cat as I held her in place with both hands.

I put the cat back inside on the floor and I leaned out the window. A van pulled up onto the sidewalk behind the car. It was either a very dirty white, or else beige before the pigeons had found it. On the side was some kind of emblem and the words CITY OF NEW YORK HOUSING AUTHORITY. Below that it said FOR OFFICIAL USE ONLY. Maybe they were coming to arrest the lesbian dance class, I thought.

Two very serious, very large men in suits and ties got out of the van. My normal everyday New York paranoia began to kick in. Paranoia was just a protective device that nature gave to anyone living in the city. Who were these guys, I wondered? Cossacks? Gestapo? Amway representatives?

The two guys were looking up at me now. They didn't smile or wave. What the hell did they want at this hour of the morning? I couldn't imagine. I didn't think I had any overdue parking tickets. I didn't even think I had a car.

I was subletting the loft, on a long-term basis, from an unpleasant Greek woman who liked me about as much as spiders. The only thing she asked of me was that I water her plants. That was the only thing I always forgot to do. Sometimes I thought of my cigar smoke as a form of incense to clear out her remaining bad vibrational traces. But she and I were locked in kind of a New York rental death dance. At the prices I was paying, she couldn't throw me out without cutting her own throat. Maybe the landlord had gotten wise to the sublet situation and was putting me and the cat out in the street. Who could I call? Couldn't call the cops. Couldn't call the housing authority . . .

Finally, a familiar figure stepped out of the car. It looked up at me and shouted: "So throw down the fuckin' puppet head!"

It was Rambam. He was an old friend of mine who'd spent a couple years on the inside. Not inside his apartment. Inside federal Never-Never-Land. Rambam was a private investigator. He was always flashing a license, but nobody ever got the chance to look at it closely. He claimed he was still wanted in every state that begins with an *I*. He knew people even Ratso never dreamed of. He had connections many people didn't even want.

I threw down the puppet head.

The two guys took a coffinlike arrangement covered with a tarp out of the back of the van. Moments later, all three of them and the large mysterious object were at my door.

"Meet your new espresso machine," said Rambam.

The two guys brought it in and began setting it up in the kitchen. It was big, bronze, and shiny like the kind you see in Italian restaurants. It had a bronze eagle perched on top of it.

"Jesus," I said, "that must have set somebody back a bundle."

"I don't think so," said Rambam with a short laugh. "You remember that girl you saved in the bank?"

"You mean COUNTRY SINGER PLUCKS VICTIM FROM MUGGER?" I asked.

"That's the one," he said. "Well, her father-in-law is Joe the Hyena."

"That's nice," I said. What else could I say?

"He wanted you to have this. These are two of Joe the Hyena's sons. They don't speak much English. They're fresh off the boat."

"The Love Boat?" I asked.

"Christ, that's funny," said Rambam. He said something in Italian to the two guys, they adjusted a few knobs on the machine, and then they nodded and left.

"I didn't know you could speak Italian, Rambam," I said.

"Just a few phrases here and there," he said.

"What'd you just tell Joe the Hyena's sons?" I asked. I lit up my first cigar of the morning and took a few tentative puffs.

" 'Get the van back,' " he said. He loaded the machine with a bag of ground coffee beans marked "Special Italian Roast." He adjusted a few more gadgets, dusted the eagle with his hand, and we both leaned back against the counter to see what would happen.

Nothing happened for a while. Rambam, the cat, and I were all watching the machine. "C'mon baby," said Rambam, "talk to me."

"Maybe it speaks Japanese," I said.

"This machine?" asked Rambam incredulously. "You kiddin'?" The machine began to hiss and hum a little. Then it started to gurgle. Then it was off to the races. "Smell that espresso," said Rambam. "Machine's worth it already. Kills the cigar smoke in here."

Heavy cigar smoking and what I liked to think of as social usage of cocaine had fairly well destroyed my beezer. But I could smell the espresso. "Smells great," I said. "First thing I've smelled in seven years."

Rambam and I sat down at the table with two cups of steaming espresso. "Good as the Caffé Roma any day," he said.

"Have to do without the lemon peel," I said.

"We'll rough it," said Rambam. He reached in his coat pocket and took out a folded copy of the *Daily News*. He handed it to me. "Looks like your pal Bill Dick's in trouble," he said. "Nobody's going to want to play his club."

"Yeah," I said. I opened the paper to the front page, and the first thing I saw was McGovern's by-line. The story carried the headline:

HANK WILLIAMS MURDERS
TWO SONGS—TWO SLAIN

It was inevitable that McGovern would stumble on to the fact that someone was sending Hank Williams songs as murder invitations sooner or later. I wondered who he'd talked to. Flippo? Cleve? Bill Dick? It didn't really matter. What mattered was that given the sensational and competitive nature of the New York press, the public interest in the case and the pressure to solve it were going to skyrocket. This was bad news for the cops. And it was bad news for me. Because it wasn't going to be an easy case to solve. And that was putting it mildly.

It was the first time I'd thought of Hank Williams all day. Of course it was only eleven o'clock.

"What do I do with Joe the Hyena?" I asked Rambam. "Send him a thank-you note or something?"

"No," said Rambam, "you already did your bit for him at the bank when you saved his daughter-in-law."

I watched the December sunshine splash into the loft and felt it chase away some of the chill. I was starting to feel pretty good. Maybe it was the espresso, or maybe it was the warming thought that I'd saved somebody's life and that people were grateful for it.

"You're lucky," said Rambam. "Most guys do their bit at the bank, they only get a toaster."

24

It was half past Gary Cooper time and I was out buying cat food. The sun was no longer anywhere to be seen. Maybe it thought it would knock off early. Get away before the rush hour. I was half-way to the grocery store when it started to rain. I never run when it starts raining. I just keep to my same leisurely pace and try to walk between the drops. You get about equally wet either way, but if you run you look stupid. If you walk you just look crazy. There's more dignity in crazy, and it's also less strenuous.

As a general concession to the rain, however, I decided to stop at a fancy little gourmet shop. About all they seemed to sell were gourmet pistachio nuts and cat food at ninety-seven cents a can. I bought four cans. They didn't give Green Stamps.

On my way back home in the rain I saw a man with his hand out and a wet cardboard sign around his neck. It said I AM A VET. PLEASE HELP ME. I gave him five bucks. He gave me a salute. I turned the corner and went home.

I fed the cat, lit a cigar, and walked over to the window. I watched the raindrops scamper down the rusty fire escapes across the street. The cat finished eating and she jumped up on the windowsill. We watched the rain together for a long time.

I felt inexpressibly lonely. "Hey," I said to the cat. "I ever tell you about the time in Vietnam . . ."

The cat kept watching the rain.

* * *

I called Gunner around dusk.

"Hello," said a breathless British voice.

"Did I interrupt something?"

"No," said Gunner, "I've been in the darkroom all after-noon."

"Grow mushrooms in there?" I asked.

"No," she said.

"Didn't think so," I said. "Want to join me for dinner at the Derby tomorrow night?"

"Let me check my schedule," she said. "Oh. I have a session at six. But I could meet you around nine."

"Fine," I said.

"Fine," she said. The last time I'd taken a broad to dinner on a Saturday night, I was a young cowboy and Broadway was a prairie. I hung up.

I had more than merely a social interest in Gunner. There were a few stray threads I wanted to gather from her Victorian tweeds. I had been gathering stray threads all week, and I was starting to feel like Rapunzel without a sewing machine. If I could've woven together all the threads I'd gathered on this case, it would've made such an unpleasant-looking web that nobody would have wanted to come into my parlor.

Murray Fishkin, the lawyer, was never in his office when I called. I didn't have the resources or the authority to corral a guy like Fishkin, but I was going to have to find some way to get to him pretty fast. Also I planned to get a little tighter with Simmons and Flippo—see if I noticed any veiled threats or new facial tics.

I poured out a shot of Jameson and downed it at my desk. Suspects were only suspects. All you could do was suspect them. When you got right down to it, there was an art to knowing when not to bang your head against the wall. I downed another shot of Jameson. I fished around in the wastebasket and found a decent-looking half-smoked cigar and I fired it up. Gives you a little buzz that a fresh one never quite comes up to.

I would wait. Let the killer make the next move in this chess game. All killers lacked one important quality. They lacked, as Holmes himself put it, "that supreme gift of the artist—the knowledge of when to stop."

Hank was bound to strike again. When he did, I planned to catch him and feed him to the iguana. I tossed off another jolt of Jameson. I'd just sit here and wait for something to happen.

Waiting was boring. Most people spend their lives waiting. For trains to pass. For princes to come. For agents to call. For ships to come in. For phone calls that will change their lives. I was no different.

I was waiting for a killer to kill.

25

The Monkey's Paw, full of stifling warmth and hollow laughter, reached out to the lonely denizens of the freezing sidewalk and pulled them inside with a greedy simian fist. A cold rain that had begun earlier in the evening had now turned to sleet. Not the sort of night to be gazing at quaint window displays in quaint little Village shops. It was too damn cold to be quaint.

General Sheridan was still there, of course, holding the fort, with sleet bouncing like enemy bullets off his greatcoat. He was about the only guy who ever hung out in the square who wasn't a degenerate. He looked proud, stern, and disapproving, even with an icicle on his nose. He might have been a mediocre general, but he made a great statue.

I arrived at the Monkey's Paw about a quarter after Cinderella's deadline.

"You're late," said Ratso. He was tucked into a far corner at the bend of the bar near the radiator.

"You never gave Marilyn Monroe that crap when she was late, Ratso," I said.

"Those were different times," said Ratso. "We were young, restless, carefree, white, liberal . . . stupid."

"You can say that again," I said.

"I can't remember it," said Ratso.

We ordered a round from Tommy the bartender. "Let's put this one on the *Lampoon*," I said.

"The rate you're going, you're gonna put it on that ugly hunting vest of yours," said Ratso.

"Put a sock on it," I said. "I'm not scheduled to perform neurosurgery for at least two more hours."

Tommy brought the drinks. I took a hearty slug of mine. Just to cut the phlegm.

"First of all, Ratso," I said, "I want to thank you for helping me the other night." I knocked off the rest of the shot.

"How?" asked Ratso.

"Remember at the loft we were talking about right-handed and left-handed shadows? I was depressed about how the case was not going anywhere? You said, 'Don't be so negative'?"

"Yeah?"

"Well, that's good advice anytime," I said, "but it's especially pertinent when you're talking about contact sheets. It's the negative, Ratso. The negative was reversed." I motioned to Tommy for another round.

"In the picture of me and Reshevsky, the white square is at each player's right hand. The next day, I went to the cop shop and got Cooperman to show me the contact sheet again. Those guys playing chess in Washington Square Park. Remember? The *black* square was at each player's right hand."

Tommy brought over a Bass ale and a shot of Jameson for me and a vodka grapefruit juice for Ratso. Ratso was under the impression that this drink would help him lose weight. I doubted if it was true, but the more he drank, the skinnier my wallet looked.

"I promise you one thing," I said. "When the murderer is caught, he'll be left-handed."

"Jesus," said Ratso, "I thought the killer came from Houston. Obviously a red herring."

"Obviously," I said.

Several grapefruit orchards later I told Ratso the nature of the "clue" I'd seen in "Settin' the Woods on Fire." The connection, as it were, between the song and Bubba Borgelt's death.

"This is a sick clue," I said. "You didn't see it in the song because you have a normal mind."

"Maybe normal is too strong a word," said Ratso.

"Ingenuous, childlike, trusting . . ."

"Yeah," said Ratso. It was only one word, but he was starting to slur it.

"What I'm going to tell you doesn't bring us much closer to the identity of the killer, but it does give us a good glimpse of his mind at work. An unpleasant spectacle at best."

"Lay it on me," said Ratso. "Maybe I'll empathize." He laughed a short, nervous laugh. I lit a cigar.

"Don't count on it," I said. I puffed at the cigar a bit. It wasn't bad.

"Okay," I said. "I knew this prison guard once, down in Texas. He was telling me about what an execution was like in the electric chair. He said that they always strapped the doomed men down to the chair much more heavily than you'd think necessary. If they didn't, he said, 'they'd get up and dance around.'

"Well, that's what happened Monday night to Bubba Borgelt. Except nobody strapped him down."

"What do you mean?" Ratso asked.

"I mean somebody wanted Bubba to dance. Somebody who looks at life through the eyes of evil.

"The killer, I imagine, rather fancied the little bridge in the song:

> "We'll take in all the honky-tonks.
> Tonight we're havin' fun.
> We'll show the folks a brand new dance
> That never has been done.

"The killer made those lines come to life in a way Hank Williams never dreamed of. He saw perverse possibilities in that old tune that would only occur to an extremely sick cowboy. We saw the 'brand new dance' on Monday night on the stage of the Lone Star. The killer employed Borgelt's body and his soul. To show the folks. To bring that spine-snapping, heart-stopping, hypnotizing, horribly out-of-control breakdance to the stage for one night only. Somebody planned it, chuckled over it to himself, carried it out without a hitch, and watched the whole hideous performance right there with the rest of us. An attractive picture, isn't it?''

Ratso sat silent for a long moment. He shook his head slowly, like he was trying to shake off a memory that you can't shake off. He tried a little laugh, but it didn't take. Ratso looked at me. I looked at Ratso.

''Shocking, Sherlock,'' he said.

26

M_y kitchen table looked like Lou Grant's desk on a bad day. It was littered with almost the whole week's newspapers, and they weren't there so I could follow octopus beak futures. I needed all the information I could get on the "Lone Star Killer" and the "Hank Williams Murders," as he and they had now come to be known.

I moved sluggishly into my second cup of espresso and lit a cigar. I looked at the front page of Tuesday's *Daily News*. The headline was PLUCK SECOND STRINGER AT LONE STAR. I settled back in my chair and searched through the pile until I found a typically amazing headline on a late edition of Thursday's *New York Post*. The article was obviously written when very little new information was coming in on the story. The *Post* headline read SECOND STAR SLAIN—LINKED TO MAYOR.

I sipped a little more espresso and puffed at the cigar. The *Times* had been a trifle late with the news, but by Wednesday it had acknowledged that indeed something out of the ordinary was occurring at the Lone Star Cafe. By Friday it had jumped aboard with both feet and was attempting to lead the way again. The headline on the story in Friday's *New York Times* was IS IT TIME TO BAN COUNTRY MUSIC?

The stories were all remarkably similar. There were interviews with Lone Star owner Bill Dick in which I learned the size of his boat—forty-two feet—and several other things about it I hadn't wanted to know, and with the Lone Star manager, my old pal Cleve, who seemed to have become an expert on criminology, electrical wiring, educating the public, and psychology in general. I'd always thought he was just a road musician who drifted into the job when his band had decided to disband.

The other name that kept popping up in the stories was that of Chet Flippo. He was a bona fide Hank Williams expert, and as such he was suddenly in great demand. "Why did the killer resort to such an odd method of communicating his death threats?" asked the reporter. "As I point out in my book . . . ," responded Flippo. And so forth.

Questions were also put to Fox and Cooperman, as they appeared to be the most prominent NYPD operatives on the case. "We have no suspects at the moment." "We are following several leads right now." "We're working on it." Things didn't look real promising.

Everybody wanted to know what was really going on. Nobody really knew except one person. And he wasn't talking.

The phones rang. I got up, made it over to the desk, and nabbed the one on the left on the second ring. A few more rings might've cauterized my brain. It was 3:04 P.M. It was Chet Flippo.

"Hi there," he said. "I'm calling to invite you to a literary event. Tomorrow afternoon between three and six at the Lone Star. It's a party for the book."

"Sounds like a lot of fun," I said.

"It's interesting," said Flippo. "Ever been to one of these literary affairs?"

"No," I said.

"You really ought to come then," he said.

"I went to a cock fight once in Mexico," I said. Flippo laughed a hearty literary laugh.

"See you tomorrow," he said.

I hung up and looked at the unopened book still sitting where I'd left it on the corner of the desk. Maybe I'd have to read the damn thing. Could a book on the life of a country singer who died thirty-three years ago shed any light on the menace of a modern-day killer who was stalking New York City? Impossible, I thought.

Highly improbable, anyway.

Nine-thirty, Saturday night. I was sitting at the little bar in the Derby on MacDougal Street, working on my third Courvoisier and waiting for Gunner. I never used to like Courvoisier but I knew somebody once who used to love it, and I used to love her. So now I drank Courvoisier sometimes and smiled to myself. If somebody was watching me drinking alone there, and smiling to myself, they might've thought I was plotting to kill my wife. But I wasn't. I didn't have a wife.

"Hello," said a voice behind me. I turned in time to catch a dazzler of a smile. "Did I keep you waiting long?" she asked.

"Yeah," I said. I employed an economy of words. Women go for the strong, silent type. Except in rare cases where they prefer the highly verbal, indecisive type. I could be either. Sometimes, in extreme situations, I would rapidly alternate the two personas in case the woman liked a guy who was confused about his identity. I didn't work at it too hard, though. I didn't really give a damn what a woman thought. That was probably the reason my personal life was a shipwreck. I treated women like everybody else, and no matter what they may tell you, that ain't the ticket. Usually.

"This is a cute place," said Gunner.

"Yeah," I said.

"Yeah?" she asked. "Yeah. That's all you say to anybody? Yeah?"

"Yeah," I said.

She sat down next to me at the bar. She put her hand on my shoulder.

"I think you say 'yeah' because you want people to think you're a tough guy," she said softly but distinctly. She was looking me right in the eyes. She wouldn't take her hand off my shoulder. I didn't mind too much. It was her hand. She could put it anywhere she wanted. "You're not really a tough guy, are you?" she asked.

"Not really," I said. I killed the last of the Courvoisier. "I just like to say 'yeah' a lot. It's part of a Beatle lyric I heard once. You hungry?"

"I'm starved," she said.

"Good," I said. "We'll order a couple of big, hairy steaks."

"Sounds charming," she said.

We took a table in the back, had some wine. I let Gunner pick the wine. Always let the woman choose the wine. Makes you look sensitive, innocent. Maybe a little vulnerable. It's also usually cheaper because the woman is trying to protect you because she thinks you're so vulnerable.

Gunner ordered a very expensive bottle of French wine. I couldn't speak enough frog to even read the label. As the waiter was opening the bottle, Gunner said to me, "Ever try this before?"

"No," I said, "I usually stick with Château de Cat Piss." She looked pretty as a picture as she laughed a little light British laugh. Just to pass the time until the guy pulled the cork. As I looked at her, she began to look even prettier than a picture. Prettier than any picture she was ever likely to take.

A fleeting thought crossed a dusty desk in my mind. Not so much a thought, maybe, as a feeling. I didn't like the feeling. It was a sort of irrational confusion heavily laced with distrust. Distrust for the vision sitting across the table from me.

What did I really know about this broad? Not a bloody lot. She looked too beautiful to be trusted. Too good to be true. I didn't even know for sure that the photos she showed us at Costello's were taken when she said they'd been. Or if she'd tampered with them first. Certainly not. But she did seem to have an uncanny knack of being nearby scenes of mysterious death. So what? I had that same little knack myself. Had Gunner left the Lone Star before somebody'd turned on the juice and cut Bubba loose? She'd stayed the whole damn night. Why leave just before the last song?

Was I just being paranoid? Probably. But if you're paranoid long enough, sooner or later you're gonna be right. The waiter was struggling with the cork and I was struggling with the notion that Gunner was holding back. That she knew something that I needed to know. But I didn't know what I needed to know that she knew. If that made any sense. I smiled at her across the table. She smiled back. What the hell. You had to trust somebody.

"I hope it's a good year," said Gunner.

"So far it's been a pretty lousy one," I said. "I don't know about you, but for me the year started fairly slowly. After a while it picked up a little steam, and life became merely tedious. Then, just when it was looking like the worm of happiness was beginning to turn my way, this little spot of bother arises at the Lone Star and throws my whole goddamn life into a hideous, murderous snarl. I don't know. . . . Maybe next year will be better. Who knows?" I gave Gunner my careless, hopeful, survivor's smile.

She smiled back. A brief, rather patronizing smile. "I was talking about the wine," she said.

27

On balance, the evening had been a success. That's what I thought as I rode up to my loft in the freight elevator with the one exposed light bulb. There is very little you can do with a freight elevator. You can't very well hang a Tiffany lampshade in it. That would be gauche.

The Hank Williams Killer was far away, I thought. You had to think of something when you rode in a freight elevator or you might as well be freight.

Inside the loft, I patted the cat and checked for any messages on the answering machine. Nobody loved me.

I put on my sarong, killed the light, and went to sleep concentrating on not dreaming about miniature babies.

The phone rang by my bedside. I hit the light and looked at the clock. It was crowding three o'clock in the morning. I was one of those guys that didn't mind getting woke up in the middle of the night. Probably should've been a fireman or a country doctor. I didn't have a wife. Didn't have any kids. Didn't have a job to go to in the morning. Didn't go to church. Didn't give a damn if somebody called me in the middle of the night.

Just as long as I didn't pick up the phone and find it was me on the other end of the line. I picked up the phone. It wasn't me.

It was Gunner.

"Somebody's broken into my apartment," she said.

Her lost-little-girl inflection combined with the British accent made her sound like one of the three bears saying, "Somebody's been sleeping in my bed." Unfortunately, I wasn't the guilty party.

"You all right?" I asked. "You call the cops?"

"Yes," she said wearily. "They've been and gone. I'm all in, I'll tell you."

"Anything missing?" I asked.

"What do you think is missing?" she fairly shouted.

"No idea," I said. "Something's missing from every life, they say."

"Well, something's sure missing from mine," she said. "And I'm scared." She sounded close to tears.

"Tell me," I said in a softer tone.

"What's missing from mine . . . is every print, contact, and negative of everything I've ever shot at the Lone Star Cafe."

28

"Where's your friend Gunner?" asked Cleve with a fairly satanic leer. The Lone Star was humming with activity. People and books and bottles of beer were everywhere you looked and a few places you didn't. Hank Williams music was blaring out of the house speakers and Lone Star Five-Alarm Chili was coming down the line as fast as Fong, the Chinese cook, could slop it into the bowls. Quite a literary event.

"Who's Gunner?" asked Downtown Judy petulantly as soon as Cleve strolled away. I wasn't sure I knew myself.

"Oh, Gunner's a photographer person I've been doing some work with," I said. Sadly, this was true. "Never above you, never below you, always by your side" was about as far as I'd got.

"Is Gunner a man or a woman?" asked Downtown Judy. She wasn't one to beat around the bush, especially if she thought the situation threatened her bush.

"Is who a man or a woman?" asked Ratso as he scurried up, balancing a bottle of Lone Star, a bowl of chili, and a book.

"Gunner," said Downtown Judy.

"She's a broad Kinky's currently hosing. She's a fucking gorgeous broad," Ratso laughed. Downtown Judy looked at me.

"She's not that gorgeous," I said. I tried to give Ratso a disparaging look, but he was busy eating his chili.

"Have I ever met her?" asked Judy.

"No," I said. "I've hardly met her myself."

Ratso looked up from his chili and winked at me conspiratorially. He was laughing so hard he couldn't eat. "Pretty good chili," he said.

Downtown Judy turned away from him and gazed into my eyes. She looked like a little puppy dog that might suddenly grow up to be the Hound of the Baskervilles. And if she did, I doubted if she'd know "c'mere" from "sic 'em."

"I didn't think you liked the chili here, Ratso," I said.

"It's the only thing on the menu today," he said. "Lone Star beer and chili. Very trendy."

"It's chic, all right," I said. "I've got to find Bill Dick. I'll be back."

I navigated my way through the crowd on the stairs and fought my way to the bar on the second floor. I didn't see anybody I knew except the bartender. Most of the people I knew were probably still sleeping off Saturday night.

I pointed to a guy standing next to me who was holding a beer bottle. The bartender got me a beer.

I looked around at the ponderous little groups of people all over the place and went out the door and on to the rear staircase. It was cooler and quieter, and no literary lions were there. I sat down on the stairs and sipped the beer. I gathered my thoughts.

I didn't have a mother-in-law. That was one of the advantages of not being married. And yet something had been nagging me all morning. Relentlessly. If it had only been a mother-in-law it wouldn't have been such a problem. I could've just called Joe the Hyena and had her legs broken. Had her left in the trunk of a Budget Rent-A-Car out at JFK.

But what was nagging me had nothing to do with the mother-in-law I didn't have. And it was very serious and very real. It had to do with Gunner.

Seven days had passed since Bubba Borgelt had been braised. The killer appeared to strike viciously, and then go into hibernation for a while, leaving no tracks. Except those he wanted us to follow. Why?

"Hey, man," said a familiar voice from under a cowboy hat. "How's the murder investigation comin'?" It was Lee, the other manager of the place besides Cleve. He looked like a black Tom Mix. His wife, Leni, ran the cloakroom setup. She was a doll.

"It's coming about as good as your chances of being elected Head Lizard of the White Supremacist Party," I said. I finished the beer. I put the bottle on the stairs.

"Don't leave it there," said Lee. "Somebody come along and trip on it and break their fool neck."

"Yeah," I said, "that on top of two murders could be bad for business." Lee smiled.

"You kiddin', man?" he asked. "You have any idea what the ring was last night?" I didn't even know what the ring was any night.

"What's the ring?" I asked.

"The ring," said Lee impatiently, "is the cash register. The amount of business at the bar. Last night was the biggest in the whole history of the club. Why you think everybody's buying this guy's book? Everybody wants to see the murder scene for themselves. Everybody's waiting for the Hank Williams Killer to hit again."

It was a little surprising what people would do. Only a little surprising.

"That's where it's at," said Lee, and he walked up the stairs. I thought it might be time I looked for Bill Dick.

He'd either be in his office or on his boat, and I hadn't brought my periscope so I thought I'd check his office first.

I saw Ratso and Downtown Judy across the balcony, waved, and headed quickly down the stairs to the first floor. At the foot of the stairs a large, polite mob had gathered around the glowing figure of Chet Flippo. He was talking, signing books, and doing a fair imitation of being gracious. Flippo didn't see me. He was looking through the whole scene. There was something in his eyes I hadn't seen before. I liked it even less than what I'd seen the last time.

Hank's lonely wail came through the speakers, but his

words went unnoticed in the din of the sophisticated, glittering crowd. The song went:

> *"Tonight down here in the valley*
> *I'm lonesome and oh how I feel*
> *As I sit here alone in my cabin*
> *I can see your mansion on the hill."*

As I made my way over to the stairs that led down to Bill Dick's office, I also overheard a few phrases from the crowd around Flippo.

"Marvelous economy of words," one said.

"The characters leap right off the page," said another.

29

"What a city!" said Bill Dick as he poured us both a glass of something from the decanter on his desk. "What a city!"

I nodded and took a sip. "It's not bad," I said.

"You're damn right it's not bad. I don't care what anybody says about it. New York has rallied around the Lone Star."

"I was talking about the drink," I said. "Drink's not bad. City's rotten." I took another sip.

"Think what you want," said Bill Dick, "but the people of New York have come through for the Lone Star." I thought of that woman who was stabbed about eighty-seven times and screamed for help for nearly an hour before she died. More than a hundred people had heard her. Nobody'd called the cops. Nobody'd helped. Kitty something, her name was, I thought, though it didn't make a hell of a lot of difference now. The same sort of ghouls who let her die were now thronging to the Lone Star Cafe.

Bill poured me another drink. I didn't say anything. Bill looked at me. "Right or wrong, Kinkster?" he asked.

My mind was still trying to think of Kitty's last name, but it was drawing a blank. "Right, Bill," I said.

"Life goes on, Kinkster. There's still a business that some-body's got to run. There's still a lot of problems to deal with."

"I can imagine," I said. "If you don't mind my asking, what are the problems? Aside from the two obvious ones. Two stiffs that used to be stars."

"They're still stars, Kinkster," said Bill Dick.

"Tell that to Gabby Hayes," I said. Bill shifted uncomfortably in his chair.

"Drawing crowds is no problem now," he said. "The problem is getting anybody to play the goddamn club."

"Can't understand it," I said.

He smiled a small, brief smile. If he'd held it a little longer you could've called it a wince. "So we're using house bands temporarily. Cleve's fronting one group. Used to have his own band, you know. Mike Simmons is booked to play a few nights. We'll get by for now, but I don't know how long we can stretch it before we'll have to get a name act in here. Pretty damn quick, I'd say. These crowds can be fickle."

"And that's a nice word for them," I said. "What other problems are you having?" I was having a problem believing anybody'd play the place again. Of course, when you needed a gig, you needed a gig.

"The other problems we can handle," he said. "Petty theft. A case of Jack Daniel's disappears. Somebody's swiped a picture from out of the manager's office. Bartenders robbing you blind. The day-to-day crap that drives you nuts."

I stood up to go. I had problems of my own. "I've got to get upstairs," I said. "Before I go, though, I'd like you to explain something to me. I don't need the details. Just nut-shell it for me. Could anybody have rigged that electrical system to french-fry Bubba Borgelt?"

If I'd wanted a one-word answer, it would've been pretty disappointing. I was glad I didn't have a train to catch.

"I know a good bit about electrical wiring," he said. "Now the guitar amp wasn't grounded. It was sitting at a potential of a hundred twenty volts AC." At this point Dick resorted to drawing little diagrams on his desk. I didn't ask any questions. I didn't know what the hell he was talking about.

"Hey," I said, "I'm not the Wichita lineman. Put the thing in layman's terms."

"Anybody could have done it," he said. "Borgelt's body completed the circuit. With that sweaty, salt-drenched outfit, by the end of the last set he was a perfect human conductor."

There was an eagerness flashing in Dick's eyes. They appeared faintly electrical and almost happy. I thanked him for his help and went upstairs.

Things had thinned out a hair. Now you could cross the room without having to turn sideways. I joined Ratso at the downstairs bar. Simmons was hanging on to him like a fungus growing out of his left elbow. We all had a drink.

"Doubles for everybody, bartender," said Simmons. "Rocks."

"What was that woman's name," I asked, "that was being stabbed to death and you know, was screaming forever, and a hundred people heard her and didn't do anything?"

"Oh yeah," said Ratso, "I remember—Kitty . . . uh, Kitty—"

"Kitty what?" I asked impatiently. The bartender brought the drinks.

"Kitty . . . ," said Simmons. "Kitty . . . I know it . . . it's right on the tip of my knife."

Downtown Judy walked up behind us. She'd taken a cigarette out of her purse and was waiting for somebody to light it.

"Kitty Genovese!" I shouted.

"You're good with names," said Ratso.

"Who's Kitty Genovese?" asked Downtown Judy.

We gravitated, if that was the word, to the upstairs bar. It was closing in on five o'clock, but it seemed like we'd spent several incarnations at the Lone Star. Einstein's theory applied. Time was relative, and time spent at literary affairs was relatively tedious.

We'd lost Simmons, but picked up Cleve and Flippo. I figured I'd play like Jack Webb and ask Cleve a few routine questions. I wasn't in much shape to ask hard ones. I'd let Downtown Judy ask the hard ones.

"So Cleve," I said, "what's the security like down there in the manager's office? What about this picture that's missing?"

"Obviously, you've talked to Bill," said Cleve. "Christ, I wish he'd get off my back about all this shit. Of course, security down there is nonexistent. What the hell does he expect?"

"What about this picture?" I asked.

"Yeah, that is a strange one," he said. "The damn thing materialized out of nowhere one morning—nobody knows where it came from—then, just when Bill tells me to have it framed, it disappears." Maybe I was imagining things, but it seemed like Flippo, sitting down the bar from us, was becoming increasingly engrossed in our conversation.

"Well," I said, "what's the big deal? Was this a valuable goddamn painting?" I thought of Gauguin's last letter, in which he stated, "I have been defeated by poverty." The letter is now owned by David Rockefeller. Why not? Flippo was definitely listening now.

"No," said Cleve. "It was hardly a case of where did Vincent Van Gogh?" He laughed a little. I didn't. "It wasn't a goddamn oil painting or anything. It was just an old photo. But it was autographed. The picture was autographed, so I guess that made it valuable. I don't know."

"Who was the picture of?" I asked. Flippo was looking away. A bit too unconcerned suddenly.

"Christ," said Cleve. "Didn't Dick tell you?"

"Apparently he didn't or I wouldn't be asking you," I said.

"It was a picture of Hank Williams," said Cleve.

30

Monday morning I was working on my first cup of espresso and looking over a little stiff chart I'd written down on a Big Chief tablet. It had been two and a half weeks since Larry Barkin had gone to Jesus. It was exactly a week since Bubba Borgelt's rather unpleasant demise. During this time Bill Dick had been able to coax only three name acts into playing the club: Jerry Jeff Walker, Asleep at the Wheel, and the Burrito Brothers. Nothing out of line had occurred on those three occasions. I considered this with a troubled spirit. Why had Hank picked on Barkin and Borgelt and let Walker, Asleep at the Wheel, and the Burritos pass by unscathed?

According to reports from Cleve and Ratso, the crowds of the curious were still coming like morbid moths to the doily of death that hung over the place. This continued to make the cash register register.

In fact, for Bill Dick, murder, unpleasant and un-American as it was, was beginning to look like a financial pleasure.

I moved thoughtfully into my second cup of espresso. I lit my first cigar of the morning and leaned back in the chair by my desk. A number of patterns were beginning to come together fairly clearly in my cranium. I wasn't a rocket scientist, but there were occasions when I was able to put two and two together and come up with something moderately wiggy.

I thought of the Hank Williams picture that Cleve had said was missing from the Lone Star. Then I remembered a snatch of conversation in which someone had told me, "He let me take a photograph." My reasoning went like this: *Gonif* is the Yiddish word for "thief." *Gonif* is Yiddish. Gunner is British. Therefore Gunner is a *gonif*.

I called Gunner.

It was not a particularly pleasant phone call, but it confirmed what I'd suspected. Gunner had lifted the photograph from the Lone Star. She had, in the words of Jesse Winchester, been "taken by a photograph" she'd seen on a desk in the manager's office. It was a photo of a "tall, gaunt man in a big white cowboy hat standing with two small boys by a sign that said HOWIE'S #1 BBQ. A contrasty print," she'd said. "A grainy texture. A large sky. A fifties feel to it."

Translated from the argot of the trendy fashion photographer, that meant she liked the picture.

"So where's the photo now?" I asked.

"That's just it," she said. "I've looked everywhere. It might have been taken along with everything else when my place was broken into. I never even got a chance to take it out of the envelope I'd put it in."

"Terrific," I said. "Do you remember anything about the picture? This is important now, Gunner." It was more important than even I knew at the time.

"This—this didn't have anything to do with what's been happening at the Lone Star, did it?" she asked with a rising note of anxiety.

"No, of course not," I said. No point in upsetting her further. It was bad enough to be known as a *gonif*. "Tell me about the picture," I said.

"I told you about the picture," she said. "HOWIE'S #1 BBQ. The man with the white hat, the small boys in cowboy suits. Did I mention that? They were dressed in cute little matching cowboy outfits?"

"No," I said.

"Standing one on each side of him by the roadside. And there was some writing, maybe a signature and a date somewhere on the bottom."

"You don't remember the signature? The date?"

"I don't recall the signature," she said, "but the date was December 31, 1952. It's my mum's birthday so I remembered it. I only saw the bloody thing for a few seconds when it was on the desk." Amazing, the things people remembered in life. Even I remembered a few things. The way Gunner'd looked sitting across from me at the Derby.

"Large sky, contrasty print, fifties feel—anything else?" I asked.

"You're poking fun at me now," she laughed nervously.

"You know who that was a photograph of?" I asked.

"No," she said, "but he had the saddest eyes I've ever seen. I can still see his eyes. Who was he?"

"Hank Williams," I said.

"Oh, God," she said. I could hear the dread in her voice. She didn't know what Hank looked like, but she'd certainly read the papers. She knew about the Hank Williams Killer. She'd been close to the scene of two of his "performances." "Shit," she said in a little, frightened voice, "you've got to be joking."

"I wish I was," I said.

Monday night I was watching *Monday Night Football* like any other good American. I had a black-and-white television set that an old dope dealer had given to me. You needed a screwdriver to adjust the volume, and you needed pliers to change the channel. The set probably would've worked better if you'd just chopped it up and snorted it.

Sometime during the third quarter the phone rang. It was Ratso.

"Hold the weddin'," I said. I put down the blower, got the screwdriver and turned off the set, found a half-smoked cigar in the wastebasket, fired it up, and picked up the blower again.

"Start talkin'," I said.

"Murray Fishkin," said Ratso. "Was that his name?"

"That *is* his name," I said.

"*Was* his name," said Ratso. "He took a brody yesterday. It's right here in the paper."

I puffed on my cigar. So the bald-headed lawyer had iced himself. I'd never even met the man, so I wasn't greatly grieved at his final passing of the bar.

"What does it mean?" Ratso asked.

"It means he'll be out of his office even more now," I said. "It means he's no longer a serious suspect, unless the murders suddenly stop. I don't think they will."

"Jesus," said Ratso.

"It also means," I said, "that the killer is almost certainly a close, personal friend of mine."

"You're kidding," said Ratso.

"Present company excluded, of course," I said.

31

It was Thursday night. Six shopping days until Christmas, and I still didn't know what I wanted out of life. I hadn't made a shopping list of things for anybody else either. You give what you get.

I'd been keeping in almost daily touch with Ratso and Cleve concerning the case and any new developments at the Lone Star. No new songs had arrived. Not many singers, either.

The holidays are a slow time for most occupational groups. It's not much different with country-singers-turned-amateur-detectives. So when I'd finished rearranging my sock drawer, I picked up Flippo's book on Hank Williams. I'd been languidly plowing through it for some time actually. Unfortunately, I'd only gotten about as far as Flippo's autograph.

I didn't much like reading biographies. Real life was tedious enough. I didn't want to read about dead country singers. I'd been to that rodeo.

I camped in the loft for several days. I survived by heating up Bill Dick's frozen Five-Alarm Chili, drinking espresso, and smoking cigars. The Beverly Hills Diet.

Everywhere I looked I saw Hank's mournful eyes.

I read.

I also organized an extensive, far-reaching telephone operation like a Mafia don in prison. When I wasn't on the phone, I was reading Flippo's book. When I wasn't reading

Flippo's book, I was on the phone. I began to gently probe the backgrounds of some of my "friends."

The only other media input I allowed myself was watching *Quincy* reruns. I had begun to regard Quincy as a close, personal friend. Not really a healthy situation, interpersonally speaking.

The book stayed with me like a bottle imp or an albatross. I read on.

Hank Williams' horse was named Hi-life. Hank's first wife was named Audrey. His second wife, Billie Jean, married country singer Johnny Horton after Hank's death. Horton also died tragically young.

It was almost two o'clock in the morning when I learned that the name Hank Williams had used when he checked into hotels was Herman P. Willis.

It was a pretty obscure piece of information. Even a knowledgeable, veteran soul like myself hadn't known about it.

I read like a demon in the night. Hank's brief, troubled life flashed through my consciousness like the meteor that it was. Lawsuits, divorce, rhinestones, guns, drugs, alcohol, pain, loneliness, untimely death.

Have a nice day.

According to Flippo's book, there was the time on the road that Hank was arrested for taking a shot at a picture of the battleship *Missouri* hanging on a wall in a restaurant. He told the arresting officers: "It drew on me first."

There was the night of June 11, 1949, when Hank electrified the Grand Ol' Opry for the first time, receiving more encores than any other performer before or since. There was the time he sold one of his songs to Little Jimmy Dickens for two bottles of Southern Comfort, and the time he bought the lyrics to "Cold, Cold Heart" from Paul Gilley.

There was the lifelong struggle between Hank's mother, Lilly, and Hank's wife Audrey for his money and his soul, roughly in that order. It was a lifelong struggle that did not stop at Hank's death. Very little stopped at Hank's death, except, of course, ol' Hank. He and Herman P. Willis were buried in Montgomery in the same grave. Hank's music and fame continued to live and grow, but Herman P. Willis was forgotten. Or almost forgotten.

Then there was the famous show on a cold winter's day in January 1953, in Canton, Ohio. The show that Hank never played. Hank's chauffeur-driven Cadillac had rolled like a death train through four southern states, through countless towns, through the morphine-hazed, broken-hearted, perpetual night that had become his life. From Montgomery to Chattanooga, where Hank stopped at a diner and tipped a waiter fifty dollars, to Knoxville, where he received several mysterious shots from an equally mysterious doctor. In Rutledge, Tennessee, a cop stopped the Cadillac for speeding. The cop looked at the figure slumped in the back and said, "Hey, that guy looks dead." The chauffeur explained that Hank was only sedated.

The Cadillac rolled through Bristol, Cedarville, Chilhowie, Marion, Wytheville, Bluefield, where Hank again stopped to see a doctor, and Princeton, West Virginia, where he stopped at a bar, Beckley, Willis Branch, and Oak Hill, where Charles Carr, the chauffeur, finally checked the back seat and realized that Hank Williams was as cold as the lonely highway in the winter night.

"Patrolman Jamey drove the Cadillac to the Oak Hill Hospital," said Flippo's book, "where Hank Williams was a Dead on Arrival. There had been another man in the car with Hank and Charles Carr. He told Jamey that his name was Donald Surface and that he was a relief driver that Carr had picked up in Bluefield, West Virginia. Donald Surface then vanished."

After the biggest funeral the South had ever seen, both of Hank's devoted wives organized country bands and hit the road, each billing herself as "Mrs. Hank Williams." A touching tribute.

By the time I'd finished the book it was almost dawn.

I rubbed my eyes and thought about the pages I'd read. It

was the first book I'd cracked in years that wasn't a murder mystery. I smiled at the ironic notion that reading it might very possibly help solve a real-life murder mystery.

I could see the sun just barely etching the warehouses to the east, like a light over the top of a doorway. The morning wasn't the only thing dawning on me. But it was a hell of a lot more attractive.

As it turned out, I'd finished reading Flippo's book barely in time to save my life.

32

Tompall and the Glaser Brothers played the Lone Star Cafe that Sunday night. Tompall had been sort of my country music godfather when I was in Nashville, and Chuck Glaser had produced my first album, *Sold American*, in 1973. The other two brothers, Jim and Ned, I had met only a few times. Tompall and the Glaser Brothers were considered by many, myself included, to be the finest vocal group ever to hit Nashville.

I went to the show with Rambam. I watched the show while Rambam cased the club for a place of concealment when they closed for the night. Hank had not sent a song to the Glaser Brothers. In fact, he hadn't been heard from in several weeks. He was overdue.

That's why, when I finally said good night to the Glasers at two o'clock in the morning in their dressing room, I was pleased to notice Rambam climbing stealthily into the belly of the iguana.

In the cab home I thought about things. I'd seen almost everyone connected with the case during the course of the evening. In my mind I went over the lot. Ratso, Cleve, Bill Dick, Chet Flippo, Mike Simmons. Also there'd been Cooperman, Fox, McGovern, Mick Brennan, and many other journalists and photographers I knew on sight. If they'd been hoping for a story, they hadn't gotten one.

The only person I'd expected to see and didn't was Gunner.

Things at the club had been pretty edgy all night. There

was almost palpable relief when the show was over and everything was all right. I was feeling pretty relieved, too.

When I got back to the loft, I poured a few shots into the bull's horn and finished 'em off. I'd taken my boots off and was sitting at the desk talking to the cat when the phones rang. I picked up the blower on the left.

"Dr. Kinky at your cervix," I said. I'd sort of been expecting a call from one of the Judys.

It wasn't one of the Judys. It was Sergeant Cooperman, and he was not amused.

And everything wasn't all right.

"What seems to be the problem, Officer?" I asked.

"Another bumpkin got waxed tonight, Tex," said Cooperman in a tired, offhanded manner.

"Jesus," I said.

"Yeah," said Cooperman, "that's what eight million New Yorkers are going to say tomorrow when they wake up and read the newspapers. Was a guy named Ned Glaser. Played the Lone Star last night. He's the brother of Tompall Glaser, who's a friend of yours I believe, so I thought you might want to know. We found him a couple of hours ago out on the West Side Highway where the construction work just sort of stops where the city ran out of funds. You know, just some columns and girders and shit. It goes nowhere. Like this case. Found him behind the wheel of a stolen eighty-two Buick fucking Skylark with a screwdriver in his back. You with me?"

"'Fraid so," I said. I lit a cigar with a surprisingly steady hand. I was a little surprised. Just a little surprised. "Find anything else?" I asked.

"Yeah. A bottle of wine and a deck of cards. No prints on either of them. No prints on the screwdriver. You get any bright ideas, give us a call."

"Okay," I said.

"Adiós," said Cooperman.

Two hours later the second call came in. I was in bed but I wasn't asleep yet. I was counting screwdrivers.

"Rambam here," said Rambam, "of the Village Irregulars. I'm at the pay phone in the doorway of Sarge's Delicatessen watching forty hookers eat dill pickles."

"Maybe they're keeping in practice," I said.

I could hear a cash register up close and a siren in the background. Those two sounds, I thought, pretty well covered the spiritual waterfront as far as New York went. And that was far enough for anybody.

"How do you know they're hookers?" I asked.

"Because they look like hookers," said Rambam. "Who the hell else would be at Sarge's Delicatessen at five o'clock in the morning eating dill pickles?" There was a pause and I heard the receiver bang against the wall a few times, and then I heard Rambam's daggerlike voice stabbing the New York night.

"Excuse me, miss, are you a hooker?" he asked. I heard a chair scrape and a woman start to say something, but I missed her response. Then Rambam was back. "I know a hooker when I see one. By the way, I got what you wanted," he said. "It says 'Tompall and the Glaser Brothers.' Big block letters."

I'd asked him to check out the Lone Star after closing hours and see what he could see. I especially wanted him to see if he could find a large manila envelope with block letters stashed somewhere in the basement offices. Apparently he had.

"You open it yet?" I asked.

"No," he said, "I thought we might share the experience."

"Is the envelope postmarked?" I asked.

"I don't see one. No. Want me to bring it over?"

"I already know what's in there," I said.

"If you do you're a fucking Houdini," said Rambam. "I haven't opened it yet."

"It's the Hank Williams song 'Lost Highway,' " I said.

"All right," he said, "let's see. And now, the envelope." There was a momentary pause, then he came back on the line. "A fucking Houdini," he said.

"It's nothing once you know the ropes," I said. Rambam began reading the contents of the envelope.

"Lost Highway, by Hank Williams," he intoned.

> *"Just a deck of cards and a jug of wine*
> *And a woman's lies makes a life like mine.*
> *Oh, the day we met I went astray*
> *I started rollin' down that Lost Highway."*

"Nice recitation," I said.

"Thanks," said Rambam. "Shall I keep this for you?"

"Yeah," I said. "We can't turn it over to the cops because of how we obtained it. I use the word 'we' loosely. But it is evidence."

"Evidence of what?" asked Rambam.

"In the words of Sergeant Cooperman, 'Another bumpkin got waxed tonight,' " I said. I puffed coolly on what was left of cigar number seven. Rambam didn't say anything.

"A little less enthusiasm, please," I said. "Before we terminate this call, Rambam, tell me exactly where you found that envelope."

"Can't you guess?" asked Rambam.

"This is getting major-league tedious," I said.

"Wait a minute," said Rambam, "let me get a pickle." I heard the receiver bang against the wall again a couple of times. Then Rambam came back on the line doing a pretty fair impersonation of a guy eating a pickle on a telephone at five o'clock in the morning. Boy had talent.

"Give up?" he asked.

"Yeah," I said.

"Want to know where I found it?"

"Yeah," I said wearily.

"Bottom drawer. Right-hand side of—"

"Goddammit, Rambam," I said, "get to the meat of it."

"—Bill Dick's desk," he said.

33

Monday afternoon Bill Dick made me an offer I couldn't understand. For some reason he wanted me to play the club. As near as I can recall the conversation ran like this:

"We want you to play the club," said Bill Dick. "You name your price."

"Money may buy me a fine dog," I said with some dignity, "but only love can make it wag its tail." I watched cigar smoke drift up toward the ceiling. What the hell did they want me for? I was too middle-aged to die.

"How about we try to wag its fucking tail five thousand dollars worth?" asked Bill Dick.

"I'm pretty busy," I said. Actually, I had enough spare time to macramé my nose hairs, but it's never a good idea to let people in New York think you're not busy.

"Busy," snorted Bill Dick.

"Yeah," I said. "I'm workin' on a tampon jingle."

"We need to overcome this idea," he continued, "that the place is jinxed or cursed. You wouldn't believe the shit-storm the media has made out of this. Boyd Matson was down here last night doing a piece for the *Today* show.

"And that was before the Glaser kid was murdered on the West Side. Anything can happen in New York. Right or wrong, Kinkster?"

"Right, Bill," I said.

"Had nothing to do with his playing the club probably, but you know how people's minds work."

"Yeah," I said, "they think they see a connection."

"Exactly," said Bill Dick. "You're the perfect guy to make New York City safe for country music."

"Right, Bill," I said.

"Bubba Borgelt's death was a freak electrical situation. I know electrical wiring inside and out, and when you're working off of a high-voltage system and your terminals . . ."

I took the receiver away from my ear and blew a peaceful stream of cigar smoke in the general direction of F. Scott Fitzgerald's letter to his little daughter at camp. It had hung framed on the wall of the loft for as long as I could remember. In the letter, F. Scott had advised his daughter not to worry about the following things: popular opinion, dolls, the past, the future, growing up, anybody getting ahead of you, triumph, failure unless it came through your own fault, mosquitoes, flies, insects in general, parents, boys, disappointments, pleasures, and satisfactions. The things to worry about, he'd said, were courage, cleanliness, efficiency, and horsemanship.

Not bad advice in a pinch.

I put the receiver back to my ear and heard Bill Dick say the words "electrical component."

I didn't say anything.

"What kind of flowers do you want?" asked Bill Dick. "In your dressing room," he laughed.

"Funny," I said, "if a bit macabre. So when's the gig?"

"New Year's Eve," he said. That particular date seemed to have a certain cloying familiarity about it, but so did numerous other things like music, motion pictures, and life on this planet.

Sometimes we do things we don't understand. Like falling in love. Like riding a subway. Like eating a sandwich that's bigger than your head at the Carnegie Delicatessen.

After all, it was for God and country music. So I took a rather fatalistic puff on my cigar and I took the gig.

"A gig's a gig," I said. I would play along with Bill Dick. I did not think the time was quite right to broach the subject of manila envelopes with big block letters.

It was closing in on two o'clock in the afternoon and it seemed to be warming up a bit. It was hard to tell what the weather was like when you never got off the telephone. I put on my cowboy hat and my hunting vest with the little rows of stitched pockets where some Americans keep their shotgun shells. I stuck a few cigars in the little pockets. What the hell? Best be prepared. I went outside.

Back in Texas it was hunting season. A good time to buy your mother-in-law a fur coat with antlers.

Now as I walked in the city, I could almost hear the random shots echoing off the Texas hills. What great sport to be a hunter. Kill things more beautiful than you. Shoot birds that flew higher than your dreams. Kill many buffalo. Once in a while you clean your gun and accidentally blow your head off. Good.

34

It was the night before Christmas. Visions of lonely, frozen bag ladies danced in my head.

I'd burned out sugarplums the year before. Along with a few synapses.

I felt a little jumpy but fairly well rested. At least as well rested as I ever felt. I was still making up for the time I stayed awake for five years once in Nashville taking pills with colorful, almost lyrical names. That's what country music was all about. Ask ol' Hank.

I put a cassette on the stereo. Chinese children singing Christmas carols. Because of my years on the road, I did not normally like to hear the sound of human voices singing. But everyone, from time to time, requires a bit of auditory phenomenon. And you make do with what you got.

It was around tennish in the P.M. as they say in Hollywood, and I'd poured close to the last shot of whatever there used to be in the liquor cabinet. I lit a cigar and sat down in the rocker.

I was sitting there trying not to think about what I was obviously getting myself into when the phones rang. It was my sister Marcie calling from Berkeley, where she was studying fish. Not too many people study fish.

I'm sixteen years older than Marcie. Old enough to be her brother. When Marcie was about four I used to play tricks on her like older brothers will do. Told her Lassie'd died. Things like that.

Marcie was one of the few people younger than me whom

I sometimes looked up to for wisdom and advice. Usually I never listened to younger people. I figured if they reached my age without hanging themselves from a shower rod, then I'd listen to them.

Marcie already knew a little bit about the "troubles" at the Lone Star. She watched the *Today* show. The Hank Williams Killer. The Lone Star Murders. I filled her in on the gory details as much as I could. Then I told her about the offer from Bill Dick.

She laughed. "You didn't take it, did you?" she asked.

"Well," I said. "Well, see, I have an idea—"

"You didn't take it," she said disbelievingly.

"Yes," I said firmly. "I took the gig."

"That wasn't exactly best foot forward, Kinkster," she said. I puffed patiently on my cigar.

"If I don't do it, it may mean the end of country music as we know it on this planet." I knew she could relate to that. She was a George Jones fan. Hank Williams was like a brother to her.

Marcie didn't say anything. There was a long-distance silence on the line. If you've got to listen to silence, that's the best kind to have. I imagined a brightly colored tropical fish swimming by in an aquarium somewhere on the left coast and my sister watching it.

"Marcie," I said, "I know enough about this person to be pretty sure he's gonna make his move. And when he does, believe me, I'll be ready for him and well protected." It didn't even sound too convincing to me.

"When's the show?" she asked.

"It's New Year's Eve," I said.

"Do you know what day that is?" she asked in a voice turned suddenly cold.

"Yeah," I said. "I think it's a Wednesday."

"That's not what I mean," she said, a note of hysteria working its way in. "New Year's Eve was the day Hank Williams died."

I suppose subconsciously I'd known it all the time. I just

hadn't thought about it, and I didn't want to think about it now. I picked up a Bic lighter that had been in the family for about forty-eight hours and, fairly calmly, lit a fresh cigar.

"Yeah," I said, "there's that."

It was about two o'clock in the morning when the phone rang for the last time. I was in the middle of an involved, vaguely sexual dream about my cat. I didn't know what the Freudian implications of it were, nor did I particularly care to find out. Like Frederick Exley said, "What good are dreams if they come true?"

I didn't like the way the phone was ringing. As if it had a will of its own. It cut across the dark stillness of the room much louder than necessary. It sounded frantic and amoral. Like the voice of a medieval witch.

I hit the lights, picked up the receiver, and heard the mournful voice of Hank Williams. It sounded like a scratchy record and it probably was. Hank was singing from either hillbilly heaven or New York City, and at two o'clock in the morning either one was bad enough.

The song, I knew, was Hank's last hit while he was still alive. The words I heard were as follows:

> "And brother, if I stepped on a worn-out dime
> I bet a nickel I could tell if it was heads or tails
> I'm not gonna worry wrinkles in my brow
> 'Cause nothin's ever gonna be alright nohow
> No matter how I struggle and strive
> I'll never get out of this world alive."

I listened to see if there was any more. There wasn't. There didn't have to be.

I picked a half-smoked cigar out of the ashtray and stoked it up. I thought of Hank's primeval, mournful voice, and the more I thought about it, the more it seemed to be mourning for me. Just what I needed.

I got up a little shakily from the chair and walked over to

the window. Outside the window I thought I heard a hoot owl call. In the distance, above the traffic, I was sure I could hear a lonesome whippoorwill.

Lonesome, however, was not my problem. My problem, it appeared, was that my three minutes were up. I poured another shot and carried it over to the window. I gazed with a sense of dread through the gloom at the rusty fire escapes across the street. I killed the shot.

It might've looked like I was smiling, but I wasn't. My lips were only sliding off my teeth.

All I'd got was a crank phone call. What the hell was there to worry about? Nobody'd sent me a song in a large manila envelope with big block letters yet.

But it's a funny thing when you're a songwriter. Sometimes you feel a song coming on.

35

It was Friday morning, the day after Christmas. Several hundred street-corner Santas were sleeping it off on the Bowery. The cat and I were in the loft, the espresso machine was gurgling, the garbage trucks were rumbling, and all was well in the world except that someone was making plans to kill me.

There'd been the "I'll Never Get Out of This World Alive" phone call two nights before, and now there was a large manila envelope that had just come in the morning's mail and was sitting smugly square in the middle of my desk.

I didn't open it right away. Thought I'd leave myself something to do when the espresso was ready. Some guys read *The New York Times* as they sip their espresso in the morning. I open large manila envelopes with big block letters and read Hank Williams songs. Different strokes.

I took the envelope, poured a cup of espresso into my *Imus in the Morning* coffee mug, and sat down at the little table in the kitchen. The cat joined me by jumping up on top of the table. It was a good thing Ratso wasn't around. He didn't enjoy seeing cats on top of tables while people were sipping their espresso and reading their death threats. Thought it was a health hazard.

As I gingerly opened the envelope I could hear the lesbian dance class starting up directly over my head again. Strangely, I found it rather comforting. Like things were back to abnormal. I wished they were.

The song was "Kaw-liga." The wooden Indian.

If you were looking for a kink, pardon the expression, that might be attractive to a sick mind, you had a hell of a lot to work with in "Kaw-liga."

Some of the lyrics are as follows:

Kaw-liga was a wooden Indian standing by the door
He fell in love with an Indian maiden over in the antique store
Kaw-liga just stood there and never let it show
So she could never answer "yes" or "no."

He always wore his Sunday feathers and held a tomahawk . . .

And then one day a wealthy customer bought the Indian maid
And took her, oh, so far away but ol' Kaw-liga stayed
Kaw-liga just stands there as lonely as can be
And wishes he was still an ol' pine tree.

In fact, the story of "Kaw-liga" is very appropriate to today's world. The futility, the miscommunications that govern life and love. If you can't empathize with Kaw-liga, you might as well not empathize at all.

I poured another cup of espresso and thought about poor ol' Kaw-liga. I knew a lot of guys like that. Knew a lot of Indian maidens. A lot of wealthy customers. I just didn't know which of my fine feathered friends was trying to kill me. I had about six days to find out who it was. It was scary, all right.

Somebody was trying to take my scalp before it got up and started crawling out the door.

In six days the Lord created the heavens and the earth and all the wonders therein. There are some of us who feel that He might have taken just a little more time.

Be that as it may, I had six days to marshal my troops, hammer out the plan, run some difficult background checks, establish what would have to pass for a rapport with Fox and Cooperman, research the data that I had—sparse and far afield as it was—and find the hidden architecture of the psyche, the twisted foundation stone of evil festering underneath the untold stories, the brick and mortar, the human facade.

Also, find the missing picture of Hank Williams, and keep Downtown Judy and Uptown Judy from bumping into each other on New Year's Eve.

Also, calibrate who was left-handed, and who, both as a child and as an adult, had been in the right place at the right time. Or the wrong place at the wrong time, depending how much of a moral judgment you wished to make.

Also, there were the usual household chores: buy cat food, toilet paper, cigars, and a bottle of Jameson. Not too many gourmet items. If I had any guests I could give them some of Bill Dick's Five-Alarm Chili, which by now looked like a hunk of black and silver frozen detritus but would probably appeal to most New Yorkers, who were constantly seeking something a little out of the ordinary.

Six days to get it all done. Christ, you could get hung up in traffic for six days. You could talk to an accountant at a cocktail party for six days. If you didn't know Leo, you could wait for a table at the Carnegie for six days.

Six days to enjoy life before you walk over a foggy little wooden bridge and meet a death's-head coming at you from the other side. It was enough to make you wish you had a week.

I got the shopping done, fed the cat, and poured myself a bull's horn full of Jameson Irish Whiskey. I downed the shot.

I was trying to fit the toilet paper on the goddamn dispenser when the phones rang. It was 2:47 P.M. I could hear her accent even before I picked up the phone. It was Gunner.

She had been reading a lot of press about my New Year's Eve performance at the Lone Star and thought it ''very brave'' of me to play the club. Would I be able to catch this Hank Williams person, she wanted to know.

I told her I was going to try unless at the last moment I woosied out and decided to take a French leave. She seemed to think it over for a few seconds. It was enough time for me to break out a new cigar and pop it into a rather vicious guillotine device given to me by my friends at the Smokehouse in Kerrville, Texas.

"Have you found my picture yet?" she asked. Interesting possessive pronoun, I thought. "The Hank Williams person and the two boys?"

"Not yet," I said.

"Humpf," she said.

"Want to get together this week?" I asked.

"I'm very busy," she said. "Maybe after the show. You know, I've never seen you perform."

"Musically speaking or any other way," I said. "Well, I may not make the show. It's kind of a country music tradition not to show up sometimes. Keeps the fans on their toes. George Jones does it a lot. So did the Hank Williams person."

"If you don't play that show Wednesday night," she said, enunciating very slowly and distinctly, "you haven't got a hair on your bum."

She hung up. Or rang off, as they say across the pond.

Maybe Gunner didn't appreciate the risk involved. Hell, maybe she did. Maybe the architecture of my personality was so displeasing to her she didn't give a bloody damn. At least two of the people she'd recently photographed at the Lone Star were now pushing up their various state flowers. I hadn't thought to ask her why she hadn't covered the Glaser Brothers show.

I puffed the cigar a bit and watched the cat, curled up, sleeping peacefully on a nearby chair. I decided I had to go through with it. I had to play the gig.

I'd never thought of myself as being particularly macho, but conversely, I didn't want anybody going around saying I didn't have a hair on my bum.

36

Rambam had had some success recently on a case in Washington, our nation's capital. He'd located a college kid from a prominent family who'd been missing and presumed spindled and mutilated by irritated Colombian drug-oriented individuals. Rambam found the kid alive and well, living out of his car and hiding from the Mob. Of course, now that he'd been found the kid could look forward to the life span of a mayfly, but nonetheless it was a feather in Rambam's cap.

I called Rambam and told him I needed a missing picture of Hank Williams found, hopefully in time to do me some good.

"Okay," he said, "where do I look?"

"I'm not sure yet," I said, "but I'll let you know."

"Okay," he said, "when do I look?" Rambam, like most private eyes, always asked a lot of questions.

"New Year's Eve," I said, "while I'm onstage at the Lone Star."

"I've got a date on New Year's Eve," he said.

"Well," I said, "you'll have to make a moral choice between your gluttonous social life and the actual life or death of one of your close friends—me."

"Let me think about it," he said.

"There's the lad," I said.

I hung up and called Ratso. Since he and Simmons seemed to be hitting it off so well, I'd asked him to do a little background work on the boy. We arranged to meet at the Derby at eight. I hung up and took a little power nap.

When I woke up I felt older and colder. I removed the cat litter box from the shower preparatory to getting in there myself. Power naps weren't what they used to be.

I got under the water and tried to shake off the gray, morphial threads. I started to feel pretty good. Not good enough to sing "I'll Never Get Out of This World Alive," but okay. I reflected upon what Conrad Hilton, the great hotel magnate, had said when someone asked him what he'd learned in his many years on the planet. He'd said: "Always keep the shower curtain inside the tub."

I followed his advice.

Before I left for the Derby I made a condolence call to Tompall Glaser at his top-secret, unpublished number in Nashville. His phone number was about the only thing unpublished about Tompall. He and his surviving brothers, Chuck and Jim, owned one of the biggest publishing houses in Nashville. They'd published many of my early songs as well. We were still on speaking terms.

"Sorry, hoss," I said when Tompall picked up the phone, "about Ned."

"Yeah," he said in a voice that John Wayne would have been proud of, "Chuck and Jim are kind of sorry, too. They're sorry it wasn't me." He laughed a raw laugh, more hollow than hearty. "I'll miss the little bastard."

In spite of the Glaser Brothers' legendary feuding, I rather thought he would. I didn't say anything.

"Why," asked Tompall, "do you think he picked on Ned?"

"I'm going to find out," I said. "I'm playing the Lone Star on New Year's Eve."

"Jesus," Tompall said. "You've got pawnshop balls, brother." There was a pause.

"Hey," he said, "Captain Midnite's here. Wants to talk to you. Thanks for calling, Kinky." I heard Tompall filling Midnite in on my forthcoming performance at the Lone Star.

"If anything happens to you," said Midnite as he came on the line, "can I have your saddle?"

"Cowboys today don't have saddles," I said. "We have answering machines, VCRs, word processors."

"How about your catalogue?" he asked.

"Midnite," I said, "you realize I may really fucking die next week."

"Yeah," he said, "I thought about that. In fact, I think about you a lot." I hadn't seen Midnite in seven years, but I still felt close to him. That was probably the secret of maintaining a friendship in country music. Stay the hell away from each other.

"Just watch your ass," he said in a softer tone. "I'm playing golf next week, and if anything happens to you—you know what they say."

"No, I don't know what they say," I said.

"You can't putt with a broken heart," said Captain Midnite.

37

Ratso and I had just dusted off two big hairys at the Derby and were now drinking coffee escorted by sambuca, which Andrew himself brought to us in appropriately stemmed glasses. I admired Andrew for never commenting on Ratso's sartorial situation. Ratso was wearing dead man's shoes, fuchsia pants, and a coonskin cap with the tail and with the little face of the raccoon mounted on the front of it. The eyes were sewn shut, and the damn thing looked pretty hideous even if you weren't a liberal.

"How's it going, Kinky?" Andrew asked in his gracious tones.

"It's going all right, Andrew," I said.

"Good," said Andrew. "The sambuca's on the house."

"Now it's going better," I said. I picked a coffee bean out of the glass and chewed on it. If you've never eaten a coffee bean out of a glass of sambuca you've never lived.

"Ratso," I said, "before we go over the minutes of our last Rotarian meeting, I'd like to ask you to please remove your hat. Not that it isn't attractive, but that dead little face keeps reminding me of what I might look like Thursday morning if anything goes wrong with my plan."

"No problem," said Ratso, and he put the hat on the rack behind him in such a manner that the sewn eye slits appeared to glare evilly at the woman at the next table. The woman glared back at the little hat with an expression as void of life and as unpleasant as the dead raccoon. Then she looked at Ratso.

"Disgusting," she said.

Ratso looked briefly at the woman, the hat, and then the woman again.

"Don't feed it," he said. I took another coffee bean out of my sambuca and chewed it thoughtfully.

"Here's the deal, Ratso," I said. "We're amateurs, but we're smart. We have basic psychological profiles of a number of acquaintances of ours. We've got this knowledge first-hand, from knowing these people for some time. But does anybody really ever get to know anybody?

"We've got clues, details, background information. More than we need. We've got to go at it from a different angle than the cops. The guy we're looking for is very smart. Got a Ph.D. in evil. You understand?"

Ratso nodded solemnly. His gaze wandered over to a dessert tray in the corner.

"On Wednesday night," I continued, "I've got to drop the mask from one of these guys before one of these guys drops a death mask on me. I'll need you, Rambam, Boris, and anybody else you can think of."

"The Village Irregulars," Ratso said. "Will that be enough?" I shrugged.

"I'm talking to Fox and Cooperman tomorrow," I said.

"We'll be ready," Ratso said. "We just don't know what we're gonna be ready for."

"I've got a fairly good idea, I'm afraid," I said. I took the sheet music to "Kaw-liga" and the Big Chief tablet out of my coat pocket. I filled Ratso in on everything I knew. It didn't take long.

When I finished, Ratso made some notes to himself on a few pieces of Chelsea Hotel stationery. "You don't miss much," I said.

"I just wanted to get down a few details," said Ratso.

"No," I said, "I mean lifting the Chelsea Hotel stationery."

"C'mon," said Ratso, "it's very high camp."

"What did you find out about Simmons?" I asked.

"Interesting," he said. "I got this from Simmons' brother, Andy. He's a couple years younger than Mike. The two of them have always been very close. Simmons is quite frustrated apparently. Hasn't gotten where he wants in country music."

"Who has?" I asked. Everybody wanted to be Hank Williams but nobody wanted to die.

"Anyway," Ratso said, "this Texas background of his is pretty bogus. He lived there all of six months once. Been a Yankee almost all of his life and won't even admit it to himself."

"Yeah," I said.

"He's had it rough," said Ratso. "Not many breaks. Never played the Opry. About ten years ago he performed for a while on the Wheeling Jamboree in Wheeling, West Virginia." He paused to slurp his coffee. "That's hard work."

"What is?" I asked.

"Wheeling, West Virginia," said Ratso. He laughed.

"That's pretty goddamn funny," I said. I thought about it for a moment. I knocked off the sambuca distractedly and said, "Very curious, my dear Ratso."

"What do you mean?" he asked.

"West Virginia," I said. "It keeps popping up. Simmons has lived there. Cleve. Flippo." I signaled the waiter for more coffee and a couple more sambucas. Ratso ordered a walnut-apple-pecan cake, the house's specialty.

"I'm reading a very strange book," said Ratso, "by John Keel, a top authority on UFOs and a personal friend of mine. The book's called *The Mothman Prophecies* and it's about these ten-foot-tall winged creatures that thousands of people have reportedly seen in the skies over West Virginia."

"At least it's not about Hitler, Bob Dylan, or Jesus," I said.

Ratso attacked the walnut-apple-pecan cake, unfazed by my remark. When he'd knocked off a good bit, and with his mouth still not quite empty, he said, "West Virginia is one of the very few places in the country that the Indians never fought over. Keel suggests it was a cursed land, a haunted area, maybe a burial ground of some kind."

"Nice place to get a postcard from, right?" I asked.

"Right," said Ratso. "It's sort of a bad-karma place."

"It sure was for Hank," I said.

"Why was that?" Ratso asked.

"Hank died there," I said.

38

McGovern had said it was very important that we meet for a breakfast engagement at ten o'clock Saturday morning at the LaLobotomy Coffee Shop on Eighth Avenue. The place's actual name was LaBonbonniere, but a gorgeous girlfriend of mine, The Lizard, had named it LaLobotomy and the name had stuck. It fit the clientele pretty well, including the way I felt myself that morning.

In spite of the fact that it was already ten-thirty and that McGovern's house was only one block away on Jane Street, McGovern was not there. Big surprise.

Charles, the owner, brought me a cup of coffee and a large glass of tomato juice without my having to order it. Charles was a real rarity, an extremely likable Frenchman, but the food was pure American greasy spoon. Best breakfast place in New York. Excluding dim sum, of course.

I was drinking my coffee and reading the *New York Post* when I suddenly saw McGovern looming in the doorway of the little place. He looked about four times as big as God.

"Hey, great," he said. "I thought I missed you."

"I'm afraid not," I said. "Have a rough night?"

"Who?" asked McGovern. "Me?" His hearty Irish laughter filled the little place to the point where a startled young homosexual couple and an incipient bag lady looked over at our table. McGovern was already perusing the menu and didn't notice. I returned their gaze with calm dignity. Saint Kinky. Patron saint and defender of large, exuberant Irishmen in small Village coffee shops.

Charles brought coffee for McGovern and took both our orders. McGovern and I drank our coffee and watched the world go by outside the windows of LaLobotomy. He'd brought a copy of the *Daily News* with him, and I of course had the *Post*. If conversation lagged, there was always reality. Or we could read the newspapers.

I didn't feel too bad bringing the *Post* with me knowing, of course, that McGovern wrote for the *Daily News*. It made him feel superior and just a little smug to be having break-fast with a *Post* reader. I liked to be supportive of my friends.

"Your show at the Lone Star," said McGovern. "They want me to do a feature on it. I know it's hard for you to give up all this press, but I think you ought to get out of it while you still can. I've got a bad feeling about it. I say cancel the show." McGovern looked un-McGovernly serious.

I sipped my coffee and watched a blind man, two identi-cally dressed homosexuals, and a nun cross Eighth Avenue against the light. Could've made a citizen's arrest but I thought I'd let it slide.

"What the hell's so funny?" asked McGovern.

"I keep looking at these damn people outside the win-dow," I said. "They look like discarded lines from old Bob Dylan songs."

"You're sure that's not your reflection you're seeing?" asked McGovern. He laughed again. A little too loud, I thought, for the small restaurant.

"Could well be, McGovern," I said. "I'm an aristocratic freak. I've earned my right to be here."

"Good," said McGovern. "So you'll cancel the gig?"

"Of course not," I said. "It's very important that I play this gig. In the words of Thomas Paine, 'I care not who makes a country's laws, if I can write her songs.' " I finished my coffee and looked at McGovern.

He got his coat off the floor and stood up to go. "You may write the songs," he said, shaking his big, handsome head sadly, "but I write the obituaries."

39

I walked the ten bone-chilling blocks to the cop shop. The world outside was not as warm and cozy as Charles' little coffee shop. I just hoped heaven looked like LaLobotomy. I looked at the street. The garbage cans whose lids runneth over. The stray dogs. Stray people. Everything was as cold as a bank lobby on the South Pole. Almost made you wish you lived in West Virginia.

The green globes of the Sixth Precinct suddenly came upon me. I felt a twinge of something akin to guilt. Maybe like a hot dog vendor operating without a license. Cooperman and Fox and I did not have an especially sharing and caring relationship. The only evidence I was legally withholding was the song "Lost Highway" that Rambam had lifted from Bill Dick's desk. I had "Lost Highway" in my coat pocket, but it'd be hard to explain without implicating Rambam, and I needed Rambam. I had such a complicated code of ethics that quite often I couldn't even crack it myself.

I gave my name to the guy who was nodding out at the muster desk, and I took a seat in a little plastic chair with a small writing arm on it. The chair was screwed into the floor tighter than the Statue of Liberty. There was another guy sitting in a similar chair in the corner. He had a mental-hospital haircut and his eyes seemed to be rolling back into his head a little more than was fashionable. One of his hands was handcuffed to the arm of the chair. Looked like he was waiting, too.

They called my number first.

I walked into the valley of death to face Cooperman and his coffee cup. Fox wasn't there. I didn't ask after him.

"Sit down," said Cooperman. I sat down.

"What do you take in your coffee, Senator?" he asked.

"Everything," I said.

He took his own cup, found another one on a nearby desk, and walked over to a Mr. Coffee machine in the corner. "I'll bet," he said.

I thought of the night, several months ago, before all this had started, when Ratso and I had been driving down Seventh Avenue and had seen Joe DiMaggio walking into the Carnegie Delicatessen at one-thirty in the morning.

"Jesus," said Ratso, "there he is."

"Yeah," I said, "looks like he's alone."

"Well," said Ratso, "he's not with Marilyn."

Joe walked into the Carnegie, and Ratso and I turned the corner at the light. "Nobody is," I said.

"You know," said Ratso, "I hear kids still swarm him for autographs, but they say, 'Mr. Coffee! Mr. Coffee!' They don't even know he's Joe fucking DiMaggio." We drove through several blocks of teeming loneliness . . . Kentucky Fried Chicken . . . a hooker or two . . . an empty skyscraper.

"I hope to Christ he gets linen," I said.

Cooperman placed the coffee in front of me and sat down heavily in a beat-up office chair on the other side of the desk.

"What's on your mind?" he asked.

Cooperman was not especially pleased to learn of my upcoming New Year's Eve gig at the Lone Star Cafe. He was even less happy to learn that the song "Lost Highway," which I'd placed on the desk between us, had been given to me by Frank Serpico.

"Christ, that's a good one," said Cooperman with a very unpleasant little fixed-wing smile on his face.

"Yeah," I said. "It was found in Bill Dick's desk—no post-mark, the envelope unopened—the night Ned Glaser died."

"Do tell," said Cooperman sweetly. "It's so nice to have this information." He took a sip of coffee. He smiled a big smile. It was the kind of smile that in a million years might have reached his eyes. I didn't have the time to wait.

"I got a song as well, in the mail this week," I said. "Ever hear of 'Kaw-liga'?"

"Black Muslim leader?" Cooperman asked.

I took a sip of my coffee and winced slightly. "No," I said. "Kaw-liga was a wooden Indian standing by the door. He fell in love with an Indian maiden over in the antique store."

"And?" said Cooperman.

"And—you know," I said. "Boy meets girl, boy loses girl, country singer loses life. Same old story." We both sipped our coffee.

"Okay," said Cooperman, "Let's have it. What have you got? Any more withheld evidence? Any hare-brained theories? Any ideas at all? Let's hear 'em." Cooperman leaned back in his chair. He took a Gauloise out of the pack on the desk and lighted it with a Zippo. I took a cigar out of my hunting vest and, in my coat pocket, found a pink Bic lighter. This one had only been in the family about twelve hours. I began the prenuptial arrangements on the cigar and I told Cooperman what I knew.

"Look," he said in a tired voice, "we now have three victims, all of them in some way involved with the Lone Star Cafe. They work there, they play there, the point is, they die there. With the exception of Glaser, who died on the West Side Highway. Now we got this baby stashed in Bill Dick's desk." He gestured with his hand to the song "Lost Highway," and an ash from his Gauloise fell on Hank's lyrics like a big gray teardrop. Nobody brushed it away. Even the French probably would've liked Hank Williams, I thought. If they ever stopped thinking about Jerry Lewis long enough.

"Then we got you," continued Cooperman, "playing this

show New Year's Eve at the goddamn Lone Star Cafe like a decoy cop calling in his backup unit. That what you're doin'?''

"Well," I said.

"Well, let me tell you, friend. The backup may not be enough."

I puffed on my cigar and started to say something, but Cooperman went on. "Then we got a perpetrator running around reading all the papers and watching the eleven o'clock news, gettin' his balls all pumped up."

Cooperman studied me for a bit longer than was pleasant, then he asked, "Ever been to a Christmas party in a ward for the criminally insane?"

"Not yet," I said.

Cooperman lit another frog butt and squinted at me through the smoke. "You're out on a limb, my man," he said. "You got yourself into this one. We'll be there Wednesday night, but I don't envy you, Tex." He smiled.

With a modified papal sign he signified that the interview was over. I headed for the door. I had the feeling that the lines were down. Very little I'd told him had gotten through. And if he knew much about the case, he wasn't saying. So much for sharing and caring.

By the time I left, the guy that had been handcuffed to the plastic chair was gone. I wondered who the hell he thought *he* was. Maybe he knew who he was and that's why he'd had to be handcuffed to a plastic chair. Maybe the only way to save ourselves was to handcuff the whole world to a plastic chair. But there weren't enough handcuffs and there weren't enough plastic chairs. And there'd be nobody left to throw away the key. Otherwise, the idea was pretty sound.

It was raining lightly as I made my way over to 199B Vandam. Christmas had come and gone like an elf out of hell. I was beginning to feel progressively more like worm bait the closer I got to Wednesday night. I hoped it wasn't going to spoil my weekend.

As I walked through the cold I thought of something

F. Scott Fitzgerald had said in *Tender Is the Night*. It was to the effect that everybody in France thinks he's Napoleon and everybody in Italy thinks he's Christ.

Well, you could chalk up another one for the Big Apple. Somebody in New York evidently thought he was Hank Williams.

40

For a horrifying, lucid moment I didn't know who I was or where I was. It was a bit like knowing what goes on in the mind of a game show host. Not a pleasant experience.

It was Saturday night. Sitting Bull was looking at me from the cover of the Big Chief tablet, which was lying on the floor. I picked him up. I sat him on the table.

The Big Chief tablet didn't have a hell of a lot to tell me. Just a very abbreviated biography of some of the people I'd been checking up on and a hurried transcript of mostly incoherent comments they'd made. My handwriting looked like the handwriting of a mouse.

"Which one of you isn't what you seem to be?" I said to the cat. The cat didn't say anything.

"Which one of you is really a fiend disguised as a friend?" Was that even possible? Well, friends, it sure looked that way. Of course, looks can be deceiving. But then again, so could friends.

From Simmons I had: ". . . grew up in Texas. Where do you think I got my Texas accent?" Simmons didn't have a Texas accent, but he thought he did. People in New York thought he had one, too, but what did they know? The way he sang was Texas, but the way he spoke wouldn't have racked up too many points with the boys in the bunkhouse.

Simmons continued: "When we were kids Dad used to take us down to the Grand Ol' Opry, and I guess some of it must've rubbed off."

Bill Dick had denied any knowledge of the manila envelope that Rambam found in his desk. I didn't want to push it
just yet. Maybe he'd only hidden the envelope in his desk
and not shown it to the Glaser Brothers so they wouldn't
cancel their gig. A coward, not a killer. But there were other
possibilities that presented themselves. When I asked him
where he'd grown up he said, "Born and raised in Brooklyn,
New York." Asked if he'd ever been in the South, he said
with some little pride, "Never been below the Mason-Dixon
line." Of course, I thought, Billy the Kid had been born and
raised in Brooklyn, too.

Cleve was very unhappy at the Lone Star. Understandably
so, I thought. We talked and laughed about some of the years
on the road when he'd been road manager for my band.
Those times were miserable enough, but now they seemed
like the good ol' days. We reminisced about a country western bar mitzvah we'd played together in New Jersey some
years back. It had been a cocaine nightmare—backyard
swimming pool, bales of hay, kids with cap guns in little cowboy suits running around everywhere.

I thought of the two little kids Gunner had told me about
in the photograph I'd never seen. More than ever I felt it was
important.

I'd gotten Cleve's background down for the hell of it. "We
grew up in Kentucky . . . moved to Virginia, West Virginia,
Tennessee, Texas—you name it." Cleve was an only child, he
said. He'd been on the circuit for a while. He thought working at the Lone Star would bring him some peace of mind.
Surprise.

It wasn't written down on the Big Chief tablet, but Cleve
had expressed grave concern about my playing the Lone Star
on New Year's Eve. He'd said it was a crazy idea of Bill Dick's
and he'd advised me to think seriously about pulling out of
the gig.

"A gig's a gig," I'd told him.

"You're a fucking idiot," he'd said.

Chet Flippo grew up in Ohio. Lived in Texas, Tennessee,

West Virginia, Texas again, and finally married and moved to New York. Had a brother a couple of years older and a little sister. Thought he was going to give himself a nervous breakdown while writing *Your Cheatin' Heart: A Biography of Hank Williams*. Seems the boy overidentified with his field of study —thought he was Hank and his wife was Audrey.

Flippo had one rather interesting thing to say. On New Year's Day 1953, when he was ten years old, he remembered waiting for a long time in a big hall in Canton, Ohio, to see a show by Hank Williams. That was the show Hank never played. Somebody'd made an announcement that Hank had died. The band played "I Saw the Light" from behind a closed curtain at the back of the stage. People who were there, Flippo said, never forgot it. That great emptiness. That sense of loss. Flippo had been fascinated with Hank ever since.

You want to be a country music hero, you've got to die at precisely the right time. And Hank's timing was damn near perfect. For everybody but him. He was only twenty-nine years old. But then again, old age wasn't usually very pleasant and it didn't necessarily ensure any measure of greatness. I thought of what Will Rogers, another guy with a sense of timing, had once said: "Longevity has ruined as many men as it's made." Of course, the way I was living, it didn't look like that was going to be my problem.

So that was the Big Chief tablet. A little geography, a little ancient history, a little psychology. Of course, I wasn't a psychologist. But I could tell a person whose Otis box wasn't rising to the penthouse. And I could put pieces together. A few pieces were starting to fit into the picture. But the picture, unfortunately, was still missing.

I thought of Gunner. I'd tried to call her the night before but her machine was on. Listening to it made you want to have sexual relations with her accent.

Couldn't be too careful in the psycho serial-murder business. Even when dealing with women, foreigners, or friends. Satan was an equal opportunity employer.

I tried to think of other suspects, someone I'd overlooked, but it just didn't fit. I was sure that one of them had to be involved. A perfect stranger couldn't have wreaked this much havoc. Too inside. Too meticulous. Too . . . intelligent.

I had a little trouble getting back to sleep. It seemed that Intimations of Mortality and Morpheus were arm-wrestling with each other on the bridge of my nose. Both would get their chance, I figured, so I didn't worry about it too much.

Just before I got back to sleep, only two thoughts were going through my head. Who would feed the cat if something happened to me? was the first one. The second one was, if a lesbian dance class was thudding on the ceiling and there was nobody in the loft below to hear it, would it make any noise?

41

It's almost as hard to get good Mexican food in New York as it is in Mexico. You've got to know what you're doing in this world or life passes you by. My pal Joel Siegel and I thought about it a while and finally opted for barbecue.

Joel took me to Smokey's on Twenty-fourth Street and Ninth Avenue. It wasn't bad for New York. But it wasn't Howie's #1.

Afterward, I stopped by Ratso's apartment. Somewhere in Ratso's apartment you could find everything in the world—a nonfunctional exercise bike, a four-foot-tall statue of the Virgin Mary, a stuffed polar bear's head, and over two hundred slightly used hockey sticks.

I browsed through Ratso's vast library of books—mostly about Jesus, Bob Dylan, and Hitler—until I found what I was looking for. An old AAA road map of the United States. Circa 1953.

It was still early when I got back to 199B Vandam but it was already almost dark. It was that lonely time in New York or anyplace else just before Sunday night becomes Sunday night. I was looking at Ratso's road atlas and smoking a two dollar and seventy-five-cent Upmann cigar. The same kind John Kennedy smoked. I wondered what kind Adlai Stevenson would've smoked if he'd been elected President. Ah, well . . .

It was 7:52 in New York; 4:52 in California. Three hours

difference in time and a few cultural differences I won't go into. As a general rule of thumb, however, if you thought of New York as a Negro talking to himself and of California as a VCR with nothing to put in it, you wouldn't be too far off the mark.

"Charlie," I said, "I got a little problem." Charles Ansell was an old friend of the family. He was also the head shrink of the San Fernando Valley and one of the foremost world authorities on sibling rivalry, dream analysis, and Lenny Bruce. He was also, so my father claims, the first man he'd ever seen hold a cigarette lighter up to his ass and light a fart.

"You just think you've got a problem," Charlie said. "After all the shit I've listened to today, you couldn't have a problem." I familiarized him with the situation.

"You've got a problem," he said.

As Charlie talked I jotted down anything I felt was remotely pertinent into by Big Chief tablet. He laid it out clearly so a fairly hip layman like myself could understand. Not too many twenty-dollar words.

"Does that help?" he asked when he finished.

"I'll let you know Thursday morning," I said. I started to hang up and then I thought of something. "Oh, Charlie," I said, "sometime ago I had a dream—"

"You think you're Martin Luther King," he said.

"This is relatively serious, Charlie," I said, "and the price is right, so let me ask your opinion about it." I told Charlie about the dream in which I'd found the miniature baby with the diaper the size of a commemorative stamp. I told him how all my friends gathered around and began insisting that the diaper be changed and how no one had seen fit to comment on the ridiculously small size of the infant.

"It means that I think I have a small penis, right?" I asked. I knew this wasn't remotely true, but it seemed to me to be a classic interpretation.

"No," said Charlie, "it doesn't mean that at all." I blew a

relieved cloud of smoke up toward the ceiling in the general direction of the lesbian dance class.

"Well, then what the hell *does* it mean?" I asked.

"It means your friends are stupid," he said.

42

It was that hour when the prince's coach turns into a gypsy cab smelling strongly of ganja.

I wandered across Seventh Avenue and stepped down into the Monkey's Paw with my Big Chief tablet and Ratso's ancient AAA road atlas firmly under my arm and a lit cigar firmly under my upper lip. A frowsy woman at the bar made frantic little fanning gestures with her hand in the direction of my cigar. I ignored her.

Ratso had said he would meet me but I didn't see him yet. Maybe he was inventorying his apartment. Mick Brennan was there and appeared to be a few drinks ahead of me.

"Where's Michael Caine?" I asked as I ordered a Bushmills Irish Whiskey instead of Jameson Irish Whiskey. Thought I'd try a little variation on a theme.

"Michael," said Brennan laughing, "is over talking to your friend Cleve at the Lone Star, trying to get a booking. He's envious of all the press you're getting."

I downed the shot of Bushmills. It wasn't noticeably different from Jameson. Of course, who could tell with one shot? "That's fairly cosmic," I said. "Michael Caine is the one guy I'm envious of. I mean, if I couldn't be me, I'd like to be him."

"Tell him when I see him," said Brennan.

"Mick," I said, "I've got another photographic query for you. This one goes back some years." I posed the problem to Mick and he confirmed what I'd already suspected. It didn't tell me much about the identity of the killer, but it was another piece in the puzzle of the missing Hank Williams picture.

Mick drifted away. I had another shot of Bushmills. I watched The Weasel, the local purveyor of marching powder, scurry back and forth from the men's room. I stayed at the bar and waited for Ratso. Satan, get thee away from my left nostril.

I was drinking a Bass ale and looking at the Alabama-Tennessee-Virginia-West Virginia section of the road atlas when I felt a presence at my left shoulder. Ratso and Boris. Boris was a Russian karate expert who could kill you in over a hundred ways without leaving any marks. Ratso reached over, took the glass out of my hand, and drank off a good portion of the Bass ale.

"Not bad," he said.

"It's only a cold sore," I said. "Don't worry, I'll check it out at the free clinic next week."

Boris, who rarely drank liquor, said, "To-ma-to juice" to the bartender in a dangerous-sounding, almost lethal accent. He smiled the kind of smile you smile when you know you can kill a man in over a hundred ways without leaving any marks.

I looked back at the road atlas and said, "Montgomery, Chattanooga, Knoxville, Rutledge, Bristol, Cedarville, Chilhowie, Marion, Wytheville, Bluefield, Princeton, Beckley, Willis Branch, Oak Hill."

"Zame to you," said Boris.

"Actually," I said, "eighty-six Montgomery and Chattanooga. We're only talkin' Knoxville, Rutledge, Bristol, Cedarville, Chilhowie, Marion, Wytheville, Bluefield, Princeton, Beckley, Willis Branch, and Oak Hill."

"That's better," said Boris grimly.

"Boris," I said, "I don't expect a person of your rich Eastern background to understand—"

"Murder?" Boris laughed. "I have seen much, much murder." His eyes were not laughing. They were gray and silent as the snow falling over Leningrad.

"So what's with all the little hick towns?" Ratso asked.

"They're not little hick towns, Ratso," I said. "They're just not New York." I drank what was left of my Bass ale.

"That's what I said," said Ratso.

"I'm working," I said, "on Hank Williams's last ride." I signaled Tommy for another Bushmills and another Bass ale. "Now, according to the date on that missing photograph, as Gunner remembers it—she should, it's her mum's birthday—we can probably exclude Knoxville, too."

Ratso bent over the bar to study the road atlas. He loved maps. I hated maps. Unless they had pins in them and were on the Pentagon wall and I was indicating with a pointer to our government leaders where I believed the giant ants would first attack the earth. I hated maps. Boris maintained a polite interest and drank his tomato juice.

"That leaves eleven little hick towns, as you say, Ratso, that Hank passed through on the last night of his life: Rutledge, Bristol, Cedarville, Chilhowie, Marion, Wytheville, Bluefield—"

"All right, all right," said Ratso irritably. "Give it a rest. What's the point of the exercise?"

"The point, Ratso," I said a bit unkindly, "is right on top of your head." I downed the shot.

"C'mon, c'mon," said Ratso impatiently. "What's the point of knowing all these little towns that Hank passed through?"

"There was a photograph of Hank taken by someone in one of these towns. That's the photograph that's now missing from the Lone Star Cafe, and I believe it's central to the case. It's a photo of two small boys and Hank at Howie's #1 BBQ, dated December 31, 1952. It's a slim lead, but if we can find the town we can check the courthouse records, if they have them, and verify which of our little friends was there at the time."

"Long shot," said Ratso. Unfortunately, he was right. And time was running out.

Boris had another tomato juice, decided he'd stop at two,

and left, promising to be at the Lone Star on Wednesday night.

"There is one more thing, Ratso," I said as we sat at the bar, the AAA road atlas lying forlornly in front of us like a forgotten woman. I opened the Big Chief tablet to the notes I'd made of my call to Charles Ansell. "The head shrink of the San Fernando Valley says it's hard to 'decode the fantasy of a psychopath.' Says often they'll 'merge—become another person.' He says 'time doesn't phase a psychopath, they're timeless, they never get over it. There's an initial trauma that they've never recovered from. Such as, a guy sees his mother hang herself and years later he hangs his wife.' "

"That's understandable," said Ratso. We got another round from Tommy.

"Okay," I said, "Ansell says there seems to be a 'self-imposed guilt situation.' What brings it about we don't know. But in the killer's case, the trauma almost certainly had its origins in childhood and has, in Ansell's words, 'kept him as a kid.' "

"Sounds like you," said Ratso.

"Also," I said, "he's fixated with a need not to let anyone eclipse Hank's success. He's Hank reincarnate. He feels threatened as he feels Hank would've felt threatened. Basic motivations for murder, we understand. Greed, jealousy, et cetera. But psychological motivations are much more difficult to comprehend. That's what Ansell says. I say it adds up to an ugly surprise and a rather tedious wig."

"You should've been a psychologist," said Ratso. "You missed your calling."

"Maybe I was out playing miniature golf," I said.

I was getting cigar ashes on the road atlas. It was damn near three o'clock in the morning. On my most recent trip to the men's room I happened to glimpse my face in the mirror. My eyes were starting to look like road atlases, too. Old ones with a lot of roads and highways that weren't even there anymore.

I was still drinking but I wasn't thinking. Ratso was talking to the woman who hadn't liked my cigar smoke. Mick Brennan drifted over, put a cold mug of Heineken down right in the middle of my AAA road atlas, and headed for the men's room.

"Goddammit, Brennan," I said. I removed the mug from the surface of the map. There was a dark circle where it had been. It extended all the way from Chilhowie to Oak Hill. I stared dumbly at the circle for a moment. Then I said: "Jesus Christ . . . Ratso . . . that's it. I've got it." I smiled a slightly crooked smile into the mirror behind the bar.

"What do you have?" Ratso asked. "Besides herpes, I mean."

I folded up the road atlas and gathered up the Big Chief tablet. "I've got the answer," I said. "I'll verify it first thing in the morning, and then Wednesday night I'll try to snare this unsavory little booger." I stood up a little shakily and put twenty bucks on the bar. I was wired and inspired.

"I'm glad," said Ratso a little unconvincingly, "but Sherlock, do you have to get so fucked up to solve a case?"

The woman who hadn't liked my cigar smoke had vanished into thin air in the fashion of cigar smoke. Other, much dearer people had disappeared from my life in almost the same way.

"My dear Ratso," I said, "you know what Oscar Wilde had to say, don't you?"

"No," said Ratso, "what'd he say?"

" 'All of us are lying in the gutter, but some of us are looking at the stars.' "

43

I made a brief flurry of phone calls early Monday morning. I called the office of the county clerk in the courthouse of a little county seat in Virginia. Yes, Virginia, there is a person in New York who thinks he's Hank Williams and is going around killing people. Yes, Virginia, there've been three stiffs already connected with the Lone Star Cafe, and now I'm going to perform there myself. Yes, Virginia, smart move.

I got the information I wanted from Virginia, and I was a little surprised about what I'd learned. Just a *little* surprised.

I called my brother, Roger, who lived in Maryland, and invited him to the show on New Year's Eve. It was arranged that he'd come right to the Lone Star from Penn Station and meet me there. I called Cleve to alert him that Roger was coming and to put him on my hit list at the door. I called Rambam and told him when and where he should look for the missing picture.

Then I thought about what I was getting myself into, and I damn near panicked.

A jolt of Jameson settled me down a bit. If I left New York now I would still have to come back and show my face sometime, and that would be difficult. Once you've lived in New York City you can't really get away. It keeps calling you back, like a perverse Hawaii.

I would stay, I decided. Didn't want anybody calling me a woosy. Didn't want anybody saying I didn't have a hair on my bum. Of course, if anything went wrong, those would be two fairly stupid reasons to die. I'd have to chance it.

But in the event that I was killed or incapacitated, who would take care of the cat?

I called Ratso. He didn't want the cat. Even for just a few days. He was worried about the cat pissing on his ten thousand books relating to Jesus, Bob Dylan, and Hitler. I told him that sooner or later, cats piss on everything. Later, he said. Some friend.

I started to call McGovern but thought better of it. You couldn't in good conscience leave a cat with McGovern. You wouldn't want to do that to a dog.

I called Mick Brennan.

"Mick," I said, "would you mind keeping the cat for a few days?"

"Not on your life, mate," he said in a quiet, serious voice.

"Thanks a lot," I said, "you self-directed, me-generation bastard." All my friends were really coming through for me.

"Look, mate," said Brennan, "who's the lesbian bird that runs the dance class in the loft above yours?"

"Winnie Katz," I said irritably. "What's it to you?"

"Nothing to me, mate," he said, "but she might not mind having a little pussy around." Brennan laughed. I thought about it. It had a lot of advantages. It certainly beat putting the cat in a pillowcase and lugging her eighty blocks uptown, fighting and scratching all the way in the back of a cab like I used to do.

I thanked Mick and hung up, and I called Winnie. She answered the phone slightly out of breath. None of my business.

"Winnie?"

"Yes?"

"This is Kinky downstairs."

"Yes?" I hoped I wasn't interrupting the class or anything.

"I may be out of pocket for a few days. I wondered if you'd mind keeping my cat while I'm gone?"

There was a silence on the phone for a moment. Then she asked, "Is the cat a female?"

"Of course," I said.

"I wouldn't want a tomcat up here spraying the whole place. Scratching up the balance beams."

"I know what you mean," I said disapprovingly.

There was another silence. This time a little longer. Then she said, "Okay, I'll take her." Interesting choice of words.

"Great," I said. "This is Monday. I'll drop her off with you Wednesday morning." I thanked her again and hung up.

The cat was sleeping on the desk under her heat lamp. I patted her on the head and said, "You're gonna have a great time. You'll be in good, safe, experienced hands. Now you won't have to ride inside a pillowcase in the back of a taxi with your eyes turning green and flashing like Satan. It's all for the best. Trust me."

The cat went back to sleep. I lit a cigar and dialed Uptown Judy. We agreed to get together that evening at the loft. I hung up.

44

Uptown Judy's recording of *Carmen* was on my stereo. Uptown Judy was on my bed. She was wearing a blue robe that fell open occasionally to reveal powder-blue panties. I liked girls with a good sense of color coordination.

I was wearing a West Point sweatshirt and my old sarong from Borneo. A heady combination of toughness and sensitivity, so important in today's world.

I turned off the light, walked over to the bed, took off the sweatshirt and sarong. In the dimness I could see the cat sleeping, almost poignantly, on top of my suitcase. I got under the covers. Uptown Judy had disrobed, so to speak, and now she struggled out of the panties and pitched them into the darkness.

I slid over a little closer to her.

"Closer," she said.

"I can't get any closer without performing the Heimlich maneuver," I said.

If you are firmly enough rooted in your masculinity, it shouldn't bother you much to have a woman on top of you. It's a good deal more relaxing, it's often more satisfying for both parties, and you can see a lot more of what's going on. Don't get into the habit, though, or you might turn into a woosy.

Later, I picked up a hairbrush and ran it through my moss a few times in the dim reflection of the mirror on the bedroom door. My moss looked pretty much the same whether or not I brushed it. It was just sort of a private ritual with me to brush my hair before I went to bed. Life was full of things that made a lot less sense than that.

"Why do you brush your hair before you go to bed?" asked Uptown Judy.

It was a hard question and I wasn't really sure I knew the answer.

It wasn't so much a matter of vanity. I think I just wanted to be sure I was really there. With a sense of dread I considered the possibility of my not ever being there again after Wednesday night. Only a lonely hairbrush combing the cobwebs of a lonely loft.

I glanced over at the peaceful form under the covers. She was a woman lying on a bed in North America. Why burden Uptown Judy with my problems? I patted the cat and got back into bed.

"I want to make a good impression on my pillow," I said.

45

I took the litter box and a week's supply of cat food and put them in the freight elevator. Then I came back for the cat, and with all our travel gear, the two of us rode up to Winnie Katz's.

Ah, Isle of Lesbos. Strange and sweet are thee. Forbidden and fragile, thy charm, Forget it, sailor.

"Come in," said a voice. I came in, closed the door, and put down the cat. Winnie was sitting at her kitchen table eating a bowl of Froot Loops and drinking Red Zinger herbal tea. A little lonely girl in a big lonely room.

"Sit down," she said. "It isn't often we get your kind up here." I pretended not to understand, but I didn't think she bought it.

"Froot Loops," she said a little disdainfully. "A long time ago, my attitude toward men. . . ." She paused. She said "men" with more disdain than she'd said "Froot Loops." She ate some Froot Loops.

"A long time ago my attitude toward men was 'Fuck 'em and feed 'em Froot Loops,'" she said. She glanced casually, coolly over at me.

"What's your attitude now?" I asked. I wasn't sure I wanted to know.

She sipped some Red Zinger and she took her time. Then she looked at me like I was a lamp and said, "Feed 'em Froot Loops."

It wasn't a healthy attitude, but it wasn't really a healthy world. Anyway, it was too late to find another place for the cat. I'd have to tough it out. I got up and walked over to the window and looked down at a limo parked next to three garbage trucks. Take me home, country roads.

"Ever been around any sisters of Sappho, Kinky?" she asked.

"No," I said, "but I've gone out with a lot of women who share your attitude toward Froot Loops."

Winnie got up from the table and came over to the window.

"You're pretty straight, Kinky," she said.

"That's why they call me Kinky," I said.

"What do people like you call people like me?" she asked. She had a lukewarm, lesbianlike smile on her face, which I mistook for a sense of humor. "Lesbians?" she asked. "Dykes?"

I smiled my interdenominational ice-breaking smile. "How about gap-lappers?" I asked.

She didn't laugh. She nodded her head a few times though, as if she understood men. Maybe lesbians were the only people who did. She was growing on me. She looked soft and small-town attractive in the morning sun from the window. I found myself empathizing with her. Maybe more. I didn't know how to say good-bye. I thought an older-brotherly farewell handshake might be in order, so I put out my hand. Winnie didn't even look at it.

She crossed both arms on her chest. The sapphic smile was back on her face.

"The cat stays," she said. "You go."

46

The green-gray reptilian scales of the creature were gleaming obscenely in the reflected lights of the city. The thing seemed to be taking on a life of its own.

"Bill Dick's got a big lizard," said Ratso. It was between sets. We were standing on the third-floor balcony of the Lone Star Cafe. I was still alive.

"Yes, he does," I said. An involuntary shudder went through me. I'd had a few shots and I was trying to pace myself for the second show, which wasn't to start for over an hour.

"Good set," said Larry Campbell. Campbell was arguably the best all-around musician in the city. He could play any instrument known to Western man and a few that weren't. He wasn't too excited about Dick's lizard.

"You guys were hot," I said.

"Decent," said Campbell. "Decent." Borrowing a phrase from the New York Rangers hockey players who often came to see the show. To them, everything in the world was either "decent" or "brutal." Not a bad way to look at life, I thought. Tonight, I suspected, would fall into what you'd call your brutal area.

Campbell wandered back into the dressing room to talk to some young female admirers. You didn't get world-class groupies at the Lone Star. I wasn't even sure that there was such a thing. Groupies were groupies. Age, sex, area of interest didn't figure into it. Adoration was one thing, but worship was enough to bore the pants off you, sometimes literally.

It was around eleven-fifteen. Still early. It was New Year's Eve, and New York was a late town anyway. The only later ones were probably Vegas and ancient Rome. So I wasn't too worried that I hadn't seen Simmons, Flippo, or Gunner yet. They might've been there all the time. It was a madhouse downstairs. A zoo and a half. Where the hell was Rambam?

Ratso took a sip of my Molson and smiled. "Well," he said, "we're halfway home."

"Where the hell's Simmons?" I asked. "I thought he was going to do a few songs tonight."

"Don't worry," said Ratso, "he's here. Said to tell you just to call on him. He said he'd play 'if the good Lord's willin' and the creek don't rise.' Nice colloquialism."

"You know who always used to say that, don't you?" I asked.

"No," said Ratso, "who said it?"

"Hank Williams used to say that at the end of his radio shows."

"That's good," said Ratso.

"What's so good about it?" I asked.

"I was afraid," said Ratso as he took another sip of my Molson, "that it might be Oscar Wilde."

Cleve had apparently spoken to Ratso. There had been a little problem already with the two Judys. Both their names had been on the "hit list," and Uptown Judy, arriving first, hadn't had any trouble getting in. But when Downtown Judy arrived, the guy at the door, not a rocket scientist, had told her, "I think you're here already."

Downtown Judy had become somewhat perturbed. The guy at the door had called for Cleve. Cleve had called for Ratso and Ratso had shown the guy that there were two Judys on the hit list. Downtown Judy had become highly agitated then, and it was at that time that Ratso, according to himself, had applied the master's touch. He'd told her,

"Kinky didn't want you to have any problems getting in, so he put your name down twice."

The dressing room was more frantic than a methadone clinic at closing time, and the overflow was spilling into the open-air patio. The iguana didn't look like it wanted any more company, and I knew I didn't. Except for Rambam. Where the hell was Rambam?

I tried to settle down and take stock of things. Cleve, Bill Dick, Simmons were all there, though I'd only seen Cleve. Where Flippo and Gunner were was anybody's-guess. Through the door to the dressing room I saw Patrick the bouncer talking to a large, squat form by the doorway. Sergeant Cooperman. My backup unit was here. Very comforting.

I figured if I stayed in one place long enough, everybody'd find me. Everybody. Even Hank Williams and Kaw-liga the wooden Indian. No point in going downstairs where the crowd was. It's never a good idea to mix with the crowd when you're performing, anyway. Tends to demystify you.

I was heading into the dressing room for another Molson. I'd just gotten inside the doorway when Bill Dick collared me.

"Kinkster," said Bill Dick, "I'd like you to meet the club's lawyer." He introduced me to a fairly glib-looking guy with a gold chain and an Italian name Thurmon Munson couldn't've caught the first time around.

We talked for a few minutes. The guy was pretty funny for a lawyer. "Like you to meet my wife, Mary," he said. "She's Irish. I'm a social climber."

The only thing I was climbing was the walls. I was starting to get real nervous. I glanced around the dressing room. Sal Lorello, dapper former manager in from Chappaqua for the show. Nick "Chinga" Chavin, country singer turned ad exec. Earl Shuman, music publisher and author of some great songs himself. Corky Laing, world-class rock drummer. Found him in the Congo, beatin' on his bongo.

I got the Molson and walked back outside onto the patio.

Had to stay away from the hard stuff just now. Had to pace myself. Didn't want to peak too soon. I could've been thinking this way before any show. Unfortunately, tonight the subject wasn't music. It was murder.

McGovern and my brother Roger were leaning on the iguana talking with each other. McGovern had a vodka tonic balanced precariously on the third toenail of the creature's left hind foot.

"I'm here for moral support," said Roger.

"Nothing's going to happen," said Ratso calmly. "Nothing's going to happen."

McGovern didn't say anything. He didn't have to say anything. The look on his face said that something was going to happen. And McGovern was a very accurate paranoid. Almost an idiot savant when it came to sensing danger. He looked worried as hell, and that made me worried as hell. It made it a little tough for me to be thinking what song I wanted to open the second set with.

It was cold on the patio. It was hot in the dressing room. But I was still alive.

There was always something to be said for that.

47

There wasn't much for me to do but stand around and look at the iguana like everybody else. Hell of a way to finish off the year.

But I had to stay out of trouble, as they say. "Don't trouble trouble till trouble troubles you, Mr. Hank," like the janitor at the sanitarium told Hank Williams. Amazing how much of Flippo's book stayed with you.

I walked over to the edge of the patio where you could look over the wall onto Fifth Avenue. Headlights were hurrying down the avenue lest they be late on their pathetic way to close out the old and ring in the new. They did it every year. But there was nothing new in New York, I thought. A few new bums on the Bowery. Maybe their New Year's resolutions hadn't kicked in yet from the year before. And yet, one kept hoping . . .

A shadow moved next to me.

It came close to me, reached into the folds of an overcoat, and handed me a Gideon Bible. It was Rambam.

"Got it," he said. "I used the old blue jeans and bucket of ice trick."

"Oh, that one," I said as my pulse began to slow a bit. "What the hell's the old blue jeans and bucket of ice trick?"

"Well, you said he recently moved to the Gramercy Park. Now, if you want to get in a hotel room, you obtain the room number from the desk. I won't go into that. Anyway, you get the room number. Then you go up to the floor the room's on. You take off your shoes, socks, and shirt and leave 'em out on the stairway. You get a bucket of ice and you walk around with your blue jeans, the bucket of ice, and an embarrassed expression until you find a maid or hotel employee and you ask could they help you, you locked yourself out of your room. Works every time."

I looked at Rambam. He was smiling. "Never fails," he said.

"What'd you find?" I asked.

"A fucking Hank Williams museum," said Rambam.

"And the picture?"

From under his coat Rambam took out a room-service menu and opened it up. There was Howie's #1 BBQ, the two kids, and poor old Hank. There was the autograph and the date, December 31, 1952.

"Watcha got?" asked Ratso. Rambam quickly started to close the menu over the picture, but I stopped him.

"No harm in them seeing it," I said. McGovern and Roger were drifting over, too. They studied the photograph.

"That's probably the last autograph he ever signed," said McGovern.

"Might be worth a fortune," Ratso said.

The moon was rising slowly over the Chrysler Building, and it lent an eerie quality to the old black-and-white photograph.

The children in the picture had that awkward, trapped, charming look common to the children of the fifties. Like kids in the audience on Groucho Marx or Beaver Cleaver and his friends.

"Who are the kids?" McGovern said with a laugh.

"I don't know," I said, "but I'm pretty sure . . ." My voice trailed off as I studied the photograph more closely.

"Yeah?" Ratso asked. "What are you pretty sure about?"

"That one of these two little boys is going to try to kill me tonight."

48

"Five minutes, Mr. Jolson," said Cleve from the door of the dressing room.

"Christ," I said. What a hell of a way to start a year. Perform an hour show for a madhouse full of brontosaurus material while you try to avoid getting snuffed by a homicidal maniac.

I put on my Nudie's of Hollywood Jesus coat that Bob Dylan had given me. It had palm trees, rainbows, pictures of Jesus, and three crosses on the back. The two outer crosses were occupied but the middle one was empty. Either the Lord had risen or he'd gone out to get a donut. The religious significance didn't bother me, only that the damn coat was too heavy to wear onstage. Had enough sequins to choke an iguana.

I strapped on my guitar.

I walked down the long narrow hallway on the third floor. The band was already onstage, and I could hear Larry Campbell launching them into "Exodus" and intricately weaving it into "Spurs That Jingle Jangle Jingle." Hell of a medley.

On the stairway to the second floor I picked up Boris and Patrick, who stayed right with me all the way to the stage. Having security not only made you feel secure, it made you feel important. Like the leader of a small African nation.

The set went extremely well. It was only forty-five minutes out of my life—fifty if you counted the encore—and it provided pleasure and entertainment to others. I wasn't Judy Garland, but I wasn't bad.

I played all the old favorites. "They Ain't Makin' Jews Like Jesus Anymore," "Get Your Biscuits in the Oven and Your Buns in the Bed," "The Ballad of Charles Whitman," "Sold American," "Ride 'Em Jewboy," "Waitress, Please Waitress, Come Sit on My Face," "Ol' Shep," "Ira Hayes," and "Ol' Ben Lucas."

There was a rather poignant moment at the end of "They Ain't Makin' Jews Like Jesus Anymore" when I brought onto the stage Lee Frazier, America's Favorite Negro, and John A. Walsh, America's Most Influential Albino, and the three of us sang harmony together. That was what I called the brotherhood-in-action segment of the show.

It was at that time that Chet Flippo made his move for the stage. Boris and Patric T-boned him directly in front of the center mike, but all he had with him was a slip of paper with a song request on it. Boris handed it up to me. It read: "Play 'Proud to Be an Asshole from El Paso.'"

I never refuse a sensitive request. I played the song. Flippo was out of it anyway. I'd known it from the time Rambam turned up with the photograph.

I called Mike Simmons up and he sang "Your Cheatin' Heart" and several other tunes that went down well with the crowd. As Simmons left the stage he said to me, "Got to see you right after the show."

"Fine," I said. I didn't mind seeing John Wayne Gacey after the show. Before the show was when I didn't want to be bummed out. Had to pace myself.

I played a few more songs, told the crowd it'd been a financial pleasure, and reminded them, if they were driving, not to forget their cars. I ended the set with "Before All Hell Breaks Loose."

Twenty-seven minutes later, it did.

49

Gunner was in the dressing room when I got there. She was sitting on the dilapidated couch, with her legs crossed, smoking a cigarette.

"Fine performance, Kinky," she said.

I leaned the guitar against a wall. "Another show in my hip pocket," I said.

I started to take off my Jesus coat but decided against it. It might bring me some clout wherever I was going next. The rest of the band was coming into the dressing room, along with Simmons, Downtown Judy, and a few others. It had been a long night, and it wasn't over yet.

I walked out onto the patio to smoke a solitary cigar under the iguana's chin. Boris was now at the dressing room door, keeping a watchful eye on me. Funny in the music business how you're either swarmed by people or left completely alone with a cigar and an iguana. There didn't seem to be much middle ground. I once thought that being alone alone was superior to being alone in a crowd. Now, I didn't see that it made a hell of a lot of difference.

Maybe God was just a nice Jewish dentist, and *Time* and *Life* and *People* were only things we looked at ever so casually and briefly in his nicely furnished, antiseptic waiting room with a little Barry Antelope music piped in.

I puffed on the cigar and looked for an occasional, wayward star that might've gotten lost somewhere between Trump Tower and the World Trade Center. I found one and made a wish. One of these days maybe Jiminy Cricket will step out of the woodwork. Then, if somebody doesn't mistake him for a cockroach and crush his back, I figure I'm in business.

I went back into the now-packed dressing room, went over to my guitar case, and got out the room-service menu and the AAA road atlas. I went downstairs with Boris to find Cooperman and Fox. Before I left the dressing room Simmons asked me to meet him in an hour or so at Marylou's. I'd told him I would.

Lee Frazier unlocked the rear door to the basement for me. I stationed Boris in the executive men's room and told him that at the first sound of trouble to come on the run. Then I met Cooperman and Fox on the back stairway of the club. It was agreed that they'd keep a close surveillance on the basement and be ready for action if necessary. I walked through the basement to the manager's office and knocked on the door.

50

"Just a minute," said a familiar voice. Then the door opened. "Come on in," said Cleve. "You want to get paid?"

"That was one idea I had," I said. We were in the little office alone. Cleve went over to the door and locked the bolt on it.

"Sit down," he said. "I'm still counting the cash. You made out like a bandit tonight. You got the five coming to you, and we went into percentages at the door. A real financial pleasure for you, pal." Cleve laughed a friendly laugh.

"Music to my ears," I said. Cleve was counting the money and I was counting imaginary worry beads and getting pretty damn nervous.

"You read Flippo's book?" I asked. I lit a cigar.

"Yeah," said Cleve. "He had some inaccurate shit in there, but on the whole it wasn't bad. If you're into Hank Williams." He kept counting the cash. I kept puffing on the cigar.

"Cleve," I said, "give it a rest for a minute. Forget the money. The only currency I value is the coin of the spirit. Take a look at this map, will you?"

Cleve spread the road atlas out over the desk. "What's this for?" he asked. "You thinking of going on a trip?"

"Not quite," I said. "Anything look familiar?" I pointed to the Virginia-West Virginia section—Hank's last ride.

"Yeah," said Cleve with a little smile.

"I know," I said. "Chilhowie, to be exact."

404

"How'd you know that?" asked Cleve, a very slight wariness creeping into his voice. The room was hot. It was also starting to feel a hell of a lot smaller than when I first walked in. My eyes went quickly, almost unconsciously, to the bolt on the door, a gesture that didn't go unnoticed by Cleve.

"You can thank Mick Brennan for it," I said. "He put his beer down on top of my road atlas last Saturday night at the Monkey's Paw. That's how Howie's #1 BBQ got to be Chilhowie's #1 BBQ."

"Very clever," said Cleve. "Go on." The color was beginning to go from his face, and there hadn't been all that much there to begin with. A nerve was twitching under his left eye.

"The time frame was right," I said. "You were there when Hank passed through on his way to Canton, Ohio. When I asked you about it earlier you told me you were an only child. Then you said, 'We grew up in Kentucky.' I remembered that and it sounded strange. So I called the courthouse at the county seat and I found the court records concerning your dead brother, Joe. Died two days after Hank Williams died. Hank was twenty-nine. Joe was ten. You were twelve. That about right?"

The twitch under Cleve's eye was getting worse. "That's ancient history," he said in a half whisper, half croak. He was staring at Chilhowie on the map, and his eye kept twitching. It wasn't getting better. The whole left eye was twitching at two-second intervals. Looked like a method actor practicing a lascivious wink in front of a mirror.

"That may be ancient history," I said, "but this isn't." I flipped the Gramercy Park room-service menu with the photo inside that Rambam had lifted onto Cleve's desk. "This was taken from your hotel room about three hours ago," I said in a cold, deliberate voice. "Want anything from room service?"

He opened the menu with all the forethought of a trained chimp. He sat there rigid, staring through the photo. His brother, himself, and old Hank stared timelessly, effortlessly back at him.

"Picture from life's other side," I said. Cleve was trembling. Whether from fear, rage, or eleven different herbs and spices I couldn't be sure. I didn't stick around to find out. I went to the door and grabbed the bolt. I didn't budge. I heard a desk drawer open. "Boris!" I shouted. "Boris!"

I turned around. The photo, the road atlas, hundred-dollar bills were falling through the air seemingly in slow motion like a one-man ticker-tape parade, and through the ticker tape, like a cadaver in high gear, came Cleve directly for me. In his left hand, sickeningly, yet predictably, was a toma-hawk.

51

When I regained consciousness, it was in a hospital bed. Like a guy swimming underwater, I could feel myself gradually coming to the surface. First, I heard voices, but the words were unintelligible. One voice had a New Yorky, rodentlike quality to it that seemed faintly familiar.

The first images I saw were two blurred figures standing by a window. When they came into clearer focus, I saw that it was Ratso and a doctor engaged in some kind of a discussion. The doctor, apparently, was explaining something, and Ratso was nodding his head very somberly. His serious demeanor was not especially comforting.

The first actual words I heard the doctor say to Ratso were, "A tomahawk wound in the groin can be a very serious thing if it isn't treated promptly." I lost consciousness again.

When I came to for the second time, Ratso was sitting on the bed eating a pastrami sandwich about the size of his head and I was in great pain. "Congratulations," Ratso said, "you're a hero."

I didn't feel like a hero. I also didn't feel like watching a man do unnatural things to a pastrami sandwich two feet away from my head. I tried to look heroic.

"Very clever, Sherlock," said Ratso between bites, "that Chilhowie business. But how'd you know to look back that far in time for the motive?"

"My dear Ratso," I said, "the pattern became fairly

obvious early on. Take a look at Hank's victims. What do you see?"

"Okay," said Ratso. "We've got Larry Barkin, Bubba Borgelt, and Ned Glaser. They were all country singers and they all had the poor judgment to play the Lone Star Cafe."

"There's something more, Ratso," I said. "It's so obvious that it's easy to miss. It's why I invited Roger down for the show and made sure Cleve knew about it.

"You see, by this time I knew that Cleve was Hank. And, as Hank, I knew that he was not just killing country singers. He was killing *brothers.*"

Ratso stared at me. He stopped eating his sandwich.

"I first saw the pattern," I said, "after Bubba Borgelt bought it. But I became even more sure when Hank spared the Burrito Brothers.

"Cleve was clearly one of the little boys in the Chilhowie photograph. He was in the right place at the right time. The real Hank Williams died sometime during the night on the same date the photograph was taken."

"Then that autograph really was authentic?" asked Ratso.

"Of course not," I said. "It was forged by Cleve. Another small step on the way to his assuming the Hank identity. In 1952 there was no way any photograph could've been developed in time for the real Hank to have signed it."

"Of course not," said Ratso.

"Two days after Hank Williams died, Cleve's younger brother Joe died. This is in the courthouse records. Whether Cleve blamed himself for his brother's death or actually killed him requires further investigation. One thing is for sure, however: He was not his brother's keeper."

"Truly amazing, Sherlock," said Ratso, "but I still don't understand one thing. Why would Hank spare the Burrito Brothers?"

"Because those brothers aren't really brothers," I said. "A rudimentary knowledge of country music always helps."

"Yeah," said Ratso. He stared at the ruins of his pastrami

408 sandwich. "It's amazing I've gotten this far in life without it."

"Look at it this way," I said. "If we ever run into a case involving Jesus, Bob Dylan, or Hitler, we're all set."

Ratso laughed. "You never know," he said.

52

Several days later I was feeling much better when Ratso came in with the newspapers, the mail, and a large number of Pete Myers' pork pies from Myers of Keswick.

"I can't believe the great press you're still getting," said Ratso. "McGovern is really having a ball with this. If you'll pardon the expression."

"How's Cleve?" I asked.

"Well," said Ratso, "aside from the fact that he thinks he's Hank full-time now and that his face is jumping around like a flea circus, he's doing all right."

"That's good to know," I said.

"The shrinks are giving him a thorough checkup from the neck up, but even his voice and his mannerisms have drastically altered. He keeps telling them he's got to move on. He's got a show to do, he says. No doubt about it, Kinkster, the boy's got a fan belt loose."

"What's in the mail?" I asked, grimacing slightly as I got up on my elbows. I still couldn't quite sit up in bed.

"Here's a nice note from Flippo. His book's gone into a second printing, largely thanks to you, he says."

"Anytime," I said.

"Here's a highly unusual photo of you that Gunner sent." Ratso passed the photo over to me. It was a shot of me sitting on a barstool looking rather dazed.

"Good publicity shot," I said. "Anything else you'd like to share with the whole class?"

"Well," said Ratso, "this is a little strange. It's a large manila envelope. Big block letters on it."

"Open it," I said.

Ratso opened the envelope and handed me the contents. It was the sheet music to the Hank Williams song, "I Can't Help It If I'm Still in Love with You."

There was a note attached. It read: "I'll always cherish the time we spent together. Let's do it again real soon. All my love, Judy."

Ratso grabbed it out of my hands and looked it over. "That's very sweet of her," he said. "You definitely ought to call her or drop her a line."

"Can't," I said.

"Why not?" Ratso asked.

"I don't know if it's Uptown or Downtown," I said.

I took out one of the cigars Ratso had smuggled into the room for me and lit it up.

"Look, Ratso," I said, "I'm almost afraid to ask, but there's one more thing."

"What is it?" Ratso asked.

"Did you save the Jesus coat?"

"Don't worry," he said. "It's safe in a closet—in my apartment." I leaned back on the pillows and took a lazy puff on the cigar.

"You're like a brother to me, Ratso," I said.

When the Cat's Away

ACKNOWLEDGMENTS

The author would like to thank the following people for their help: Tom Friedman, Earl Buckelew, Marcie Friedman, and Larry "Ratso" Sloman; Esther "Lobster" Newberg at ICM; James Landis, Jane Meara, and Lori Ames at Beech Tree Books; and Steve Rambam, technical adviser. The author would also like to express his thanks to the following officials of the Garden Cat Club: Vicky Markstein, Peter Markstein, and Elinor Silverman.

One magic midnight show
She taught you how it feels
Once, oh so long ago
When rock 'n' roll was real

For Kacey Cohen,
The angel on my shoulder

1

Winnie Katz's lesbian dance class was like God. Mankind never saw it, but you always knew it was there.

Of course, Moses had seen God. In the form of a burning bush, interestingly enough. Then he took two tablets and went to bed.

There are people who have seen God since, but we have a place for them. It is called Bellevue and the area around it, for a twenty-block radius, is regarded as having one of the highest violent-crime rates in the city. That's because it's impossible to tell who's insane in New York.

Every seven minutes they let a perfectly normal-looking guy out of Bellevue. He walks a block or two, buys a pretzel on the street, asks somebody what time it is, then has a flashback to the Peloponnesian War. He takes out a Swiss Army knife and cuts some Korean woman's head off. Uses the wrong blade. The one you're supposed to cut nose hairs with. Of course, it isn't his fault.

Not everybody's had the opportunity to be in the Swiss Army.

I listened to the rhythmic thuddings in the loft above me. I wondered what the hell was really going on up there. If somebody's wayward daughter from Coeur d'Alene, Idaho, was being broken down like a double-barreled shotgun, it'd be a hell of a lot of early ballroom lessons gone to waste. On the other hand, what did I know about modern dance?

It was a chilly evening in late January and I was sitting at

417

my desk just sort of waiting for something besides my New Year's resolutions to kick in. If you're patient and you wait long enough, something will usually happen and it'll usually be something you don't like. I poured a generous slug of Jameson Irish whiskey into the old bull's horn that I sometimes used as a shotglass. I killed the shot.

Like my pal McGovern always says: get rid of the toothpaste taste.

I was dreaming the unisexual dreams of the everyday houseperson, when the phones rang. There are two red telephones in my loft, both connected to the same line, at stage left and stage right of my desk. When you're sitting at the desk they ring simultaneously on either side of what you're pleased to call your brain. While this may upgrade the significance of any incoming wounded you're likely to receive, it can also make you want to jump into your boots and slide down the pole.

I woke with a start, which was a good thing. Daydreaming while smoking cigars can be a fire hazard. It can be as dangerous as drugs and booze unless you know what you're doing. If you know what you're doing, it can be as safe as walking down the street. Long as you're not daydreaming within a twenty-block radius of Bellevue.

2

I watched the phones ring for a while. I'd been dreaming about a girl in a peach-colored dress. Another couple of rings wasn't going to hurt anybody. I took a leisurely puff on the cigar and picked up the blower on the left.

"Spit it," I said.

A woman was sobbing on the other end of the line. I tried to identify her by her sob but I couldn't. Maybe it was a wrong number.

Finally, the voice collected itself somewhat and said, "Kinky. Kinky. This . . . this is Jane Meara." Jane Meara was a friend of mine, a pretty, perky, intelligent girl and one of the authors of the book *Growing Up Catholic*. At the moment it didn't sound like she'd grown up at all.

Grieving women are not my long suit. I have found, however, that a direct, almost gruff demeanor is usually quite effective. Anyway, it was all I had in stock.

"Jane," I said, "pull yourself together. What the hell's the matter? Your guppies die?"

This, apparently, broke the dam. A heartfelt wail was now coming down the line. I put the blower down on the desk. I puffed several times rapidly on my cigar. When I picked up again it was just in time to hear Jane saying, "I wish, I wish my guppies *had* died."

"C'mon, Jane," I said, "what is it? You're cuttin' into my cocktail hour."

I could hear her shoulders stiffen. She sniffled a few more times. Then she said, "My cat's disappeared."

"Relax, Jane," I said. "We'll get it back. What's the cat's name?"

"Rocky."

"What's he look like?"

"It's a she."

"Fine."

I got the pertinent details from Jane. Rocky was yellow and white with four white paws. According to Jane she "looked like she was wearing sweat socks." Rocky'd disappeared—vanished into thin air—right in the middle of a cat show at Madison Square Garden. Jane had stepped away for just a moment and when she'd returned the cage was empty and the cat was gone.

I pressed Jane for a little more information, made some reassuring noises, and gave her my word I'd hop right on it.

I hung up, walked over to the kitchen window, and watched the gloom settle over the city. Monday night and it looked like it.

The cat show, according to Jane, would be purring along all week and would be closing each night at nine. It was now nudging seven o'clock. I'd have to work fairly fast.

If the cat was still in the Garden, there was always a chance. She might wind up on the wrong end of a hockey stick, but there was a chance.

If Rocky'd gotten out of the Garden and into the street, getting her back would be tough.

Almost as tough as getting back a girl in a peach-colored dress.

3 Finding lost cats is not the most romantic, macho experience a country-singer-turned-
amateur-detective might get into. But there was
something rather poignant about the hopelessness of Jane
Meara's situation that I couldn't bend my conscience quite
enough to ignore.

I puffed on my cigar and reflected that I'd never much
liked cats myself. Until one winter night about eight years
ago in an alley in Chinatown when I'd met the first pussy
that ever swept me off my feet.

Now I have a cat. Well, that's not quite accurate. A cat and
I have each other. We inhabit a large, drafty loft on the
fourth floor of a converted warehouse at 199B Vandam, New
York City.

In the summer the loft is hotter than Equatorial West Top-
syland. In the winter it's so cold you have to jump-start your
electric toothbrush. The landlord has promised to do something about it. The cat and I live in hope.

Cats, country music, and cigars have become the three
spiritual linchpins of my life. Actually, I have a few other
spiritual linchpins and they also begin with a *c*, but we won't
go into that now.

If I was going to find Jane's cat, I'd better get cracking.

I called Ratso, a friend of mine who, over the past few
years, had accompanied me in solving several rather ugly
murder cases in the Village. Ratso was loud, garish, and fis-
cally tight as a tick, but he was also warm, loyal, and blessed

with an ingenuous spirit. He was as worthy a modern-day Dr. Watson as I was every likely to find. Good help is hard to get these days.

Ratso was not home so I tried him at the office. He was the editor of the *National Lampoon*. Maybe he was working late, I thought. He answered the phone himself.

"Leprosarium for Unwed Mothers," he said.

"Ratso," I said, "it's Kinky. I need your help. I'm looking for a lost cat. It got away at the cat show down at the Garden."

My words were greeted by laughter and hoots of derision. It became quickly apparent to me that Ratso had put me on the speaker phone. I could hear Mike Simmons, the other editor of the magazine, shout, "If you find that pussy, give me a call." There was more laughter. I was beginning to run out of charm.

"Ratso," I said, "either you're coming or you're not."

Simmons shouted again, "That's what she told him last night." That one seemed to crack up the whole office.

"Listen, Kinkster," said Ratso, "you and I've got better things to do than run around New York looking for a lost fucking cat. You're a hero, Kinkster." I winced slightly and took a puff on the cigar.

Ratso continued, "You solved the Worthington case. You got McGovern off the hook. Remember?"

" 'Fraid so," I said.

"You saved the girl at the bank from the mugger."

"Anybody could've."

"But anybody *didn't*—you did. That's why you're *somebody*. You're hot. You're happening! You can pick and choose, baby."

"Look," I said, "it's just something I've gotten myself into. I'll go down there alone."

There was a moment of silence on the line. Then Ratso said, "All right, I'll meet you at the Garden. Window eleven. Fifteen minutes."

"Make it ten," I said. "We take any longer, this cat's gonna be out at LaGuardia asking for an aisle seat in the nonsmoking section."

As I hung up I heard Ratso mutter something to himself. It sounded very much like "Fucking cat."

I put on my hat and my old hunting vest and took three cigars for the road. I put them in the little stitched pockets of the vest where some Americans keep their shotgun shells.

"You see," I said to my own cat as I left for the Garden, "he's not such a terrible Watson after all."

4

Ratso was waiting for me at window 11. He looked like an amiable pimp. He wore a coonskin cap minus the tail, fuchsia slacks, and red flea-market shoes that, as I often pointed out to him, had once belonged to a dead man. To round it off, he wore a blue sweatshirt that said NATIONAL LAMPOON COHABITATION TEAM.

"Nice outfit," I said. "You look like the Don Juan of all ticket scalpers."

"Thanks," he said. "Wardrobe by Hadassah Thrift Shop."

We walked down the corridor toward the Felt Forum, with most of the people going in the opposite direction. They looked like harmless, happy cat fanciers. A few of them carried cats in cages, but under close scrutiny none of the cats were wearing little sweat socks.

Jane Meara was standing by the entrance to the exhibition hall. She looked like a biker gang had just raped her Cabbage Patch doll.

I introduced Jane to Ratso and the three of us made our way into the hall. The whole place had the air of a carnival that couldn't make up its mind whether or not it was leaving town. All around us people were either packing up their cages or preparing their cats for last-minute judging. Every few moments someone would race by with a cat on his upturned palm like an Italian waiter with a rush-order pizza.

Rocky's empty cage had food, water, a litter box, a bed, and lace curtains. If the rents kept going up, I might check in there myself.

Rocky seemed very gone indeed.

A woman came up beside us wringing her hands. "This is terrible," she said. "I'm Marilyn Park, the producer of the show. This is the first time anything like this has happened at one of our shows. I know how you must feel, Jane, dear."

Jane nodded and let go with a little sob.

"Look, Miss Park—" I said.

"*Mrs.* Park," said Mrs. Park. "My husband and I produce the shows together and I told Stanley security here at the Garden should've been tighter."

"Mrs. Park—" I said.

"Call me Marilyn," she said. "And we *will* find the cat. We have people checking right now into all the places a lost little pussycat could go."

"Marilyn," I said, "do you think the cat is loose in the Garden or do you think someone could've *taken* Rocky?"

"All the cats," she said, "have identification numbers. They're checked coming in and leaving the exhibition hall."

"Well," I said, "do you think . . ."

I stopped.

Something was winking at me from beneath the lace curtains in the corner of the cage. It was too short to be a Times Square hooker. It was too small even to be a cat. I reached into the cage, put my hand under the curtains, and withdrew a metal object.

It was the key to room 407 of the Roosevelt Hotel.

I turned the key over in my hand. I put my arm around Jane Meara.

"I don't think Rocky's in the Garden," I said.

The cab ride over to the Roosevelt was a bit strained. Jane appeared to be fighting off a mounting hysteria. Ratso was behaving like a self-appointed member of a lost-cat support group.

"We'll find him, Jane," he said. "We'll find him."

"He's a her," wailed Jane.

"Don't worry," said Ratso. "There ain't a cat alive that the Kinkster can't find . . ."

"That's what I'm worried about!" sobbed Jane. "Whether she's alive!"

". . . blindfolded," continued Ratso, in a stubborn, almost toneless voice.

I was trying not to listen to them. I was trying to think. Why would someone want to steal Jane Meara's cat? I couldn't make head or tail of it.

Marilyn Park had told us that the Roosevelt Hotel was where all the out-of-town cats were staying for the cat show. Almost a thousand of them. One of the few hotels in the city that allowed cats.

As we got out of the cab in front of the Roosevelt, I looked up at the hotel. It looked like a giant gray ship in a children's book, and I imagined hundreds of little cat faces staring down at us from the portholes. I wondered what was waiting for us in room 407.

We crossed the hotel lobby and took the elevator to the fourth floor. Room 407 was down the hall to the left. The hallway was gray, dusty, and smelled like buildings used to smell when you were a child.

I knocked sharply on 407.

Nothing. Not even a meow.

I inserted the key into the lock and opened the door. I hit the lights and we took a look around. The room was not quite empty.

On the bed was a note scrawled on Roosevelt Hotel stationery.

It read: "What's the matter—cat got your tongue?"

5

We put Jane Meara into a cab. Exposure to a distraught woman was not healthy for Kinky. And my increasing surliness wasn't likely to calm Jane's heart. Somewhere there was a guy who could comfort her. A guy who could take her in his arms and tell her, "Don't worry, honey, everything's going to be all right." Unfortunately, the guy probably sang in the Gay Men's Chorus.

Ratso and I crossed Forty-fifth at Madison, took a left, and walked halfway up the block to JR Tobacco, home of the Jamaican "A" cigar. The Jamaican "A" has been aged for one full year. The cigar has more breeding than some people I know.

"Scratch one tabby," said Ratso moments later as the two of us were walking down Fifth Avenue smoking our Jamaican "A's." "Eighty-six one mange-ridden mouser."

"Not particularly spoken like a cat fancier," I said.

"I hate the precious, preening, putrid little bastards."

I took a puff on the cigar as we walked along the avenue in the cold. "They speak very highly of you," I said.

"I mean it," said Ratso, poking the air vehemently with his cigar. "I hate the little bastards."

"You're not alone," I said. "Brahms used to shoot them from his window with a bow and arrow. Napoleon hated cats as well."

"The French hate everyone."

"Except Jerry Lewis. Hitler hated cats, too."

"He wasn't real partial to Jews, either," said Ratso.

"No," I said.

We walked along in silence at a fairly brisk pace until we got to Thirty-fifth Street. I pointed to the right in the general vicinity of some old brownstones. "That's where Nero Wolfe lives," I said.

Before Ratso could say anything, a dark blur shot through the street directly across our path. A black cat.

Ratso made a hard right up my leg and tried to nest in my vest pocket. I didn't think he was a Nero Wolfe devotee, so I had to assume that he was avoiding the path of the black cat. Couldn't blame him.

We were only a few blocks from the Garden and I felt I would be remiss in my responsibilities as a friend and country-singer-turned-amateur-detective if I didn't go back and look for Rocky one more time. Not that I figured we'd find anything.

I bribed Ratso to come along with me to the Garden. I offered him three cigars and promised I'd buy lunch next time at Big Wong, our favorite Chinese restaurant. It was almost shameful to have to tempt an adult in this way, but as Ratso pointed out, he hardly knew Jane Meara, and his dislike of cats was long-standing and rather intense. It would've been useless to try to reason with him.

In fact, the whole little affair didn't seem to be making a hell of a lot of sense. Somebody, it would appear, was playing a pretty mean prank on Jane Meara. And Jane Meara was the kind of person who didn't have an enemy in the world. Never much liked that kind of person myself. Still, I couldn't imagine hating her. Evidently, someone could and did.

Or maybe it was Rocky they were after. But Rocky, from what I understood, was more of a house pet than a grand champion. Outside of her four little sweat socks, there wasn't much about her that would whip your average cat fancier into a sexual frenzy. Of course, cat fanciers had been known to have rather strange appetites. Stranger even than the menu at Big Wong.

We got to Eighth Avenue and entered through the side doors of the Felt Forum. It was nudging nine o'clock and there was a steady stream of cage-carrying cat fanciers and assorted spectators leaving the Garden area. We had almost gotten to the entrance of the exhibition hall when I noticed a worrisome knot of people gathered in a corner off to the left-hand side of the lobby. At the center of the small crowd stood a big, burly man with a little notebook.

He looked unpleasantly familiar.

A large woman carrying a large cat in a large cage blocked my field of vision for a moment. When she stepped out of the way, I caught a brief but sufficient glimpse of the malevolent mug of Detective Sergeant Mort Cooperman from the Sixth Precinct. Sufficient to remind me that Cooperman and I were not exactly chummy. And sufficient to tell me that something was terribly wrong at the cat show.

If they'd found Rocky, somehow I didn't think it was going to be pretty. I was glad Jane Meara wasn't around.

"Ratso," I said, "I think we're too late."

"Too late? What do you mean?"

"I mean I think we've got a dead cat on the line."

6

When you look for something in life, sometimes you find it. Then you find it wasn't what you were looking for. Then you wonder why the hell you went looking for it in the first place. Just curiosity, you figure. You rack your brains trying to remember what curiosity did to the cat. Did it make him healthy, wealthy, and wise? Did it help him get the worm? Oh, Christ! It killed him!

But by now it's too late. You catch your reflection in a stolen hubcap—you're a cat. The specter of curiosity, which looks like a large, seductive venetian blind, stalks you across miles and miles of bathroom tiles . . . across the cold and creaky warehouse floor of your life . . . across a candlelit table in a restaurant that closed twelve years ago. Shut down by the city for being too quaint.

I killed what was left of the Jamaican "A" and Ratso and I walked across the foyer to where the people were standing. We were just in time to hear Marilyn Park say to Sergeant Cooperman, "Nothing like this has ever happened at one of our shows."

Ratso nodded solemnly and winked at me. I watched the man standing next to Marilyn Park, a shadowy fellow whom I took to be her husband, Stanley Park. The one who thought the security at the show was adequate. He was introducing a third man to Cooperman.

"Sergeant," said Stanley Park, "this gentleman is Hilton

Head. He's in charge of all our public relations. The spokesperson for the whole show."

Head was a nervous, rather effeminate young man who
ran a limp hand through limp hair and kept repeating the
phrase ". . . such a pussycat . . . such a pussycat . . ."

Cooperman glowered at the young man and scribbled a
thing or two in his little notebook. You can always tell a cop
with a notebook from an angry young novelist with a notebook. Both of them are angry, but the novelist opens his
notebook from the side while the cop flips the pages over the
top.

Cooperman flipped a page over the top and looked up
from his notebook. He was not pleased to see me standing
there in the small crowd of cat fanciers.

He tried to pick me up by the scruff of the neck with his
left eye.

"Jesus Christ," he said, "talk about a bad penny."

"Did you find the cat?" I asked.

"Did we find the cat?" said Cooperman with a smile.
"Yeah, we found the cat."

"Where's the cat now?" I asked.

"Where's the cat now? The cat's right back here in this
office." He jerked his thumb toward what looked like a small
cloakroom.

Cooperman had a fairly sick smile on his face that I
couldn't quite cipher. I wasn't sure I wanted to.

"Wanna take a look?" he asked.

I shrugged and motioned to Ratso and the two of us
followed his trucklike body into the small room adjoining
the foyer. At first I didn't see anything because a camera
flash went off practically right in my eyes. When I could
see, I couldn't believe what I was seeing. The room was
a beehive of activity. Cops and technicians all over the
place. Rocky was nowhere in sight. But something else
was.

On the floor in the center of the room was the body of a

man. His chest was so red it looked like E.T.'s little heart-light.

There was a blood-encrusted, gaping hole where you kind of expected a mouth to be.

"How do you like that?" said Sergeant Cooperman cheerfully. "Looks like the cat's lost his tongue."

7

If life is but a dream, death is but a night-mare. That information notwithstanding, I was pleased to find, when I woke up Tuesday morning, that my cat was still in the loft and my tongue was still in my head. All things considered, not a bad way to start the day.

I fed the cat, put the espresso machine into high gear, and lit my first cigar of the morning. I looked out the window at the sun-dappled, grimy warehouses across the street. The billboards were glistening with dew. The rust was shining on all the fire escapes. It was a beautiful morning.

I sat down at the kitchen table for a quiet cup of espresso. If you ignored the constant rumbling of the garbage trucks, everything was fairly peaceful. One of the appealing things about this case, I reflected, was that a dead man with his tongue cut out couldn't give you any lip.

I sipped the espresso from my *Imus in the Morning* coffee cup. I puffed the cigar and watched a blue wreath drift upward toward the lesbian dance class. Pretty quiet up there just now. Maybe they were getting into their little lesbian leotards. Or out of them. The whole world loves a lesbian, I thought, and nobody knows dick about her. Of course, when you've got 'em thudding on your ceiling all day long, even lesbians can lose a little magic.

If lesbians were a mystery, so was the dead man at the Garden. But I knew a little more about him. Just a little more. His name was Rick "Slick" Goldberg. He had a cat entered in the cat show. When he hadn't been busy entering cats in cat shows, he'd been a literary agent.

I had not gotten this information from Sergeant Cooperman. When I'd asked him who the dead man was, he'd asked me if I was next of kin. I'd told him I didn't know because I didn't know who the dead man was. He'd told me to wait till tomorrow and ask a newsboy. That was that.

But if you hang around a few crime scenes you usually learn a thing or two, besides not to hang around crime scenes. Once you get behind the police lines into the crime scene search area, it is assumed that you belong there. Like being backstage at a rock concert—once you're actually there, nobody questions your presence. So I'd gotten the information from a uniform who was standing there listening to his hair grow.

I poured myself another cup of espresso and thought it over. Rick "Slick" Goldberg. Cat fancier. Literary agent. Current occupation: worm bait. Nothing too slick about worm bait—we're all worm bait waiting to happen. It's what you do while you wait that matters.

Unless you wanted to count my laundry, there were only two things that I needed to do at the moment: find out all I could about the tongueless stiff at the Garden, and find out who'd occupied room 407 at the Roosevelt Hotel yesterday. I decided to call the Roosevelt Hotel.

Rick "Slick" Goldberg would keep.

8

"Good morning," said the blower on the left, "Roosevelt Hotel."

"Can I speak to the cashier, please?" I said.

"One moment, sir."

"Fine."

I waited. I puffed patiently on my cigar as I sat at the desk. I was going to get only one take on this and I knew it'd better be a wrap. I didn't think the "cat got your tongue" note and the stiff *sans* tongue at the Garden were just one of death's little coincidences. It was past time to turn the note over to Cooperman, but I wanted to take one little shot at the situation first. Maybe I'd hit the side of the barn.

"Cashier," said an irritated, almost petulant voice. It was the voice of a woman you wouldn't care to meet.

"Mornin', ma'am," I said in a bright voice. "This is the FTD florist in Fort Worth. Chuck speakin'." Try to disarm her with a little southern charm. I thought briefly of how John Kennedy had once described Washington, D.C.: "Northern charm and southern efficiency."

"Yes?" she said impatiently.

"We're havin' a little booger of a problem down here, ma'am. I thought like maybe you could help us with it."

"Yes?" Sounded like she was warming up to me.

"Seems we sent our Silver Anniversary Cup Bouquet—it's been a real popular item for us—we've got a lot of retired folks down here . . ."

"Sir . . ."

435

". . . sent it out yesterday mornin' to a Mrs. Rose Bush from here in Texas—I think they said she was related to the Vice President—second cousin or somethin' like that. . . ."

"Sir! What exactly do you want?"

"Well, now, we sent it to Mrs. Bush—to her room there at the Roosevelt Hotel—and somebody signed for it and took it and now I hear from the boss that Mrs. Bush never did get it. Boss's madder'n an Indian who's trying to take a peepee and can't find a teepee."

There was a silence on the line. Finally, the cashier asked in a rather curt voice, "What room was the—uh—Bush party in, sir?"

"Well now, let's see. . . . The Silver Anniversary Cup Bouquet was sent to—hold the weddin', I'll find it—here it is —room 407."

"Just a moment, sir." There was a pause while the cashier checked her ledger. "There must be a mistake, sir. There's no Bush party registered."

"Well, I'll be hog-tied and branded."

"Will that be all, sir?"

"Well, now, you see, if I could get the name of the party that *was* registered in that room—just for our records, you see—I'd be off the hook. As the catfish said to Little Black Sambo."

There was a deep and somewhat disgusted sigh on the other end of the line. Then a silence. Then an abrupt decision was apparently made. "The party registered in room 407 was not from Texas," said the cashier in an almost haughty voice. "The party was from Connecticut. The party's name was Fred Katz."

I took a thoughtful puff on my cigar. "Care to spell that?" I asked.

9

They say that death is just nature's way of telling you to slow down a little bit. Whether or not that is true, it can certainly add a slightly bitter taste to your espresso.

I listened to the lesbian dance class starting up over my head and I listened to some of the darker thoughts dancing around inside my head. Somehow I did not think that Fred Katz was related to Winnie Katz. In fact, I doubted that he was related to anyone. I doubted that he existed.

The name was obviously a rather humorous alias. Or at least it might've been if Rocky hadn't been missing. And if they hadn't found a stiff in the Garden with his clapper torn out. Little things like that can kill a laugh pretty quickly.

I thought over the whole situation. Somebody's cat was missing and somebody's literary agent had gone to Jesus. Which was more important depended on how you looked at the world. In the case at hand, however, the cat and the agent were closely interrelated. Whoever'd heisted the cat had written the note, and whoever'd written the note had iced the agent. He'd probably done a few other things, too. Could've picked up sticks. Buckled his shoe. Well, whatever he'd done and whoever he was, he had to be declawed and neutered fairly rapidly or things could get ugly.

The first step, I decided, was to drop by the Sixth Precinct and lay the "cat got your tongue" note on Sergeant Cooperman. It promised to be an extremely tedious little visit, but if I didn't go soon, I might be obstructing a lot more than my own slim likelihood of having a nice day.

I had not forgotten about Marilyn Park, Stanley Park, Hilton Head, and the hundreds of other cat fanciers down at the Garden. They'd be there all week. I hadn't forgotten that an agent like Rick "Slick" Goldberg had probably made a lot of enemies over the years. If he was like most agents I knew, half his clients would've liked to have croaked him.

I remembered a little story my pal John Mankiewicz had told me about a writer in L.A. who came home to find his house burned to the ground. A neighbor came over and said, "Your agent came by. He raped your wife and daughter, killed your dog, and torched the whole house." The writer was stunned. He stumbled through the ashes of his home and all he could say was "My agent came by?"

I'd put on my hat, coat, and hunting vest, stuffed the note in the vest pocket, left the cat in charge, and was almost out the door when the phones rang. This was good for two reasons: one, I'd forgotten my cigars; and two, it was one of those calls that can change your life. I went back to the desk, picked up a few cigars, and collared the blower on the left.

"Start talkin'," I said.

"Kinky!"

"Yeah."

"This is Eugene at Jane Meara's office. I'm her assistant." Jane, I knew, was an editor now for a large publishing house.

"Yeah?"

"Jane would like you to come over here right away if you can."

The cat had jumped up on the desk, and as I stroked her, a little shiver went jogging down my spine. "What seems to be the problem, Eugene?"

"Well, this may sound crazy—like something out of Agatha Christie—but Jane just got back from lunch and there's—"

"Get to the meat of it," I said irritably.

"There's a butcher knife on her desk. It's covered with blood."

I stroked the cat one more time and tried to collect my thoughts. I fitted the last cigar into the little stitched pocket of the hunting vest.

"Sharp move," I said.

10

I took the Otis box to the seventeenth floor of Jane's building, bootlegging a lit cigar the whole way. Things didn't get ugly till fourteen, when a woman with a hypersensitive beezer got on and sniffed me out. Nothing lasts forever.

I escaped into a small lobby and practically ran into the back of a tall, snakelike figure who'd been doing a fair impersonation of a man studying gourmet cookbooks in a glass showcase. The figure uncoiled and sprang toward me just as the elevator doors closed.

"What took you so long, Tex?" it hissed. It was Detective Sergeant Buddy Fox, Sixth Precinct.

"Waitin' for my nails to dry," I said. Fox was probably my second favorite American. My first was everybody else.

"I understand," said Fox, "you been squirrelin' some evidence in a homicide. Maybe you oughta fork over this purloined letter we been hearin' so much about. Or would you like to hang on to it till Valentine's Day?" There was a smile on Fox's face but it seemed to lack a certain warmth.

I reached into my vest pocket and handed him the note that Ratso, Jane, and I had found in room 407 of the Roosevelt Hotel.

Dear Jane, I thought. Dear, sweet, innocent, little cat-loving Jane. Right then I could've killed Jane Meara with a pair of numb-nuts, or whatever they're called. Any exotic North Korean martial-arts device would probably do. She'd gotten me into this mess by appealing to a sense of compassion I didn't even know I had. Now, albeit unwittingly, she'd thrown me to the dogs, pigs, jackals, lions, wolves—whatever animal you'd choose if you could be any animal you wanted to be. As for myself, I felt like a swallow that had gone down the wrong way and stopped at a service station for directions to Capistrano. I needed either a road map or a Heimlich maneuver and I wasn't sure which.

Fox escorted me down a maze of hallways to a small office. He motioned for me to go in, stuck his head in the doorway after me, winked, and said, "Wait here, Tex."

I looked around the room. There was a sofa and a cluttered desk. On the wall were various book jackets. There was a little bulletin board with pictures of Jane Meara at a baseball game and several shots of a cat. I noticed rather grimly that the cat was wearing four little sweat socks. Rocky. I took down one of the snapshots of Rocky and slipped it into my pocket.

I didn't need Frank and Joe Hardy to tell me I was in Jane Meara's office. I looked carefully at the desk. I did not see a bloody butcher knife. Of course, it's a little hard to see one if it's sticking in your back.

Actually, I thought, it was nobody's fault. Self-pity could be an important trait in a country singer, but in a detective, it was about as attractive as a busted valise. Maybe the whole, rather tedious situation was just one of the little tricks God plays on us from time to time. Like being born with freckles or coming back from Vietnam on a skateboard.

I was pondering this when a large, vaguely evil form darkened the doorway behind me. Without acknowledging my presence, Cooperman walked around the desk and sat in the chair. Fox slithered across the threshold and motioned me seductively toward the sofa. I walked over and sat down. Still not looking at me, Cooperman took a pack of Gauloises from his pocket, shook one out, and lit it with his Zippo lighter. I took out a cigar and lit it with a Bic. Nobody said anything. If silence was golden, we were closing in on the Klondike.

11

An hour and a half later I was ready to bring my brain over to the French cleaner's and tell the head frog I wanted light starch. I'd given Cooperman everything I had on room 407 at the Roosevelt Hotel, which was not a hell of a lot. He'd wanted the key to the room and to know precisely how I'd wheedled the name Fred Katz from the desk at the Roosevelt Hotel. "I have my methods," I'd said. He was not pleased.

Things went downhill from there.

Cooperman warned me off the case. He told me I could go and look for all the stray pussy I wanted but this was a homicide. Not a missing cat. Once I left this office, he said, he did not wish to see me for at least a couple years. Maybe three or four.

I got up to go and he said, "We're not through with you yet." I sat back down on the sofa and puffed on my second cigar. The cigar was well past the midway point already. I didn't like to smoke a cigar too far past the midway point, but then I didn't like a lot of things. Cooperman, for instance.

I asked Cooperman about the knife and he told me it was already at the lab. Knowing what he did *now*, he said pointedly, he had little doubt that it was the murder weapon.

It was at about this time that Cooperman had Jane Meara brought in, sat her down next to me on the sofa, and told her in very graphic terms for the first time exactly how the charming implement had been employed prior to its arrival upon her desk. She hadn't even known about the stiff, much less the tongue, and she turned white as a Klansman on the Fourth of July.

Cooperman asked her another question but he got no answer. When you pay your nickel you're supposed to get a nickel ride. All Cooperman got was an autistic stare.

Cooperman killed his fifth Gauloise in the ashtray. I began the pre-ignition procedures on my third cigar. It wasn't really a contest, of course, but I liked to keep up my end of things. The conversation had begun to lag a bit.

At a signal from Cooperman, Fox went out into the hallway and brought in Jim Landis, the publisher Jane worked for, and Eugene, her assistant editor. Cooperman asked Landis where he'd been for the past few hours. Landis said he'd been at a nearby restaurant. Fox took the name of the place and said he'd check it out.

Eugene said he'd been at his desk all through the lunch hour and several authors and would-be authors had stopped by Jane's office while she was out. He had their names on memo slips at his desk.

"Would you be so kind as to bring them to us now?" Cooperman asked in a sweet, sarcastic voice. Eugene went out with Fox. I smoked my cigar. Jane sniffled quietly next to me. Landis fidgeted. Cooperman glared at the empty doorway.

Eugene came back and handed the memos to Cooperman. Cooperman handed them to Fox. "That's it?" he asked.

Eugene nodded. Then he seemed to remember something. "Oh, wait," he said, "there were some people here right after you left, Jane. They said they were from the cat show and they wanted—"

"Cat show?" said Cooperman.

"Cat show," said Eugene.

"Names?" asked Cooperman.

"I—I didn't get their names," said Eugene. He was starting to wither visibly.

"You didn't get their names!" shouted Cooperman.

"Well—they said they'd be back to see Jane. I didn't think —is it important?"

"No," said Cooperman, "it's not important. We're just here having a little fun at the office today. We're playing visitor trivia."

With a snarl, Cooperman gestured viciously toward Eugene and shouted, "Fox! Take this guy outa my sight and get descriptions."

Cooperman picked up his cigarettes, waved Landis out with his hand, and told Jane Meara she could have her office back. Jane shuddered. Cooperman stood up. I stood up. Cooperman looked at me. His eyes were a curious admixture of pity, malice, and maybe something just a little more unsavory.

"Penny for your thoughts," I said.

Cooperman gave out with a dry, gritty chuckle. Sounded like a guy trying to start his lawn mower in 1957.

"I'll be seeing you around, Tex," he said.

12

Tuesday night. Ten o'clock. Ratso and I walked into the Carnegie Delicatessen, our home away from home away from home. It smelled great—like pastrami and perfume, salami and cigars. The Carnegie warmed your heart like a matzo ball in January and that, in fact, was what I had my dial set on when we walked into the place. Matzo-ball soup with a matzo ball about the size of McGovern's head. McGovern was my friend who wrote for the *Daily News* and sometimes, rather grudgingly, helped me gather crucial data on various and nefarious individuals. McGovern had the largest head in North America.

Leo met Ratso and me at the door like a white Joe Louis. He owned the Carnegie, but his greetings were so effusive he could've fooled you. He was equally enthusiastic even if you'd just been in the place that same afternoon. Of course, I hadn't been in Leo's place. I'd been in Sergeant Cooperman's face.

"Kinky! Kinky!" said Leo, as he rushed over and took my hand warmly in both of his own. Shucking all modesty, I had to admit that very few patrons were greeted in this warm a fashion. Several customers looked up from their blintzes.

"When you playin' at the Lone Star again, Kinky?" Leo asked.

"Well, not for a while Leo, if I can help it," I said to the back of Leo's head. He'd turned away from me to greet Ratso. Probably asking him how the magazine was going. Maybe admiring his wardrobe. I passed the awkward moment admiring the salamis in the window and presently Leo's attention turned back to me. Patience is always rewarded.

"So Kinky," said Leo, "so how's the Broadway musical coming along?" I had written the score for a Broadway musical comedy but my collaborator, Don Imus, had been dragging his feet on the book for about four years. Lately, Imus had been showing a little bit of progress.

"Yeah . . . well," I said unenthusiastically, "we hope to have a few homosexuals tap-dancing by late summer."

"Great, Kinky!" said Leo. "Great."

Leo called a waiter over and got us a table. As Ratso and I sat down we heard Leo, in the best tradition of the stage whisper, shout to the waiter, "Give 'em linen!"

Ratso and I were seated across from each other in the middle of a long table, with people on both sides of us. The guy on my immediate right was so close that when he ate his smoked fish I could spit out the bones. Everybody at the table had paper napkins with the Carnegie logo: a picture of Leo holding a tray and saying, "I make a gooooood sandwich." I ordered seltzer and coffee and began looking over the miles of menu. Ratso began working on the bucket of pickles that was always on the table. Then the waiter brought our linen.

It created a mild ripple effect. A bit of whispering. A nervous chuckle here and there. A little resentment. A look of wonder on one lady's face before she went back to her chopped liver. I put my linen napkin on my lap but Ratso, in an embarrassingly ostentatious gesture, tucked his into the neck of his shirt like a lobster bib. Each to his own, I thought.

But mainly, it felt good. In fact, it felt gooooood.

Possibly very few people attach as much importance as I do to being given a linen napkin at the Carnegie Delicatessen. Most people, of course, spend their lives caring about the wrong things. They worry about South Africa or Nicaragua. They spend so much time finding themselves that they lose their taxicabs. They don't see that what kind of napkin you get at a delicatessen is a matter of much significance in the world today.

That's why they don't get linen.

I'd knocked off a bowl of matzo-ball soup and Ratso had eaten an obscenely large piece of gefilte fish and a pope's nose, which isn't obscene but should be because it's a turkey's ass. We were both still hungry. Ratso studied his menu like a handicapper looking at a racing form.

"A little more interesting crowd's starting to drift in here now," I said. "They look like either theatrical types or hookers."

"Or Puerto Ricans from the United Nations," Ratso said, looking up from his menu. "So tell me about the investigation."

I told Ratso about Fred Katz. I told Ratso about the bloody butcher knife. I told Ratso about the cat show people who had come by Jane Meara's office while she was out. I told Ratso I couldn't make up my mind what else to order.

"So what're you going to do?" Ratso asked.

"I don't know," I said. "I'm caught between corned beef and pastrami." I looked at the menu.

"I'm talkin' about the case," said Ratso. "What're you going to do about the case?"

"Nothing," I said. "Sergeant Cooperman warned me off."

"Ah, c'mon," said Ratso, dismissing the issue with a wave of a pickle. "You're not gonna let a little thing like that stop you, are you? This is America. This is 1988." He took another bite of the pickle and thought about it for a moment. "This is the Carnegie Deli," he said.

"I know all that," I said. "I just don't want to think about it right now. All I want to think about is what I want to order." I looked down at the menu again.

Leo hovered in from the left like a Huey chopper, with his rotors rotating. "Kinky! How ya doin', Kinky? What can I get you?"

"I don't know, Leo," I said. "I'm somewhat confused as to what to order."

"I know the perfect thing," said Leo. "I'll be right back. Just a moment."

He veered off in the general direction of the kitchen. When Leo came back he was holding a large, rather unpleasant-looking, purplish object.

"Here," he said. "How about I cut you a nice tongue?"

13

That night, back at 199B Vandam, I had a heart-to-heart talk with my cat. I was sitting at the desk. The cat was sitting on the desk. So was a bottle of Jameson Irish whiskey and the old bull's horn.

I'd had a few shots. The cat hadn't touched the stuff. Probably pacing herself.

"Have you ever wondered," I said, "why Negro undertakers always drive white hearses and white undertakers always drive black hearses?"

The cat looked at me and blinked her eyes.

"I know it's a tough question," I said. While the cat thought about it I poured another generous slug into the bull's horn. Then I poured the bull's horn into my mouth.

"I'm not afraid to die," I said. "I'm not afraid to live. I'm not afraid to fail. I'm not afraid to succeed. I'm not afraid to fall in love. I'm not afraid to be alone. I'm just afraid I might have to stop talking about myself for five minutes."

The cat yawned.

"It's not easy being who I am," I said. "Sometimes I think of myself as a country singer. Sometimes as a Broadway composer . . ."

The cat shook her right front paw in an unmistakable gesture of irritability.

". . . sometimes as a private dick," I said.

The cat stood up on the desk and stretched. Starting to get restless. I pretended I didn't notice.

"I'll tell you," I said, "it's lonely in the middle."

On an impulse I picked up the cat and held her close to me. Cats, like everybody else, are a fairly perverse lot. They wish to be held only by those who don't wish to hold them. By the time I remembered this it was too late.

The cat scratched me severely on my right wrist. Then she jumped down and bounded away. I chased her, cornered her, and hit her with my open hand on top of her head. She screamed and ran under the couch. I glanced down at my arm. Looked like a nearly successful adolescent suicide attempt.

"You asshole!" I shouted. The cat had come a little way out from behind the couch so she could enjoy watching me. Technically, I thought, the cat was not an asshole. As my friend Biana is fond of saying, "Assholes are people [or cats] who don't know that they're assholes." By this standard, the cat was not an asshole.

Neither was I.

I went back to the desk and poured another jolt into the bull's horn. There are those who would say, I thought bitterly, that it is not right for a 170-pound man to hit an 8-pound cat. Even with an open hand. It's not fair, they'd say. Hardly the appropriate response to the situation, they'd snivel.

Well, it didn't make me especially proud to be an American, but you couldn't always turn the other cheek. Life is a game of give and take. Dog eat dog. Cat scratch man. Man hit cat.

Hell, it'd be all right. Couple of days, everything'd be back to merely strange. Anyway, it was none of their goddamn business. It was an act of passion.

I looked down at my wrist. I glared across the room at the cat. It didn't bring me a hell of a lot of satisfaction, though, because the cat had closed her eyes and was curled up asleep in the rocking chair.

I sighed, picked up the bull's horn, killed the shot, and lit a cigar. I watched the smoke drift away and disappear like the dreams of a child who always wanted to be a fireman.

14

Wednesday morning I was doing a pretty good impersonation of a busy little New Yorker. I had the espresso machine, a cigar, and the blower on the left all going simultaneously. Somewhere out there was a lost cat. Somewhere out there was a killer. My plan, with or without the help of the police, was to find them both. If you had to have an impossible dream, you might as well make it a good one.

On the other end of the line, Jane Meara was telling me how sorry she was to have landed me in hot water with the police.

"They told me to tell them *everything*," she said.

"Forget it," I said. "I'm still on the case, in spite of Cooperman's warning."

"Kinky," she said falteringly, "I don't think—"

"This is America," I said. "This is 1988."

"This is dangerous."

"I like danger. It gives me a buzz. It's supposed to be good aerobically." I puffed a few times on the cigar.

"It was horrible about Slick," she said. "You know, I had lunch with him that same afternoon."

"Didn't know that. What'd you talk about?"

"Oh, just the usual. The big deals he was working on. Who he was touting this week."

"Who was he touting this week?"

"Oh, some guy who'd written a book about how there's an inordinate number of mass murderers who have the middle

452   name Wayne. The author feels that their fathers overidentified with John Wayne, named their sons accordingly, and
thus passed along a sort of festering internalized violence as
well.''

"Coffee table job?''

"No. It's a long-winded psychological tome. I passed.''

"So did Slick,'' I said. I paused to glance over at the
espresso machine. It looked and sounded like it was preparing to fly to Jupiter. "What kind of guy was Slick?'' I asked.

"Well,'' said Jane, "he wasn't particularly well loved.''

"Apparently not,'' I said.

Jane put in a fast plug for finding Rocky, said she had to
run, and then we ciao-ed off. I beat a path to the espresso
machine, poured a cup, went back to my desk, sat down, and
took a sip. It was a lot of work for that hour of the morning.

I leaned back in the chair and thought about agents.
Agents were people, too. Just like cats. Maybe not quite as
thoughtful or sensitive sometimes. But who was?

Pieces were beginning to fall together. For one thing, the
person who called himself Fred Katz had quite conceivably
never occupied room 407 at the Roosevelt. He'd just left the
"cat got your tongue'' note there and headed for the Garden
to take Rocky, leave the room key in the cage, and dispense
with Slick Goldberg. That would make for a busy afternoon
and it didn't leave a lot of time to decide what to do with
Rocky before inking Slick's final deal. Of course he could've
taken Rocky back to the hotel, but how would he get into the
room without a key? And obtaining two keys, under the circumstances, would've risked arousing the desk clerk's suspicion. So Rocky must've been set loose on the street or dispatched to kitty heaven in a rather rapid fashion. It'd be too
big an order to kill the agent without letting the cat out of the
bag, so to speak.

I took a deep breath and called McGovern at the *Daily
News*.

"National Desk," said a familiar voice.

"Yeah, National Desk," I said, "I'd like to report a runaway garden slug out here in Westchester."

"Is it an exclusive?" McGovern asked.

"McGovern," I said, "this is Kinky. I need a favor."

"No shit," he said. I took a patient puff on my cigar. It was important that McGovern not go into a snit. If he did, it could be unpleasant.

"It's really a small thing," I said, "but you could get it done a lot faster than I could. You've got the connections. Besides, I'm working on a case and I've got to be somewhere soon."

"Where do you have to be?"

"The cat show at Madison Square Garden."

There was no response.

"All I want is for you to place an ad in the *Daily News* for a lost cat."

There was a stunned silence on the line. It was followed by hearty, incredulous Irish laughter. McGovern was one of the few people in the world who, even when being incredulous, could be hearty. He was always Irish.

I figured I'd rush him with the ad copy while he was still laughing. "Okay," I said, "it runs like this: 'Fred Katz—all is forgiven. Return Rocky and no questions will be asked. Call Kinky—555-3717.'"

"You know," said McGovern, "I'm a little disappointed in you. Just a *little* disappointed." He laughed again.

"What's the big deal?" I asked. "I'm busy this morning and I thought—"

"I've covered every beat there is," said McGovern with some intensity. "I got the exclusive on the Richard Speck murders in Chicago. I spent six weeks covering Charles Manson. I got the most in-depth story ever on Lieutenant Calley. . . ."

"Rusty?"

"Yeah," said McGovern, "good ol' Rusty. I've spent over two decades covering major news stories. My whole career—

454 my whole life—has been building, building up to this moment, when a country singer I know calls me to place a want ad for a lost cat. Kind of makes it all worthwhile.''

Dealing with McGovern had turned out be at least as tedious as calling *Daily News* advertising and placing the ad myself, which I should have done in the first place. But you dance with who brung you.

"So you'll do it," I said. I waited.

"Sure, ol' pal," said McGovern a bit wistfully.

"Thanks, pal," I said. "You're a great American."

"You could do me a little favor, too," said McGovern.

"Sure," I said, "what is it?"

"You can tell the Pulitzer committee they can go back to bed now," he said.

15

That afternoon Ratso and I went to the Garden to weed out a killer. Ratso had taken a renewed interest, indeed a fascination, in the case from the moment he'd seen the stiff. Death is a hot ticket. For rubberneckers on an expressway viewing a tragic accident or for would-be Watsons, the specter of death is compelling. It requires the subtlety of a more Sherlockian mind to appreciate the finding of a lost cat.

That morning, before I'd left the loft, I'd spoken to Eugene in Jane Meara's office, described the people I planned to interview at the Garden, and discovered, not to my total wonderment, that the cat show visitors to Jane's office bore a strong similarity to Marilyn and Stanley Park and their spokesperson, Hilton Head. Of course, they could've been Marilyn and Stanley Park and Hilton Head impersonators, but somehow I rather doubted it.

I assigned Ratso to plague the three of them with his presence. I told him to insinuate himself into their lives and find out all there was to know. For myself, I had other ideas.

I figured I would start in the area of Rocky's disappearance, talk to people and cats, absorb the ambience of the place. Where was Rocky? What made the Cheshire Cat smile? What made some people kill? I wanted to know more about cats in general. More about God and man. Less about William Buckley.

The Garden looked spectral as Ratso and I got out of the

cab, almost evil. The afternoon was cold as blue eyes that didn't love you anymore. It was starting to rain.

I grudgingly paid the driver, who was allergic to cigar smoke and probably a number of other things. Pretty smart to get a job driving a hack in New York City if you're allergic to cigar smoke. Of course, as a child, the driver probably hadn't wanted to be an allergy-prone cab driver. No child wants to be that. Just as no child wants to grow up to be a critic for *The New York Times*. Children want to be something good and meaningful in life. Like the fire chief of Spokane.

I lit a cigar and Ratso and I walked silently through the gray day like two mothmen drawn to the bright flames of death.

I walked around in the Garden for a while, focusing on the vague area where Rocky'd disappeared two days earlier. I combed the area thoroughly and didn't come up with as much as an ear mite. Every time I saw a receptive face I'd take out the snapshot I'd liberated from Jane Meara's office and ask the person, "Ever seen this cat?"

None of them recognized Rocky. However, once I identified the cat as Rocky, many of them commented on her abduction. No one seemed to think the cat could have wandered off. No one had seen anyone strange hanging around.

Of course, the cat owners themselves were such a strange-looking lot it would've been hard to notice anyone who had looked strange.

I was about ready to call in the dogs as it were, piss on the fire, and go find Ratso, when I saw her.

She was wearing a David Copperfield cap and between her hands she was stretching what appeared to be a large white rat. Beneath the cap her face looked beautiful and vaguely ethnic in a childlike, poignant, American kind of way, like a parade in New York for a country that, for all practical purposes, no longer existed.

She looked half of something pretty weird and I just hoped

it wasn't Turkish. Their only major export was knives that went around corners.

"Sexy weather we're havin'," I said. I'd gotten that one from a male cab driver one rainy evening at the Vancouver Airport.

"What do you want?" she asked.

"Well, I don't want what's between your hands," I said.

She smiled a mischievous smile and turned a beautiful, cold shoulder on me. She carried the large white rat over to a table and placed him on it. Like a confused Pied Piper, I followed the rat.

I stopped a little distance away and looked at the two of them. The rat still looked like a rat, but the broad looked like a killer. What the hell, I thought, I was looking for a killer.

We carried on a rather strained cocktail conversation without the cocktails and I learned a number of things. Her name was Leila. She was half Palestinian. She was a judge at the cat show. She had not been holding a large white rat. She'd been holding a purebred hairless Sphynx. She'd heard of Rocky's disappearance and she'd read about the murder in the newspaper, but she could offer no new information about either. The last thing I learned was that she did not wish to join me for a drink.

I caught up with Ratso right in front of a veterinarian giving a slide show on diarrhea. Ratso was having a rather animated discussion with Hilton Head. I walked up just in time to hear Head say "I hope you're satisfied!" and to see him prance away.

"There goes a very unhappy young man," I said.

"Yes," said Ratso, "and he's gonna miss the rest of the slide show."

"So are we," I said.

I would like to be able to say that I felt a slight prickling effect on the back of my neck as Ratso and I started to leave the Garden. It would've been nice if I'd noticed the hairs on the backs of my hands standing up like little Sandinista soldiers. Unfortunately, all I noticed was that I'd spent several hours asking people about some cat many of them had never heard of and daydreaming about a sensitive relationship with a Palestinian harem girl. I didn't know if I'd be seeing Leila again or under what circumstances that event was to occur. I only knew that if I succeeded in tearing away the veil from her heart, the two of us might have a decent chance of erasing six thousand years of bad karma.

"Well, what'd you get, Rats?" I asked as we walked down the hallway from the Felt Forum to the Garden proper.

"Hilton Head is a born-again Christian."

"Mildly unpleasant."

"Yeah, and it's kind of funny, too."

"Why is that?"

" 'Cause he doesn't look like a born-again Christian."

I stopped briefly to light a cigar. "What about Marilyn Park?" I asked.

"She's a vegetarian."

"Good detective work," I said as I blew on the end of the cigar. "Were you able to learn what her favorite color is?"

"No," said Ratso, "but I did find out something rather strange about Stanley Park. His wife and Head say that the three of them went by Jane Meara's office yesterday."

"So?"

"Park says it's the first he's heard of it. Claims he was here supervising the judging all afternoon."

"Interesting discrepancy."

"Yeah," said Ratso. "So who was the third man? Maybe our old friend Fred Katz?" The only times I'd ever seen Ratso that animated were when somebody else was paying for his lunch.

"Well, you might have something there," I said. "Or . . ."

"Or—what?"

"Or . . . nothing."

"Terrific, Sherlock. I've just discovered what could be a vital clue. What've you turned up?"

We walked out the front doors of the Garden and down

the walkway toward Seventh Avenue. I thought about it for a moment. Then I told Ratso about Leila.

"I don't see how your wanting to jump the bones of a female camel jockey is relevant to the case," he said.

I shrugged. "She and I could be the last hope for peace in the Middle East," I said. Ratso was not impressed and responded with a fairly ethnic hand gesture.

We were nearing the end of the walkway when a figure stepped out from behind a portico. It was wearing a garish mask not dissimilar to the ones worn in the Broadway show *Cats*. There was something rather frightening in its manner—like catching a Jekyll entering the on-ramp to Mr. Hyde. There was also something rather frightening in its right hand.

It was a gun and it was pointed at my heart.

16

Everybody dies an early death sooner or later. I'd always hoped mine could've been a little later. Dying's not what it's cracked up to be. But in all fairness, very few things are. Body surfing, for one.

The figure adjusted the mask and I adjusted to the notion that I might've gotten linen for the last time. The Jamaican cigar I was holding like a lifeline in my right hand might be the last Jamaican cigar I'd ever smoke. I'd probably never go to Jamaica now. I'd probably never even go to Big Wong.

Funny the things you think about when your life hangs like a stray gray thread on Ratso's Hadassah Thrift Shop coat. Maybe it continues to cling there and you continue to live. Or maybe some well-meaning, neurotic broad puts down her plastic cup of white wine at a SoHo gallery opening and says, "Just a minute, Ratso, honey, you've got a thread hanging on your coat." She picks off the thread and you die. The landlord finds a new tenant and raises the rent. The cat goes to the city pound. The girl in the peach-colored dress calls, hears your voice still on the machine, leaves a message, and wonders why you never got back to her. Serves her right for waiting so damn long to call.

Answering machines tend to take on a life of their own. I remember the time the pope called Mother Teresa and told her she was needed in Los Angeles. Mother Teresa thought it was an unusual assignment, but the pope told her there were many poor people in the *barrios* there who needed her help. So, about three months later, the pope called Mother Teresa in L.A. She wasn't home but he got her answering machine. The message said, "Hi. This is Terri. I'm away from the phone right now . . ."

It's amazing how much time you have when you're out of time. Strangled images struggled through Kentucky Fried synapses under my cowboy hat. What used to be. What might have been. A dark and beautiful girl in a little blue car —the prettiest girl in the world with a flower in her hair . . .

And there was Leila. Brown eyes sharing sweet and sour secrets of Semitism. Fragile Arabian ankles I would never be familiar with. I hated to pass the Middle East peace baton back to the Henry Kissingers of the world. Let them try to sleep counting tiny little Cambodians. Soon I would probably be a tiny little Cambodian, too. Any moment now. . . . Leila again. . . . Brown eyes . . . as my friend Chinga Chavin says . . . that look like handcuffs . . . . And the espresso machine I leave to Ratso. . . .

Suddenly the cat behind the mask gave forth with a sharp, chilling sound—half feline, half fiendish—somewhere between a cynical, human meow and the noise a cat would make if it could laugh.

Then it pulled the trigger.

17

When I came to there were two green garden snakes coming out of my stomach and three Ratsos sitting by my bedside. All of them looked hungry. The three Ratsos were eating bagels, and whatever the green garden snakes were eating I didn't want to know, so I went back to sleep.

When I woke up the second time, there was only one Ratso and he was eating a large slice of pizza from John's of Bleecker Street, the best in New York. Ratso ate like a starving boar-hog but he had taste.

"Where are the other two Ratsos?" I asked. I didn't know if it was night or day, but it was beginning to dawn on me that I was in a hospital. Hell would have to wait.

"The other two Ratsos?" he said uncertainly. "Maybe they're out playing with the other two Kinkys."

I thought about it for a moment. My mind was clearing a little more slowly than my vision. It took a while to think about the other two Kinkys and the other two Ratsos. "Maybe they're working on a case," I said.

"Could be," said Ratso, nodding his head. "What kind of case do you think they're working on?"

"Maybe they're finding the little missing children on the milk cartons," I said.

"Maybe," said Ratso. I could tell he was worried, because he'd stopped eating his pizza. "Look, Kinkster," he said, "you just rest here a minute. I'm going to go find the doctor."

Ratso walked out into the hall and I looked around the

room. Everything came back to me like a buzzard on the highway. Obviously I'd been shot. Obviously I wasn't dead. Obviously I was in a hospital room. Obviously my friends hadn't sent a hell of a lot of flowers.

The tendrils of my brain were becoming a little less fuzzy and they were damn close to grasping onto something important. I tried to think again and this time I connected. Whoever'd shot me must've known I was at the Garden and must've known what I was looking for. That brought it down to a very small group of people. The Parks. Hilton Head. Leila?

I credited myself with enough native sensitivity to rule out the people I'd shown the Rocky pictures to. I'd seen nothing in their eyes beyond the pale of innocence, sympathy, admiration, boredom—each a normal cat fancier, if such an animal existed. I'd learned to beware of "normal" and "harmless" types. It was the "normal" and "harmless" types that usually did you in. And the women.

My spirits sagged a bit as I enlarged the field of suspects to practically everybody I'd shown the photograph to and his kid sister. And God knew what Ratso had stirred up interviewing the Parks and Head. It was hopeless. For all I knew the veterinarian could've shot me for walking out on his slide show on diarrhea. Men have been shot for less.

I shook my head, cleared a couple cobwebs, and my spirits lifted again. There had been something familiar about the figure behind the cat mask. I wasn't sure exactly what it was. I wasn't even certain whether it'd been a man or a woman. But whoever it was, I was very conscious of one thing. It had seemed to know me. That narrowed the field.

I was trying to remember what it was that had been familiar when the doctor came into the room briskly with Ratso tailing after him like a large jet stream. The doctor looked like Robert Young on a bad day. He adjusted a few knobs on something that looked like a sound system, put a stethoscope to what I'm pleased to call my heart, fondled one of the garden snakes, and smiled.

"You had a close call," he said. "A very close call. I'm going to keep you here for a few more days."

"Well," I said, "at least we'll find out if my Blue Cross has wheels on it."

Robert Young laughed the same friendly, hollow laugh that he always used to tag the Sanka commercials with. The nervous window-washer who works on the ninety-seventh floor has just switched to Sanka. Robert Young asks how he's feeling now. He says, "Great, now that I've switched to Sanka." Robert Young laughs, ha-ha-ha. You didn't exactly trust that laugh, but it was comforting.

"You know," he said, coming nicely off the laugh, "you've been unconscious for over twelve hours." Of course I hadn't known it. I would've had to be the Three Faces of Kinky to have known it.

"Yeah," said Ratso, "you were almost the Rip Van fucking Winkle of the Village."

I looked at Robert Young. "Did you get the bullet out?" I asked.

Robert Young looked at me. Then he gave forth with another friendly, indulgent little chuckle. "There was no bullet," he said. "You were shot with a tranquilizer dart."

"A tranquilizer dart?" I couldn't believe it.

"A tranquilizer dart," said Robert Young. "The kind they use on the big cats."

18

I spent Friday afternoon in a hospital bed dreaming of cigars. But I took a little time out to empathize with a dead literary agent whom nobody had liked and to overidentify with a lost cat whom one person loved.

But then, I was more sensitive than most Americans. In fact, most Americans were more sensitive than most Americans.

I'd had a phone hooked up in the room and I'd been working it like a hyperactive croupier most of the morning. I like telephones. On some occasions, I love telephones. They sometimes make it possible to travel cross the darkness in the distance of a dream. I like cats better than agents but I wanted to be fairly scientific about the thing, so I'd begun my calls in alphabetical order; that is, I made the calls pertaining to the dead agent prior to those pertaining to the lost cat. An organized mind solves an organized crime.

I called Esther "Lobster" Newberg, an agent I knew, and learned the worst. *Everybody* had hated Rick "Slick" Goldberg. Lobster didn't wish to speak ill of the dead, and she didn't wish to speak ill of other agents (many disgruntled writers would consider this to be the same thing), but even she had not much liked Rick "Slick" Goldberg. If I could've paged his mother at the Shalom Retirement Village, *she* probably wouldn't've liked Rick "Slick" Goldberg. Well, it was a murder case, not a popularity contest.

I made another call or two and then called my friend

466 Ted Mann in Hollywood, the glitzy graveyard of all talent. Things were going so poorly, Ted said, that he'd had to hire a non-Jewish agent.

He'd never heard of Rick "Slick" Goldberg, so we talked cats coast-to-coast for a while. Ted said he'd once had a cat named Puss-Puss who'd lived to be twenty-five years old. Outlived most of his friends, he said. When I hung up, it was not without a certain pride. It wasn't the kind of thing you'd really want to crow about, but I *had* outlived Puss-Puss. Of course, a few more tranquilizer-dart incidents like the day before and I might not beat out Puss-Puss by too much.

I was at St. Vincent's Hospital, I discovered. According to Robert Young, the contents of the tranquilizer dart had been sent to the lab for analysis. He was eagerly awaiting the results. I told him I was, too. Everybody needs to look forward to something.

Earlier in the afternoon, I'd sent Ratso over to 199B Vandam to get some cigars and fresh clothes, feed the cat, tell her I'd be home soon, and check the messages on the answering machine. It didn't seem like that difficult an assignment, but he still wasn't back. Maybe he'd passed a garage sale on the way.

While I waited for Ratso, I took stock of things. There was only so much you could do from a telephone in a hospital bed. I needed to get out of there before I began relating to Robert Young as a father figure.

But the very fact that I was in a hospital bed and the sequence of events that had put me there were matters of significance in themselves. It all meant that I was getting pretty damn close to whoever it was I was looking for. It also meant that this dart-shooting devil was looking for me. And I had the unpleasant feeling that the hand that had fired the dart had already taken a life, nipped a cat, and severed a tongue.

19

In winter, men's thoughts turn to Palestinians. I was not a great sympathizer with their cause, but why hold the sins of an entire people against one broad? This was not a time for ethnocentric thinking. Nonetheless, when dealing with foreigners of the female persuasion, it's better to be safe than sorry, though it's often more fun to be sorry. I decided I'd have Leila's background checked. It wasn't that I thought she was spy for the PLO. It was just that some women are sometimes a little more adept than men at wearing masks.

I called Rambam, a friend of mine in Brooklyn who was a private investigator and a couple of other things. Rambam knew the kind of people most folks only watch on the late-night movies. I liked to think of him as a rather militant Jewish Jim Rockford. He was charming and likable, but there were aspects of his life you didn't want to know about. Could land you in a hospital bed.

When I reached Rambam at the offices of Pallorium, his security company, I told him where I was and how I'd got there. "Interesting," he said. I told him about the unsavory demise of Rick "Slick" Goldberg. "Even more interesting," he said. I described my meeting Leila and told him she was half Palestinian.

"Forget her," he said.

I told him Leila and I could be the last hope for peace in the Middle East. It wasn't a bad line, but it was starting to wear about as thin as the Gaza Strip.

468

"Forget her," he said.

"Okay," I said, "but while I'm busy forgetting her, I'd like you to run a little background check on her."

"No problem," said Rambam. There was a certain finality to the way Rambam said "No problem" that was always comforting to hear. Especially when you thought there was a problem.

I was shaloming off with Rambam when Ratso came careening through the door like a bordertown dog. He was obviously excited about something, but if I knew Ratso he was probably going to make me fish for it. I was right.

"Fresh clothes," he said, putting my New York Rangers hockey bag on the table. "Probably won't get you into the embassy ball, but they're not as foxed out as whatever you're wearing."

"They shoot clothes horses, don't they?"

"That's a thought," said Ratso. "Hey, maybe the guy with the dart gun was aiming for me."

"Not likely," I said.

Ratso shrugged it off. "Here's your toilet kit," he said. "A modern man-about-town can't live without his toilet kit. . . ."

"My dear Ratso, I'm eternally grateful to you for bringing my toilet kit, but what is it that you're holding back?"

". . . Oh yeah, and the cigars. I didn't forget the cigars. But you must promise not to let Big Nurse know that you have them."

"I'm more worried about the big nerd who's standing here not telling me something I ought to know."

Ratso feigned injury at my words but he recovered quickly. "Now really, Sherlock, the doctor says for you to relax and not—"

"My dear Ratso, you're as transparent as a toilet seat cover, though not quite as hygienic. What aren't you telling me? Spit it, goddammit."

"Well, there were some messages on the machine—one from a broad in Texas—"

"Where in Texas?"

"Texas. I don't know . . . Houston, Austin . . . one of those places."

"Did you get her name?"

"Yeah. It begins with an *L*, I think."

"Linda?"

"No."

I looked over at the cigars affectionately. "Lydia?"

"No."

"Leda?"

"No, it's kind of a Texas sort of name."

"Bubbette?"

"No. It begins with an *L*. Keep goin'."

"Lola?"

"No. You really know all these broads?"

"I do very well with women whose names begin with an *L*. I don't know why. All except Lady Luck, of course—she can be a mean-minded, vacuous bitch. . . . Leila?"

"Keep dreamin'."

"Wait a minute . . . I know who it is. That's great."

"What's so great about it?" Ratso asked.

"It's the girl in the peach-colored dress," I said.

"I wouldn't know about that. On an answering machine," said Ratso, "all dresses sound gray."

As it turned out, there'd been one more message on the machine. Ratso described the voice as toneless, flat, and with something almost not human about it. Like death itself, he told me. The voice alone had given Ratso a chill, he said, as he handed me the message he'd transcribed onto a scrap of paper. I didn't have the voice to work with, but the words I read did not radiate warmth to the little hospital corners of my bed. The message read as follows: "Hey, Kinky. When the cat's away, the mice will play. The next time you sleep, it may be forever."

"Fred Katz?" Ratso asked, looking over at me.

I read the words again and nodded somberly. "And I was just starting to like the guy," I said.

Martin Luther King had a dream; I had a nightmare. It involved Fred Katz, a man I didn't know.

In the dream, Fred Katz's face was weak, fairly handsome, and characterless. He looked like the kind of guy you might see driving a Rolls-Royce around in a small town. But his eyes looked like two angry hummingbirds coming at you beak first. The smile didn't look too healthy either.

He walked over to my hospital bed and spoke to me, but the words were unintelligible. His lips were beginning to look like a flower on Mars. Something even the FTD florist in Fort Worth wouldn't have in stock. Maggotlike tendrils began growing out of his face—not entirely unattractive—and they wriggled like the pale toes of a woman you once loved. He stepped forward quickly with a shiny knife and cut the two green garden snakes in half. Something in mauve from the Dairy Queen began oozing out.

From the corner of my eye I saw him put the knife away and pick up my toilet kit. A deep, biblical-sounding voice, heavy on the echo chamber, boomed out from the sky of the hospital room. It said: "A modern man-about-town can't live without his toilet kit."

Katz took the toilet kit and headed for the door. I reached out from the bed to stop him, but suddenly I was tired as hell. Tired of life. Tired of hospitals. Tired of looking at a face that was as ragged as a death mask.

"Sleep well," the face said.

Maybe I slept for just a few hours. Maybe it was long enough to fall in love, get married, have kids, get divorced, and fight for the custody of a seven-year-old child who looked, laughed, and acted exactly like the spouse you despised. It was only time, and time was just a magazine, and it cost two dollars, and you only had a dollar, and that was life, and life was just a magazine, and who the hell believed what they read anyway?

Eventually, I found myself swimming upward into the rather brackish waters of consciousness. Appropriately, I was doing the American crawl—back from a track-lit, neon nightmare into the pale careless light of the twentieth century. Coffee-colored cobwebs began to clear from my mind. The green garden snakes were back in place. That was nice. What passed for New York sunshine was streaming sluggishly in through the window. But there was something new in the picture.

I didn't know if she was an angel of the morning or a straggler from the *Arabian Nights*, but she was sitting on my bed wearing the naughtiest smile I'd ever seen and not a hell of a lot else.

"Jesus Christ," I said.

"Try again," said Leila.

20

There is something very attractive about the prospect of eating, or hosing, forbidden fruit. Leila wasn't exactly forbidden fruit, but she was close enough for color TV. She was wearing a very diaphanous blouse and on her head was a red-and-white sort of scarf that looked like it'd started out in life as a tablecloth in Little Italy.

"I've got two questions for you," I said, as the smile drilled right through me into the bed where it belonged. "The first one is, what is that thing you've got on your head?"

The naughty smile turned a bit mischievous, I thought. "We call it a *kaffiyeh*," she said. I nodded as if I'd just been told some highly important piece of information. Her breasts filled out the front of the blouse like the humps of a small camel. Not the kind you smoke, but the kind you ride.

"The second question," I said rather gruffly, after a small pause to study the terrain, "is, how in hell did you get here?" It's a good policy to keep up a relatively tough-guy exterior. There's always the broad who thinks she's the only one who sees the gentle, sensitive side of you. Whether or not you even have a gentle, sensitive side is pretty much irrelevant. Women like guys who are hovering at death's door, who've just been shot with a tranquilizer dart, or who've committed some particularly sickening heinous crime that no sane mind on the planet could sanction or absolve. My advice is, if they want to think they see this gentle, sensitive side of you, let them. There'll be plenty of other people in your life who, when you're doing what you believe to be right, will think you're a shmuck.

"Maybe I'm just an ambulance chaser," she said, "who's a day late. They wouldn't let me see you yesterday. After I was so curt with you I changed my mind and decided I'd like to get to know you." She kept studying me. Her eyes were bold and curious.

"C'mere, baby," I said, "let me show you where the rabbi bit me."

She laughed. She may have blushed, but I doubted it. If she did, it got lost in the sunset somewhere west of Mecca. She leaned back on the foot of the bed. The camel rumpled its humps attractively as it crossed the linen desert. Leila had stopped smiling. You could tell she was one of those women who, when they wanted to, had pouting staked out.

Neither of us said a word as she pulled her knees up to her chin and sat on the bed gazing casually through the sheets. She had a beautiful bucket, and I knew damn well that I wasn't the only one who could see that side of her. The construction worker on the ninth floor could see it from the other side of the street.

I thought I'd go for a laugh. Break the implicit sexual tension.

"Speaking of ambulance chasers," I said, "my friend Sammy Allred in Austin, Texas, knows a hotshot lawyer who once got a charge of sodomy reduced to following too closely."

"That sounds nice," she said.

I might have blushed. If I did, fortunately, it was lost in the implicit sexual tension.

Leila proceeded to explain how, though I'd been rude when she first met me, she'd been strangely drawn to me. Then, as she was taking a break from the cat show, she'd seen the ambulance, and somebody'd told her that I'd been shot. She'd felt terrible. She'd had to see me.

When I asked her for her phone number, she looked at me

in an Old World sort of way. Her eyes looked like clear beads on an abacus. Then she smiled, reached into her purse, took out a pink felt marker pen, and looked around either for a piece of paper or to see if anyone was watching.

"Give me your hand," she said.

I did.

With an almost nasty, jerky little smile, she wrote for a while on the palm of my right hand, then put the pen away, picked up her purse, and stood up to go. My hand felt hot where she'd held it.

"I'll call you when I'm better," I said.

"No," she said. "Call me when you're ready."

She walked to the door and I looked at my hand. Never be king of the Gypsies, I thought. Couldn't even read my own palm. The writing looked like some kind of blurry, hot-pink hieroglyphics.

"Leila!" I shouted in a commanding, sandpaper voice.

She turned at the door and faced me. Her expression might have been one of fetching mischief. It might have been one of childlike wistfulness. I figured I'd wait until I got the lab report before I decided which. And something told me I might have to wait longer than that. There are some women you can never really get to know until you're dead, and even then you can't be too sure.

"What the hell does this say?" I asked.

"Can't you read it?" she asked playfully. "It's Arabic numerals."

21

I remember once reading a newspaper on a sunny veranda on the left coast of our nation. I was having a mimosa cocktail and eggs bend-my-dick and reading an article about what certain prominent Californians planned to do on the Fourth of July. The mayor of Los Angeles was planning to attend a picnic in the park. Cal Worthington, the used-car dealer, was going to lead a parade in Pasadena. But when they asked Henry Miller what he planned to do on the Fourth of July, he said, "Sleep through it like a bad dream." That's what I'd planned to do with my Sunday morning. St. Vincent's is a long way from St. Patrick's.

I would've followed Henry Miller's advice if it hadn't been for McGovern. McGovern, for all his warm and easy-going nature, was positively brutal when it came to smelling a good, unsavory story. I don't know how McGovern got on to me or knew where I was, but it didn't take him long to go for the jugular. He called and wanted to know if the dart gun rumor was true, if it was connected to the murder at the cat show earlier in the week, and if they both were connected to the lost cat I was looking for.

"The hipbone is connected to the assbone," I said.

"Well, obviously," said McGovern, "you're not in the hospital from overwork and exhaustion." He laughed. "So the dart gun rumor must be true."

"Okay," I said, "say it is."

"Now we're getting somewhere," said McGovern.

"That's what I'm afraid of." It was bad enough that the cat show was over and most of my suspects were probably scattered to the winds. I didn't need McGovern alerting them further with sensational speculation in the *Daily News.*

"Did you get any response to the lost cat ad?" asked McGovern.

"None of your beeswax, corn bread, or shoe tacks," I said coolly.

"I can't believe you're saying this. We're in this thing together. MIT . . . MIT . . . MIT . . ." MIT was the name McGovern and I had once given to the "Man in Trouble Hotline" that we'd established so that if either of us died at home it wouldn't take them eight months to find the body, like it did with some guy in Chicago that McGovern had read about. When things got unpleasant, we'd call each other and say, "MIT, MIT, MIT."

"McGovern," I said, "the problem is that inquiring minds want to know, and if you write about it, inquiring minds may want to hurt Kinky."

"Okay," said McGovern, "this is off the record. Just between us girls. Who was that stone fox who came to see you at the hospital yesterday?"

"Jesus up a Christmas tree, McGovern. What are you doin'? Payin' off the orderlies here?"

"You have your sources; I have my sources," said McGovern with some little dignity. "I just heard that this mystery woman visited you in your room and evidently I heard right. They said she was fucking beautiful."

"McGovern, I've got something for you," I said. "It's something you can print."

"What?"

"Every time you see a beautiful woman, just remember, somebody got tired of her."

Sunday had three other high points, if you wanted to call them that, besides the call from McGovern. The first one was the lab report. It looked like a doozy, because Robert Young brought it in himself from the eighteenth hole. At least I hoped he'd been playing golf. If not, he was working a string of hookers out of Times Square. Golf is the only opportunity that middle-aged Wasps have to dress up like pimps.

I had been shot, apparently, with an animal tranquilizer named supercalifragilisticexpialidocious. Or something equally as long and tedious.

"Enough to put a lion under," Robert Young told me and Ratso. "You can imagine what that would normally do to a man."

"Kinky the Lion-hearted," Ratso laughed. I smiled. I was kind of proud of myself in spite of it all. Maybe the years I'd spent abusing my body with drugs on the road had finally paid off—my system was conditioned to it.

"I think you have a very strong will," said Robert Young.

"I want to live," I said. "I want to paint."

"Nevertheless," he said, "I've spoken to Ratso here and he's going to be keeping a close eye on you for the first week. You can go tomorrow, but Ratso will stay with you for a while."

The idea of my being Ratso's ward was not a pleasant one, but it looked like the only way Robert Young was going to let me out of the hospital. Ratso had moved into the loft with me for a few weeks several years before, when I had been trying to help McGovern out of a hideous snarl he'd gotten himself into. I'd had a little urban hunting accident. Ratso had been dedicated at that time, even devoted. He'd stood up well in the face of death threats, my incapacitation, and harassment from the police. But he was still pretty far down on the list of people on this planet that I'd like to have for a roommate.

To put it kindly, Ratso lacked certain social graces. In fact, he lacked all social graces. And people who lack social graces are the very ones who don't know what you're talking about when you tell them they lack social graces. Anyway, it's not very polite to tell somebody he's a gluttonous, niggardly, unhygienic animal. About all you can say is what a dowdy, humorless woman once told Ratso when he was burping rather loudly in an Indian restaurant: "Pardon the pig."

"This could be the end of a beautiful friendship," I said. "We've done this before and it was most unpleasant."

"Well, we're doing it again," said Ratso.

"Pardon the pig," I said.

22

It was Sunday night, my last night in the hospital, and Ratso had gone home to pack his Gucci luggage for the big slumber party. Maybe I was being too hard on him, but at least I *knew* I was being an asshole and that meant that I wasn't an asshole.

I'd had a few more visitors by this time. Jane Meara had come by. She was still pining for Rocky and she said what had happened to me was her fault. I said it wasn't her fault. Cooperman came by and asked a few questions. I said I felt like hell and he said he'd see me there. He left. Unfortunately, Leila did not return.

I gazed lovingly at the unsmoked cigars in my toilet kit on the nearby table. There had already been one rather ugly altercation involving myself, the nurse, and the nurse's supervisor over smoking cigars in the hospital room. I argued that cigars smell better than hospitals, but they disagreed. That's what makes for horseracing. In my weakened state, I was hardly a match for them and I lived in fear that they might tell Robert Young and he might keep me at St. Vincent's till the Fourth of July. I decided if I just played my cards right and practiced a certain Gandhi-like abstention, in twelve short hours I would be home smoking like a factory in New Jersey.

I was persevering as best I could when the last call of the day came in. It was Rambam.

"The girl, Leila—the one who's half Palestinian—I checked her out."

"Great," I said.

"Not so great," said Rambam.

"What is she?" I asked. "Yessir You're-a-Fart's aerobics instructor?"

"The fact that she's half Palestinian is nothing. It's the other half that's the problem."

"What could be worse?"

"Think about it."

"Kraut," I said.

"Worse."

"Frog."

"Worse."

"What could be worse?"

"Try Colombian," said Rambam. "She comes from a big, wealthy, powerful Colombian family, with the emphasis on the word *family*. And believe me, they don't get their money growing coffee beans."

By the time I hung up, I could see the red flag standing up like a small erection in the parking meter of my mind. I didn't know if it meant "danger" or "your time is up," but either possibility seemed sufficiently unpleasant.

I thought of Leila and a chill came over me. It started hot and ended cold. If I knew myself at all, like Ferdinand the Bull, I would probably soon be charging that little flag. And that, on top of everything else, could be very dangerous indeed.

It was a long time before I got to sleep that night. I kept hearing Rambam's last words over and over again: ". . . they don't get their money growing coffee beans. . . ."

Where was Robert Young when I needed a cup of Sanka?

23

For a fairly large, cold place, the loft seemed surprisingly cozy. After a stint in the hospital, of course, Houston International Airport would have seemed cozy. But I was glad to be back. And the cat was glad I was back. But the cat was not pleased to see Ratso moving his luggage into the loft.

Cats are a fairly right-wing group politically. They are lovers of the status quo. They don't like anything that might represent change. They hate marriages, divorces, moving days, graduations, bar mitzvahs, bill collectors, rug shampooers, painters, plumbers, electricians, television repairmen, out-call masseuses, Jehovah's Witnesses, and just about everything else, most of which I agree with them about.

Ratso, possibly for the first time in his life, was an agent of change.

The trouble began innocently enough on the first night we were back, with the cat taking a Nixon in one of Ratso's red antique shoes. This is the kind of behavior that, while it may be rather incommoding to the guest, is usually seen as mildly amusing by the cat fancier. It makes the guest feel uncomfortable but it makes the host feel, in a somewhat peculiar, roundabout way, wanted.

"It's just the cat's way of saying, 'Welcome, Ratso,' " I said, as Ratso threw open the kitchen window to the grim February morning and dumped frozen feline detritus onto the heads of a mother and her two children down on the sidewalk. The sidewalks of New York are famous for many reasons, and one of them is that people have been dumping frozen cat shit onto them for over a hundred years. Pedestrians think its sleet or some new kind of weather condition. They find it bracing and invigorating.

Ratso's comments will not be recorded here as they do not further the narrative or much of anything else. It is enough to note that they were the kind of ill-humored, unfortunate remarks that one often regrets no sooner than one has uttered them.

By nightfall things were getting back to what passes for normal in New York. Ratso, operating in a rather pioneer mind-set, was under the impression that we might be snowed in for months. Food was his number one priority and I heard him putting in large to-go orders with Joe at Big Wong and with my friend Herb at the Carnegie Deli.

I did not feel that the moment was quite right to tell Ratso we were running low on cat food.

Ratso screened all incoming calls and in general treated me, to my extreme displeasure, like a convalescing maiden aunt.

"You'd make a very good male social secretary, Ratso," I said. "Have you ever thought about that line of work?"

"Not really," said Ratso. He was busy unpacking large books about the life of Jesus as an adolescent and other arcane subjects. Ratso was ignoring my comments and complaints in much the manner that he ignored the presence of the cat. The cat and I were merely two large, troublesome gnats in Ratso's life. For all practical purposes, the cat and I no longer existed. Ratso's domineering manner created a certain resentment in me and I could tell the cat wasn't too keen on it either.

Ratso went to the kitchen and began moving pots and pans and plates around—something the cat disliked intensely—like a predatory insect laying up supplies for the winter. The to-go orders from the Carnegie and Big Wong were due any moment and Ratso was becoming increasingly animated.

He turned to me with a frying pan in his hand and said,

"I'm not just staying here until you're well. I'm staying here until we discover who it was that shot you."

It was a frustrating but somehow poignant sentiment. I looked at Ratso and shrugged.

"You're going to make somebody a fine homosexual pancake chef," I said.

The food Ratso had ordered took longer to arrive than you'd think. It always does. The guys at the Carnegie were probably still shaking the matzo ball tree, and the guys from Big Wong were probably still scouring the neighborhood for a small black dog. Matzo ball trees do not fare well in this country, but the small black dog *is* a Chinese delicacy.

Ratso stood by the window staring gloomily into the gloom. In his hands he nervously juggled the little Negro puppet head with the key to the building in its mouth and the brightly colored parachute attached. I sat in the chair by my desk, puffing on a cigar.

"Careful with that," I said.

"Don't worry," said Ratso. "It's the best little head I've had in a while."

As it happened, both deliverymen arrived at almost precisely the same time. I don't know who was first, but they came up on the same puppet head. With the two delivery guys standing in the doorway, Ratso came over to me and spoke in a voice he thought was a whisper.

"Give me about eighty bucks for the slope food," he said.

"That's pretty steep," I said. "Where's it from—Mr. Chow of Beverly Hills?"

"Just give me the cash. . . . Look, I'm pitching in, too. I've got to tip these guys. You'll get something coming back."

"Sure."

The truth was that every time Ratso and I had ever split a check, I'd gotten hosed. Then Ratso would always demand the receipt, which he maintained was necessary for his taxes. Once, I tore up the receipt rather than give it to him, and it made Ratso so sad that I vowed never to do it again. So, with the two deliverymen doing an impatient jitterbug in the doorway, I christianed Ratso down to sixty-five bucks and let it go.

Ratso tipped the deliverymen, they left, and he started sorting packages all over the kitchen. "I think," said Ratso, "we'll hold the Jew food till the morning and go with the slope food tonight. Or we could mix the two and have sort of a bicultural smorgasbord. Anyway, there's enough here to last us awhile."

"Wait a minute. How'd you pay for the food from the Carnegie?"

"I worked out a deal with Herb," Ratso said shiftily.

"What was the deal?"

"He put it on your tab."

"Good work, Fatso."

"Don't mention it, Shylock."

24

At two o'clock in the morning, the cat jumped on Ratso's balls. I'd been waiting for the other shoe to drop, so to speak, and when it happened, I didn't have any trouble recognizing what it was. I didn't see it happen, but hearing a cat jump on somebody's balls is about as down-home an experience as you can have, next to having a cat jump on your own balls.

I leaped sideways out of bed, went into the living room, and saw Ratso holding his testicles and looking around for a weapon. The cat, quite wisely, was nowhere to be seen. So, without the cat, I just had to deal with the Rat.

I had to calm him down first. "Don't personalize it," I said. "It's a territorial situation; it has nothing to do with what the cat thinks of you." This, of course, was blatantly false, but when a cat jumps on your houseguest's balls you don't rub it in.

"If I find him I'll kill him."

"It's a female."

"Might've known."

"Sanka?"

"Piss off."

Ratso was understandably upset. He'd given up his bed and his ten thousand books relating to Bob Dylan, Jesus, and Hitler. He'd sacrificed his cable television set, which included forgoing the thing he loved most in life next to food, watching hockey games in a disreputable pair of woolen pajamas. He'd taken a few days off work, moved into a rather strange locus, and possibly put his own life at risk. He'd done all this to help a convalescent country-singer-turned-amateur-detective. And what thanks had he gotten?

But that didn't make things any better for me. I was still weak and subject to periodic dizzy spells. I was trying to locate a killer and a cat before somebody drowned me in a bag. And now I had to cope with a petulant and somewhat torpedolike houseguest.

Being an urban hermit is not the easiest thing in the world to be when you grow up. You feel either crowded or lonely as hell. But at least you feel something. I was feeling like a shot of Jameson.

I walked over to the counter and poured a medicinal portion into the old bull's horn. Ratso was already back on the couch. I noticed he was sleeping on his stomach.

I downed the shot and thought about Jane Meara, whom I ought to check on. I thought of Fred Katz, whom I ought to find before he found me again. I thought of Sergeant Cooperman, whom I ought to talk to but didn't want to. I thought of Leila, whom I wanted to see. I wasn't better but I was ready. I thought of lots of things, lots of people, lots of reasons why I was me. Maybe someday I'd fall victim to marriage, suburbia, puttering with my lawn, but I couldn't really see it. I'd long ago come to the conclusion that you're born alone, you die alone, and you might as well get used to it. Nothing that Thoreau or Kerouac hadn't already found out, but it was comforting to realize that nothing had changed.

I took another shot and looked over at my boots standing by the desk. They were long and narrow, like my mind. I visualized a person standing in them. Another Kinky, but not like the other Kinkys I'd seen when I first came to in the hospital. It was the Kinky that I could be with a little bit of luck and a hell of a lot of guts. He was a little weatherbeaten but he looked all right. You could tell that he didn't have time to be lonely.

There's not that much time left, I thought. There never had been that much time. Never enough to spend the rest of your life looking at the bland face of a child in a yellow station wagon.

The road could've ended anywhere, but it didn't. So you keep driving life's lonely DeSoto, looking ahead into the rain and darkness with the windshield wipers coming down like reaper's blades just missing your dreams. And you don't stop till you're damn well ready. Till you come to the right place. Till you come to the right face. The place may be New York or Texas or it may be somewhere painted with the colors Negroes use in their neon lights.

The face will be smiling. So you take the key out of the ignition and you see if it opens her heart.

25

The phone call from Eugene came at about 6:15 A.M. It was a trifle early and it was also a trifle unpleasant. "Our little friend," according to Eugene, had not been idle during the night. Whoever he was, he was continuing his campaign of terror against Jane Meara. Eugene was at Jane's place now because she was frightened to be alone. They wanted to meet me. They had something for me.

I didn't want anything. Maybe another twelve hours of sleep.

I agreed to meet them in an hour at a little Greek coffee shop on Twenty-eighth Street around the corner from Jane's office. I hung up, got dressed, found and fed the cat, and found and lit a cigar. I put on my old hunting vest, my hat, and my coat and I tiptoed across the living room like a guy sneaking out of the house for a poker game. It was my house —I could sneak out of it if I wanted. I locked the door to the loft behind me.

One rule I always follow in life is "Let sleeping rats lie."

Vandam Street was windy, cold, and empty in the early morning. There was just a little old lady trying to hold on to a little pink hat and me trying to hold on to my cowboy hat. Deserted as it was, the place had an aura of urban prairie to it. Of course, these days I usually rode two-legged animals.

I drifted up Hudson and hailed a hack. Through a frosty window that wouldn't quite close, I watched the city waken.

A stout woman with a shawl unlocks an iron gate. A man in a woolen cap unloads a crate of oranges from a truck. Down the street another man sits by the gutter next to a whiskey bottle and blows on his hands. Two little children in mackerel-snapper uniforms come out of a building with a doorman. A man wearing a coat walks a dog wearing a sweater.

People walk dogs in Dallas. People walk dogs in California. But in New York sometimes you can see a real man walking a real dog, and there's something timeless and rather beautiful about it. It's performance art.

My mind was starting to wake up a little bit, too. A lot of things were happening to Jane Meara and she wasn't the kind of person things always happened to. She wasn't the kind of person whose junkie boyfriend beat her up or who didn't know that her apartment was being used as a crack kitchen or who found a serial killer in her shredded wheat. She was normal as a blueberry blintze.

So why had somebody kidnapped her cat? Why had somebody left her a crank note at the Roosevelt Hotel? Why had somebody put a bloody butcher knife on her desk? I didn't have any hard answers, but a garish mosaic was coming together in my mind's eye and it wasn't the kind of thing you'd want to hang in your sitting room.

The cab screeched to a halt at Twenty-eighth Street next to a man who was vomiting on a police car. The police car was empty and pretty soon so was the man. Make a nice picture postcard. I paid the driver, got out of the hack, and started walking up the street.

Halfway up the block I found the little Greek coffee shop. It wasn't hard to find the place. You seen one Greek coffee shop, you've seen 'em all. Life imitates John Belushi.

It was a little after seven but the place was already crowded. Eugene and Jane were sitting at a table by the window and waved me over. Jane looked fragile. Eugene looked nervous. The waitress came to the table, Frisbeed a menu at me, and said, "Whad'll you have?"

I said, "Coffee."

She took the menu and went away faster than a dream you weren't sure you had.

"I'm glad you were able to come," said Jane.

"Let's not get personal," I said. As a rule, I tried never to appear too sophisticated until the coffee arrived. Jane looked like she was practicing her smile for the first time and Eugene made a let's-get-on-with-the-show gesture.

The waitress brought my coffee. I took a sip and waited. Eugene looked at Jane and Jane looked at Eugene. I looked into my coffee cup and wished I were on a little Greek island instead of in a little Greek coffee shop.

"All right," I said finally, "spit it."

"Well, first of all," said Eugene, "there's something I think you ought to know. I didn't tell the police about it the other day for obvious reasons, but I've talked it over with Jane and I think I ought to tell you."

"Spit it," I said.

"Well, Jim Landis is my boss. I work with Jane, but he's both of our boss. He's the publisher. He's got his own imprint. You know what that is?"

"I've heard the word."

"It means he runs his own publishing company."

"So?"

"So he wasn't in a restaurant like he told the police—he was in Jane's office." Eugene looked at me nervously. I'd have to check it out but it seemed a bit too easy.

"Maybe I'll order some pie," I said.

"Landis can't know we talked to you," said Eugene.

"Autism is my middle name," I said. "What else have you got?"

Jane reached into her purse, came out with a cassette tape, and handed it across to me. It was an incoming message cassette for an answering machine. "It's the last message on side B," she said. "It came in late last night—about two o'clock in the morning, actually."

"Okay," I said. Two o'clock in the morning was about the

time the cat had jumped on Ratso's balls. The two incidents were probably unrelated, but it was a time-frame.

"It's a silly message, I know," said Jane, "but it scared the hell out of me at the time. In fact, it still does."

"What was the message?"

"Meow," said Jane.

"I've heard the word," I said.

26

By the time I got back to 199B Vandam, it was pushing eight-thirty and Ratso was dunking a bagel into a bowl of wonton soup. The cat was sitting on my desk. Neither of them looked pleased to see me.

The cat knew I was not carrying a grocery bag of cat food. She had a habit of looking in the cupboard with me every time I went to feed her, and she knew we were down to just two cans of Southern Gourmet Dinner. The cat hated Southern Gourmet Dinner.

The cat was merely petulant, but Ratso's expression combined equal components of fury and disgust. I knew he was truly angry when he left his food and began pacing up and down in the kitchen. I was glad I didn't own a rolling pin.

"You are not to go out," he said with eyes blazing, "especially these first few days, without first checking with me. Even if you do check with me, I still don't want you going out on the street alone. I'm to know where you're at at all times. Do you understand?"

I took the cassette tape out and put it on the desk. "Lot of rules for such a small company," I said.

Ratso continued to stare at me. "You're goddamn right," he said.

"Why so hostile?"

"Because you're being an asshole."

"That's Mr. Asshole to you, pal."

The bickering went back and forth for a while with the cat watching it like a slightly bored tennis fan. I played it out for a few more minutes and then Ratso somewhat grudgingly agreed to listen to the cassette tape with me.

I took the ceramic hat off the top of the large Sherlock Holmes head I kept on my desk and reached inside for a cigar. The Sherlock Holmes head had been given to me by my friends Bill and Betty Hardin at the Smokehouse in Kerrville, Texas. I kept my cigars and other valuables in there. Ratso often said that it was hardly a safe place for valuables, but I always invoked the words of my friend Goat Carson: "Sooner or later, cats piss on everything." The way things were going, the cat probably would've pissed on everything by now if it weren't for the little ceramic hat.

I took the tape out of my own answering machine and popped Jane's in. I rewound the tape. Then I pushed the play button. The first voice we heard identified itself as Jim Landis's. It sounded brusque and irritated.

"Jane, it's Jim Landis. . . . It's nine-thirty. . . . What *is* this shit? A monograph on the Flathead Indians of Montana? You think they're happening? You think anybody gives a shit about the Flathead Indians of Montana? I can't believe you sent this on to me—the writing stinks, too—the whole thing sucks. Send the guy to the *National Geographic*. What the fuck's the matter with you, Jane?"

"Pleasant guy to work for," said Ratso.

"He's got his own imprint," I said.

"If I worked for him I'd put my imprint on his forehead."

"Listen." There was one hang-up and a message from Jane's mother. Then we heard it. It began in a high register and cascaded evilly down to a bone-jarring growl. The same fiendish, half-feline half-human sound we'd heard at the Garden a moment before I'd been shot.

"Any question?" I asked.

"Not a doubt about it," said Ratso.

I lit my cigar with a rather feeble Bic. I'd had the Bic for four or five days. That was already pretty old in the lifetime of a Bic. I puffed thoughtfully on the cigar.

"I agree," I said. "That's our man."

"Or woman," said Ratso.

27

"I'm not tailing Hilton Head," said Ratso as we sat around the kitchen table later that same day. "I've already spent too much time with that little fruitcake."

"That's an alarmingly homophobic attitude, Ratso," I said. I was working on my fifth or sixth espresso and I was starting to get a little buzz.

We haggled back and forth for a while and gradually a division of labor was established. Ratso would, without alerting the parties involved, get a current rundown on Head and the Parks. Head lived in New York, but the Parks had several homes and it wasn't even clear whether they were still in the city.

For my part, I would explore the Fred Katz situation and the "meow" situation and I would contact Sergeant Cooperman. My investigations were to be conducted telephonically. At least for now, Ratso would do the legwork. It was a reversal of roles that neither of us particularly relished.

It was Tuesday evening, about dusk. In New York in February, of course, it looks like Tuesday evening about dusk most of the time. Ratso was heading for the door with about half of Canal Street on his back. His shoes, pants, shirt, coat, and hat all were exclusively flea-market items. You could say that, in a rather seedy way, he was impeccably dressed. He was a man with deep loyalties to his clothier.

"Don't give up your day job," I said.

"Don't worry."

"Just check around a bit. I'd just as soon no one else knows about the dart incident or that we're pressing on with the case."

"I know what to do."

Ratso had the door of the loft open when I thought of something else. "Oh yeah," I said, "there's one more thing."

"What?"

"Would you mind picking up some cat food?"

Ratso closed the door.

Alone in the loft at last, I sat down at my desk and thought things over. If a Gray Line tour had come through 199B Vandam that night, it would've provided a colorful, rather eccentric portrait for the tourists. They would've seen a man sitting alone at a desk in the New York wintertime, smoking a cigar, taking occasional medicinal shots of Jameson from an old black bull's horn, and saying "meow" repeatedly to himself. But there was no Gray Line tour. Only gray.

The case, as I saw it, was pretty much at a dead end. The cops, according to what I'd read in the papers, had no new leads on the Rick "Slick" Goldberg murder. In the case of a murdered woman, I'd once read, at least 85 percent of the time the killer is the lover. In the case of a murdered literary agent, the killer could be half the civilized world. Using the word "civilized" advisedly, of course.

I didn't see what I could do to draw out Fred Katz that hadn't already been done. Maybe skywriting would work. And as for Rocky, well . . .

The slender thread of hope that Jane clung to was probably spurred on by the note, the knife, and the phone message. Maybe Jane thought someone had kidnapped Rocky and was keeping her for ransom or reasons unknown. It was possible, but I doubted it. I'd heard the "meow" sound twice. Once in person and once on tape. There was something in the nature of the sound itself that made it hard to tell much about the identity of the speaker. There was only one thing that came across loud and clear to me. And that didn't bode well for Jane Meara.

It sounded as if the person didn't like cats.

28

Three cigars and half a bottle of Jameson later, the only thing that really seemed to be clicking was the lesbian dance class. The combination of the Irish whiskey and the residual lion tranquilizer was starting to feel pretty good. It was a rather unorthodox method of mixing drugs and booze, but if everybody did everything the same way it'd be a boring old world.

I was feeling almost numb enough to call Sergeant Cooperman. The game was afoot all right, but with Ratso's new rules in effect it would be impossible, not to say tedious, to try to go anywhere in the next forty-eight hours. Not that there was anywhere to go.

I picked up the blower on the left and dialed the Sixth Precinct.

The desk sergeant sounded tired and frazzled. Tough to be a cop, I thought. But I knew about tough, too, in a different way. Once you've been a country singer on the road for a while, there's not a lot of things in life that you'd think of as tough. Maybe ordering from a wine list.

I gave my name to the desk sergeant, told him I wanted to speak to Sergeant Cooperman, and got put on hold. I'd been there before. In fact, I'd been on hold for some pretty important people in my time. Now I was on hold for a cop.

But on hold was on hold. I knew what to do. I took a few lazy puffs on my cigar and let my imagination fly like an

endangered crane. I saw the world through the eyes of Aga-
memnon, flying into LAX, walking off the plane onto a carpet of blood-red Astroturf. I was Davy Crockett at the Russian Tea Room, fighting off literary agents with my salad fork.
A little imagination can be a dangerous thing. You can just
have met someone and ten minutes later you're sitting cozily
together in a breakfast nook listening to Arthur Godfrey. You
can miss a lot of life that way, but it will kill some time when
you're on hold.

A gruff, gratingly familiar voice came on the line, bringing
me down and back to Vandam Street.

"Well, well," said Sergeant Cooperman, "how's Bomba the
Jungle Boy?"

"Hangin' in there," I said.

"The doctor said you were too ill to talk, but much to our
joy here at the station house, you seem to've pulled
through."

"Sorry, officer."

"Maybe you'll do better next time. What do you need,
pal?" You can say the word *pal* or you can spit it. Cooperman spit it like slow-moving phlegm from a fast-moving
pickup.

"Well, Sergeant, you know I've been looking for this missing cat of Jane Meara's."

"Yup."

"And this guy that shot me, just before he shot me, he said
the same thing someone left on Jane Meara's answering machine last night. I was wondering if we couldn't make a
voiceprint or voice comparison of some kind and—"

"It's inadmissible. What's the phrase?"

"What?"

"What's the *phrase?*"

"Well, it's just a word, actually."

"Impossible. What's the word?"

"Meow."

There was a long silence on the line. It was so long that I

thought maybe he'd gone out to answer a ten-four or something. Finally, he spoke.

"Bow-wow," he said.

"You don't have to bark at me."

He hung up.

29

It was 11:30 P.M. Ratso was still not back and the cat was not in a very talkative mood, so I picked up the blower on the left and dialed a number I'd recently conjugated from my right hand.

"Hello," came a sleepy voice.

"Shit," I said. "Are you asleep?"

"Kinky?"

"How'd you know?"

"I could smell your cigar," she said dreamily.

"Leila—you really like the way my cigars smell?" It was too good to be true.

"I love it." What a wonderful girl.

One thing about cigars is they save a lot of time with broads. If you find a girl who likes your cigar smoke, it usually means she likes a lot of other things, too. And most of the time, but not always, it means you've got her in your hip pocket. Either she's the kind of broad who loves not to like it, or she's unconsciously trying to get closer to her grandfather who smoked cigars and was run over by a trolley when she was six years old.

In either case, forget the Freudian implications, which is always good advice. What you're left with is a wholesome, earthy, soulful, open-minded, old-fashioned, sensuous person of the female persuasion.

It also means you can smoke your pie and eat it, too.

When I hung up, Leila and I had agreed to get together at

502 eight the following night at her place, which was fairly close by in the Village. She gave me the address.

I put on my Borneo sarong from Peace Corps days, killed the light, and got into bed. I'd given up waiting for Ratso and I wasn't worried about how I was going to slip out of the loft the following evening.

I was just thinking about a certain Middle East hot spot that, with a little bit of shuttle diplomacy, was soon going to explode.

30

I did not dream of Leila that night. I dreamed of androgynous-looking cats doing a form of St. Vitus's ballet around my bed. Many times during the night I willed them to go away. Jump on Ratso's balls or something. Wherever he was.

The cats would disappear for a while, but then they'd return, doing poisonous little pirouettes in ever-tightening circles inside my brain. They all wore masks, of course. And hideous Day-Glo leotards. They were supple and sinuous—sexy in a feline sort of way. The little bastards were macho about being androgynous.

When the dancing cats had finally buggered off into the darkness, it was almost dawn and the garbage trucks were beginning to gnash their teeth outside my window. I was tired as hell but I couldn't sleep. All I could seem to do was think. And what I was thinking was not very pleasant.

By dawn's surly light I was all but convinced that the androgynous dancing cats had been trying to tell me something. They were trying to tell me that all of this fit together somehow. It seemed as easy as connecting the dots that were dancing before my bloodshot eyes.

There was no room for coincidence now. The man who called himself Fred Katz was a very sick puppy. He'd left the "cat got your tongue" note at the Roosevelt and he'd killed Goldberg and gotten *his* tongue. I felt certain it was he who was behind the series of pranks that had occurred—the knife, the phone message. Fred Katz had also, I believed, tried to kill me.

Find Fred Katz, I thought, and you'd have the cat and the killer. The more I thought about it, the more desperate and deadly the situation seemed.

I wasn't worried about what was going to happen to Rocky anymore. But I was worried—very deeply worried—about what was going to happen to Jane Meara.

31

It took me longer than the prime of Miss Jean Brodie to find Leila's street. I didn't mind the little walking tour of the Village, though. It was a clear night and cold as hell. "Bracing," as they say. It doesn't matter how horrifically cold it gets in the city, New Yorkers always think it's bracing. That's one of the reasons New York isn't Buffalo. In Buffalo, they think it's cold.

I was just thankful to be out of the loft where there was nothing to do but stroke the cat and Ratso's rapidly developing ego. He seemed to be overidentifying with his Dr. Watson role. That morning we'd killed the remaining wonton soup and knocked down about seven espressos at a breakfast power caucus.

Ratso's appetite for the case had increased dramatically. It was just over a week ago that I'd had to drag him by the heels to the Garden to help me find a missing cat. Now he couldn't wait to get back on the track of the mysterious Parks and Hilton "Fruitcake" Head. Amateur detectives are hard to figure.

The other thing that had been irritating about Ratso at the power caucus was how close to the vest he'd played his cards. It was an "ongoing investigation," he'd said. He'd "fill me in when he knew more." Almost like talking to Sergeant Cooperman.

The good thing about Ratso's active involvement in the case, however, was that I had no trouble slipping out to meet Leila. I didn't even feel too guilty about breaking the house rules. Besides, I was starting to feel better. It only hurt when I meowed.

By the time I found Leila's street the numbing cold had put Jane Meara's situation out of my mind. I lit a cigar with a new pastel-purple Bic I'd bought from a rather hostile Pakistani at a corner grocery store. Now I was looking for street numbers and trying not to freeze my *huevos* off. Three more blocks and I stumbled on the place.

Leila lived in a fairly modern building named after a French painter who'd once been fairly modern himself. That was over a hundred years ago and now he was dead and famous enough to have a wino urinating on a building named after him. A nice touch, if you belonged to the Impressionist school.

I walked into a small lobby with a large doorman. He planted himself directly in my path.

"Can I help you?" he asked. His eyes looked like little locked glass doors.

"Twelve-K," I said.

"Name of the person you wish to see?" he asked, looking at my hat.

"Leila."

"And your name is—?"

"Kinky."

He went to the house phone, dialed a couple numbers, and said, "Mr. Kinky is here."

He listened, nodded, put down the phone, and motioned me in. I bootlegged my cigar into the elevator and pushed twelve. I stood back to enjoy the ride. Took a few puffs on the cigar. Thought neutral elevator thoughts.

I took a left on twelve, found 12K at the end of the hall, and knocked on the door. After a moment the door opened. It wasn't Leila. It was a stockily built, swarthy man with a large mustache. Looked like an organ grinder who'd just stomped his monkey to death.

"Come in," he said.

32

I peered around Jerry Colonna and saw a red sparkle-topped tennis shoe resting casually on a glass coffee table. A bare Arabian ankle was growing luxuriantly out of the tennis shoe like the stalk of a sexy tropical plant. I'd have to look it up in *National Geographic* sometime and find out if it was a man-eater. The guy backed up a little and I stepped into the room.

The place looked like a whorehouse in *Architectural Digest*. There was a lot of glass, a lot of metal, mirrors everywhere, and a forty-foot couch done up entirely in bullfight-poster red.

"Understated," I said to the man with the mustache.

He didn't say anything. His eyes looked hot and distant. Staring at his face was like flying over a forest fire in the middle of the night at thirty-seven thousand feet. You knew it couldn't burn you, but you also knew that one of these days they were going to have to land the plane.

"It's okay, Hector," said a familiar feminine voice. The guy stepped to the side and I saw that the bare ankle was attached to an equally bare, slightly thin, sinuously gorgeous leg. Leila was attached to the leg.

"Kinky's harmless," she said with a smile. She was wearing a pair of faded, delicious-looking cutoffs and a tight pink T-shirt that said something in one of the Romance languages. I gave her a harmless wink.

I walked a little closer to the couch. "What's a Hector?" I said.

She gave a little papal sign with her right hand and Hector nodded once and left the room. "Hector works for my brother," Leila said.

"Maybe your brother's taking being an equal opportunity employer a step too far."

She smiled a top-drawer mischievous smile, crooked her finger, and beckoned me around the coffee table.

"Maybe I've got a job for you," she said.

"Like what?" I asked as I sat down next to her.

"I don't know," said Leila, "but you'd look pretty cute handing me a dry towel."

You might say that a forty-foot-long couch isn't very cozy and you'd be right. But given a spiritually horny American and a rather randy Palestinian, it can be just about everything else.

Leila had turned the lights down to low interrogation. She had turned me on to the point where I was one step away from making water wings out of her cutoffs. We were both trying to chew the same piece of Dentyne when a slender, vaguely sinister figure appeared in the hall doorway. When the lights came up we hardly noticed. Dentyne can be a very sexy gum.

Leila recovered first. "Kinky," she said, ". . . this is my brother, Carlos."

"Carlos?" I said. I sat up. It was a chore to get my breath back.

"Carlos," said Carlos. His expression hadn't changed since I'd first seen him standing there. His face looked like a sweet, evil puppet that enjoyed pulling all the strings itself. I didn't know if Colombians liked guys practically hosing their sisters on forty-foot couches but I doubted it, so I tried to leaven the situation.

"Carlos," I said. "Carlos . . . wait a minute . . . not Carlos the international terrorist?"

His eyes took on the unmistakable glint of primitive obsid-

ian tools used to bring death to small animals. A rather unpleasant hissing noise came from Carlos's mouth. Then he
was gone.

"I don't think he considers me a prospective brother-in-
law," I said.

"He'll get over it," said Leila. "Wait right here."

I waited. Leila got up and walked out of the room into the
hallway. Nice bucket, all right. I heard a door open and close.
I took out a cigar and lit it and looked at a picture of the sad,
lonely face of a bull in the ring. I didn't like Spanish-speaking
peoples because they were mean to bulls. Of course, maybe if
the Krauts, Turks, and Communists had had some bulls
around they would've left the Jews, Gypsies, Armenians,
Cambodians, and everybody else alone. I puffed on the cigar
and watched the reflections of smoke disappearing in one of
the mirrors across the room. Life is but a dream.

I waited. You'd think Hector would've come in and asked
me if I'd like a nice cup of Colombian coffee. I waited.

The next time I looked up I saw a vision coming toward
me in a light-pink afghan coat with a red-and-black-checked
Italian tablecloth on its head.

"Nice gefilte," I said.

"Kaffiyeh," said Leila.

She put a rectangular cloth bag on the glass tabletop. It
looked like a Gucci shoeshine kit. She opened it and began
taking out some of the most ornate drug paraphernalia I'd
seen this side of the East Village. A two-pronged silver coke
spoon in the form of a sacrificial maiden with arms out-
stretched. A large seashell container with a mirror on one
side and an inch of what looked like diplomatic-pouch-qual-
ity snow on the other. Finally, she took one end of a tubelike
device that branched into two silver globes and handed it to
me. The other end remained in the Gucci shoeshine kit.

"This is for you, Kinkster. Do you know what it is?"

"Looks like a stethoscope for a pinhead."

Unfortunately, I did not need a great deal of coaxing. I put

510 one silver globe against each nostril, inhaled sharply, and simultaneously blew my brains out.

It was so good it was very dangerous. Just like all the other good things in life.

33

I don't remember how I got out of that room. Maybe I flew by Jewish radar. Maybe the faces of John Belushi and Lowell George guided me like Sherlock Holmes carriage lamps shining through the mist. Whatever it was that got me there, I was glad to be outside.

It was America. It was 1988. I didn't know it, of course. The right lobe of my brain was just beginning to recouple with the left lobe. I could feel the clumsy, gloved hands of Russian cosmonauts slowly piecing the machinery together somewhere in space.

I could hear Leila's voice, soft and intimate, somewhere next to me. Cocaine always sends men and women to different planets. "I could go for a man who doesn't wear running shoes," she said.

I did a few impromptu deep-breathing exercises and looked around to get my bearings. Incredibly, we were still on Leila's block, just a few houses down from where she lived. It was hard to believe that I'd felt brain-dead for what seemed like an eternity. How could I have almost allowed my childhood dreams, my dearest hopes for the future, my very existence on this planet to be reduced to a mere fossil record on the dusty, forgotten desk of some mildly interested, science-oriented graduate student who'd gone out for a pizza without anchovies?

The wind began to blow a little harder and a lot colder. I began to notice a few things. Two of them were Leila's legs.

As the wind whipped up her coat I saw she was still wearing the cutoffs underneath. Her legs looked as pink as the house where The Band used to practice with Bob Dylan.

"Your legs look cold," I said. I took her hand and we walked a little farther. She didn't say anything.

"Maybe I could blow on them," I said.

"Maybe."

We were each lost in our own thoughts on our own different planets when we came face to face with Sergeant Mort Cooperman and Sergeant Buddy Fox. They appeared to be in a hurry.

"One side, Tex," said Cooperman brusquely. Fox looked appreciatively at Leila, we both stepped aside, and they continued at a brisk pace up the sidewalk.

Standing in the gutter I turned and saw cops getting out of several unmarked cars and heading in the same direction as Cooperman and Fox. Four of them were carrying a long metal pole with a sort of phallic knob on the end of it. There were two handles on each side. It was a battering ram.

They all went into Leila's building and they didn't seem to be having any trouble with the doorman. I took Leila's arm and hurried her farther down the street and around the corner.

"What do you think's happening?" she asked a little too coolly.

"I don't know," I said. "Maybe somebody tore the tag off their mattress."

34

Thursday morning broke cold, grim, and gray in New York. My hangover and I stepped gingerly around the cat litter box, which was blocking the doorway to the bathroom. I usually kept the cat litter box in the shower, except, of course, when I was taking a shower. The reason for the cat litter box displacement soon became evident.

Ratso was taking his biannual shower. It was sort of a purification rite with Ratso and he followed it almost religiously whether he felt he needed it or not.

And he was singing.

Because of my years on the road as a country singer, I had come to hate the sound of the human voice singing. To make matters worse, Ratso was singing some half-punk, half-rap song by his favorite new group, Smoking/No Smoking. Unfortunately, or perhaps fortunately, depending on how you looked at it, both the song and the band would be passé before Ratso stepped out of the rainroom, a visual experience I did not wish to have at that hour of the morning.

I went to the sink, wiped some steam away from the mirror, and saw that my hair was standing straight up in the shape of a rocket ship. It was a fairly current New York hairstyle but it didn't blow my skirt up too much. I got a brush and ran it through my moss a few times, brushed my choppers, drew a bye on shaving. My eyes would've looked good in a stuffed rabbit's head.

Ratso showed no signs of departing the rainroom, so I

opted for a little trick I'd picked up on the road. It was known widely in country music as the Waylon Jennings Bus Shower. You stand close to a sink and splash water on your face and your armpits. If there's soap around you can use it, but then you have to splash a lot of water on your armpits to get it off.

There was soap and I used it. The results left my sarong and the bathroom floor pretty wet, but when you thought about it, it was a small price to pay for being well groomed.

I went back into the kitchen and looked out the window at the bleak warehouse walls and rusty fire escapes across Vandam Street. The hangover was starting to go, but I still didn't feel like putting hotcakes on the griddle and taking down the ol' fiddle.

I stoked up the espresso machine and fed the cat.

While I waited for the espresso I paced back and forth and thought about what had transpired on the previous night. It was the kind of situation where you hated yourself in the morning but you were still pretty damn glad that you'd done it.

Before I knew it the espresso was ready.

I poured a cup, lit my first cigar of the morning, and sat down at the kitchen table to read Ratso's copy of the *Daily News*. On page 2 I saw a headline that almost made the espresso come out my nose. It read:

MAJOR COKE RING BUSTED
COUNTRY SINGER THOUGHT TO BE FINGER

35

"**G**reat follow-up," said Ratso from over my shoulder. He was wearing some kind of New Wave bathrobe that hurt my eyes. I turned my attention back to the story.

"Terrific sequel," he said.

"What the hell are you talking about?"

"Terrific sequel," he said, "to 'Country Singer Plucks Victim from Mugger.'" At this point Ratso leaned over and began to read the story aloud.

"Let's see," he said. "'Although law enforcement officers refused to comment, an informed source revealed that a well-known country singer was seen leaving the premises just prior to the time of the raid. The Texas singer, who has often performed at the Lone Star Cafe, is known to have been involved with crime-solving on an amateur level in the past. . . .'" Ratso stood up straight and put his hands on my shoulders.

"What you need is an agent, Kinkster," he said excitedly. "What you need is a manager."

"What you need is a muzzle for Christmas," I said.

Ratso looked hurt. He stood beside the kitchen table like a large, wounded sparrow. I didn't let it get to me.

Ratso had carefully cultivated that hurt look and he was pretty damn good at it. When I was hurt, I only looked confused, nervous, or angry. So a hurt look wasn't a bad thing to have. Could keep you from getting hurt sometime.

"You see, my dear Ratso," I said, "there was only one

mugger. Surely you realize there must be thousands of Colombians in New York whose mustaches intersect in the illegal drug trade."

Ratso thought about it for a moment. So did I. The cat jumped up on the windowsill and watched a few toxic snowflakes crash-land on the East Side, far corner of the pane.

"You don't really think," said Ratso, "that they'd put all of this together and come looking for us, do you?"

I got up from the table, poured another shot of espresso into my Imus in the Morning coffee mug, and watched the cat watch the snow.

"As Albert Einstein used to say, Ratso, 'I don't know.' "

As the snow drifted down, our conversation drifted to other matters. I was midway into my second cigar and finishing my third espresso when Ratso unburdened himself of the results of his adventures in the past few days as an amateur detective. I listened politely.

To hear Ratso tell it, he'd run a very thorough-going investigation into the three parties in question. Unfortunately, I hadn't thought about them in so long that they seemed like characters in an old Russian folk story. It was beginning to dawn on me that, even for an amateur, I had not been very professional. I had let Marilyn and Stanley Park and Hilton Head, as well as the better part of caution and common sense, be pushed to the back of my mind by Leila's beautiful legs.

". . . and so Stanley Park's been missing in action for almost a week," Ratso was saying. "Nobody's seen him, and get this . . ."

"Don't talk while you're eating."

". . . Head may not be as much of a winkie as we at first thought," Ratso continued.

"I'll take that dry towel now."

". . . at least three occasions coming out of Marilyn Park's building . . ."

"Yes, you can borrow my toothbrush, but in some cultures it means we're engaged."

". . . and on a fourth occasion—are you listening, Kinkster?—coming out of his own place with . . ."

"Leila!"

"That's right. Hilton Head was coming out of his own place with Leila. How'd you know that?"

"Call it cowboy intuition," I said. "She was too good to be true."

It figured.

36

As Archie Goodwin, Nero Wolfe's famous sidekick, once observed, "No man was ever taken to hell by a woman unless he already had a ticket in his pocket, or at least had been fooling around with timetables."

I hadn't been taken to hell yet, but I could sure see it coming. A lot of things were going on and I didn't like any of them. If I was going to solve this case and live to hear Ratso take credit for it, I'd better be damn careful and lucky. Of course, if I'd really been lucky I'd've been in a park somewhere in Oregon throwing a Frisbee to a dog with a bandanna around its neck and I never would've gotten Jane Meara's phone call in the first place. Of course, then I never would've met Leila.

Around eleven Ratso went out for a while to check on things at his apartment. When you've got a stuffed polar bear's head, a four-foot-tall statue of the Virgin Mary, ten thousand books relating to Jesus, Bob Dylan, and Hitler, and a couch with skid marks on it, you can't just run off and leave things.

After Ratso had departed I hopped off the espresso and poured a stiff shot of Jameson into the bull's horn. I toasted the cat rather briefly and killed the shot. I called Leila's old number and got a recorded message saying that it had been disconnected.

I called Rambam. He wasn't home, so I left a message for his machine to call my machine and maybe the two machines could get together and have lunch at the Four Sea-sons. I also mentioned for Rambam to be sure to read page 2 of the *Daily News* and let me know what he thought about it.

The more I thought about it myself, the less likely I be-lieved it was that members of a major Colombian cocaine cartel, as the *Daily News* described the operation, would take the time and effort to identify one country-singer-turned-amateur-detective. It seemed to me, as I sat in the loft that Thursday afternoon and knocked back another shot of Jame-son, that it was even less likely that they would take any action. They had plenty of bulls to fight, and if they ran out of bulls there was always each other.

As the morning wore on, I started to feel a bit more secure about the whole thing. I just wouldn't throw the puppet head down to anybody wearing a big mustache.

About noon I opened the refrigerator and was able to lo-cate a residual bagel behind a small city of Chinese take-out cartons, some of them dating back to before the Ming Dy-nasty. The bagel was in surprisingly good shape. In fact, it felt better than I did.

I took the bagel and a bottle of Dr. Brown's black cherry soda over to the desk, and with the cat, two telephones, and an old typewriter, I had lunch. Fairly pleasant dinner com-panions, as they go.

After lunch I opened the day's correspondence with my Smith & Wesson knife. There wasn't a hell of a lot to open. If you want a pen pal, you've got to be a pen pal.

There was something that looked unpleasantly like a wed-ding invitation. I slit it open and sure enough it was. A girl I used to know named Nina Kong was getting married. In or-der to do this she must have straightened out her act in more ways than one. The guy she was marrying was Edward S. Pincus, a rising young urologist. The wedding was at the Pierre Hotel. Reception to follow.

Apparently the happy event had taken place two days ago. You know the mails.

I started to throw the invitation out and then thought

better of it. Placed flat on the desk, it made a pretty fair coaster for the Dr. Brown's black cherry soda.

A house isn't really a home without a coaster. I gave the cat a crooked smile. The cat smiled back.

It was downhill from there. A form letter from a Catholic priest in Nicaragua, which had come addressed to "Occupant." A bill from Con Ed. A letter from a militant lesbian coalition called Sisters of Sappho, which I inadvertently opened before I realized it was for Winnie Katz.

Bringing up the tail end of the day's correspondence was a postcard from the Pilgrim Psychiatric Center. It was from my old friend Cleve, the former manager of the Lone Star Cafe. It read as follows: "Don't believe the doctors. There's nothing lamp carrot rocking-horse wrong with me. Wish you were here."

That was the lot. One of these days I'll reverse my zip code and see what happens.

I called McGovern at the *Daily News* and he vehemently denied having anything to do with the story on page 2. He asked me if I'd been at the scene of the bust. I vehemently denied having anything to do with it. We both vehemently hung up.

I got a screwdriver and turned the old black-and-white television set that was missing a knob on to *Wild Kingdom.* I moved to Ratso's couch and the cat moved to her rocking chair. I lay down for a little power nap, and an idea gradually began forming in the back of my mind amidst all the debris that Leila's legs had recently kicked there. The idea rose like a phoenix, no doubt from the ashes of several rather charred brain cells. It started off a little shaky, but it looked like it was going to fly.

I did not especially like *Wild Kingdom.* I always felt that the feeling was Mutual of Omaha. The cat, however, always seemed vaguely to enjoy the show, so I turned it on every now and then for her enjoyment.

It wasn't a great sacrifice for me. Just part of the give-and-take of daily life. A little adjustment we make in order to ensure that the world becomes a better place for our children and our kittens. On the other hand, it could've been that, subconsciously, these little kindnesses I performed were a trick I was playing on God to make Him think I was a more sensitive American than I am. But could any man play a trick on God? Whose *Wild Kingdom* was it anyway? Was it God's or Mutual of Omaha's? Tune in next week.

Ratso walked in just about the time I got the phone call from Sergeant Cooperman.

37

After I'd established that Ratso was not going to interrupt his journey to the refrigerator to answer the phones, I walked over to the desk and collared the blower on the left.

"Start talkin'," I said.

"Goodbye, Tex," said Sergeant Cooperman.

"Going somewhere, Sergeant?"

"Yeah. Funeral of a guy. Used to be a country singer. Tried his hand at a little amateur crime-solving now and then. Got lucky a few times. Then he got in over his head. Colorful character, he was. Gutsy guy, too. Never liked him too much, personally. . . . Never got off on funerals much, either. I'll take a fucking wake any day."

"I know what you mean. I'd rather go to an Irish wake than a Jewish wedding. They're more fun."

Ratso looked over at me inquiringly from the refrigerator. I shrugged and took a fresh cigar out of Sherlock Holmes's head.

"Got a mick in the woodpile somewhere, do you, Tex?" While I listened to Cooperman chuckle I began preignition procedures on the cigar. For a while I thought he had the chuckle on an endless loop, but it subsided neatly right about the time I had the cigar ready for lift-off.

"Gonna wear a Colombian necktie to the funeral, Tex?"

"I must assume, then," I said, "that this call's in reference to 'Country Singer Thought to Be Finger.' " I took a not-so-relaxed puff on the cigar.

"Let me tell you something you obviously don't know," said Cooperman. "These guys don't operate like the Mafia. They don't make a precise, targeted hit. It ain't like the Tongs either, where they let the honky customers continue eating their sweet-and-sour pork while they blow away the enemy slopes at the next table. These are the kind of guys that like to waste the grandmother in the wheelchair, the dog, the cat. They see a two-month-old baby in a crib, they ice it. And believe me, they don't pick the rattle up off the floor. If they come for you, every bag lady and hot-dog vendor on Vandam Street will go with you. You're not dealing with Ricardo Montalban here."

The chuckle was gone from Cooperman's voice. Even the malice was gone. Things were worse than I'd thought. I needed a drink.

"You know," Cooperman continued almost wistfully, "when I think of two Jewish meatballs like you and your pal Ratso trying to stay ten steps ahead of a private army of bloodthirsty spics with an intelligence network that's probably superior to the FBI . . ."

Cooperman sighed. I tried to swallow. Sometimes it's harder than it looks.

"You might have been set up, pal," he said. "Or maybe somebody's using you for a tethered goat. I can't prove it. In fact, if anybody asks, I didn't even say it."

"Maybe you're wrong," I said. "Maybe they won't figure it out. Maybe they won't bother to come after us."

"Maybe I'm a nigger jet pilot," said Cooperman.

I put my cigar down in the middle of a big, Texas-shaped ashtray. It looked lonely there, burning away deep in the heart of Texas. I hardly noticed Ratso, who, by this time, was hovering close to the desk like an expectant father.

"Well," I said, "other than renting a stateroom on the *Titanic*, what do you suggest we do?"

"Absolutely nothing. And keep your fingers crossed. I got to run."

"One more thing," I said. "What's a Colombian necktie?"

524   "That," said Cooperman, "is where they slit your throat vertically, pull your tongue out through the opening, and let it hang down your neck. Colombian necktie."

"Nah, don't think I want it. Too trendy. It'd clash with my hunting vest."

"Wear whatever you want," said Cooperman. "It's your funeral."

38

When I finally got to sleep that night, I dreamed I was in the office of a beautiful female psychiatrist. Apparently things hadn't been working out too well for me and I was seeing this lady shrink to find out what was wrong.

"Have you ever been involved in joshman?" she asked. She lowered her voice slightly when she said the word *joshman.*

"What is joshman?" I asked.

She seemed a little surprised that I didn't know. She looked at me for a moment. Then she said very clearly and distinctly, "Joshman is when a man kisses another man on the knees."

I woke up suddenly. I'd heard a sound that I didn't think belonged in the dream. I hit the lights and checked the clock by my bedside. Closing in on 3 A.M. I listened.

Except for Ratso's rather unpleasant snoring, there was nothing. I was almost ready to kill the light and get back to my joshman dream when I heard it again. Sounded like a muffled clang. Maybe it was a shy trolley. I walked over to the bedroom window and looked, but it didn't do much good. No one had opened that window or even seen through it in forty-seven years. Not that there was much of a view. Garbage-truck docking area.

Grime was a nice word for what was covering the outside of the window. It was rusted shut tighter than some people's minds. The window worked about as well as everything else in the loft. I kind of liked it that way. Always live in a house that's older than you are.

I heard the sound again. This time I had it. A drunk throwing rocks against the fire escape. It was as common in New York as crickets in the country. Then a shrill voice that sounded like it was coming all the way from Brooklyn shattered the night.

"Hey, Tom fucking Sawyer! Throw down the goddamn puppet head!"

It was Rambam.

I walked across the cold floor of the loft, past Ratso's torporous body, past the cat stirring slightly in the rocker, to the kitchen. I turned the kitchen light on. If the Colombians wanted me, I figured they could dream up more creative methods than shooting a man standing at a window.

The puppet head smiled down on me from on top of the refrigerator. The puppet head always looked like it was smiling. You'd look like you were smiling, too, if you had a large house key wedged in your teeth.

I picked up the puppet head, opened the window, and read Vandam Street like a gutsy quarterback who was playing hurt. Rambam came out of the darkness from my right at a measured pace. Throwing into the wind, I tried to lead him, but the parachute didn't hang quite as much as I'd expected. He had to run into the gutter and halfway onto the street to make the catch.

"Complete to Rambam," he shouted.

I closed the window before I froze to death. Through the window, I watched Rambam with no little degree of fascination as he spiked the puppet head in the gutter.

Rambam came in the door wearing his green Israeli Army jacket just about the time I was getting into my old hunting vest. East meets West. Or, if you spoke with a Yiddish accent, East meets vest. It wasn't terribly funny. It was just the kind of thing you think of when you don't want to think about everything else.

"Parked way up the street," said Rambam, as he flipped me the puppet head. "In case the Colombians try to put a potato in my tailpipe."

I examined the puppet head carefully. It looked happier, more alive, and more purposeful than many faces I passed on the street every day. And it didn't use the word *marvelous* too much. I was starting to get kind of attached to it. I placed it gently back on top of the refrigerator.

"Alas, poor Yorick," I said, "you have a head the size of a LeSueur pea."

I took the bottle of Jameson and two appropriately stemmed glasses and sat down at the desk with Rambam. We had a round or two and I ran down for him everything that had happened in the last twenty-four hours. Leila's apartment, Leila, Hector, Carlos, meeting Cooperman and Fox on the street before the bust, the *Daily News* story, and Cooperman's phone call earlier in the evening. The only thing I didn't tell him about was the joshman dream. I didn't think it was pertinent to the case. Also, I didn't want any spurious rumors flying around New York about unfounded joshman episodes in my past. Even one can ruin a guy.

When I'd finished telling Rambam everything I knew about the Colombians, which wasn't a hell of a lot, he sat back in the chair and thought about it for a moment. Then he took the bottle and poured us both another shot.

"You're leaving tomorrow," he said. "You and Ratso. You're going back to your ranch in Texas and you're going to stay there. I'll pick you up and put you on a plane. All you got to do is pack, check the plane schedules, and call me and I'll pick you up. Any problem with that?"

"Well," I said.

"Fine. That's it." He stood up. "Look," said Rambam, "the average detective, third grade, earns about thirty-six thousand a year. The average Carlos character spends more than that a *day* just on payoffs. They know all about you already. You've got zero chance. I'll pick you guys up tomorrow."

"You want to crash here?"

"Where the hell am I gonna sleep?"

"Well," I said, "you could sleep on the couch with Ratso."

"Or?"

"Or you could sleep in the bedroom with me. There's only one bed, but we could put a guitar case between us like we used to do on the road with the band to keep us from accidentally hosing somebody in the middle of the night."

"Thanks for the offer," said Rambam. "It's very attractive, but I don't want to wake up with a Colombian butterfly."

"What's a Colombian butterfly?" I asked.

"That's where they take your lungs out of you while you're still alive, and leave them suspended outside your body."

"Charming," I said.

"Sweet dreams," said Rambam.

After he'd left I walked over to the kitchen window and looked out into the nothingness of the New York night. It almost didn't matter whether all this stuff was real or not. It was bad enough either way. I didn't know what to think. I didn't know what to do.

I stared into the darkness again and I thought of Wyatt Earp's brother Virgil's last words. All of the Earp brothers were very close and they were said to have believed strongly in life after death. The legend is that when Virgil was dying after a gunfight, Wyatt knelt by his brother's side in the dust and asked him what he saw.

"Wyatt," he reportedly said, "I don't see a fuckin' thing."

39

New York's a tar baby. Once you're here, it's hell to get away. Like most New Yorkers who plan to leave the city, we didn't make it.

Everyone thinks they're not going to die in New York. Everyone thinks they're going to die someplace nice like St. Penisburg, Florida. Everyone is wrong.

There are some interesting, if not particularly relevant, exceptions. Of course, when the subject is death it's sometimes hard to say what might or might not be relevant. Maybe nothing's relevant. Be that as it may, Damon Runyon—born, of course, in Manhattan, Kansas—wanted to die in New York and did, and had his ashes scattered over Broadway from a small plane flown by Eddie Rickenbacker. George S. Kaufman, the playwright, wished to die in New York and he also got his wish. Kaufman, however, requested in his will that his ashes be thrown in the face of the theater critic for *The New York Times*.

The only other guy that ever did anything very significant with his ashes was Joe Hill, who was wrongfully tried and hanged on a trumped-up charge in Utah. Joe Hill's ashes were scattered, at his request, in every state of the union except Utah. Never cared for Utah much myself.

The lesson in all of this, I suppose, is that it's a good thing to get your ashes hauled as much as possible before they're finally scattered.

Ratso was waking up.

It was not a nice thing to see.

I busied myself with feeding the cat some tuna and the espresso machine some ground coffee beans while Ratso proceeded with his morning ablutions. By nine o'clock Friday morning, Ratso and I were drinking cups of espresso and looking at each other across the kitchen table like Ward and June Cleaver.

I filled Ratso in on Rambam's visit and told him what Rambam had advised. He seemed to take it soberly enough.

"We've been warned twice now," I said. "Once by Cooperman and once by Rambam. Of course, you don't have to stay here in the loft or go to Texas. You could leave now and go to your place or lie low somewhere else."

"Yeah," said Ratso, "but if their intelligence network is superior to the fucking FBI, they already know more about me than my mother. I think we're in this one together, Kinkster. And I don't really believe these guys are going to come after us. Anyway, it's too late to run and they don't have bagels in Texas."

"Great," I said. "So I'm joined at the hip to a guy who wears a coonskin cap without the tail and a dead man's shoes."

"It could be worse," said Ratso. "There could be a dead man standing in your shoes."

I got us both another round of espresso and extracted my first cigar of the morning from Sherlock Holmes's head.

"You know," said Ratso, "I wonder if these guys—these Colombians—could have been in this thing from the start. After all, you met Leila at the cat show. Then, very shortly after that, you're shot with a dart filled with a lethal dose of lion tranquilizer. And these guys, from everything I've read, aren't all that far removed from the jungle themselves."

"I've considered that." I lit the cigar and watched the smoke dance in the sunshine that was coming in the window. It was a cold but beautiful February day and there wasn't a Colombian in sight.

"And then," Ratso continued, "there's this Colombian

necktie business.'' My hand went unconsciously to my throat.

''Go on.''

''Well, I don't know if these guys have a tongue fetish or what, but there seems to be some common ground between the Colombian necktie and what happened to Rick 'Slick' Goldberg.''

''My dear Ratso, I don't know what I'd do without you.''

''So you think they iced Goldberg.''

''Actually, my conclusions are quite the opposite of that.''

''What do you mean?''

''I mean these are early days, Watson. Too early in the case to idly discuss it with you.''

''You're a sharing, caring kind of guy, Sherlock. It's inspiring to work with a guy who gives so much of himself.''

I puffed on the cigar a bit and looked at Ratso. ''As Marco Polo said on his deathbed in 1324: 'I have not told one half of what I saw.' ''

''Yeah,'' said Ratso, ''but those were the Dark Ages. Today inquiring minds want to know.''

''In this case,'' I said, ''curiosity might just kill the rat.''

Not long thereafter, Ratso departed the loft in somewhat of a snit. I let him go. It was probably safer on the streets of New York than it was these days at 199B Vandam. Who the hell knows what's safe anymore? Some people claim the smoke from my cigar is drifting over to them and creating a health hazard, but I don't let it bother the Kinkster. The main health hazard in the world today is people who don't love themselves.

To cover all bases, I went to the desk, got the number of American Airlines, and gave it a call. All the American agents were busy so I had to listen to some tape-recorded Musak by the Captain and Toenail. Where were the Disappointer Sisters when you needed them?

It would be somewhat ironic if I were to net myself a

532   Colombian butterfly while waiting for the next available agent to answer the phone. For about two or three minutes I listened to the kind of crap that would make an elevator blush. Then I just said to hell with it.

40

The call that was going to change my life did not come that afternoon. There were two others, however.

The first was from Rambam, who felt I was laying my life on the line by not going to Texas. I told him I was laying my life on the line every time I ate a frankfurter at Madison Square Garden, but I wasn't leaving town because a cop and a private investigator were getting a little nervous in the service. He said something, probably to relieve his frustration and disgust, and then hung up.

It was a gorgeous day, as we say in New York, even if you're standing at the kitchen window of your loft anticipating that many men will come hurt you. The buildings looked gorgeous. The pigeons looked gorgeous. The prostitutes looked gorgeous. Actually, these things always have had an inherent beauty, but people have just tried too hard to look at them wrong. You come to see what you want to see.

I wanted to see this whole tension convention blow over. I wanted to continue with the case—find Slick Goldberg's killer, find Rocky. I wanted a lot of things and it didn't look like I was going to get them. I had about as much chance of coming out of this situation a happy American as Oliver Twist had of getting more.

The phone call that was to fling us headlong into something that nobody would think was gorgeous came at around three-fifteen that afternoon.

Interestingly enough, it was from Jane Meara.

41

It was Friday evening and the shadows were beginning to fall on Central Park as Ratso and I, who had reached at least some form of rapprochement, stood looking at a tall building on the corner of Seventh Avenue and Central Park South.

"Too bad," said Ratso. "We're only two blocks from the Carnegie Deli."

"If we get through this alive, I'll buy you a bowl of matzo-ball soup."

"I really wanted a Reuben sandwich."

"Fine."

It was cold and dark and it was getting colder and darker and I was trying to explain to Ratso what we were doing there.

"Jane Meara called me today and she was quite distressed."

"So what's new?"

"My dear Ratso, one would think you could dredge up a little more sensitivity for a person who's lost a cat."

"Go on, Mr. Sensitivity."

"Well, Landis called Jane in and said her work was falling down since all this started, and Eugene was coarse enough to suggest she forget about Rocky and get a dog."

"How thoughtless." Ratso's eyes were straying in the direction of the Carnegie Deli.

"But the real reason we're here is that Jane was supposed to have lunch today with an editor from another publishing house whose name is Estelle Beekman. I know Estelle slightly myself. She's the author of a recent, critically acclaimed novel and she's sort of a recluse, but a very responsible person in the publishing business. She comes from an extremely wealthy family and she lives in this building. One of the things she wrote about in her novel is that she had been deathly afraid of cats since she was a child. To this day, she abhors them.''

"I like her already," said Ratso. "But why are we here?"

"She did not show up for her luncheon meeting with Jane, no one at her office knows where she is, and her telephone has been busy for about four hours now."

"Maybe she's talking to her shrink about a Tom and Jerry cartoon she once saw when she was a child."

"I don't think so, Ratso. There's no conversation on the line. I checked with the operator myself."

"Why don't we call the police?"

"It may come to that, but with this broad and this building, Jane thought it might be better if we were to run a quick check on the situation first ourselves. We wouldn't want to create any social embarrassment, would we?"

"Of course not," said Ratso in a voice that was possibly not quite as sincere as one would have hoped.

"Okay," I said, "there's about fifteen doormen and all of them are surly. I'm going to call a friend of mine who also lives here and then we'll go up and see the lay of the land."

"The lay of the broad is what we'll probably see," said Ratso.

"This is a very respectable broad, Ratso. She told me once that she hardly believes in social intercourse, much less sexual. I'll be right back."

I went to a pay phone on the corner of Seventh Avenue next to the building and put in two bits. Nothing happened. No dial tone. No change. I took it in stride. The more storms one rides out in life, the better the captain one becomes of one's soul.

I tried the next pay phone. This wasn't easy because an

escaped gorilla had ripped the receiver completely off the machine and left the wire dangling in the night air like the withered arm of a peasant.

The third pay phone worked fine and after three rings I got through to my friend. What hath God wrought?

Nick "Chinga" Chavin, the guy I was calling in the building where Estelle Beekman lived, was a country singer turned ad exec. I knew the building, one of the poshest in New York, because I'd stayed a couple times with Chinga as his house pest there before I grew up and rented a loft and had to deal with house pests of my own.

One of the things Chinga liked to do late at night was to fire Chinese bottle rockets from his fourth-floor balcony at the New York Athletic Club just across Seventh Avenue. According to Chinga, the New York Athletic Club has, to this day, never admitted Jews or Negroes as members. They don't much like Chinese bottle rockets either. But on many occasions I'd witnessed Chinga laying siege to the club, aiming particularly at the Aryan shadows jogging along behind the tinted glass.

Now, Chinga agreed to call down to the concierge and tell him Ratso and I were his guests so we could get past the fifteen surly doormen.

He did and we did.

I told the elevator guy to take us to the sixteenth floor. We found the stairs, walked up three, didn't meet anyone. We wandered down a hallway awhile and found 19G, Estelle Beekman's apartment. The door was slightly ajar.

"Oh, shit," I said, "I don't like to see this." I'd seen some things behind slightly ajar doors in my time, and none of them had turned out to be a free trip for two to Acapulco.

"What is it?" Ratso asked.

"We're about to find out," I said.

I opened the door.

42

We walked in as gingerly as two astronauts stepping onto the moon. The place was quiet as a library and almost as big. We listened. There was a soft but persistent electronic sound coming from somewhere on our left. It was quiet and discreet, but it was there. Sort of like a coke dealer's beeper going off at a backgammon tournament.

We followed the sound for about half a mile and wound up in the kitchen. The telephone receiver was lying forlornly on the drainboard. I took my snot rag out of my hip pocket, picked up the phone, and put it back on the hook. Sorry, nobody home.

We wandered back into the living room. It was dark, so we turned on a few lights. There were several big ornate lamps. There was track lighting. None of it removed the gloom, the visceral sense of foreboding that seemed to cover the pores like sweet, death-scented, coconut sun-tan oil. There was death all over the place. The only thing missing was the body.

Ratso and I made a cursory tour of the lushly furnished living room. It was like a rather macabre open house where you couldn't find the homeowner but you knew she must be hanging around somewhere. Or lying in one of the bedrooms. Or tied up.

There was expensive-looking chrome and leather furniture, Persian rugs, several large pieces of sculpture that must've meant something to somebody somewhere. Large vases, jade carvings.

"Jesus Christ," said Ratso, gazing at a picture on the wall, "look at that."

"Yeah," I said. "That's nice."

"You know what it is?"

"Sure," I said. "That's a picture of some fat naked ladies dancing with each other." I took a cigar out of one of the little stitched pockets on my hunting vest.

"It's a Matisse," said Ratso.

"It's a triumph of art over life," I said, as I lit the cigar.

"I'm glad you appreciate it," said Ratso. I blew a cold stream of cigar smoke in the direction of the painting.

"I don't," I said. "I just think those fat, naked ladies dancing with each other have outlived Estelle Beekman."

We walked from one posh room into another. No Estelle. Even the bathroom was something to see. She didn't have a twenty-seven-foot jade toilet seat like Kenny Rogers, but it was definitely a five-star pissoir.

"Since there's no dead body in the bathtub," said Ratso, "I think I'll use the facilities here."

"Well, I'm sure it's all right with Estelle, wherever she is. It could be seen as a trifle gauche under the circumstances."

"I've got to urinate like a racehorse." Ratso unzipped his fly and I zipped out into the hallway.

"Don't whiz in the bidet," I shouted through the partially closed door.

"I'm surprised you even know what that is."

"Of course I do. Bidet lived a little before the time of Matisse. Many people feel that Matisse stole a lot of Bidet's ideas. Bidet had a splashy style and Matisse was kind of jealous—"

"All right," shouted Ratso, "that's enough. But what's she doing with a goddamned bidet if she doesn't believe in sexual intercourse?"

"We find her, we'll ask her," I said. Never trust a person who's afraid of cats.

I walked into Estelle Beekman's bedroom and turned on the light. There was no dead body on the bed either, but lying on the floor there was a key that I didn't particularly like the look of. I was about to pick it up when I heard a sound that turned my blood to Perrier on the rocks with a little twist of something I didn't need at all.

It was a cat's meow. It was coming from the closet.

I listened. It came again. It was joined by another meow.

Normally, the cat's meow does not turn my kneecaps to Smucker's. Even after the dart gun incident and the meow message on Jane Meara's answering machine, I had not felt that the voice of the cat could be, in itself, a manifestation of evil. Now, in this place, I wasn't so sure.

I got out my snot rag, picked up the key, and opened the locked door of the closet just as Ratso came walking in from the boudoir. For a moment, nothing happened. Then two scrawny street cats came toward us as if they were walking out of a Disney movie. One of them purred and rubbed itself against Ratso's legs. He moved away in disgust.

"What're these two cats doing in here?" Ratso fairly screamed.

"Maybe they're two homosexuals and they're just coming out of the closet," I said.

I turned on the light switch in the closet with my snot rag. Nothing happened. I stepped inside the closet. Ratso followed. It was a big closet, crowded with furs and long evening gowns, and it wasn't easy to see with the subdued lighting of the bedroom. I took out my Bic and I gave it a flick.

What we saw on the floor of the closet did not look like a Disney movie at all. It looked more like something brought to you by the people who killed Bambi's mother.

Estelle Beekman's eyes were wide as shiny new nickels, and they reflected pure, polyunsaturated terror. The body was already cold to the touch. The face was blue; the throat muscles looked constricted. One hand had scratched the wall repeatedly in several places, somewhat reminiscent of wall markings I'd heard about elsewhere. For a moment I had a fragment of a picture of an old man walking into a gas chamber playing a violin. Then the Bic became too hot and I let it go.

A few minutes later, I'd opened the sliding door to the private balcony and we were breathing the cold night air and looking down on the New York Athletic Club.

"Let a little of the cigar smoke out of here," I said. "When I call the police I'm going to strive for anonymity."

"So she was frightened to death," said Ratso. "Killed by two cats."

"More likely by Fred Katz. Or the person we think is Fred Katz."

For a few minutes we watched a horse and buggy and a driver in a top hat fighting their way through the taxis, buses, and limos down Seventh Avenue. Happy trails.

Ratso was shaking his head, leaning on the railing. "Literally frightened to death," he mumbled, half to himself, half to Central Park.

I didn't say anything.

"It's a shame," Ratso said. "Estelle Beekman leaving behind all that beautiful shit she's got in there."

We'd only been out on the balcony for a few minutes, but I was feeling colder than I had in years.

I took a last puff on the cigar and flicked it across Seventh Avenue at the New York Athletic Club.

"You never see a luggage rack on a hearse," I said.

43

It was after eleven when Ratso and I climbed out of the hack a few blocks past Sheridan Square and began walking briskly up Vandam Street. It had been a rather gnarly night, cold enough to make a penguin remember his mittens, and it wasn't over yet.

I'd asked Ratso to put a sock on it conversation-wise, so I could use the walk home to sort things out a bit. Sometimes a walk in brutal weather could freeze extraneous sensory input and make you AWOL upstairs, leaving you with the ice-cold truth. Sometimes all you got was a runny nose. But that, along with not leaving fingerprints, was what snot rags were for.

I let my mind run free. I thought of Eskimos. Two Eskimos rubbing their noses together. Nine months later they'd probably have a little booger. I thought of icebergs. I thought of Goldberg. Goldberg had liked cats. He'd been killed. Estelle Beekman had been afraid of cats. She'd been killed. Jane Meara loved cats. Her life, it appeared, was in danger.

Something was wrong here, I thought. I'd have to call Lobster and find out more about Slick Goldberg. Maybe cats weren't the common denominator here. If not—what was? . . . And Leila . . . why in the hell hadn't she called? I knew she might be lying low after the bust and the *Daily News* story, but I missed her. Maybe even . . .

"Kinkster," said Ratso suddenly, "the fucking door to the building's open."

It was true. It was nudging eleven-thirty at night and the large metal door to the building was standing wide open. You left a door open in New York, you'd be lucky if a family of Rastafarians was all you got.

"Could be a careless lesbian," I said.

As we rode up in the freight elevator with the one exposed light bulb, the hairs on the back of my neck began to rise as well. I was visited by a trapped, desperate, doomed feeling. It's hard to run away when you're in a freight elevator.

"Next time," I said, "remind me to take the stairs."

"If there is a next time," said Ratso.

When the doors opened on the fourth floor we fairly leaped out of the elevator into the dimly lit hallway. I already had my key in the door of the loft when something made me stop. I looked back and saw Ratso standing stiff in his coonskin cap in the middle of the hallway like a chunky, slightly Semitic statue of Davy Crockett. With his right hand, he was pointing at the door.

On the door to the loft was a paw print of what looked like a jaguar or a large jungle cat. It was red and still dripping and, almost certainly, done in blood.

"Careless lesbian?" Ratso asked.

"Maybe somebody knocked too hard," I said.

44

In pre-Colombian times, life was much simpler.

That was the thought that was in my head when I woke up early Saturday morning with a ringing in my ears. It was the blower.

I grabbed the blower and looked at the clock by the bedside. It was 6:15 A.M., a fairly obscene time for anybody to be awake. It was also, it emerged, a fairly obscene phone call.

"I want you," said Leila. She sounded like she was right next to me in bed with no guitar case between us.

"Do I have your little heart in my hip pocket?" I asked. That was as coy as I got at six-fifteen in the morning.

"Yes," she said, "but I have you right here."

"Where's here?"

"I'll give you a hint—it's right where I want you."

Great waves of passion rolled over me. I didn't know if it was Leila's Palestinian, Colombian, or New York background that enabled her to have such an effect on me. All three cultures seem to have sort of a jaded, hedonistic attitude toward love and sex. Thank God I'm a country boy.

"Hold the weddin'," I said.

"Wedding?" said Leila. "This is awful sudden. I need some time. If we do get married, though, I think I'm going to make you wear a veil." She laughed confidently.

"Castrating bitch."

"I'm not a castrating bitch," she said. "I just want the West Bank."

"It's yours," I said, "if you promise to always walk ten steps behind me." I got out of bed, took off the sarong, and put on some jeans. I managed to zip them up without killing myself.

"Honey," said Leila, "Carlos promised me he's not going to hurt you. He may just try to scare you a little."

"Yeah," I said. "He scared me a little last night."

"Don't worry, my brother won't hurt you. They're having some kind of meeting tonight, but I'll keep you posted. Everything's going to be all right."

"Where are you?" I asked.

There was a pause. Finally, Leila said, "I'm with my Uncle Abdul—don't laugh, that's not his real name. I have to be very careful just now. We can't be seen together. There is another family that hates our family and would do anything to harm me and those I love."

"Okay, Juliet."

"It is a little like that, isn't it?"

"Yeah," I said, "except all the warring families are on your side."

"I don't want to get you in any trouble. I don't want anything to happen to you. And Kinky—"

"What?"

"I think I love you."

There was a long pause and Leila might've been crying.

As I hung up, I wondered why I couldn't just meet a broad at the mailbox on the day her Visa card arrived. Why did things always have to be so melodramatic and convoluted?

"One of these days," I said to the cat, "they're going to make a life out of my movie."

45

Maybe I should've driven my car into a tree in high school, but I didn't. Jesus or Allah or somebody wanted me to be drinking hot chocolate in a drafty loft and watching freezing rain slant down by the window at 8 A.M. that Saturday morning. I thought I'd give the espresso machine a rest. When you drink too much espresso, you think too much. When you think too much, you can't see the forest for the tree you should've driven your car into in high school.

I felt I was close to achieving peace in the Middle East, but no matter what I felt for Leila, I couldn't let her assessment of her brother, Carlos, determine whether I was to live or die. According to her, Carlos was merely a macho practical joker. He had nothing better to do than go around scaring people who weren't too secure to begin with.

What if she didn't know her brother as well as she thought she did? Maybe because she loved him, she couldn't see what he really was. Maybe because she thought she loved me, she was shielding me from the truth. Maybe because I thought I loved her I was placing myself, Ratso, the cat, and an innocent lesbian dance class in grave danger.

That didn't say much for love.

Something else was bothering me, too. I tongued a few more mini-marshmallows out of the hot chocolate. Had to keep in practice. I ate the marshmallows and thought about it. The bloody paw print on the door. I'd seen it before somewhere.

I fed the cat some tuna. They say if you feed a cat tuna all the time, you'll turn the cat into a tuna addict. Makes the cat finicky and irritable. I say, "How can you tell?" My cat happens to have always been finicky and irritable and I've always been finicky and irritable and we don't need other people telling us how to run our lives.

Hot chocolate and mini-marshmallows go well with cigars and rain. Of course, just about anything goes well with cigars and rain except asparagus tips or whatever they call them. Bean sprouts. I was sitting in the rocker, working on hot chocolate number three and cigar number one and watching Ratso sleep, when I remembered where I'd seen the red paw print.

So as not to wake Ratso, I padded quietly, like a jungle cat, over to the desk. Then I picked up the blower on the left and dialed a number in Austin, Texas.

46

Back when Margaret Mead was jumping rope in the schoolyard, Jim Bone and I had taken Anthropology 301 together at the University of Texas at Austin. Of course, now he was Dr. Jim Bone, but I didn't hold that against him. Jim had retained everything he'd learned in the anthropological field, traveled the world, and gone on to become one of the foremost experts on ancient, obscure, and lost cultures. I'd repressed everything I'd learned, traveled the world, and become a country singer who, some cynics would say, is probably also an expert on lost culture.

Jim had spent considerable time exploring in South America and had been the first white man to do a lot of things. One of them was hosing a piñata. It was only 7:30 A.M., Texas time, but in New York, I had the spiritually debilitating feeling that time was running out.

"Jimbo! Leap sideways!" I said. "Somebody put a red paw print on the door of my loft."

Jim sounded a bit grumpy but coherent. "Bit obsolete," he said. "People haven't been doing that for a thousand years."

"Yeah, well, somebody did it to me last night."

"I'll tell you what it's *not*," he said.

"What?"

"A 'Happy Bar Mitzvah' sign."

What followed was a long and somewhat ill bout of laughter. Only idiots or geniuses laughed that way at seven-thirty in the morning. It was dealer's choice.

When the maniacal laughter had subsided, Jim gave me a crash course on the lowland Wachíchi, many of whom had been jaguar priests, and all of whom appeared to have vanished from the face of the earth in the space of one week, over a thousand years ago.

The Wachíchi worshiped a god called Kukulcán, the cat god, who some believe was an early spaceman, and who disappeared into the skies forever in 986 A.D. The Wachíchi were seagoing colonists, contemporaries of the Aztecs, Incas, Babylonians, and ancient Romans. The tradition of wearing masks so the sun couldn't see their faces originated with the Wachíchi, was later borrowed by the Iroquois, and was even later taken on by many disingenuous Americans who still didn't wish the sun to see their faces.

The jaguar priests of the Wachíchi, in their darker moments, were said to dress up as cats. It is known that they dealt with the structure of evil, not the structure of accomplishment. The information, according to Dr. Bone, comes from the *Chilam Balam*, which are roughly the New World equivalent of the Dead Sea Scrolls—except, again according to Dr. Bone, that they are about one hundred times spookier.

"So you've become involved with a cat lately," Jim said.

"You've been readin' my mail, brother. Several weeks ago a friend of mine's cat disappeared during a cat show at Madison Square Garden and very little's been the same since."

"Sounds about right. Any South or Central American types in your life currently?"

"You're battin' a thousand."

"Are they maybe Colombians or Peruvians—?"

"Colombians."

"Sorry to hear that."

"So am I."

"Let me get a cup of coffee. Hold the line. I want to think about this for a moment."

While Dr. Jim Bone got a cup of coffee in Austin, Texas, I took the opportunity to move smoothly into hot chocolate number four and to perform the prenuptial arrangements on cigar number two. I lit the cigar and tongued a few more mini-marshmallows. There was a certain sweet afterglow to the combination that I'd never felt before in my life. Jim was back on the line.

"No one knows for sure," he said, "what happened to the Wachíchi. Did they disappear? Did they sail somewhere and recolonize? But around 1000 A.D. the Norse fought many wars with a group they called the cat people. This occurred in the New York-New England area. One of the results was a tribe of Indians that spoke a combination of Old Norse and Quiché. Quiché, of course, was the language of the Wachíchi."

"This is," I said, "no doubt fascinating. But how is it relevant?" This is one of the problems you encounter in dealing with anthropologists and archaeologists. They prefer the past to the present. How stupid of them.

"What I'm trying to establish in your adult brain," Jim said rather irritably, "is that there is a long tradition for the Wachíchi to be visiting New York City."

"Unpleasant," I said.

"Not from an anthropological view."

"Fine."

"I'm not trying to scare you, but people have traveled a lot farther for a lot stupider reasons than finding a cat."

"Certainly this is a bit farfetched."

"Jason and the Golden Fleece. The quest for the Holy Grail. Hell, the Egyptians went all the way to Tunisia for a missing finger ring. It's not that strange."

It was that strange.

Art Linkletter was right, I thought. People *are* funny. Of course, they're not quite as funny as Art Linkletter, but they're funny enough to make you die laughing.

"Listen to me," he said. "Can't you understand this? Am I here alone? Am I driving through a ghost town? You may be on the verge of a major anthropological discovery."

One of the little difficulties with the world is that it's riddled with anthropologists who travel to the far corners of the earth and bore people with their theories. My father once told me that in Greenland every family has five kids, three dogs, two chickens, and one anthropologist.

"Like what?" I asked. "Finding a fossilized turd in the litter box?"

Dr. Jim Bone was not amused. "Wake up, man. Don't you know what that red cat strike on the door means?"

"That's why I called you, Jim."

"Well, I'll tell you," he said evenly. "That's the standard Wachíchi mark of death."

"I'll jot that down in my field notes," I said. But I knew I wouldn't have to jot it down to remember it. If I'd had any field notes and if I'd tried jotting something down in them, I couldn't've been sure my hand wouldn't shake.

"That cat you're looking for," said Jim. "The one that's missing. That cat wouldn't have four white paws, would it?"

I felt like an ancient civilization had come crumbling down on top of me while I'd been out in the field looking for arrowheads. For a moment I was speechless, a rare occurrence indeed. Then that good old twentieth-century indifference came roaring back. Man is nothing if not resilient. Only sometimes there's little enough to be resilient about.

Four little white sweat socks, I thought.

"How," I asked, "in the name of Kukulcán, did you know that?"

"Because the Wachíchi had another name for Kukulcán."

"Yeah? What?"

"They sometimes called him," said Dr. Jim Bone, "the God Who Stands with His Feet in the Clouds."

47

The telephone works in mysterious ways. Sometimes it brings you cheerful little insipid greetings from cheerful little insipid people. Sometimes it leaves you just a little to the north of scared shitless.

I was cleaning the red paw print of Kukulcán off the door of the loft with hot water and Ajax when Ratso almost stumbled on the bucket on his way into the bathroom.

"What the fuck are you doin'?" he asked. "You're gonna want lab tests, aren't you?"

"The only thing I want a lab test on is your brain," I said a bit unkindly.

"Yeah, but if it's human blood, or animal blood, that might tell us something."

"It's already told us something," I said. I gave Ratso a quick rundown on the phone call I'd had with Jim Bone. When I finished he tried to whistle but it was too early in the morning. He settled for looking pale.

"The last thing the cops want to hear," I said as I continued washing off the blood, "is some yarn about ancient civilizations. Cops are not anthropologists. They find other ways of being tedious."

"I still don't think you should've washed it off."

"It's either that or look at the son of a bitch every time I come in. It's probably nothing anyway."

Ratso didn't look convinced.

As I paced up and down the loft and listened to him gargle,

cough, and flush the toilet about seven times, I didn't think I was too convinced either. All of us will be relics someday, I thought. Let's just hope somebody nice finds us. It was probably too much to ask that somebody nice should find us while we're still alive.

Ratso came out of the bathroom, got dressed, and put on a pair of telephone repairman's rubber boots that almost went up to his waist.

"I hate rain," he said.

"I love the rain," I said.

The cat, who was sleeping peacefully on the rocker, didn't say anything, but it was safe to say, I thought, that she loved the rain, too.

I looked at the open door of the loft. There was still a ghostly shadow where the red paw print had been. It didn't look like the kind of thing Ajax and hot water would get rid of. I doubted if Mr. Clean was going to cut much ice either. I was going to have to get a new door or a new loft.

No matter what I did, I had the feeling the ghostly shadow would always be there. If not on the door, in the nightmare of my mind's eye.

48

The snow was beginning to mix with the rain as Ratso and I walked along Twelfth Street that Saturday night. It was just a little after eight o'clock and young men were picking up young women for dining engagements. Young men were picking up young men for dining engagements. Young women were picking up young women for dining engagements. You are what you eat.

It was Saturday night. It was the Village. It was America. It was 1988. It was cold. About the only thing it wasn't, was very pleasant. In the far reaches of my peripheral vision I could see a specter lurking. I could feel the frostbitten wings of angels occasionally brushing against my cowboy hat. Something besides rain, snow, cheap perfume, and roasting chestnuts was in the air. It was death—possibly the only dinner guest more unwelcome than Sidney Poitier.

As we crossed Fifth Avenue, the rain seemed to let up and the snow began to fall more heavily. In the white-and-gray dimness I could just make out the giant iguana on the roof of the Lone Star Cafe one block up the street. It stood like a beacon to rather ill pilgrims. Even in that weather, I felt the chill it gave me.

It'd been a little over a year ago that I'd played the Lone Star. It had been the performance of my life and damn nearly the last performance of my life. Now everything was back to normal at the Lone Star except that Cleve was sending me postcards from the mental hospital, and when I wanted a waiter to bring my check I seldom used the phrase "Drop the hatchet" anymore.

On the other side of Fifth, a cat jumped out of a garbage can. From force of habit, I tailed him a little way down the block. It wasn't Rocky. Kind of hard to keep your mind on a missing cat when you knew that soon you might be missing your lungs.

We banked a sharp left in the middle of Twelfth between Fifth and University and went down a few steps and through a couple doors into Asti's Italian restaurant, where the waiters, bartenders, busboys, and the guy that checks your hat and coat all sing opera.

As we came in the place, Augie, the owner, was behind the bar banging out "Dixie" on the rows of bottles. Then he moved over to the cash register and played a few more choruses, using the keys to ring up the melody and sliding the cash drawer in and out for percussion.

"Versatile," said Ratso to a group of well-dressed European tourists. They looked at him like they thought he'd just flown in from the coast and hadn't bothered to take a plane.

Saturday night is not the best night to go to Asti's. There're a few too many tourists from Iowa, Japan, and the Upper West Side. But if it wasn't for tourists in New York, they'd probably have to close the Empire State Building, the Staten Island ferry, and the Statue of Liberty, because the locals would stay away in droves.

My knowledge of opera extends to *The Student Prince*, which I know isn't really opera but is very good, and sometimes *La Bohème*. Asti's draws heavily from both of these, some show tunes, some long-haired, fat-lady type songs that are good to get drunk by, and medleys of things like "Dixie," "When Irish Eyes Are Smiling," and "Hava Nagila," which say something to everyone but Japanese businessmen.

Asti's was founded by Augie's father on the date Caruso died. You can't urinate in the place without coming face to face with autographed photos of Toscanini sailing for

America and Caruso singing an aria. Augie assures me Caruso did not die after he ate there.

Augie finished playing the cash register to thunderous applause and showed the Rat and me to a table near the small stage. Vittorio, in his little Russian cap, was singing "If I Were a Rich Man" when a large form came lumbering up to our table.

"May I join you girls?" it asked. It was McGovern.

"How the hell did you know we were here?" I said a bit irritably.

"Got a tip from Reuters," said McGovern, as he sat down with us and ordered a Vodka McGovern from a passing waiter. "That's vodka, orange juice, soda, with lime. Vodka McGovern."

"No problem," said the waiter.

"I'll have a Vodka McGovern, too," said Ratso.

"I'll have some kind of obscure, expensive cognac," I said. It was a good thing to warm the blood and I wasn't happy enough with McGovern to order a Vodka McGovern, or even to eat one of my favorite dishes he cooked, Chicken McGovern. In the back of my mind still lurked, despite his denials, the thought that my old pal might've put my life in jeopardy.

"So tell me," said McGovern, "about that giant red claw mark you found on the door of your loft. That must've scared the shit out of you two."

I looked at Ratso and Ratso looked at me. We both shrugged.

"How'd you know about that?" Ratso asked, suddenly nervous.

"I have sources," McGovern laughed, "among the gay terpischorean community."

"Goddamn poufters," said Ratso.

"Alarmingly homophobic," I said, as I sipped a little of the obscure and expensive cognac. "As Rita Mae Brown says, 'If Michelangelo had been a heterosexual, the Sistine Chapel would have been painted basic white with a roller.'"

Ratso looked at me. "I didn't know you were into such highbrow writers," he said.

I sipped the cognac. It tasted like semiviscous airplane fuel from the Amelia Earhart era. I didn't respond.

"Better than no brow at all," said McGovern.

49

I was working on a linguine with red clam sauce when Pasquale hit the stage simultaneously singing Figaro and demonstrating how to make a pizza. He threw the spinning dough in the air repeatedly until it reached a diameter of about three feet. Then he put it on his head like a scarf and sang a verse of "Don't Cry for Me, Argentina."

Pasquale now tore little balls of dough from the pizza and threw them to various diners seated around the place. Eddie, the piano player, kicked into high gear and the patrons threw the dough balls back toward Pasquale, who, holding a tambourine in front of his face like a hoop, caught them in his teeth.

Through this hail of dough balls walked a figure in a business suit carrying an attaché case. It sat down at our table and ordered a double shot of Bushmills. It was Rambam.

He set the attaché case down on the floor beside his chair and reached across the table to take one of Ratso's Shrimp Puccini.

"I like your Wall Street drag," said Ratso.

"Not everybody has your vast wardrobe, Ratso," I said.

"And not everybody wants to go around looking like a Sonny Bono impersonator," said Rambam.

"Is that why you're affecting that attaché case?" Ratso said.

"No," Rambam laughed, "that's my Uzi submachine gun."

He took the double Bushmills with one large gulp. "Not bad," he said.

At the next table were some opera buffs. One guy was pretty friendly and gave me periodic little nods when a song was performed particularly well. I could kind of cue off of him so I knew how much enthusiasm to applaud and bravo with. He probably took me for an eccentric but willing-to-learn non-opera buff in my cowboy hat, for we exchanged knowing little nods throughout the course of the evening.

There existed, of course, the possibility that he was a homosexual. But opera buffs, like cowboys, are probably a dying breed in this busy world and whatever they choose to do is okay with me. If you ever had to sleep with one of them in the same bed, it might be smart, however, to put a cello case between you.

Augie came by the table. "Would you gentlemen like a round of drinks on the house?" he asked.

It was an offer McGovern couldn't refuse and he appeared as happy as a young gentile on Christmas morning. None of us refused the offer, actually, but some of us were more subdued in our enthusiasm. In a world of empty gestures, coming from Augie at Asti's, this was a real one.

"Shall I check that briefcase for you?" he asked Rambam.

"No, he'll keep it," Ratso said delightedly. "It's his Uzi submachine gun."

Augie laughed. Rambam laughed. McGovern laughed. Even the opera buff at the next table laughed. I went to the men's room to grab a Republican by the neck and watch Arturo Toscanini sail to America.

When I returned to the table, Rambam was on the subject of South American hit men. "Dixie cup kids," he said. "That's what they call them. Completely expendable. Anything happens to 'em, they buy their family a few acres and a couple of pigs and everybody's happy."

"This conversation's off the record, of course," I said to McGovern.

"Of course," said McGovern, his eyes twinkling.

Before we left, we said goodbye to the opera buffs, the piano player, Vittorio, Pasquale, several bartenders and waiters, and, of course, Augie. It was like leaving home. And, unlike Gallagher's Steak House, Asti's lets you wear your hat indoors if you're a cowboy. One of the few things cowboys and Jews have in common is that they both wear their hats indoors and attach a certain amount of importance to it. Hank Williams wore his hat indoors. So did Davy Crockett. A friend of mine, Bob McLane, who was the former chairman of the Gay Texans for Bush Committee, told me that George Bush always took his hat off when he came inside a place. That's another good reason for wearing a hat indoors.

Ratso and McGovern, having already hosed me on the check, were up front getting their coats. I was still dealing with the check, paying the guy at the other cash register, the one that didn't play "Dixie" but just took your money. Ratso circled back briefly, requested and received a receipt for the meal I was paying for, and walked back to the door. Sometimes Ratso could take the word *chutzpah* to a whole other level.

Rambam was having a last drink at the bar as I walked by to get my coat.

"Have one with me for the road," he said.

As I ordered a shot of Jameson, I noticed his attaché case resting on the barstool next to him. "What *is* in the attaché case?" I asked.

In the background a man and woman were dancing together on the stage and singing a duet of "The Surrey with the Fringe on Top." Rambam watched the stage with a faraway expression. When he spoke he had all the even-mindedness of the Mahatma.

"An Uzi submachine gun," said Rambam.

50

We were standing outside Asti's on the sidewalk. McGovern, Ratso, myself, Rambam, and Rambam's attaché case. Either the music and the magic of Asti's was staying with me or it was the red clam sauce.

We drifted with the snow down toward Fifth Avenue. My thoughts skittered like snowflakes through all the cold nights and all the winters of the past. I was wearing my old blue David Copperfield greatcoat that I'd had forever and that Ratso'd always coveted. I'd bought it down the street from the Greyhound station in Albany, New York, shortly after I'd been de-selected from my first Peace Corps program. I thought of Leila with her David Copperfield cap. Maybe someday, if we both lived long enough, we'd take off our David Copperfield clothes and put them together in a warm closet somewhere. Then we could twist away the summer. Be happy Americans. Raise cute, gypsylike children who'd grow up realizing that their parents loved each other. I put my hands down into the big pockets of the coat.

There was something in the right pocket that hadn't been there when I'd left 199B Vandam. It was a package of some sort, but I didn't like surprises and I didn't think it was my birthday.

I took the parcel out and looked at it. It was the size of a thin brick or maybe a somewhat undernourished videocassette. It was wrapped in brown butcher paper and tied with twine. Scrawled in pencil on the butcher paper were the words PERLA YI-YO.

"Maybe it's a valentine present that's a little slow out of the chute," said Ratso. He grabbed the package out of my hand.

"Gimme that," said Rambam. He took the package from Ratso and headed back in the direction of Asti's with it. About halfway there, he found a doorway with steps leading down below ground level. Rambam took out a knife and disappeared from sight.

Ratso, McGovern, and I stood around the little doorway watching Rambam down on the ground fooling with the package. "Under the circumstances," he said, "this could be a bomb."

"Why don't you see if it's ticking?" Ratso said.

"That big-alarm-clock shit went out with the Russian Revolution, Ratso," said Rambam. "Today, they use a little Timex or something—you couldn't even hear it until it's too late."

"If it's our guys," I said, "they probably used a Rolex."

"Very funny," said Rambam, as he gingerly poked the knife into the side of the package. "You want to be very careful, you see, not to mess with the twine. We'll know in a minute . . . one way or another."

I looked over at Ratso and he wasn't there. One moment he was standing between McGovern and myself, and the next moment there was nothing but McGovern's large head blocking out Fifth Avenue.

"Maybe you should call the bomb squad," came a voice from about forty feet away. Ratso was standing in the street on the other side of a parked car.

"Hate cops," said Rambam.

"Maybe you should put those feelings aside," said McGovern, "till this whole thing blows over."

"An unfortunate use of words," I said. "I'm concerned about your use of the language, McGovern. You know what Hemingway said about journalism, don't you?"

"What'd he say?" asked McGovern as both of us backed slightly away from the doorway.

"He said, 'It blunts your instrument.' "

"And hanging around a bullring can sap your semen," said McGovern.

"Holy shit," said Rambam. McGovern and I moved a little farther away. Rambam might be right or he might be off the wall, but it'd be pretty ugly if all of us were to wind up literally off the wall.

"What is it?" called Ratso.

"Come over here and find out," I said.

McGovern and I inched a little closer to the doorway. Rambam had cut a small hole in the side of the package. He'd cut through the butcher paper and through a thick layer of plastic, revealing what looked like a white chemical substance.

"What the hell is it?" asked McGovern.

"Could be potassium chlorate," said Rambam, "a very popular ingredient in explosives today."

It was about at this time that I put my hand back into my coat pocket and found the little card that had apparently fallen off the package.

"Hold the weddin'," I said. "It ain't a bomb. Take a look at this. It's a note that came with the package."

Rambam, knife in hand, came over to me. So did McGovern. Even Ratso found his way back from the street and looked over my shoulder at the little card. It read as follows:

I hope you enjoy this little token of my gratitude. I have great admiration for what you have done. Soon I shall meet you.

THE JAGUAR

"Nice-looking business card," I said.

51

I was standing on a sidewalk in the Village at 11:30 P.M. on a Saturday night, holding in my hands a brick of cocaine whose street value, when cut, would probably exceed a quarter of a million dollars. Want a toot?

I'd been in the presence of that much cocaine before on several occasions, though I doubted if the quality had been commensurate with the current batch. Once in L.A., I'd been sort of house-sitting for a rather shady friend who was off somewhere in the Caribbean. I knew the guy had a few too many Tiffany lamps but I didn't figure it out until I stumbled on a large briefcase full of off-white rocks the size of puppet heads.

Years later, I'd related this story to a well-traveled, coke-dealing Brit in my hotel room in New York and he had not been too impressed. "I've seen the factory, mate," he said.

"Let Ratso hold that shit," said Rambam. The two of them whispered back and forth as my hands trembled.

"Obviously, the Jaguar is Carlos's bitter enemy and believes what he reads in the *Daily News,*" I said, looking pointedly at McGovern.

"I'm not Deep Throat," said McGovern.

Fortunately, the weather was keeping sidewalk traffic to a minimum, but it was still a very strange feeling holding what could surely be my certain death and destruction in my hands. Of course, I'd have some fun before I'd go.

"Better let one of us keep it," said Rambam, like he was talking to a child.

"C'mon," I said. "I haven't touched the stuff in almost seventy-two hours now. I had to quit when Bob Marley fell out of my left nostril." I was breaking out in a sweat.

I had torn off some more of the butcher paper and the plastic and run a little taste test to establish that it wasn't potassium chlorate. It wasn't.

I gripped the packet tightly until Ratso took it away from me. But I remember gazing at it under the streetlamp. It looked as beautiful as fish scales in the moonlight.

And memories came back to me like snow falling on snow.

52

Sunday started as a busy day on the blower and ended with my almost getting blown away. But first things first.

I got up, fought back a desire to strangle Ratso to find where he'd hid the cocaine, thought better of it, and made some espresso. No point in having hot chocolate. It wasn't raining.

I fed the cat. Tuna in any weather.

I walked over to the desk with the espresso and sat down. When I took the top off Sherlock Holmes's head to get a cigar, I looked inside to see if Ratso had stashed the cocaine in there. Of course, it was a ridiculous notion, but there you are. It wasn't there. Neither were Sherlock's brains and I had the feeling I was going to be needing them before this mess was over. I would deal with the Jaguar when he came. I would deal with Carlos when he came. I would deal with Leila when she came. A man's not a man until he's given multiple orgasms to a Palestinian terrorist. Of course, Leila wasn't a real terrorist, but she had done some things under a comforter that damn near scared me. I'd been the comforter, of course.

The first call I made was to a colorful, mysterious friend of mine named Dangerous Dan, who was an authority on powders, the Latin American import-export business, and just about everything else that nobody really knows about. Since I spoke to Dangerous, he has left us and gone to Jesus, and I hope and trust that he's made heaven a happier place since he's arrived. But if somehow he got de-selected from heaven, I've always felt I could do a lot worse than waking up in hell next to Dangerous Dan.

Dangerous said that *perla* meant "pearl" and *yi-yo* was an Indian word that did not compute into the white man's mind. Taken together, he said, they meant "the best of the best." Where had I seen that phrase? he wanted to know. I told him the men's room at the Lone Star Cafe. Which stall? he wanted to know. There was only one stall, I told him. He told me to be careful. I told him I'd do my best.

I miss Dangerous Dan and I think of him, in human terms, as perla yi-yo.

I didn't know what Dangerous Dan thought of cats, but Slick Goldberg had liked cats and Estelle Beekman had hated cats and someone had killed them both. So what did that tell us? Not a damn thing. Or maybe it did.

For the next half hour I made a series of calls to information operators in Connecticut, finally hit pay dirt, and called my party. Things were just about what I'd expected. We talked for a while and arranged to get together in the city soon for a drink.

Forty-five minutes is a long time to be on the blower but I was used to hard work. Anyway, the alternative was to look around the loft for some perla yi-yo that I didn't really want to find, because it would fry my remaining synapses in about four seconds and then they would be holding memorial services for my brain in New York and Los Angeles. I got another cigar and another espresso and I made my last call of the day to Jane Meara.

I told her she wouldn't be having lunch with Estelle Beekman anymore. I gave it to her pretty straight. She held up as well as could be expected. In fact, she was starting to show a toughness I didn't know she had.

I told her if the cops called her, and I didn't think they would, she never talked to me about Estelle Beekman. She said she understood.

I asked her if there'd been any news on Rocky from her

end. She ticked off an extensive list of everything she'd done to find her. Net result: no Rocky.

I was reading Jane a story from the *National Enquirer* about a cat named Tom who'd walked 773 miles from Harrison, Arkansas, to his home in Detroit, when I noticed that Sleeping Beauty had awakened from the couch and was walking toward the television set with a screwdriver in his hand. I told Jane to be very careful. I had a few little problems of my own right now, but we'd wrap this whole business up quite soon, I was sure. There wasn't much else to say, and it wouldn't have been very easy anyway because Ratso had, by this time, turned the set up quite loud.

I walked over to where Ratso was sitting and looked at the screen. Many men carrying long sticks were moving rapidly across a great expanse of frozen tundra. At either end, there was a large figure wearing a Wachíchi mask.

"Ranger game!" Ratso shouted.

53

By Sunday afternoon at four-thirty, Ratso, myself, Rambam, and Rambam's attaché case were having lunch at Big Wong on Mott Street in Chinatown. Just before I'd left the loft, Leila had called. She had not heard from her brother Carlos as she had expected, and she was worried. She knew the feds had not picked him up in the bust and she couldn't understand why he hadn't contacted her. I told her if I saw him I'd tell him to call her.

There followed a conversation of a rather sweet and personal nature that was rudely punctuated by Ratso's loud and prolonged curses as the Rangers lost the hockey game. Apparently Ratso'd taped the game at his apartment the previous evening and brought his VCR over to the loft. Nice to see him staying on top of things.

Big Wong was like dying and going to heaven at this time of the day. It wasn't crowded, the food was great, and the waiters treated us like old friends, doing humorous things like bringing Ratso one chopstick. Ratso never found this to be very funny, but I always got a good chuckle out of it. Rambam thought it was pretty funny, too. I don't know what Rambam's attaché case thought. It was sitting in its own chair, not saying anything. I didn't know it at the time, but it would be talking a blue streak before the night was over.

Big Wong is a little different from most places in Chinatown. It isn't fancy and the menu is not very extensive and not very expensive. The food could be equated to that at a very good all-night truck stop, if the Chinese culture had such things as truck stops, country music jukeboxes, and rubber machines, which of course it does not. It does have Big Wong.

But occasional honky faces are beginning to pop up among the clientele these days. Soon some guy with a bow tie from *The New York Times* will stumble onto the place, write a trendy little piece on it, give it a couple of stars, and it'll all be over. When that happens, you might as well order out from Eggroll King in Columbus, Ohio.

It was starting to get dark by the time we got out of Big Wong. We walked down the sidewalks of Chinatown past ducks hanging upside down in the shop windows, past the Chinese dwarf painting pastel pictures of a distant homeland, past the fish markets along the sidewalk, past stalls selling strange-looking vegetables that appeared as if they'd been grown on another planet.

At this time of day and at this time of year the city was gray. But there was something very vital about things that were East. You could see, hear, and smell them, and they renewed the senses and the spirit. The whole scene was reminiscent of the time I'd spent in Kuching, the capital of Sarawak in Borneo. *Kuching* was a Malay word, I reflected as we crossed Canal Street, that, interestingly enough, meant "cat."

We walked up Mulberry Street, bought a few cigars at Louie's. "Hey, it's Buffalo Bill. Look, there he is," Louie said to the other customers in the little shop, mostly elderly Chinese buying lottery tickets, "the Gene Autry of Canal Street." I wasn't sure if Rambam appreciated Louie as much as Ratso and I did. Rambam was half Italian and Louie was about as close to home as you could get without somebody telling you to take out the trash.

We had cappuccino, espresso, and cannoli at a little sidewalk café next to a store that sold Mussolini T-shirts.

"One thing I have very little use for," I said, "is a Mussolini T-shirt."

"Neither does Mussolini," said Ratso, as he took a rather large bite of cannoli.

* * *

In the growing dark we walked through SoHo past stores that sold nothing but pillows, and a ghost town of galleries and industrial lofts taken over by narrow-tied, suspendered New Wave artists. A small group of musicians played chamber music inside a restaurant that served Art Deco chicken-fried steak. SoHo was one of the last places on earth where a break dancer could still draw a crowd.

The closer we got to 199B Vandam, the darker and colder and seedier everything became. Sort of picked up my spirits.

There was a black limo parked on a side street just down from the loft.

"Whose car is that?" Rambam asked.

"Garbage czar from New Jersey," Ratso said.

"Vandam Street's a major garbage-truck staging area for the city," I said, not without some little pride.

"I can see," said Rambam, as he kicked his way through the swirling newspapers and crap along the sidewalk.

We drew a bye on the freight elevator and legged it up the stairs to the fourth floor. I opened the door of the loft, let Ratso and Rambam in ahead of me, and turned on the lights.

A thin dark man dressed in black was standing very still with his hand inside his coat. He looked like Johnny Cash in 1952. He looked dangerous. He was standing next to the hat rack, but it didn't look like he was planning to grab his hat and run.

There was another guy across the room from us standing by a window. He had a smile on his face but it was about as thin as airline coffee.

The rocking chair, which faced away from the door of the loft, was rocking slowly back and forth. It wouldn't have been so bad, except it didn't look like anybody was in it.

54

Somebody was.

A dark figure slowly uncoiled itself from the chair and stood up to face us. It moved toward us in silence. If Joel Siegel had mated with Gene Shalit's daughter, and if their offspring had been a male child born with a luxuriant mustache, it might've looked similar to the cookie duster under the beak of the approaching apparition.

The figure came closer. Upon inspection, it had five shining emerald studs in its left ear. It had flat, dark, death-where-is-thy-sting eyes.

"I am the Jaguar," it said.

There is almost nothing very humorous you can say in a situation like this. If raw courage is the ability not to let others know you are afraid, it could be said that I was very courageous. Because there was something about the presence of the Jaguar, despite his seemingly softspoken, refined manner, that transparently went against the grain of what it is to be human.

"You find the key I left for you?" I asked.

"The Jaguar doesn't use a key. For the Jaguar, there are no doors," he said.

With a chill I thought about the story I'd read of a guy in Houston, a Colombian coke dealer, whom the cops had pinpointed, trapped, and tried to bust three times, only to find that he'd disappeared into thin air on each occasion. He was known as the Wizard, I believe. The Wizard. The Jaguar. There are many names for death, I thought.

Rambam moved up a few steps. He was still carrying the attaché case, but I figured by the time he could open it and take out the Uzi, we'd all be pickled herring.

My eyes flicked wistfully over to Rambam and the attaché case and then back to the Jaguar. The Jaguar continued to look straight ahead like a malicious Buddha.

"That won't be necessary, my friend," he said. Then he paused and added, "Or very effective."

"Depends how you look at it," said Rambam. He was holding what looked like some kind of high-tech police revolver in his right hand and aiming it placidly at the Jaguar's gonads.

I looked over my right shoulder and saw that Johnny Cash was now sporting a thin, gray cigar-box contraption with a long handle and a rather unpleasant-looking black nozzle extending from it. It was pointed at the back of my head and the guy was smiling.

It was an ugly situation at the very best. Rambam continued to look challengingly at the Jaguar. The Jaguar only licked his chops. I hazarded a side glance at Ratso. He did not look like a happy camper.

There were a couple other places I could think of that I'd rather be myself. Almost any of those bumper stickers that you always see would be fine. I'd rather be sailing. I'd rather be playing golf, though it bores me to death. The only good balls I ever hit was when I stepped on the garden rake. I'd rather be hang gliding.

Most of all, though, I'd rather be in a Jacuzzi one night many years ago under the stars of Malibu with the most beautiful girl in the world with a flower in her hair from Vancouver. The girl was from Vancouver, not the flower. I'd given her the flower. She wanted to make love in the Jacuzzi that night under the stars, but, coming from Texas, I was a bit inhibited. Today, of course, I'd hose her in a heartbeat, but that, unfortunately, would be quite impossible. She's wherever Dangerous Dan is, and I'm standing here in the loft with a man pointing an unusual-looking weapon at the back of my head and smiling like an airline stewardess.

I looked at the five shining emeralds in the Jaguar's ear and all I could think about was how much I missed the stars shining over Malibu. How much I missed somebody. How much I missed.

"Well?" said the Jaguar. He was smiling now, but the smile had all the humanity of an upside-down tragedy mask.

I looked at Johnny Cash. I looked at Rambam. I looked at the Jaguar.

"Colombian standoff?" I asked.

55

The Jaguar issued forth a thick, throaty, animallike laugh and gave Johnny Cash a sign with his emerald-ringed finger. When I looked around, the weapon was back under Johnny Cash's coat and Johnny was still smiling, though not quite as much as when he'd thought he was going to get to use it. Rambam shook his head like a fireman who's seen too many false alarms and quietly slipped the gun back into a shoulder holster.

A little color was coming back into Ratso's face and he began, for the first time, to breathe perceptibly. I was starting to feel a little better myself.

I took out two cigars, offered one to the Jaguar, which he accepted, and then I walked over to the desk and guillotined the butt off my cigar in one rather decisive, macho movement. I motioned for the Jaguar to use the guillotine on his cigar. He shook his head and walked over to the kitchen table near where Ratso was standing.

From his breast pocket, the Jaguar took out a white object, gave it a dextrous flick, and walked close to Ratso with a bone-handled straight razor in his hand. Ratso looked like an extra from the cast of the movie *Coma*. He didn't turn a hair as the Jaguar moved past him, put the cigar on the table, and cut the end off like a master surgeon working with warm butter.

"Jesus," Ratso said almost involuntarily. "Do you shave with that?"

The guy by the far window said something in Spanish. The Jaguar and Johnny Cash both laughed.

"What'd he say?" I asked.

"He said," said the Jaguar, "if you shaved with it, you'd cut your lips off."

It was pretty clear to me what the thing was used for, but as long as the Jaguar was slicing cigars and not working on passageways for lungs, it was okay by me.

"It is so sharp," said the Jaguar, holding up the straight razor, "that when you cut someone with it, they do not even know that they're cut for sometimes twenty seconds." He folded the straight razor and put it back in his breast pocket.

"Sometimes," I said, "I bet they never find out."

"That is true," said the Jaguar. "But that is only when the Jaguar wishes to be kind."

The small talk had pretty well run its course. The Jaguar took out an expensive-looking gold lighter and lit his cigar. I took out the pastel-purple Bic I'd bought from the Pakistani the night I'd gone to Leila's apartment and met Carlos. If Bics could talk. That particular Bic had now seen two major cocaine-cartel kingpins, one very dead body in Estelle Beekman's closet, and one very live and lovely body when I'd lit a cigarette for Leila afterward. It had led a very exciting life for a Bic. Five days it had been with me and it was still going strong. That was longer than some marriages. Unfortunately, the lifespan of the Bic and my own mortality had in common a rather evanescent quality.

I lit the cigar. For a while the Jaguar and I stood around and quite literally blew smoke. Then he reached over and picked up a package from the seat of the rocking chair.

"It is good what you have done to Carlos," he said, as he watched me closely. "Carlos is no good. Carlos's people are no good. Did you receive the perla yi-yo?"

"Yes," I said, "but—"

The Jaguar silenced me with his hand. "Here," he said, "is

another token of appreciation from the Jaguar. Some say it is even better than the perla yi-yo.''

Ratso rolled his eyes but didn't say anything. The Jaguar held the package out for me to take.

"Beware of geeks bearing gifts," said Rambam in a stage whisper from my left.

I walked over to the Jaguar, thanked him, and took the package. He was one gift horse I wasn't even going to think about looking in the mouth. I carried the package over to the kitchen table. It was wrapped in the same butcher paper as the perla yi-yo. I tore off the paper.

If the Jaguar hadn't been a smarmy, evil, Freon-blooded killer, the gift would've been almost poignant.

"What is it?" Ratso asked. "Heroin?"

"No," I said, as I threw the package over the counter to Rambam, "Coffee beans."

Rambam went to work with the grinder and the espresso machine and pretty soon the loft was filled with an aroma so rich even my beezer could tell it was the McCoy. The whole place was threatening to become Kinky's Kosher Cajun Coffee Kitchen.

Suddenly, we heard the kitchen window break as if five or six baseballs had been thrown through it in extremely rapid succession. There was no other sound until Johnny Cash slumped to the floor. He was still smiling, but it looked like somebody'd crocheted his face.

Mustaches were moving along the fire escape.

It looked like it might be a while before anybody was going to have a cup of coffee.

56

The cat jumped over the moon, the Rat scurried for the hallway, and I ducked behind the kitchen counter. I could hear more invisible baseballs crashing through the windows, making no sound but for the breaking glass. I couldn't see Rambam. I couldn't see the Jaguar either, but I could imagine what he was thinking. Set up.

Then the lights went out. I glanced up and saw little cometlike tongues of fire coming through the windows. Wherever he was, it looked like the Jaguar had his hands full for the moment. It was a good thing, too, because the idea of the Jaguar stalking the Kinkster with a bone-handled straight razor in a darkened loft was enough to keep the sandman away for the rest of my life. Which, under the circumstances, might not be too long.

Strangely enough, I was not afraid. Or else I was so afraid that my fear had become a kind of quiet rage. If nothing else, I was determined to outlast the Bic.

I peered over the top of the counter into the semi-darkness. I saw several red flashes. A window crashed, and two mustaches bit the fire escape. But there were more, I suspected, where they came from. The Dixie cup kids.

There was a large crash from the direction of the bedroom that sounded like the wreck of the Hesperus. I took it to be the window that wouldn't open. I never said it *couldn't* be opened. I could see dim figures moving around in the bedroom. Men were shouting in Spanish. Strange sounds erupted like Paul Bunyan zipping and unzipping his fly many times in rapid succession. More figures crouched on the fire escape. The place sounded like a bullring with a rather small crowd. It looked like an urban Alamo.

Obviously, the Jaguar's boys were coming in from the west side of the building, and the other guys—who belonged to either Carlos or Santa Anna—were coming in from the front or south side. Directions can be important when you're lost in the woods in the dark. Without them, you might never get to Grandmother's house.

There was a strange aroma in the air—a heady, acrid, robust mixture of gunpowder and Colombian coffee. Very distinctive. You couldn't fool this crowd with Folger's crystals.

I didn't know how long I could stay there between the counter and the espresso machine before I caught a bullet, or realized twenty seconds too late that I'd been cut cleanly in half with a very sharp knife. I didn't want to be there, but everywhere else seemed worse.

Someone grabbed both my arms from the back in an iron grip. I looked around expecting to see a smiling mustache, and was somewhat relieved when I didn't. It was Rambam.

"Time to go," he said. "But stay down low."

"Where to?" I asked.

He extended his hand toward the door of the loft like a maître d' showing me to a table.

"This way, Mr. Kennedy," he said, "right through the kitchen."

57

There is a rhythm to fear.

It's not something you pick up at Arthur Murray. It's measured in the statistical velocity at which the head and the feet can fly toward each other when the guts disappear. It's something you feel when you stand in a dark hallway and realize you may be about to die.

It has a sickly, draconic, not quite Caribbean flavor that can be very catchy when you see the cotton-candy-colored specter of death pressing its evil, childlike nose against the frosted glass of your mind. By then, of course, the party is o-v-e-r.

On the stairwell below I could hear the sound of a man dying in another language. I didn't plan to stick around for the translation. I was moving on up faster than the Jeffersons when Rambam caught me on the landing between the fourth and fifth floors. He had the Uzi on a strap around his neck. He handed me the police revolver.

"How do I use it?" I asked.

"You see anything that even faintly resembles a spic, you pull the trigger," he said.

"Fine." I didn't like this at all. Where the hell were the sirens? I wondered. I wanted sirens. I needed sirens.

"They're using MAC-10's with silencers," said Rambam. "That's the noise like a zipper you keep hearing."

"Until they make contact," I said. "Then it sounds like somebody caught his shvantz in his Jordaches."

"That gap-lapper with the dance class still up here?" asked Rambam as we hit the fifth floor.

"Yeah," I said, as I looked at the pistol in my hand and at Rambam with his Uzi and Israeli Army jacket. "But I'm not sure if she's ready for the raid on Entebbe."

As we listened to the freight elevator creak ominously through the gloom, Rambam banged once on the door of Winnie Katz's loft, turned the knob, and threw it open.

If you're going to interrupt a lesbian dance class, you can't insist upon no surprises. We were ready for just about anything and that's just about we got.

There was a Colombian lying barely inside the doorway. A bright red worm was crawling out of his head and moving in the general direction of the kitchen. Winnie Katz was standing over the body in a powder-blue warm-up suit, holding a MAC-10.

"How do you reload this cocksucker?" she asked.

There were sirens in the distance now, but I could see shadowy figures moving around on the fire escape. A fag in leotards came leaping by and two hysterical girls were cowering in the kitchen. Nothing wrong with cowering in the kitchen, I thought. I was just starting to look around the place when a barrage of shots forced us all to the floor and took out a large mirror on the wall behind us.

Rambam killed the lights, took up the Uzi, and cleared the fire escape, taking out every front window in the place. A quiet, uncertain moment followed in which everybody's ears rang and cold air and colder fear poured into the loft in about equal quantities. I looked outside but I didn't see any movement on the fire escape.

"You oughta get a silencer for that thing," I said.

Rambam was looking out of one of the broken windows. "Still a lot of action down there," he said. "I'll stay here. You check the bedroom."

I walked across the darkened studio with my pistol out, like a gunfighter walking into the bar where the bad guys were. I didn't think anybody was in the bedroom, and I was pretty sure Rambam didn't either or he wouldn't've sent me in there. It was like sending seven different people to get blankets when you're treating a drowning victim. Gives everybody something to do, and maybe somebody shows up with a blanket in time to cover the guy before he dies of shock. If everybody shows up with blankets, you send them out again for beer and fried chicken and you have a picnic by the riverside.

Halfway to the bedroom I saw something move down by the floor under the desk. I crept closer and pointed the revolver in front of me. As I got very near the desk, a taut white face looked up at me. It was Ratso.

"What the hell are you doing?" I asked, dropping the gun to my side.

"What the fuck do you think I'm doing?" said Ratso. "I'm calling 911!"

"Jesus Christ, Ratso, how long does it take to call 911?"

"I'm on hold," he said.

I walked over to the bedroom, prepared to take a quick, cursory look around. I walked in about four or five nervous steps. There wasn't even a bed in the place, just one of those tofu mattresses. Lesbians are weird, all right.

As I turned to leave the room, a figure suddenly detached itself from the far wall and flew at me like a desperate bat. It was too dim in the room to tell if it faintly resembled a spic, but it had a long, shiny knife in one hand so I pulled the trigger. The knife seemed to flutter against my throat like a steel moth and then it fell away. At that distance, with Rambam's big gun, even Mr. Magoo would've been deadly. The bat bit the tofu.

I hit the lights and looked at the body. It was very dead. The first life I'd ever taken. A line came into my head from the poet Kenneth Patchen: "There are so many little dyings, it doesn't matter which of them is death." I turned the body over with my foot.

582 It was Carlos.

I stood there for a moment breathing like the guy who came in 791st in the Boston Marathon.

"Call your sister," I said.

58

I crept back across the studio like an anxietous crab. Rambam was peering out of the doorway into the hall and motioned me to join him. Two dark figures had forced the doors of the freight elevator, and a third was firing down into the shaft with a MAC-10. The wall switch for the elevator had been thrown and apparently it had stopped between floors. There was no roof to the freight elevator; it was little more than a grimy cage with a light bulb hanging from two crossbars. It was like shooting fish in a barrel, except that the fish were screaming and cursing in Spanish, and the racket was echoing in the elevator shaft.

It sounded, to quote my pal Tom Waits, "like Jerry Lewis going down on the *Titanic*."

After the fish began to sound more like ceviche, the three figures turned from the elevator and Rambam field-stripped them with the Uzi. He stepped over the bodies, threw the switch, and pushed the down button, which sent the stiffs in the elevator to the ground floor.

"Lingerie," he said.

We could hear cops in the hallway now and random shots being fired in the street. We went back into Winnie's place and collected Ratso.

Winnie seemed calm and cool. "You want some Red Zinger tea?" she asked.

"No thanks," I said. "I've got some coffee downstairs."

Rambam casually gave his Uzi to the dead Colombian by the doorway.

"Illegal," he whispered to me.

"I see," I said. I gave the revolver back to him.

By the time Rambam, Ratso, and I got back to the loft, the cops were swarming all over the place. There were more crushed Colombian Dixie cups lying around than I'd thought, but, like Rambam said, they were expendable.

I conducted a rather agonizing search for my cat, finally locating her in the closet in the bedroom. She was fine. Just a little pissed off. I gave her some tuna.

I took out about forty-nine cups and poured coffee for anyone who wanted it. I guessed that it would be a long, tedious debriefing, or whatever they called it, and I was right.

I got myself a cup of coffee and walked through the loft surveying the damage. It didn't look too bad. Of course, it hadn't looked too good to begin with.

I was able to observe only one casualty on our side: The puppet head had taken a direct hit.

There was one other thing I noticed that bothered me almost as much as the loss of the puppet head.

There was no sign of the Jaguar.

59

Two days later, on a crisp, cold Tuesday morning, I was having breakfast with Eugene in the little Greek coffee shop at the rather obscene hour of 8 A.M. I had asked for the meeting, not the other way around. I wanted to get this Rocky-Goldberg-Estelle Beekman situation spanked and put to bed. The sooner the better. Eight o'clock in the morning was a little early for my blood, but some people work for a living and Eugene was one of them. I wanted to meet with him away from the publishing house.

"Eugene," I said, "I need your help."

"What can I do?" he asked.

You can stop wearing that yellow knit tie, I thought. I sipped a hot cup of coffee and mulled it over. "I need someone," I said, "on the inside, so to speak. Someone more familiar with the publishing business than I am."

"Why don't you talk to Jim or Jane?"

"I'm going to talk to everybody, but Landis is being uncooperative and Jane is the one I'm worried about."

"I'm worried about her, too," said Eugene. "I gave her a manuscript over a month ago and she hasn't finished it yet. That's not like her."

"What was the manuscript?"

"A novel I wrote."

"No kiddin'? What kind of novel?"

"It doesn't matter," he said. "Nobody's ever going to find

out, the way things are going. If Hemingway were around today he'd probably be writing ad copy.''

"You're right," I said. And he was. Van Gogh had been able to sell only one painting in his lifetime. The painting was *The Red Harvest* and he sold it to his brother, Theo. Good ol' Theo. Franz Schubert's estate at the time of his death was valued at twelve cents. He didn't have a brother around to buy the *Unfinished* Symphony.

"It's frustrating," said Eugene. "Jane's just got to come to grips with reality. She's got to realize that that cat is *gone*. It's not just affecting her work—it's affecting her mind.''

"Yeah, I said. It was affecting my mind, too.

Eugene did not know Goldberg. Eugene did not know Estelle Beekman. Eugene had to get to work. Fine.

If Eugene had not been my ideal choice for a breakfast companion, Hilton Head for brunch was worse. I had to talk to these people. The battle of the Colombian drug cartels on Sunday night had convinced me that the Kukulcán angle, the possibility that the Colombians were behind Goldberg's and Estelle Beekman's demises for some reason that was connected with Jane Meara's cat, was very doubtful to say the least. Men who kill with silenced MAC-10's, who perform Colombian neckties, who perform Colombian butterflies, would be more creatively cruel and clever than merely to cut a man's tongue out. And it had been a sloppy job at that. I didn't see the mark of the Jaguar there, so to speak. But who knew?

Sunday night had also convinced me that the Baby Jesus wanted me to live for some reason. To save Jane's life? To find Rocky? I didn't know, but I doubted if the reason was so that I could have brunch with Hilton Head.

I had brunch with Head in the Village. Wanted him to feel he belonged. We ate at some chic European rabbit-food place that blew in more ways than one.

I browbeat Head about what Leila was doing coming and going from his apartment. Finally, he told me.

"Just delivering a little shmutz," he said, He pronounced it like "fruits."

"Shmutz?"

"Cocaine," he whispered irritably.

"Oh, yeah," I said. "Shmutz."

It was not uncommon, I'd learned, for people to give harmless little names to very deadly, dangerous things. Ted Mann had once told me about an heiress he'd known, from some spiritually bankrupt family, who also called cocaine shmutz. She'd snort about eight grams a day and drink about four bottles of vodka. She'd destroyed her mind entirely and her very life was hanging on a thread and here she was still calling it shmutz. "I'll just have a little shmutz." Well, we all have our blind spots.

The only other interesting thing that emerged from the Head brunch was that Hilton, several years before he'd come out of the closet, had dated Estelle Beekman for a while. He didn't seem in great grief about her death. He seemed more to think it was rather pathetic.

I wasn't a professional checkup-from-the-neck-up kind of guy. Just your normal dimestore Jungian. But I really thought Head's sexual evolution let him off the hook. I couldn't see a guy who'd finally come out of the closet ever wanting to put somebody else back into it.

60

I had lunch back at the loft with Ratso and the cat. I'd already had two meals, if you wanted to call them that, and I was still hungry enough to eat a tofu mattress.

Ratso and I ordered in from a Nip place he wanted to try. Several hours later it nipped us back pretty good. It was a meal that would live in infamy.

The cat had tuna.

Ratso and I used chopsticks. The cat did not.

I'd always felt that the Chinese were smarter than the Japanese, and one of the arguments that I frequently used to support this thesis was that they ate Chinese food instead of Japanese food.

"So how'd it go with Hilton?" Ratso asked, affecting a slight lisp.

I told him.

"Could be some clues there," he said.

"Your rather obsessional quest for what you call clues, my dear Ratso, can sometimes be counterproductive, not to mention tedious. What we must ask ourselves is this: If Jane Meara is the killer's next intended victim—and I, for one, believe she is—what does that tell us? What kind of pattern presents itself?"

"Yeah," said Ratso, "but what about Estelle and Head having an affair? What about your friend Leila running cocaine to Head? What about the discrepancy over whether or not Stanley Park ever visited Jane's office that day?"

"Pace yourself," I said. "These things, I think you'll find, are what we in the business of detection commonly refer to as red herrings."

"I've heard the term," said Ratso in a somewhat miffed tone. "What about the possible involvement of the Colombians, though? What about Carlos?"

"That's a dead herring," I said. "Ratso, when this case is solved, I don't think the killer will be a Colombian. It'll most likely be a normal American just like you or me. It'll probably be an average member of the white larval middle class. Of course, we may, in a deeper sense, never find the killer. There are those of us who feel that life itself may be a red herring."

"Let's not get too metaphysical," said Ratso. I poured us each a cup of the finest Colombian coffee in the world.

"Is perla yi-yo," I said. "Speaking of which, where the hell's the other perla yi-yo?"

"I'll make you a deal," said Ratso. "You solve the case by the weekend, I'll tell you where in the loft I hid the perla yi-yo."

"You're not asking for much, are you?"

"Is it a deal?"

I took another sip of Colombian coffee. I shook Ratso's hand grimly.

It didn't give me a hell of a lot of time. Of course, I didn't *have* to solve the damn thing by the weekend. But it would be nice.

61

"It's nothing," I said. "I've just got this special knack for being in the wrong place at the wrong time."

Jane Meara and an attractive friend of hers, Lori Ames, were both cooing over a McGovern-bylined article on page 1 of the *Daily News*. It was part two of a multipart series about how a country singer who was a close personal friend of the journalist had almost single-handedly brought about the downfall of two of the largest Colombian cocaine cartels operating in the city.

"You're hot shit," said Lori Ames.

"Thank you," I said.

We were sitting in a restaurant on Mulberry Street in Little Italy. It was late Tuesday afternoon and I was eating lightly. Sending some Wop food down to try to straighten out the little eruption by the pesky Nips. Or maybe it was the brunch with Hilton Head that had done it. Normally, I could eat anything without getting upset. I thought of Leila. She hadn't called in several days now. Never trust a Palestinian.

The restaurant the three of us were in was called Luna's and was one of the best in Little Italy. It was run by a woman named Yola and I can't remember how many times I'd seen Ratso, on very crowded nights, walk up to the front of a long line of people waiting to get in, and wave to Yola. She'd come over and get us a table right away. The people would mutter while we spread bread with butter.

Luna's was also the last place Ratso and I had had dinner

with our friend Mike Bloomfield, the great blues guitarist, before he died. It was also where he'd once taken my friend Dennis McKenna, who on that occasion had been a very drunken Irishman. When the *capo* of one of the city's major crime families had suddenly appeared, wearing vaguely sinister Old World garb, the whole place had gone silent. That was when McKenna had called out to the man, "Nice hat!"

"The ASPCA has been very helpful," said Jane Meara.

"What?" I said.

"In trying to locate Rocky."

"Yeah," I said. "If there's a way to run her down, they ought to know it. Pardon the expression."

"You don't think we'll find her, do you?" asked Jane.

"I think we'll find out where Rocky is when we find the killer. We could find the killer by this weekend," I said. Of course, Dallas could melt by this weekend.

"Jane," I said, "why haven't you read Eugene's manuscript?"

"Oh, he told you, did he? That little brat. He's bugging me to death about it. I'll read it when I find out about Rocky."

"You may find out something you don't want to," I said. I thought of how Rocky might look dying in an alley, the victim of a Colombian butterfly.

"I'll take my chances," said Jane.

Lori Ames had been reading the *Daily News* piece while Jane and I had been yapping. Now she looked up at me and, shucking all modesty, there was admiration in her eyes.

"You know something?" she said.

"What?"

"You're hot shit."

"Don't put me up on a pedestal," I said.

I'd been on the human rodeo circuit long enough to know that you couldn't change people's minds by telling them the truth. If McGovern's articles had half of New York believing I was a hero who'd cleverly and courageously contrived to bring two major drug cartels to their knees, who was I to say it wasn't true? If I'd told Lori Ames the truth of how I'd

stumbled into the whole mess, she probably wouldn't've believed me anyway. So I might as well enjoy the ride.

As the three of us left Luna's, something Sherlock Holmes
once said came into my mind. Sherlock was explaining to
Watson his hesitance to reveal his methods, because once
he'd done so, he'd in effect demystified himself. When he
revealed his methodology to his clients, they tended to be
somewhat blasé about the results. They said things like "Oh,
I could've told you that."

What Sherlock actually said to Watson was "What you do
in this world is a matter of no consequence. The question is,
what can you make people think you have done?"

As the weekend grew ever closer, I'd probably have to borrow a page from Sherlock. If things got really rough, I
thought, maybe I'd lift the whole book.

62

As it evolved, I borrowed a page from Nero Wolfe before I borrowed a page from Sherlock. It was like borrowing a cup of sugar from a yesterday that never was, but if certain things had worked for Sherlock and Mr. Wolfe, why not for the Kinkster? Indeed.

The problem was that I was not a fictional person and I was not dealing with fictional people. When you work with flesh and blood, as God probably found out on day eight, things tend to break down a little. In real life, Cinderella tires of the prince and has an affair with the boy who comes to clean the swimming pool. In real life, Sleeping Beauty his insomnia. Of course, on the other hand, the Village was one of the few places, outside of certain dense forests in Ireland, where fairies could still often be seen. Sometimes they'd even grant you a wish. Like get out of your way so you could park your car.

Late Tuesday night, after a couple of shots of Jameson, I told Ratso my plan. He was somewhat skeptical, but every Jesus needs a Doubting Thomas to sort of keep him on his toes. Not that I thought I was Jesus, of course. I was having enough trouble with Sherlock Holmes and Nero Wolfe.

"Here's the plan," I told Ratso. "Thursday night at eight o'clock we invite all the principals in the case here to the loft. The Parks, Head, Jane, Landis, Eugene, and maybe a special guest or two. We'll also have Cooperman here. We'll have Pete Myers cater the affair. You with me so far?"

"Sure," said Ratso. "It's the only invitation I've gotten all week."

"Okay, now we get these people over here—"

"What if they don't come?"

"Oh, they'll come all right. Not showing up would amount to a tacit confession of guilt. Besides, who the hell are they? George Jones? Greta Garbo? Of course they'll show. They wouldn't dare *not* show. Anyway, when they get here, in the manner of Nero Wolfe we sit them all down, serve food and drinks, and then, with a little incisive probing and a little normal human interaction, we'll get some interesting results.

"Now, I've got some work to do myself tomorrow, so I'd appreciate it if you'd call the list and get the whole thing set up."

"You're out of your mind," said Ratso. "You can call me a homosexual pancake chef, but I'll be damned if I'll be your male social secretary."

"You can't very well expect Nero Wolfe himself to make the calls. Our guests would find it highly unsatisfactory, not to mention rather gauche. This is really quite juvenile, Archie."

"Archie? Who the hell's Archie?"

"Archie Goodwin," I said patiently, "was Nero Wolfe's assistant. If you read anything other than books relating to Jesus, Bob Dylan, and Hitler, you'd've known that."

"God," said Ratso, "what a horrible cultural gap in my very being. All because I didn't read a certain dime-novel whodunit."

"It is the kind of gap," I said, "through which a clever killer can sometimes escape."

I poured a healthy shot of Jameson and puffed on a cigar. Ratso walked over to the door of the loft and bolted it.

"Why are you doing that?" I asked.

"Well, Mr. Wolfe, you forget that there's a Jaguar out there somewhere and he's familiar with this address."

"Ah, but Archie, you know that for the Jaguar there are no doors."

"I know that," said Ratso, "but we don't have to make it a fucking cakewalk for him."

I killed the shot. I killed the light. I killed the temptation to say something to Ratso. I walked into the bedroom, put on my sarong, and went to bed. As luck would have it, I did not dream.

63

Wednesday morning while Ratso slept, I ran a routine search for the perla yi-yo, just in case I didn't find the killer by the weekend. I didn't know what I'd do with that much cocaine if I found it. I wasn't even sure I wanted any amount of cocaine. But I knew it was there somewhere in the loft. It was kind of like finding the *afikomen*.

I didn't find anything but an old letter I never sent to a broad I never really got to know. Nothing lost. A lot of things in life fall behind dressers and get lost in the cobwebs and we don't even know the difference. Of course, there's a lot of hip spiders walking around somewhere.

At 10 A.M., the time all good agents should be in their offices, I lifted the blower on the left and posted a call to Lobster.

I wanted Lobster to rifle Slick Goldberg's files personally. Both those on his current clients, if you wanted to call them that, and his reject-letter files. Slick had worked for a large agency where, as was the rule, nobody really knew what anybody else was doing. Lobster's job was to get into his office on any pretense, even that of seeing another agent, and finding the goods. Also, I requested that she worm her way into Estelle Beekman's old publishing house and check those files as well. I told her what to look for and that I needed it by the weekend.

"I'm going to do this for you just this one time," said Lobster. "I don't really know why."

"Maybe it's my rural charm," I said.

I left the Nero Wolfe party list on the desk where Ratso would be sure to see it, and I went out to lunch. I dined at a swank and fairly unpronounceable French restaurant on the Upper East Side where I had to take my hat off to get in.

Normally, I wouldn't have stood for that, but then, normally I didn't have lunch with Fred Katz.

64

Wednesday night I stayed up late with the cat and what was left of the bottle of Jameson. Ratso, having called the list and ordered a roast and two dozen pork pies from Pete Myers, had gone to play hockey. I sat at the desk. The cat and the bottle sat on the desk between the two red telephones to keep me company. I wasn't an alcoholic. Alcoholics drink alone.

I was reading a clipping a friend had sent to me several weeks before. It wasn't related to the case at hand. Well, let's say it wasn't directly related to the case at hand. The article looked like it was from the *New York Post* or the *National Enquirer*, the kind of paper that occasionally has the guts to print things that are not fit to print.

The source of the article was *The Compendium on Continuing Education for the Practicing Veterinarian*. The part of it that jumped out at me was a statement to the effect that "57 percent of cat owners confide in their cats about important matters."

"What in the hell," I said to the cat, "have I gotten myself into?"

The cat didn't say anything. I downed a shot of Jameson from the old bull's horn.

"What in the hell," I said to the cat, "am I going to do if nothing happens tomorrow night?"

The cat demurred. I poured and killed another shot.

"And what do you think of Ratso?" I asked. "In his own stubborn, neurotic, New York way, he believes in me. His loyalty is almost poignant, don't you think? Kind of like a gynecologist daydreaming of his wife . . .''

The cat licked her paw a few times and closed her eyes. I wondered what percentage of cats gave a shit about the confidences of their owners.

I knocked back another fairly stiff one.

"Nice of you to listen to all of this," I said rather facetiously.

The cat yawned. I poured another shot.

"The way I see it," I said, "we've been looking in the wrong places for the wrong things. We've misconducted the case in the same manner that most of us misconduct our lives. Of course, this time we've had more than our share of red herrings and blind alleys, but still, there's no excuse. I think I see the solution. And it's really very simple. The problem is going to be how to prove it without somebody punching Jane Meara's dance card for the river Styx.

"Look at it this way. What strategy would Tom Landry, the coach of my second favorite team, the Dallas Cowboys, have used if he were alive today? Are you listenin'?"

The cat was sitting with her back to me, which was something she occasionally did when a person or a situation greatly displeased her.

I ignored this rude behavior.

"Maybe I should've been a Buddhist or a dusty old Navajo. Maybe everything would seem clearer then. I just don't understand people today. There's a sign on the highway near our ranch in Texas that says 'Waterfall for Sale.' You ever hear of anything like that? Guy thinks he can sell a waterfall. Hell, maybe he can. You in the market for slightly used waterfalls? How about a guy who never quite made it to the top as a country singer so he tries his hand at something much more difficult and deadly? Sometimes it looks like a guitar picker just can't tell what to pick. He rambles around the world until he suddenly stumbles head first into a situation that makes him a hero with feet of Play-Do.

"If I'm wrong tomorrow night, well . . . we can go on the

600 road again. You and me and the old guitar and the pillow-case. You never did like traveling in a pillowcase much, but who said life on the road was gonna be easy? A middle-aged misanthrope and his cat playing county fairs and ro-deos . . ."

I killed the last shot. I looked at the cat. The cat was sound asleep. By the time Ratso got back from his hockey game, I was, too.

65

Thursday night rolled around like a battered beach ball. The loft, however, looked like a million bucks. Two rows of mismatched furniture, including folding chairs, the rocker, and a hassock that appeared to be left over from *The Adventures of Ozzie & Harriet*, were arranged neatly in front of my desk. Nero Wolfe would've been proud.

The windows sparkled. That was because they were new windows, put in to replace the ones blown away by Rambam and the boys from Brazil or wherever the hell they came from.

I was wearing my formal black Italian tuxedo jacket, which had once belonged to a Puerto Rican coke dealer. A little class never hurt anything.

Pete Myers was standing in the kitchen with a long knife, cutting what looked like an obscenely large portion of a farm animal into paper-thin slices. Pork pies from his shop on Hudson Street were laid out all along the counter with hot mustard, chutney, and a few other things I didn't recognize. Also, there were several large bottles of the ever-present HP sauce. I thought, but did not verbalize, the sentiment that a famous frog had once expressed: "In England there are sixty different religions, and only one sauce." It would've been in questionable taste.

"These friends of yours coming tonight, Kinkster?" asked Myers in his soft, northern English Lake District accent.

"'Fraid not," I said.

"One of 'em's a murderer," said Ratso in his rather rodent-like, grating Queens accent. "Tonight Kinky's gonna unmask the fiend. Right, Kinkster?"

"Right," I said a little shakily as I reached for a bottle of Guinness.

"Pour enough of that stuff down your neck and you may unmask yourself," said Myers.

"Wouldn't be the first time," said Ratso.

"Right," I said with a measure of dignity.

I took the Guinness and walked over to the kitchen window. With the puppet head out of commission, Ratso and I were going to have to do a lot of legwork going down to the front door each time to let the guests in. Of course, if you want to entertain, you have to be prepared to make sacrifices. I poured a little Guinness down my neck and looked out at the empty street. What if Nero Wolfe gave a party, I thought, and nobody came?

By ten-thirty only two pork pies and two detective sergeants were still hanging around. The two detective sergeants were leaving and Ratso was putting the two pork pies into the refrigerator.

"See you around, hero," said Cooperman.

"Call us when you get another bright idea like this," said Fox. I let them out the door, poured another Guinness down my neck, and sat down at the desk facing two little rows of disheveled, empty furniture.

Everyone had come and everyone had gone, and now everything was quiet except for a little garbage-truck activity starting up on Vandam Street. Like someone going over the minutes of a past Rotarian meeting, I ticked off the high points of the evening in my mind. During the course of the little affair I'd also managed to tick off some of my guests, but that can't always be helped. Being a society host is not my long suit.

Jim Landis had shown up about half an hour late. As a result, he'd had to sit on the *Ozzie & Harriet* hassock and he wasn't any too happy about it. Something else was eating him, too, but whatever it was, he didn't want to share it with the whole class. Relations between Jim and Jane, and Jim and Eugene, seemed rather strained. Some internal politics were going on that did not look very pleasant, but what they were was anybody's guess.

Jane and Eugene, for their part, said very little, though leading questions were asked and touchy subjects and confrontations were common during the course of the evening.

When I asked Eugene if the Parks and Hilton Head were the three people he'd seen up in the office the day the butcher knife was found on Jane's desk, he said yes to Marilyn Park and Hilton Head and no to Stanley Park. Who was the third person? I asked. No reply.

Stanley Park became slightly *agitato*. In fact, the ugliness became so thick you could've cut it with a knife.

Finally, Head cleared the air. The third person had been his "friend." Who was the friend? He'd rather keep the friend out of it.

I let it pass. The friend was out of it anyway. It was something the Parks could squabble over, or Head could fret over, on their own time.

Everyone was alert to questions regarding Estelle Beekman or Slick Goldberg. Many of them had probably read Nero Wolfe, too.

I was creative, clever, crude, caustic, conciliatory, conniving, and just about everything else that starts with a *c*, but none of them snapped their wigs and ran madly for the door into the waiting arms of Sergeant Cooperman. Everybody played it cool. Everybody had alibis for the times when Goldberg and Beekman had gotten aced.

It was quite a three-cigar problem. I watched for hands tensing, facial muscles twitching, other signs of noticeable discomfort, but it was hard to watch seven Americans at once. I learned little that I didn't already know.

The only one in the room who seemed to be legitimately socializing was the cat. She turned her back on Marilyn

Park's advances and walked over to sniff at Jane Meara's boots.

"Kinky's cat has a leather fetish," said Head. Landis chuckled. Most of the group, being cat fanciers, found little humor in the remark.

The cat walked over to Eugene and leaped into his lap. He tried to push her away, but if you've ever tried to push away a cat who doesn't want to go away, you know it can't be done. She preened herself, rubbed up against him, and pawed at his stomach in a friendly cat manner. Eugene, though obviously a bit stiff and uncomfortable about this sudden feline attention, held up pretty well under the circumstances.

"Enjoy it, pal," said Cooperman. "It may be the only pussy you'll get tonight." Fox laughed. Marilyn Park pursed her lips in a little moue of distaste.

Just as the natives were starting to get restless, I introduced Fred Katz to the group for the first time by name. This brought about the strongest reaction of the night. Many in the small group were convinced from my *Daily News* advertisement and from talk they had heard that Fred Katz was the villain of the piece. I observed reactions carefully. Jane looked horrified. Nobody grabbed him by the throat, but Stanley Park and Eugene were both on their feet in outrage. The cat went flying. She rubbed herself against my leg in an effort to regain her dignity.

I hushed the crowd. They returned to their seats. "Fred Katz is no cat-napper," I said. "Nor is he a murderer." The crowd oohed and ahhed a bit. I puffed on cigar number three.

"Fred Katz is a financial consultant, which, in some quarters, might be regarded as equally odious. But, for our purposes, he is innocent. The only thing he's guilty of is checking out and leaving his key in his hotel room."

The cat jumped back into Eugene's lap. Eugene took the ordeal rather stoically this time. Cooperman leaned his mug into the group and said, "Hey, buddy, at least get her phone number."

Jim Landis announced he'd "had enough of this charade" and he was leaving. Others got up to go. Some said thanks and good night. Some just beat it out the door. I poured another Guinness down my neck.

At the door, I hugged Jane Meara and whispered to her to be careful, we were getting close. She looked at me like I was an outpatient.

Now I gazed across the tiny ocean of empty chairs and puffed languidly on what was left of cigar number three. Ratso came over and slumped down across from me in the rocker. He looked at my face closely, almost sadly.

"Looks like a washout, Mr. Wolfe," he said.

"Quite to the contrary, my dear Ratso," I said. "Quite to the contrary."

66

Early Friday afternoon, while I was waiting around for Lobster to call, I made the mistake of telling Ratso about my joshman dream. Now, as he walked back into the room wearing his hockey kneepads, I began to wonder about the wisdom of my disclosure.

"There's nothing wrong with being a latent homosexual," said Ratso, as he adjusted his kneepads and walked over to the refrigerator.

"I'm not one," I said curtly. "It's just . . . the gentler, more sensitive side of me manifesting itself. The actual dream definition of joshman means nothing. It just reflects a longing."

"Tell that to Hilton Head," said Ratso. "I'm sure he's quite an authority on joshman."

"Forget it," I said. "It was just a dream."

"I wouldn't worry about it none," said Ratso, as he took a pork pie out of the refrigerator. "Them ol' dreams are only in your head." He closed the refrigerator door. "Bob Dylan," he said.

"That's an unusual source for you to quote from," I said. "Beats Rita Mae Brown."

The phones rang. It was 1:15 P.M. It was Lobster and she had the goods. It was just as I expected. I put down the blower and allowed myself a deep sigh of relief. I took a cigar from Sherlock's head and lopped the butt off it with the guillotine.

Then I called Jim Landis.

Fortunately, he wasn't at lunch or at a sales conference, the two places where people like him seemed to spend most of their lives. Unfortunately, he didn't want to speak to me.

"This is a matter," I told the secretary, "of life or death." I was put on hold.

I made a cup of espresso and found and put on my brontosaurus foreskin boots while I waited. What you do with the hold time in your life is an index of how successful you'll be when your call finally comes through. A wise old judge told me he'd once heard of a Jew, an Italian, and a person of the Polish persuasion who all had been sentenced to twenty years in prison for bank robbery. The Jew had wanted a telephone, the Italian had requested conjugal rights, and the Polish individual had demanded four hundred cartons of cigarettes in his cell. Twenty years later, the Jew had built a worldwide corporate empire, the Italian left prison with a family of eight, and the person of the Polish persuasion came out of his cell with an unlit cigarette dangling from his lip and said, "Got a match?"

At least I had a match. I lit the cigar. The secretary came back on the line.

"Mr. Landis wants to know *whose* life or death," she said.

"Tell him *his* life or death," I said with some intensity. "If he doesn't pick up the phone right now, I'll call a hit on him by the Jewish Defense League. And don't think I can't."

This is the kind of thing you get used to when you're dealing with professional people in general. They have their lives just a little out of perspective and sometimes you have to tell them what is important and what isn't. You have to be aggressive.

"Yes, Kinky?" Landis said like a patronizing aunt.

"Where's Jane?"

"Out," he answered brusquely.

"Sorry about last night," I said. "You don't like charades?"

"Only with eccentric, best-selling British mystery writers in drafty old manor houses."

"I can see how you'd be disappointed," I said, "but the little charade had its little purposes. You see, it helped me identify the killer."

Landis didn't say anything. I took a puff on the cigar and looked over at Ratso. He was sitting across the room on the couch with the screwdriver in his hand. He'd been ready to turn on the television, but my last sentence apparently had gotten his attention. Now he looked over at me. I nodded to him.

"Jim," I said, "tell me about this manuscript that Eugene supposedly has given Jane and that Jane supposedly's been squirreling away, threatening to read for over a month."

"Oh, that," laughed Landis. "I looked at it once briefly when it was lying on Jane's desk. Eugene's masterpiece."

"What was it about?"

"It was a book about dogs," said Landis lightly. "The *Jonathan Livingston Seagull* of dog books."

"That tears it," I said grimly. "Jim, this is important. *Where is Jane?*"

"She's been acting a little spooked lately, so I let her take the afternoon off. I think she went to the circus at Madison Square Garden. Maybe she thinks she'll find her cat. Is anything wrong?"

"Yeah," I said.

I got my coat and two cigars for the road and walked over to Ratso. I looked at the overly large hockey kneepads he was still wearing.

"Either take those fucking things off or put on the rest of the uniform. And hurry."

"Where we goin'?" he asked.

"Back to the Garden," I said. "The circus is in town in more ways than one."

67

There is a time to live and a time to die and a time to stop listening to albums by the Byrds. Now, as we hurtled uptown toward the Garden at high speed in a hack that rattled like a child's toy, I only prayed that my unorthodox assemblage of what Ratso still rather archaically referred to as clues was correct.

I thought of the last phone call I'd made just before we'd left the loft. It had been to Sergeant Cooperman and it had made the previous call to Jim Landis seem like spu cotton candy.

Heroes, it seemed, had a rather short wingspan in New York. Either that, or Cooperman did not believe what he read in the *Daily News*. I felt like Sly Stone's lawyer. When Sly had suddenly found his house surrounded by police cars, he'd called the lawyer and reportedly said, "You get over here now. And you better be heavy and you better be white."

Being white is an accident of birth. Being heavy is spiritually relative. What I had to be, in no uncertain terms, according to Sergeant Cooperman, was right. And right is sometimes the hardest thing to be in the world.

As we stepped out of the hack and into the throng, I wondered, not for the first time, if I could be making a terrible mistake. It was the kind of case where logical deduction hardly followed logical deduction. Philip Marlowe, with his dogged perseverance, would've had a better shot at cracking it than Hercule Poirot, with his little gray cells. I'd started looking for a cat, stumbled across two stiffs along the way,

610 gotten shot by a lion tranquilizer dart, been sidetracked by a Jaguar, and now, with any luck, I was finally closing in on the killer.

Train schedules and comments by the butler were not going to catch a murderer in 1988 in America. We'd been to the movies. We'd grown up on television. And to make things even harder, in the words of Mark Twain: "There is no distinctly native American criminal class except Congress."

And yet, when I went over it again in my mind, I was sure I had it right. Like Inspector Maigret, walking the rainy streets of Paris, smoking my pipe, my hands in my pockets, watching the people caught up in the problems of their lives, I would solve this case. After all, like Maigret, I was a serious student of human nature. And, come to think of it, not-so-human nature.

I didn't see Cooperman or Fox in the foyer, but there wasn't a hell of a lot of time to waste, so I gave Ratso forty bucks, told him to buy two tickets, and then I went over and talked to a uniform who was picking his nose near the doorway. I told him Detective Sergeants Cooperman and Fox from the Sixth Precinct were on their way, and I told him the vicinity where I thought Ratso and I would be. That was the best I could do under the circumstances.

Ratso returned with the tickets. I don't know what circus tickets cost these days, but I didn't see any change. Maybe Ratso threw in a service charge.

We went in.

Going to the circus as an adult is not the same as going to the circus as a child. The difference is, when you're an adult, all the clowns tend to look like John Wayne Gacy.

It was now pushing two o'clock, when the show was supposed to start. Martha Hume, a sassy, southern, circus-going friend of mine, had told me some time ago that there are holding cages in the basement where you can see the animals up close before the circus starts. The place is called the menagerie, and if I was right, I thought, as we headed down the

Dantean ramps into the noisy bowels of the Garden, it would certainly be one today. If I was wrong, Jane could be sitting in the third row eating peanuts and watching normally rational animals making fools of themselves for other animals who already were fools. Life's a circus, or it's a carnival, or a whorehouse, or a wishing well. Or a winding, muddy river. One of those things. About the only thing we know life isn't is a Norman Rockwell painting. But don't tell your dentist that. Dentists have their dreams.

We were coming to the end of the last ramp, and the suspicion I held was getting stronger as we progressed downward. Evil has its logic, I thought. Mental illness has its patterns. I was betting Jane's life that I had accurately gazed into the mind of a maniac.

I hoped Cooperman and Fox would show up soon. If not, it looked like Ratso and I were going to be working without a net.

68

"Looks like it's closed and we're hosed," said Ratso, as we tried vainly to open the two locked doors at the end of the ramp.

"Think, Ratso," I said. "You're a pro at getting backstage at rock concerts. What do we do?"

"I'll tell Dumbo the Elephant that I know Ron Wood," said Ratso.

I banged loudly on the metal doors. Nothing. It was two o'clock. Upstairs, we could hear the grand parade kicking off. There had to be somebody around. I kept pounding the doors.

Finally, an old man with a funny hat opened the doors. It could be said that Ratso and I were wearing funny hats, too, but we were wearing very serious faces.

"Detective Sergeant Cooperman," I said. "Sixth Precinct. Undercover." I flashed the idiot button inside my wallet at him. It was a courtesy badge that had been given to me by Lieutenant Scott Grabin of the NYPD, one of the few cops on the force I still enjoyed good relations with. That was because I rarely saw Grabin. He worked out of a precinct in Harlem. Maybe if somebody burned a watermelon in my front yard we'd have the opportunity to work on a case together.

"This is Sergeant Fox," I said quickly, nodding toward Ratso. "We're looking for a small boy who's on special heart medication. Been missing for over an hour. We're runnin' out of time."

The only other occasion on which I'd ever used the idiot

button was when I'd gotten drunk once in a Mexican restaurant and tried to arrest some of the patrons. It hadn't worked then and it didn't look like it was going to work now.

Then Ratso, drawing heavily on his New York background, pushed the old man to the side and shouted authoritatively, "C'mon, gramps! Get out of the way!" The old man did. Ratso and I walked purposefully through a length of empty corridor and started searching around. We didn't look back.

"Not especially kind," I said.

"It gets results, Sergeant."

We turned a corner and entered what seemed like a large, dank, dark hall. The circus music coming through the ceiling sounded distorted and rather eerily similar to something the hunchback of Notre Dame might've selected for his Walkman.

"Smells like a zoo in here," said Ratso.

"That's what it is, Sergeant."

We came to a cage with a lone elephant. As Ratso walked up to it, the animal gave forth with a loud fart, apparently signaling its displeasure.

"You've made a friend for life, Ratso."

"I have that effect on people."

I had stopped downwind from the elephant and was lighting a cigar when I first heard the laughter. It was toneless and void of joy and it came cascading out of the gloom with the chill and suddenness of a Texas blue norther. It was the kind of unearthly, almost unspeakably evil sound that caused ice to begin forming along your spine.

"My God," said Ratso. "That better be a fucking hyena."

"It is," I said. "But I'm afraid it's of the two-legged variety."

When you're frozen in your tracks, one of the easiest things to do is listen. We listened.

The next two sounds we heard, if it is at all conceivable, rattled our cages even more.

The first was the roar of a lion.

The second was the scream of a woman.

69

"Damn everything but the circus" was the way e. e. cummings had once put it. Now, as Ratso and I dashed into the gloom, I was more than ready to throw the circus into the pot with everything else.

The only thing I wasn't ready for was the tableau of horror that lay in a pool of sick, yellow light at the end of the hall. Jane Meara's body was lying on the floor of a cage and the biggest lion I'd ever seen in my life was turning her over with a bloody claw.

I approached at a run and grasped the door of the cage. The lion tracked my movements with ancient, ruthless, storybook eyes. It was staring right at me and licking its chops.

The cage itself was a fairly small enclosure—about the size of your average apartment in the Village—only it probably didn't cost fifteen hundred dollars a month. Whatever it cost, it was going to be a bitch to collect the rent.

I looked around frantically for something to put between me and two thousand pounds of biblical hate. I found a metal folding chair.

When you know you'll soon meet a lion in person with no bars between you, a lion's eyes can tell you things about yourself that you might not pick up in a philosophy course at the university. How different in some ways, and yet how similar these eyes were to another pair of primeval orbs I'd recently encountered—the Jaguar's. One pair at least had the physiognomy of a human being, while the other belonged to a beast of the jungle. And yet both had a flat, glinting, mesmerizing quality. Of the two, it was Leo's eyes that held more compassion, more humanity. Made you think twice about the theory of evolution.

But there wasn't time to think even once. The lion roared. A soft moan came from Jane Meara's body.

It was ironic, I thought, I wasn't even a Christian.

I opened the door.

The lion stood its ground and there was something in its eyes akin to the cool, unwavering gaze of a hooker sizing up a potential john on the street. For my part, I thought of Earl Buckelew, the famous water witcher of the Texas hill country, knocking down a hornets' nest with a straw cowboy hat. I thought of Tchaikovsky or Stokowski or whatever the hell his name was, who used to walk onto the conductor's podium oblivious to the world. They say that if a brick wall had been erected across the stage, he could've walked right through it.

Whether it was a hornets' nest, an audience, or a lion, you had to use Judy Garland's little trick—pretend it wasn't there. Shake it off completely. Play only for the silent witness.

The lion roared and I damn near dropped the chair. I was edging a little closer to Jane when the beast suddenly came at me with a jungle version of a left hook. I twisted my body sharply but I still caught some of it and my right arm went completely numb. I watched the metal chair go crashing against the bars. I watched the bright red blood splattering against the concrete floor. I didn't feel too much like Judy Garland and this didn't look a hell of a lot like Kansas.

Suddenly, the lion's attention seemed to be drawn to the far side of the cage. I looked over its shoulder and saw what appeared to be a human jack-in-the-box jumping up and down. It was Ratso.

Incredibly, he was getting results. Even the lion appeared to be amazed to see somebody hopping up and down like a piston, waving a coonskin cap between the bars, and shouting, "Yo! Yo! Raw meat! Check it out!"

616 The lion leaped for the side of the cage, viciously swiping at the hat. I grabbed Jane with my good arm and dragged her to the door of the cage. I let go of her and awkwardly struggled to open the door, praying that Leo's attention span would stretch for a few more seconds.

It did. I got Jane out of the cage and closed the door behind us.

Ratso was down, my arm was beginning to throb, and Leo was sitting in the middle of the cage chewing peacefully on the coonskin cap.

"Everything's going to be all right," I said to Jane.

Her eyes fluttered open and I watched them turn into mirrors of horror. I looked over my shoulder and saw it coming out of the shadows toward us.

It was another big cat, but this one walked on two feet and was carrying a gun.

70

"She wouldn't even read it! She wouldn't even look at it!"

The voice seemed to echo dully in the room like a horrifying, atonal sob. The figure moved closer and into the light, trapping Jane and myself between the gun and the cage. The gun, which we couldn't get away from. The cage, which we weren't about to go back into.

In the unhealthy, yellow light the garish cat mask looked like it came from a steam locker in some forgotten corner of hell. The gun, as near as I could tell, was not a tranquilizer gun this time. It looked a little like Rambam's revolver, only smaller. But when a gun is pointed at you, the most important thing to be aware of is that a gun is pointed at you. The size and make and model can be established later. If there is a later.

"Back in the cage! Both of you!" the creature screamed.

"No," Jane said. Her voice sounded like that of a small tired child who'd suddenly realized it was past her lifetime.

"Yessssss," hissed the voice, like an obscure Hindu demon.

Suddenly, the mask was off and flying against the bars of the cage. The face that was revealed looked familiar yet unfamiliar. Like someone you always thought you knew but never did. It was cold, pale, twitching, and terrible. Almost like a mask under a mask.

"Eugene!" said Jane with a sharp intake of breath.

"Who'd you expect?" he said in a low, gravelly voice. "Robert Ludlum? Stephen King?" I couldn't be sure but it seemed as if he was frothing a bit at the mouth.

"Looks like the cat's out of the bag," I said.

Eugene smiled. Right then he looked like the meanest son of a bitch who ever put on shoelaces.

"None of you helped me!" he shouted. "You stood in my way with all your little cats! Now look what's happened to you!"

He pointed the gun straight at my head.

"Eugene," I said. "Eugene . . ."

"Good-bye," said Eugene. He paused. ". . . Kinky," he added. I could see the muscles in his face tighten at the same time his hand tightened around the trigger.

You never know what's going to happen in life. You could pick up a newspaper and see where Lady Bird Johnson was caught swimming naked in the pool at the Holiday Inn. That's what keeps us all in the game.

Jane and I held our breath.

A shot rang out.

Eugene spun around in an awkward little last waltz and hit the sawdust.

In the shadows I saw Sergeant Cooperman slowly rising out of a crouch. He and Fox walked over to us.

"Nice show," said Sergeant Fox.

Jane, Ratso, and I were taken by ambulance to the same hospital. Ratso was fine. In fact, as he told the doctor, he'd just gone along for the ride. Jane was kept overnight for observation, and by the time I called in the morning she'd already been released. They treated my arm, said it was a flesh wound, gave me a few shots and a few prescriptions, and Ratso and I went home.

Eugene had not been as fortunate. He'd taken a ride in the stiffmobile to a nice refrigerated drawer.

Ratso never got his hat back and, quite uncharacteristically, he never even asked about it.

71

My attitude about life is you should always take the good with the bad. The game, of course, is to see if you can tell which is which.

It was Sunday night, two days after our little trip to the circus, and Ratso was packing.

"Seems like I've lived here a long time, doesn't it, Daniel?" said Ratso. Daniel was what Ratso had taken to calling me in the days immediately following my brief excursion into the lion's den. The name wasn't that humorous, but it was shorter than Nebuchadnezzar.

"Maybe Alex Haley will do a story about your stay here," I said.

I was sitting at the desk smoking an eleven-dollar Cuban cigar I'd once bought in Vancouver. I'd been saving it for a special occasion and this was it. Getting rid of a house pest. The cat watched dispassionately from the kitchen table as Ratso packed his things. She wasn't going to believe it until she actually saw him leave.

"Uh, Daniel," said Ratso, "I can accept the idea of a spiritual hunch about Eugene and the circus, but run it by me one more time just how and when you began to suspect him."

"I told you, Ratso, the pattern was there all the time. Slick Goldberg, Estelle Beekman, and Jane Meara all had in common that they were literary types. They were in one way or another involved in the publishing business.

"Eugene said something rather strange when he told Jane

she should forget Rocky and get a dog. A more normal, if still somewhat insensitive, suggestion would have been to get another cat.

"After Estelle Beekman got aced, I was convinced the killer lay somewhere within the literary community with which we were dealing. Then, when Eugene told me he'd written a novel that he was having trouble getting published, he really tipped his hand. I asked him in the coffee shop that morning what the novel was about. He sidestepped the question and went into some monologue about 'if Hemingway were around today he'd probably be writing ad copy.'

"Now I ask you, Ratso, from what you know about human nature, have you ever heard of a novelist—especially an *unpublished* novelist—who, when asked what his book is about, declines to tell you? There ain't no such animal. It's almost clinical recall with these people."

"So you knew," said Ratso, "that there was something strange about Eugene."

"Either something strange about Eugene," I said, "or something about that particular manuscript that he didn't want me to know. So I had Lobster find out if he'd ever been a client of Goldberg's. He had, and Goldberg had dropped him. Also, he'd submitted the manuscript to Estelle Beekman, who'd rejected it. Meanwhile, here is Jane talking endlessly in the office about her cat, and taking forever to even read the thing. Then I find out from Landis that Eugene's book is about *dogs.* A major opus—'the *Jonathan Livingston Seagull* of dog books,' Landis called it—that conceivably might've taken Eugene years to write.

"When I heard that, it absolutely tore it. A book on dogs."

"Amazing," said Ratso, shaking his head as he packed up his hockey equipment. "I guess that means a foul wind is blowing for the future of my horse book."

"Sorry about that," I said.

I got up and walked over to the kitchen, poured out a shot of Jameson into the bull's horn, and killed the shot. I paced back and forth in the kitchen, leaving a rich trail of pre-Castro smoke in my path.

"But aside from all of this," I said, "what really nailed Eugene had nothing to do with human logic or human perception at all. It was an inversion of Sherlock Holmes's famous case of the dog that didn't bark. Our case features a cat that *did* take action."

"Rocky?" Ratso asked.

"Not Rocky, my dear Ratso, but this very cuddly little creature"—here I picked the cat off the kitchen table and briefly held it in my arms before it twisted away and tried to claw me on its way to the floor—"this cuddly wuddly little . . ."

"Spare me," said Ratso.

". . . creature who once jumped on your balls. Remember?"

"It's emblazoned on my scrotum forever."

"Well, the cat was telling you something. When the cat took a Nixon in your red antique dead man's shoe, it was also telling you something. Now you're packing up and leaving and the cat is happy."

"So am I," said Ratso.

"Well, I'm sure in her own way the cat will miss you."

"Fuck the cat," said Ratso.

"It hasn't got that bad yet. Now, as I was saying, there are some things that men still don't and probably never will understand about animals. For instance, beavers. Beavers build underground exits in their dams in late summer and early autumn and they seem to know just how thick the ice will be long before the winter ever comes. It's amazing, if you think about it. I saw it on *Mutual of Omaha's Wild Kingdom.*"

"That's what I tried to tell my ex-girlfriend," said Ratso. "Man still doesn't know a lot about beavers."

"Humorous, if somewhat crude," I said. I walked back over to the desk and sat down again. The cigar was killer bee.

"Now, if you will, my dear Ratso, cast your mind back to last Thursday night, the little get-together that, in your words, was 'a washout, Mr. Wolfe.' That night was no wash-out, though at the time I let it be seen as one. Actually, it was a great, if somewhat accidental, triumph. One that I had nothing to do with, but was able, at least, to observe. Fortu-nately, seeing was believing.''

"What the hell are you talking about?"

"I'm telling you the cat went right to the murderer. It jumped in his lap several times; it pestered him; it wouldn't leave him alone. Any cat owner will tell you how perverse cats can be. Quite often, they won't come to people who like them. They seem somehow to know just who of all your guests might have asthma, or be allergic, or be afraid, or be uptight. Thursday night was like a living lie detector test, and Eugene, fortunately for us, failed. There was something about him that we couldn't see, that was strange, evil, not right. I've seen the gentlest animals in the world become very upset around people who aren't quite right in their heads.

"Animal behavior, Ratso—very important. Not only can animals predict earthquakes and natural disasters, but some-times they can unmask the cold, cruel mind of the killer among us."

I took a rather languid puff on the cigar and watched the smoke drift upward toward the lesbian dance class.

"Now, where," I asked, "is the perla yi-yo?"

72

If you've ever emptied a tray of cat litter, you know that you hold the tray at arm's length and turn your head away as you dump the contents into the trash can. It was in this manner that I had managed to throw out possibly a quarter of a million dollars' worth of perla yi-yo sometime earlier that weekend.

"Easy come, easy go," Ratso said, after I'd returned from checking the trash Dumpster on Vandam Street. It was as empty as the sky in California.

I wanted to kill Ratso. I wanted to kill the garbage men.

"Look at it this way," Ratso said. "You're probably the only guy in New York who's bitching about prompt, efficient garbage collection."

I killed off the bottle of Jameson mouth to mouth, lit a fresh cigar, and walked over to the window.

"And now it would appear," I said, "that I'm about to lose a house pest."

"Don't worry," Ratso said. "I haven't left yet."

73

It had been raining cats and dogs all evening. One of them must've literally fallen from the sky because on this night, at the windy tail end of March, Jane Meara provided me with the other bookend to the story.

I had stocked up on liquor and tuna and I was just kind of sitting around, not quite feeling sorry for myself, when the phones rang. I went for the blower on the left. It was Jane.

"I told you never to call me at home," I said.

"You won't believe it!" she said.

"You finished reading Eugene's manuscript?"

"Stop it, Kinky. I went to a hockey game tonight at Madison Square Garden with a friend. . . ."

I sat back and listened as Jane told me her story. When she'd finished, and I'd cradled the blower, I put my feet up on the desk and smiled to myself. All I remember thinking was, I wish I had another Cuban cigar.

"But it wasn't really Rocky?" Ratso asked, as we stood close to the bar in the Monkey's Paw. It'd been about an hour since Jane's call and Ratso and I had already had a few rounds.

"All I know," I said, "is that it followed her from the Garden for five blocks with a glint of triumph in its eyes. Then, when Jane got to her car—"

"Brahms shot it with a bow and arrow."

"No, Ratso. It jumped in the car with Jane. She took it

home, went to work on it with soap, water, and a washcloth, and guess what?"

"What?"

"Four little white sweat socks."

"Jesus Christ," said Ratso. "It's enough to make you believe there's a God."

"Not necessarily," I said. "There are many things in nature that we don't understand. There's an old dead tree on our ranch in Texas that my dad won't let anybody chop down because the hummingbirds live there. My mother always used to love the hummingbirds. Every year, right around March fifteenth, you can see them start to arrive. They fly all the way from South America to that same old dead tree where they were born."

"Well, that proves there's a God."

"No, it doesn't."

"What does it prove then?"

"It proves, my dear Ratso," I said, "that there is a hummingbird."

Later that night, back at the loft, I was having a quiet conversation with the cat. The place looked oddly empty without Ratso's belongings strewn all over the couch.

I was sitting at my desk when I got the call from Sergeant Cooperman.

"Tex," he said, "I don't know how close you were to that Palestinian broad. You remember the one?"

"Yeah," I said.

"She got whacked by one of the Jaguar's boys. Happened sometime earlier this week, we think. She left a package, though, and it's got your name on it. We went through it, of course. But I'll send a car over with it now, if that's all right."

"Thanks," I said.

"Sorry, Tex."

I put down the blower very slowly. There wasn't really any hurry now. It was like being on spiritual hold without even being on the telephone. I waited.

In time, a squad car pulled up in front, a uniform got out, and I went down and got the package. I brought it back upstairs and opened it on the desk.

It was Leila's kaffiyeh.

I put the kaffiyeh around my shoulders. It was a little cold in the room. I walked over to the kitchen window and stood there for a long time. The cat came by and jumped up on the windowsill. Everything was quiet on the street. Maybe the garbage trucks were observing a moment of silence.

Together, the cat and I watched the world. I pulled the kaffiyeh a little tighter around me and gently stroked the cat. Sort of a sad, scythelike Pakistani moon was falling in the west over the warehouses.

"Next year in Jerusalem," I said.

I was folding the kaffiyeh and putting it in the desk drawer when Ratso came barging into the loft with a copy of the *Daily News*.

"Jesus Christ," he said, "look at this." He put the newspaper down on the desk and pointed to an article. The headline read: MCGOVERN NOMINATED FOR PULITZER PRIZE.

"I don't believe it," said Ratso. "It's for his series about you and the cocaine cartels."

"McGovern's got talent," I said with some little satisfaction, "among other, rather more tedious qualities."

"Yeah," said Ratso, "but a *Pulitzer*?"

"Maybe there *is* a hummingbird," I said.

A short while later, Ratso was pillaging an order, on my tab, from the Carnegie Delicatessen, and watching some obscure sporting event on television. I was sitting at the kitchen table with a bottle of Jameson, the bull's horn, a tube of epoxy glue, and some black paint.

I was repairing the puppet head.

It was a very satisfying, almost meditative sort of work. Repairing a little black puppet head when you couldn't repair your own.

Maybe the problem was that now I was between cases. Or

maybe the problem was, as Sherlock himself had said, "I have never loved." But that wasn't really true for me. I had loved. I could've loved. It just didn't look like it was going to come my way again. Not everybody finds their Rocky in life, I thought. Some of us just find the courage to face the world alone.

The phones rang.

"I'm not here," I said. Actually, it wasn't too far from the truth. In the background, I heard Ratso talking to someone on the blower.

"You're kiddin'," he said. "What took you so long?" I kept working on the puppet head.

"I don't believe it," he said. "Jesus." I kept working on the puppet head.

"Kinkstah!" he shouted. "It's for you."

"Who is it?" I asked.

"It's the girl in the peach-colored dress," he said.

I stared intently at the puppet head on the table.

"What the hell's going on?" shouted Ratso. "Aren't you gonna talk to her?"

I turned the puppet head a little to one side and then a little to the other. You couldn't even tell it had been wounded.

"I'll speak to her," I said, "when the glue is dry."

ABOUT THE AUTHOR

The leader of the real-life country band, Kinky Friedman and the Texas Jewboys, proves that art imitates life in his Manhattan-style mysteries based on a country western singer. Splitting his time between Texas and New York, he continues writing novels, including *Frequent Flyer* and, most recently, *Musical Chairs*. He is also a frequent guest on the popular radio show, *Imus in the Morning*, based in New York.